First published 2020

First printed edition published 2024 by Drollery Ltd.

Copyright © Alice Coldbreath, 2020

ISBN 978-1-916736-08-5

The Vawdrey Brothers Series:

Book 1: Her Baseborn Bridegroom

Book 2: His Forsaken Bride

Book 3: An Ill-Made Match

The Brides of Karadok Series:

Book 1: Wed By Proxy

Book 2: The Unlovely Bride

Book 3: The Consolation Prize

Book 4: Her Bridegroom, Bought and Paid For

Book 5: An Inconvenient Vow

Book 6: The Favourite

The Victorian Prizefighter Series:

Book 1: A Bride for the Prizefighter

Book 2: A Substitute Wife for the Prizefighter

Book 3: A Contracted Spouse for the Prizefighter

This book is dedicated to Becks, who I hope will be reading this at her favourite castle location! From Alice x

Caer-Lyoness, May Day Celebrations

For god's sake, thought Armand despairingly as his opponent swung wildly, overextended, and nearly lost his balance. If he wasn't careful, he'd end up winning this bout. He feigned a slide even though the grass was dry and parched and dropped to one knee, letting his sword fall with a clatter. Surely even Farleigh couldn't fuck this up. He watched the other's eyes light up behind his visor as his competitor bore down on him with wild enthusiasm. At this rate, he'd end up losing an ear to this bloody young fool!

"Do ye yield?" Farleigh panted, clumsily setting the point of his blade at Armand's throat.

"Watch my chin, for fuck's sake, Farleigh, you oaf! Of course I bloody do!"

Someone in the crowd booed and others followed suit. *Too bad*, Armand thought, clambering to his knees. The crowd always hated it when he lost. But they'd had good entertainment from him this past quarter of an hour, and no one could say they had not. He always put on a good show, and it wasn't like his life had not been endangered. Not with an inexperienced hand at weapons like Farleigh.

He pulled his helmet from his head and shrugged eloquently to the masses. A few lackluster cheers went up for him, though they turned to boos again as Farleigh held up his sword, turning in a circle for adulation. Feeling a stab of pity, Armand grimaced and approached his foe to hold up his arm in a show of sportsmanlike defeat.

Farleigh looked gratified as the crowd cheered for that gesture at least. He'd better make the most of it—whoever faced him in the next round would surely beat the living daylights out of him. As Armand knelt for the royal box, he scanned the crowd for that weasel Fulcher, who owed him half of his takings. He was sure it would be a fat purse this time. After all, he had been runner-up at Tranton Vale and placed highly in the last three rural tournaments. No one could have predicted Armand de Bussell would go crashing out in the first round to a nonentity like Sir Douglas Farleigh, even if his form was sadly unpredictable.

"De Bussell!" He gave a start, noticing that Farleigh was hissing at him out of the corner of his mouth.

"What?" he snapped irritably.

"The King speaks!" the other said hoarsely.

Oh. Armand lifted his head and noticed King Wymer had come to the front of the royal box.

"…grave disappointment," the King was finishing. "But you must take heart. Fortune may be a fickle mistress, but I have no doubt she will smile on the House of de Bussell again one day soon."

Armand arranged his expression into one of brave and noble suffering in the face of defeat. For some reason, Wymer usually gave him some word of favor at these events. Probably on account of his great-grandfather being one of Wymer's grandfather's staunchest supporters back in the day or some such thing. Besides, people always did like Armand. He was damned if he knew why.

His gaze wandered from the King, who was sadly shaking his head, to the Queen regally waving to the crowd, to the third figure seated in the box, the reviled northern princess. Armand winced. What the hells was that monstrous headdress, which stuck out like two cow horns on either side of her head? She looked totally out of place in the royal box, jarringly foreign with her barbarous trappings of a bygone age and utterly incongruous in comparison to the sophisticated Argent royals.

It was ironic that it was her forbears, the Blechmarshes, who had been the ones to actually build this palace, while Wymer's ancestors were merely poor relations. *Funny how the world turns.* He wondered if the wide and rigid construction she wore could possibly be fashionable in the north. It made her look more like a pavilion than a woman. She looked three times as wide as Queen Armenal, and that peculiar mass of frizzy hair didn't help matters. For a moment he felt something akin to pity for the frumpy royal cousin. For a few years, it had been touch and go whether she would keep her head on her shoulders after the northern forces fell. It was dangerous having rival claims upon someone else's throne. Inconvenient for the King that her claim was legitimate. Armand found himself wondering for a moment if she could possibly be as placid and bovine as she appeared, considering the blood of warlike kings that flowed in her veins.

Then a trumpet blasted, and he was jerked out of his reverie. He needed a drink. And to find that rat Fulcher before he started spending their winnings.

*

"A pity, a great pity," Wymer tutted as he sat back in his gilded seat. "If only de Bussell could conquer this wild inconsistency in his performance, he could be a fine champion one day."

Queen Armenal, sat at the King's left, did not bother responding, so Una, sat on a seat behind the two of them, leaned forward to give a murmur of agreement to her royal cousin.

"He looks a fine figure of a man, cousin," she commented in her most colorless tone. She did not lie, for not only was de Bussell's build athletic and muscular, his tanned face was also undeniably handsome. He looked the very image of knightly prowess, and it was a sad fact of life that appearances could often be deceptive.

Wymer gave a bark of a laugh. "You'll catch cold looking in that quarter. His family has been loyal to the Argent throne for centuries," he said, jutting out his chin.

Which meant they have also been an enemy of mine, thought Una. Wymer never failed to rub such things in her face where he could. If only he knew how much she loathed any loyalty to her own family's cause, she thought with wry amusement. Northern followers were the bane of her existence. Their insistence that she was the true ruler of all Karadok had nearly sent her to the executioner's block on several occasions over the years.

Would her royal cousin, as she was now bid to call him, ever forgive her for existing? She had such hopes for reconciliation when she had first come to court eighteen months ago. But now, her only wish was to marry some provincial knight and be allowed to sink into obscurity, tucked away in some remote spot where she could at last be free of her bloody heritage.

She felt her stomach lurch as the next two combatants took to the field. Surely that was Otho. What on earth was Otho doing here? And why, oh why, would one of her own half brothers be fighting in a contest to find her a bridegroom? It made no sense! Craning her ears, she made out the name the herald announced: Sir Bavistock of Leigh. Una's heart sank; he was fighting under

4

a false name. What on earth was she going to do if he made it through to the final? Could she really denounce Otho, the only one of her father's numerous bastards who she actually held some affection for? She certainly could not marry her own brother!

"Never heard of this pair," Wymer muttered irritably, jerking her out of her thoughts. "Northerners?"

Una hesitated. "I do not know them, cousin," she answered and wondered if she was, once again, setting her head on the axman's block with this lie. *Would it never end?*

Wymer waved a hand and a servant darted forward. "Fetch me Vawdrey," he said plaintively, asking for his chief advisor.

Una's heart sank. Most people knew Earl Vawdrey was also His Majesty's spymaster. She felt a good deal of anxiety whenever she caught sight of his tall, elegant figure about court, dressed head to toe in unrelenting black. What if he recognized Otho as one of her half-blood siblings? She wouldn't put such knowledge past him. He knew so many unexpected things that people sometimes whispered he was in league with imps and demons. Not that Una believed in such things. She was all too aware of the horrors men were capable of to start inventing ghouls and beasties to account for them.

"Can you not go one morning without consulting Vawdrey?" Queen Armenal sniped with a roll of her eyes.

"Why should I?" Wymer asked shortly. "Besides, he organized this May Day debacle." He shifted restlessly in his seat. "It's an insult having this damned bunch of no-names competing!"

"You're just cross because de Bussell went crashing out," Armenal said with a tinkling laugh. "All because he looks exactly to you as a knight should. Did you wager on his

5

winning?" She sighed. "You never learn! Just because he looks the part, you're determined to back him, despite all evidence to the contrary."

Wymer's glower increased, and Una guessed the Queen was right about the wager. A footfall behind them had Wymer swiveling around in his seat. "There you are, Vawdrey!" the King cried out as Earl Vawdrey appeared next to him with a smile on his handsome face. He bowed his dark head to Queen Armenal, who nodded coldly, and to Una, who responded in kind.

"Your Majesties," he murmured. "Are you enjoying the festivities?" He swept a hand eloquently toward the competitors. Before the competition of arms, there had been dancing of maidens around a pole decked with ribbons and accompanied by musicians. In the north this was traditionally done around a white hawthorn tree, but things were different here in the south. Or maybe it was just here in the palace that they dispensed with trees. Una wasn't sure.

"Enjoying it, be damned!" burst out Wymer. "I don't know half of these fellows who have thrown their hat in the ring! What do you mean by allowing these nonentities to compete for my cousin's hand?" He glanced at Una. "She's a princess of the blood, I'll remind you!"

"I'm not likely to forget," Vawdrey answered coolly. "But you must allow the criteria for entrants has prohibited many of our brightest competitors from entry." The King frowned. "If you recall," Earl Vawdrey added mildly, "they must be unwed, distinguished by birth, own their own estate, and be loyal to the Crown." He counted the points on his long, elegant fingers.

"And?" barked Wymer, clearly in a confrontational mood. "What of it? Admittedly Orde and your brother are out of the running, but Kentigern's not married to my knowledge, and neither is de Crecy. Even young Renlow is conspicuous in his absence. Where are they, sirrah?"

"Perhaps they do not wish to be saddled with a wife?" suggested Queen Armenal, sotto voce.

Una was glad that she was not easily put to the blush. The implication was clearly that they did not wish to be saddled with her.

"Renlow does not own his own estate," Earl Vawdrey put in smoothly. "He's a younger son. As for Lord Kentigern…he was a prominent figure during the war, was he not?" he suggested delicately. "It would perhaps seem impolitic for him to compete."

Una did flush at that. Lord Kentigern had suffered grievous wounds in service of the Blechmarsh forces. His lands and his ancient seat had been confiscated after crushing defeat. Doubtless looking on her face every morn would serve as an unpleasant reminder of all he had lost. She did not blame him one bit for shunning this tournament. Who would?

"And de Crecy?" Wymer snapped.

Oswald pursed his lips. "I have heard a rumor that Sir Jeffrey is already married, sire, though as to its veracity, I could not say."

"Humph!" The King sat back in his chair. "I suppose I shall have to accept these sundry excuses," he said grudgingly. "But I am sorely vexed there are not more prominent knights of the realm to be seen this day. What of Bevan of Knollesley? Or Sir James Attley?"

"Alas—" Vawdrey spread his hands wide. "Unforeseen circumstances do arise, Your Highness."

Una stared straight ahead of her, grateful for the stiff-jeweled collar that kept her head upright and the cumbersome headdress that meant she could not see the Queen's expression unless she fully turned her head. No doubt Armenal would be vastly amused. The Queen did not appreciate having to share the dais with another female these days.

Una hardly blamed her for her knowing smirk though. 'Twas obvious to all present that these southern knights did not wish for the dubious honor of being wedded to a dethroned princess, besmirched with ill fame. Even her dubious royal status would be lost as soon as they married her.

Her unpopularity at court probably did not help either, she acknowledged unflinchingly. She had heard echoes of some of the cruel jibes and whispers about her, though no one dared say to her face that they found her ugly, her accent unattractive, and her northern manners stiff and outdated. She had heard the court jester refer to her as "the northern mare" or "the warhorse of Blandivar" and the guffaws that had greeted these words, though she had pretended to be quite oblivious.

Fortunately for her, Una's upbringing had been so dire that a few tittering courtiers were hardly enough to make a dent in her armor, which had been twenty-four years in the making. For someone who had spent the latter part of their childhood dragged from one battlefield to another, and had languished the last three years under house arrest, being shunned at court was like a flea bite after being savaged by a pack of ravenous wolves.

She found her stoic calm mostly unruffled by the experience, although it wasn't pleasant to be a social pariah. It beat waking every morning in draughty fortresses to the clash of swords, never knowing when she might feel a dagger at her throat or be forced to mount the gallows as a traitor.

"Sir Bavistock?" mused Earl Vawdrey, rousing her from her reflections with a jolt. She noticed, uncomfortably, that his gaze was trained on her now rather thoughtfully. "I do not think I've ever heard tell of him before today. Now, what was the name of the other?" he said, casting his eyes down a list he carried. "Ah, yes, Sir Walter Skeffington. I fancy the Skeffingtons are descended from the Borlois family, a minor branch of less distinction."

"Indeed?" the King grunted. "Well, Sir Walter looks a spindle-shanked fellow. This other—" He waved a hand irritably, clearly having forgotten Otho's assumed identity.

"Bavistock," supplied Vawdrey helpfully, a smile playing about his lips that made Una uneasy. He surely could not know him for her baseborn brother, or he would say something, would he not?

"This Bavistock will soon have the best of him, I'll wager." When no one argued, King Wymer looked disgruntled. He soon cheered up though, when after a few moments of swordplay, Otho beat the unfortunate Sir Walter in an ignominious defeat. "There, did I not say so?" he demanded, gratified to be proved right.

Earl Vawdrey inclined his head. "Just so, sire," he said, smothering a small yawn.

The King drummed his fingers against the arms of his chair. "Who else competes?" he barked. "Surely there is some half-eligible knight who will win my cousin's hand outright?"

Wordlessly, Lord Vawdrey passed him the list of competitors. Una watched with some perturbation as Wymer's face turned increasingly more purple as his gaze traveled down the list.

"Intolerable!" he burst out at last. "Not to be borne! I don't recognize a single name among this bunch of hedge-born churls!"

"My King," said Queen Armenal reproachfully. "You cannot blame Earl Vawdrey entirely for this fiasco, for it was you yourself who set the criteria. You alone insisted it must be a combative knight who must win her hand in marriage."

Wymer's jaw thrust out angrily. "I am aware of that! But I had thought—" He broke off impatiently. "However, that can't be helped. They did not come to compete, and it appears I cannot force them to." Una's color blazed and she realized she could be mortified after all. "Not one of these low-born knaves can be permitted to win my royal cousin's hand!" the King hissed. "It's an insult to sovereignty!"

"Your Highness—" Vawdrey began placatingly.

"I won't have it! A damn bunch of country yokels with nary a decent connection between them! Half of them could scarcely have been presented at court!"

"I am persuaded that you are not in earnest," Vawdrey said calmly. "For you gave your word the princess's hand would be awarded at the outcome of this event, and every man present knows the King's word is law."

The King's face turned even more violently purple, and Una felt a sudden alarm that he might be taken off by apoplexy. She turned her eyes on the Queen, but Armenal was murmuring behind her hand to one of her ladies-in-waiting.

"You must not upset yourself, sire," Vawdrey said with a shrug. "For there is always some way of negotiating around these things, if needs must."

Wymer looked up sharply. "I do not take your meaning," he barked, a gleam of hope now in his eyes. "Do you tell me you've hit upon some way out of this damnable mess?"

Earl Vawdrey smiled a rather wintry smile. "Let me consider the matter, Your Majesty."

Wymer grunted but relaxed back into his chair. "Aye, well, see that you do, that's all!" he said pettishly. "For I won't abide by the winner of this piece of mummery, and so I warn you!"

Una risked another glance at Lord Vawdrey and found him looking thoughtful. She glanced back down at Otho, who raised his sword to the restless crowd. They, too, did not seem happy that there was no clear favorite to cheer for. It seemed almost that they picked up on their King's palpable displeasure and took it for their lead.

None of these competitors knew how to play to the crowd like the seasoned favorites did. In the last eighteen months, Una had come to a pretty shrewd knowledge of how fond these southerners were of their pageantry. Caer-Lyoness was used to the flamboyance of the King's Champion, Sir Roland Vawdrey, or the proud Jeffrey de Crecy. If they were to cheer for an antihero, they preferred the arrogance of Sir Garman Orde or the brutality of Lord Kentigern.

To them, Otho was naught but a grim-faced northerner who fought without flair and only a dogged determination that gave them precious little by way of entertainment. There was no pomp or colorful display in his mud-colored shield or glamor in his plain helmet without plume. He carried no banner and barely seemed aware it was a spectator sport.

They had vastly preferred the extravagant loss of that good-looking fellow from the first round, Una thought wryly. *What was his name? Sir Armand de Bussell.* He had danced around

11

for all the world as if he were on a stage. Feigning, he would go left, and then going right, staggering from blows against his shield and tumbling to the ground as though grievously injured, before rolling to his feet mere moments later, rallying again.

The crowd had responded with glee to his antics, cheering and then sending up terrific groans when he had been bested by what seemed a lucky circumstance by his opponent. Since he had been defeated, the crowd seemed glum and depressed in spirit.

The announcement of the next combatants' names evinced no ripple of interest, and so the afternoon proceeded. Una could not be impervious to the growing disquiet or the fact the mood was turning uglier as the day wore on. She glanced uneasily at the King, but Wymer's expression showed just as much disgust as the rest of the audience. The Queen, complaining of a headache, had disappeared after the first hour, and Wymer had gestured for Una to move up into Armenal's seat.

It seemed an inauspicious thing to do, but she was the subject here, so Una duly moved her stiff-structured skirts along and lowered herself with the usual attendant difficulties onto the Queen's seat. Her ceremonial robes were hard to maneuver, for they were stiff and rigid from the framework underneath. Wiping her brow, which was perspiring under the heavy headdress, she wondered how many more bouts they were to sit through before the eventual winner emerged.

The sun beat down on them as the contenders were eliminated one by one. To Una's horror, Otho proceeded from round to round until there seemed a certain horrible inevitability about his ending up in the final two. With a sort of dull, resigned pain, she watched the very last opportunity of escaping from her cruel fate trickle through her fingers. She had always known her bloodline would be the death of her.

Quite apart from the impediment of their close blood tie, Otho was ineligible for the tournament on every single score. He had no loyalty to the southern king he had been raised to despise, no estate to his illegitimate status, and he was competing under a false name. She had no doubt that these facts would be swiftly discovered in a matter of mere days, if not hours, and then what would happen? A double execution?

Una gave a faint moan and pressed a scarf to her mouth. She was sweating in earnest now, though she wasn't sure if it was from the hot sun or pure unadulterated fear. Were her last living moments to include being married to her own brother, and then summarily executed? Just when she thought the history books held all the shameful chapters of her blighted family's misdeeds, she found there was room for yet more infamy and scandal.

As though on cue, his current opponent yielded, and the crowd stirred restlessly to see Otho stand his ground, the final victor. A pugnacious expression on his face, he raised it to the royal box and Una gazed at him in despair. *You wretched fool, Otho!* Una thought bitterly, clenching her fists. *Why would you do this to me? I was so close. So, so close to renouncing my title and finally losing this cursed name!*

Just then, she noticed some commotion down on the sidelines. Earl Vawdrey was barring the announcer from entering the ring to confirm Otho's win and was instead sending in a group of entertainers. They looked a ragtag bunch of jugglers and acrobats, and in the center of them all was a swaggering court jester resplendent in trailing robes of red and gold.

"What the hells?" Wymer growled, sitting up in his seat. "Now what's afoot? Why's the fool entered the fray? I thought he wasn't appearing till the feast. Blessed if I can make heads or tails of this business!"

Una could only deduce that the court jester did not usually bring his revels to the competitors' field and heartily regretted that he had done so now. He was the one person at court who dared to be downright rude to her face with impunity. She surveyed him now with dismay as he leapfrogged onto one of the acrobats and rode him like a horse about the arena with a demented look upon his face.

The crowd immediately erupted into laughter. The jester dismounted and performed three forward rolls upon the ground before leaping up like a jackrabbit.

"Hold, my good lords, my good ladies, gentles all!" he shouted, his voice carrying far and wide. "I must protest most heartily at being left out in the cold from these proceedings. For His Majesty, the King, must needs grant me a boon on May Day, as is the custom." He directed a look up at the royal box, and the King rolled his wrist in assent.

"Aye, that is true enough," Wymer acknowledged grudgingly. "Good master Robkin."

"Aha! Aha!" The jester bounded about the ring, appealing to the crowd. "Didst not thou hear that good King Wymer did promise me a boon?" The crowd murmured back an assent, curious at this late turn in proceedings. "Then, this I ask of thee, my King," the jester suddenly boomed. "That I am given sway over this tournament, in my official office of Lord of Misrule!"

Una felt the sudden frisson of excitement that ran throughout the audience. *Lord of Misrule?* That put a different slant on proceedings. Suddenly, Robkin held his hands out before him and clapped for attention. "Bring forth the prospect," he yelled.

The acrobats and jugglers all looked around in great confusion, before suddenly converging on poor Otho, who was stood watching from the sidelines with some bemusement. They seized him now by the arms and bore him to stand in front of the fool.

"This?" howled Robkin. "You dare bring this before me? Nay, say it is not so!" The crowd reacted with amusement as he walked around Otho examining him like a bull at the fayre, prodding him with his long bauble stick. "No, no," he said, shaking his head sorrowfully. "This will never do!" He held up his hand for silence as the sounds of mirth grew from his audience. He stood a moment, cupping his chin as though in rapt concentration. Suddenly he spoke with great deliberation. "His legs, in truth, are not bandy enough to make him a goodly man in the stable," he announced, slapping Otho's calves until he was forced to jump from side to side to avoid the jingling stick as the crowd dissolved into gales of laughter. "No, no," he added, walking around to Otho's back again and gesturing toward his thighs. "I mislike his stance. I' faith, 'tis too wide! He'll ne'er stand guard at the stable door, in truth, he's more suited to a pigsty!"

Wymer guffawed, then seemed to remember his company. "Foolish fellow," he said lamely.

"This groom," the jester pronounced grandly, "is a fat-kidneyed fustilugs, unfit to mount so fine and spirited a filly." Una could have sworn that every eye present swiveled to look at her. They knew full well her unkind nickname. There could be no mistaking that she was the butt of this joke. "I like him not!" yelled Robkin. "I'll see that northern mare saddled by a worthy rider, you just see if I do not!"

Una tried to not let her dismay show as the crowd erupted in howls and whoops of laughter. The time she had spent in the company of rough soldiers had helped her to turn a deaf ear to many a bawdy joke or rough speech. Even so, she had to make a concerted effort not to stiffen in the face of such impertinence, if not downright insult.

"I invoke the law of reversal," the fool said, knocking his staff against the ground three times. A whispering started about the arena.

"The law of reversal?" Wymer repeated slowly. He looked at Una blankly. "What does the fellow mean by that?" Una could make no answer, for her heart was suddenly in her throat.

"He who is first, is now last," proclaimed Robkin triumphantly. "And he who was cast down in that lowest of positions is, by misrule magic, elevated now to the most revered and fortunate of men!"

A wondering chatter began in the stalls as everyone whispered and nudged each other in speculation.

"He who is first is now last," repeated the King with a fierce frown. "I don't think I quite…"

Una peered down at the ring and saw Earl Vawdrey gesturing to some guards. For one horrible moment she thought they were going to arrest Otho, but instead they plunged into the audience, and Una watched with a sort of horrified fascination the bizarre turn of events that saw them drag, a moment later, another knight altogether into the ring. He still held a flagon of ale to his lips and held a half-eaten pastry between his fingers. He had now shed most of his armor, but still wore the shoulder plates and his chainmail vest.

"Eh, what's all this?" she heard Sir Armand de Bussell ask as he was marched into the center of the ring by an armed guard.

"Good Lord!" thundered King Wymer. "Last place was de Bussell!" He reached out a hand to grab her sleeve and wag it. "De Bussell, I say!" Una looked at him speechlessly. Clearly the King was in the grip of some deep emotion. His eyes glistened and his face glowed. "By gads, I'll give Vawdrey a dukedom for this!" he said, his voice rasping. "Or mayhap," he reflected, "he'll want a title for that rackety youngest brother of his. Viscount Vawdrey or some such thing."

Back in the ring, the jester was turning somersaults before he approached the bewildered de Bussell.

"Sir Armand de Bussell," announced Robkin, puffing out his chest. "Have I got glad tidings for you this day!" He looked about him slyly at the audience, who were starting to break out into cheers. "For you thought you were cast down in the doldrums, the lowest among this fine company." He struck up a benevolent attitude. "Little did you expect, the miraculous transformation of your fortune!" Trumpeters blasted at this point, having picked up some cue, and a banner unfurled from the royal box. Una leaned over and, to her astonishment, saw the large green wyvern of House Blechmarsh hanging in all its glory. She blinked, reflecting that this particular standard had not been displayed in a southern palace in some five hundred years. True, they had expunged the golden crown that should sit at the beast's brow, but even so, it was an astonishing turn of events.

"I don't quite follow…" She faltered, not able to believe that she was to be offered a reprieve from the cruel fate that had so nearly befallen her. She started again. "Am I to understand—?"

But the King was not attending her, instead he was snapping his fingers to attract the attention of one of his pages. "Fetch us some refreshment, boy! Honeyed mead and cakes!"

Una turned back to gaze down at Sir Armand, whose expression of affable bewilderment was now being replaced with one of stunned disbelief. He was saying something now, his hands waving. It looked very much like a spirited denial of the great honor done him. Una swallowed and dragged her eyes away from his protests. *Poor man.* She felt bad for him, indeed she did. Doubtless this unlooked-for distinction was quite unwelcome to him, quite the opposite of what she herself felt. With his own patent lack of experience in the field, he could not have expected to win her hand. He must have entered simply for the experience, and now he found himself saddled with an unwanted bride.

For Una's part, she felt almost sick with relief. Her eyes scanned the arena anxiously as she sought out her half brother. She saw his expression darken with rage as Earl Vawdrey drew him to one side. Otho was bright red with anger, his mouth working furiously as he gave vent to his wrath. How like their father he looked at this minute, Una thought despairingly. She had seen their royal father's rages too many times to think this storm would pass quickly.

Una watched tensely as the King's chief advisor appeared to quietly listen for a while, then all of a sudden lift his head and say something that made Otho's expression blanch. Otho staggered a little, his face white as chalk as he stared at Lord Vawdrey, who was now all smiles again. Was it purely a figment of Una's imagination or did his smile look a little…sinister? Una didn't think she was fanciful, but certainly something about his expression and his stillness was disconcerting.

Looking at Otho, she could see he felt it too. He looked like a stunned fish, opening and closing his mouth. Lord Vawdrey's arm extended and she saw him passing something that looked like a purse of monies. For a moment, she caught her breath, thinking Otho would likely fling it back in his face. But to her surprise, he took the purse, gave a nod, and turned on his heel, disappearing into the crowd, leaving Earl Vawdrey standing to watch after him with an enigmatic expression.

If she did not know better, Una would have thought Otho had been paid off.

*

"Come now, Una!" Queen Armenal called from the other side of the screen. "You must surely be in your shift by now? You've been long enough to undress three times and the groom's party will be approaching soon."

Una sighed as she unbuckled the last of the straps that held the great structure of her underskirts together. It was an exhausting business climbing in and out of her royal regalia, and these southern women had no idea of the awkwardness of the wide panniers Una was forced to wear, which made it so difficult to negotiate narrow doorways and corridors.

"I won't be much longer," she replied as she stepped out of the wicker cage and, from the giggles and laughter on the other side, guessed that the Queen was likely rolling her eyes with impatience.

"I'm sending someone in to help you," Queen Armenal replied testily. "Jane, do please go and move things along!"

Una bit back her instinctive refusal of help. She had only ever had one attendant, her dear Estrilda, who had dropped dead with extreme old age after they had been only two months in residence at the winter court. She had been Una's mother's attendant before her and a dear creature, her protector, and her most loyal friend. She was irreplaceable, and since she had gone, Una had been fending largely for herself.

It was not that she did not like Jane Cecil, the Queen's favorite, for she had the nicest manners and had only ever been scrupulously polite and deferring toward her. If Una thought it a little odd that the Queen's favorite should be sister to the King's acknowledged mistress, she kept this thought to herself. Recently Lady Helen Cecil had been forced to retreat from court to the country estate the King had gifted her, for she was clearly increasing with child and without husband.

Everyone at court was fully aware of the fact, and Una could not say why precisely she found it all so distasteful. Her own father had had a parcel of bastards, but as her mother had died when Una was a few days old, there had been no question of them having to coexist in close quarters. She supposed it was no wonder that the Queen could be a little sharp somedays. After all, she had given Wymer no issue, so perhaps she felt her position precarious, though he already had a son and heir by his first wife, good Queen Eleanor.

Lady Jane swept behind the screen with an apologetic expression on her face. "Allow me to—oh!" She stared at Una in frank astonishment, and then at the pile of heavy fabrics and the complicated wooden structure fastened together with leather straps, then back to Una again.

Una cleared her throat. "My royal costume is quite elaborate in its underpinnings. Very different to the southern royal fashions," she explained.

Jane nodded. "Yes, indeed," she agreed faintly. She touched the wicker structure that Una had worn laced around her waist with one slippered toe. "It must have been vastly uncomfortable," she marveled.

Una nodded. "Yes," she agreed simply. "But now I am no longer a princess I need never wear it again." She gave a swift smile to the surprised Jane. "Perhaps it would be helpful if you could assist me after all?" she suggested, drawing her heavy linen shift up and over her head. Jane hurried forward obligingly to help drag it off her arms, and Una let out a relieved breath to be finally down to her last layer.

20

She stood now in the very thin strappy garment that was worn against her skin. She knew it to be rather sheer, but as the custom always used to involve placing the bride naked into the bridal bed, she could not see that it would signify much. She rethought this, however, when she saw how Jane stared at her.

"This, too, is very different to your own?" she ventured, gesturing to the translucent slip.

Jane swallowed and turned very pink. "Indeed," she gulped. "Why, it has no sleeves at all!"

"No," Una agreed. "We generally wear a second shift on top of it that has the sleeves. This one is just for next to the skin."

"Do you sleep in that?" Jane asked, reaching out a hand to touch the filmy fabric of the skirt. "Would you not..." She hesitated, her cheeks flaming. "Fall out of it?"

"If it is cold then I would leave on the outer shift also. As for falling out of it..." Una glanced down at her deep bosom and then back at Jane, who was girlishly slight. "I never have."

Jane's lips formed an *oh* before she gave herself a slight shake. "Are you ready to—"

Una shook her head and pointed to her frizzy yellow hair. "First I have to remove my wig," she explained.

"Wig?" squeaked Jane, and Una nodded. "You—you wear a wig, Princess?"

"Of course," Una said, shrugging. Her father had worn one and her previous understanding was that all royals did. Now, at Jane's incredulous reaction, it dawned on her that in this, as in all things, the Blechmarshes were distinct in adhering to the most uncomfortable and rigid of practices. She sighed and sat on the wooden chair, taking up the little bowl she reserved for this purpose and, reaching up, began removing the headful of hairpins she wore to secure the false mane in place. After a moment or two of stunned silence beside her, Jane joined her in the task, and Una was glad to find her fingers were gentle as she extracted pin after pin and added them to the bowl.

"Wearing all these must give you a blinding headache," Jane murmured as she extracted the last of the clips.

"My scalp does get very tender," Una admitted. "But again, after today I will be free from this also, so…"

Finally, the hairpiece felt looser on her head, and Una gave it a tentative tug until the whole mass of tight yellow curls came away in her hands. Jane covered her mouth with her hands and stared at her. Una flung the wig on top of the pile of discarded brocade, leather, and wood that comprised of her former self. "There lies Princess Una," she said softly. Jane turned and looked at the castoffs almost fearfully. Indeed, Una had to admit, looking at the heap, that it almost looked like the poor northern princess had collapsed in on herself, especially with the distinctive wig sat atop of the sprawling mass.

"It almost seems like we should bury it," Jane blurted.

Una gave a laugh, surprising her companion greatly. The expression of humor sounded rusty and out of practice coming from her lips. Indeed, she could not remember the last occasion she'd had to use it. "Hello," she said. "I'm Una." Jane's eyes grew rounder. "And you must not call me princess anymore."

Jane made a strangled sound in her throat. "We…we had better see to your hair," she said, uneasily. Una nodded, and together they removed yet another mass of hairpins until her auburn hair was unfastened from the tight braids wound about her head and hung down to her waist in a thick fall of dark reddish brown.

"I can scarce recognize you," Jane breathed.

"How much longer will you be?" Queen Armenal demanded. "You've been an age, I vow! Bring her out, Jane! The groomsmen must nigh be upon us!"

Wordlessly Jane took her hand, and Una allowed herself to be led around from the screens toward the center of the room, where a large bed lay on a raised platform, covered in rose petals.

"Finally—" the Queen began before another of her ladies let out a shriek. There must have been seven ladies stood in the room, spreading petals and draping garlands of flowers over the four-poster so it looked like a bower more than a bedchamber. Every one of them turned now to stare at Una with frozen expressions of varying stupefaction.

"That's never the princess!" Lady Fenella Vawdrey cried, dropping her end of the garland. "Whatever have you done to her, Jane?" For her part, Una rather liked the country-born countess who seemed such an odd choice of wife for the elegant Lord Vawdrey. She invariably said the wrong thing but was exceedingly kind for all that. Against all odds, her husband positively doted on her. She hurried forward now to clasp Una's hand. "You look so much better without those awful cumbersome clothes! I suppose that extraordinary hair was really a wig, then?"

"I can take no credit," Jane answered, serious as ever. "For the princess wrought this change herself."

The Queen was the first to recover from the shock, clapping her hands together. "Bring her to me," she ordered summarily, setting down her goblet of wine with a thump. Obediently, Jane obeyed her summons, and Una meekly followed until she was stood before Queen Armenal.

Una waited while those shrewd dark eyes summed her up. Much like Robkin the jester had circled her half brother earlier, the Queen paced about Una taking in her altered appearance. This time, it seemed the northern stranger was not found wanting. The Queen's lips spread into a slow smile as she came about to face Una again. "But this is charming," she pronounced. "Our princess was under a dark spell, and now she is freed by the kiss of true love."

The ladies gasped and twittered at this, clearly as taken with the notion as the Queen herself.

Una colored. It trembled on her lips to point out that the only kiss she had received thus far from Sir Armand had been a chaste salute placed clumsily on her fingers after their vows had been exchanged. His eyes had been bleary and his smile somewhat vacant. It seemed to Una's seasoned eye that her groom was sotted and small wonder, for every time she had caught a glimpse of him before the ceremony, someone had been pressing a goblet of wine into his hand.

"Quickly!" the Queen cried, for her sharp ears had caught the sound of the bridegroom's party approaching. "Set the crown of flowers on her head, then get her under the covers!"

Una found herself rushed toward the bed as the Queen's ladies hastened to set a flowered wreath over her head, while dragging back the sheets for her to clamber into the wide bed.

"I wonder what Sir Armand will say to such a transformation?" one lady gasped out before she was shushed and dragged to stand against the dressing room door. Apparently, the southern tradition was for the bridal party to prepare the bride, and to then retreat as the groom's faction approached. It seemed there would be some crossover as the Queen's party lingered at the far end of the room, eager for a glimpse of the bridegroom.

24

Three ceremonial knocks were heard on the bedchamber door and an upraised voice shouted out impressively, "The bridegroom has arrived!"

Lady Fenella cleared her throat discreetly, then called back, "The bride awaits her groom within!"

Then the door burst open and Sir Armand was dragged into the room, his arms slung around two supporters who were big enough to support his frame. Una huddled under the blankets as a stream of groomsmen noisily followed. They seemed a loud, inebriated bunch, and her heart sank when she saw her nemesis, the court jester, prancing about at the foot of the bed telling what, she could only guess from the raucous laughter, was a bawdy joke.

"Good luck, Una," called Fenella with an encouraging nod as the ladies hastily backed out of the room.

The King remained by the door, deep in conversation with Lord Vawdrey, though the earl seemed to be watching his wife as she whisked out of the dressing room door. Una had noticed whenever his countess was around, he had precious little attention for anything else.

"That's it! Take off his clothes!" the King boomed as Sir Armand was lowered onto the bed face-first. "No need to stand on ceremony. She's his wife now and will have to suffer him in worst states than this!" He guffawed and nudged his companion in the ribs. "Eh, Vawdrey? You should know, you've no head for spirits yourself!"

Earl Vawdrey looked a little pained. "'Tis sadly true, sire."

Una watched the King's eyes drift over the flower-strewn bed until they reached her and practically started from his head. "Good gods." He faltered.

25

"Your Majesty?" she heard Vawdrey inquire. A hush fell over the room as everyone present caught the direction of the King's stunned gaze and followed it to where Una sat huddled. Robkin's bauble stick hit the floor with a jingle and a clatter. The jester let out a surprised yelp.

"Ah, Lady Una," said Lord Vawdrey politely. He alone seemed quite unaffected. "I trust you are more comfortable, now you can abandon the royal trappings of the House of Blechmarsh."

Una's fixed smile grew a little warmer. She appreciated he was the first to address her without her old title. "Yes, my lord," she agreed. "Indeed, it is a great relief to me."

"I can only imagine it would be," he responded and turned back to the King. "Perhaps, Your Highness, you might suggest we now withdraw and leave the married couple to their nuptials."

"Eh? Oh, er, quite," Wymer agreed, still looking like he had suffered something of a shock. "Everyone out!" As they turned to go, she heard him murmur to Lord Vawdrey, "What the hells happened to all that hair!"

The court jester was the last to tear his gaze away, and in keeping with his character, he tripped over his stick on the way out. Una wondered if he felt obliged to exit all rooms in such a fashion. Either way, when the door was finally shut after them, she breathed a sigh of relief. Only then did her eyes travel down to where her naked husband lay sprawled on the covers. *Oh my.*

Slipping out of the bed, Una crossed to shoot the bolt across the door and then returned to try to haul the inert body up the bed so she could cover his nakedness with the sheets. To her surprise, he roused from his stupor sufficiently to aid her in this task. It was just as well that he did, for she would have stood no chance without his cooperation, for his body was large and heavily muscled.

26

She tried not to stare as she pushed and rolled him over the bed. She was no sheltered maiden, despite the distinction of her birth. A lifetime of military campaigns meant she had been fully exposed to all the privations of the battlefield. She had seen men's bodies before, whether it was a flash of buttock as they peed in a field, or stripped for the attention of a surgeon. She had never seen one "stark ballock naked" up close though, as she believed the term went. She could not help stealing a few glances at him now as she maneuvered him between the sheets.

He may have little prowess in the field, but his body was truly magnificent, she acknowledged. No wonder the King thought he looked the part of a bruising knight. With such mighty limbs, muscle, and sinew, any onlooker would be fooled into thinking him a serious contender. What a pity he could not actually deliver in the field. She bit her lip as her eyes wandered down over the expanse of muscular stomach and below.

Pragmatically, she considered the likelihood that the equipment between his legs would be just as ineffectual after his afternoon of heavy drinking. She had frequently heard ribald talk between men and had some hazy awareness that the efficacy of their pizzle was somehow related to the quantity of drink they had consumed.

Certainly, he was not "hard," that much was evident, though he seemed to be of impressive proportions down there as everywhere else. Unkindly, it crossed her mind that perhaps in all areas of his life, Sir Armand de Bussell might look the part, but otherwise be lacking. Robkin the jester had sworn the northern mare needed a stallion to master her, but in the end, it seemed he had given her naught but a gelding after all.

Strange to say, her heart squeezed with sudden sympathy for the handsome sot. She knew only too well what it was like to be considered one of life's disappointments. She drew the covers carefully over him before walking around to the other side of the bed and climbing in.

To her surprise, Sir Armand rolled over the mattress toward her, one arm closing about her, to draw her body to his. She could only suppose him well accustomed to a sleeping companion. Indeed, with a face like his, why should he not be? Even at close quarters, she could see no flaws in those handsome features.

She had fully resigned herself to a night of failed consummation when he shifted over her and began sloppily kissing her neck. His breath was hot and his mouth wet, and though she should find his drunken handling distasteful, she was shocked to find she did not. She was relieved he kept the brunt of his weight off her as one hand came to squeeze her backside while the other fondled her breasts through the filmy material. He fumbled a moment with the neckline of her undershift, unable to find access under the close fit of the material.

"Wait a minute," Una said, struggling to slip the thin straps down over her shoulders before peeling the garment down to her waist.

He gave a noise of husky approval as he lowered his face to her breasts and she awkwardly patted his head. She felt oddly touched he was even bothering to cuddle and kiss with her like this. She had heard enough soldiers' talk to know that such things could be dispensed with during a coupling.

After a few moments of this, however, she started to wonder if he was going to get to the main business. He didn't seem in any hurry, and his movements were definitely slowing now. She was beginning to suspect he was going to fall asleep, facedown in her bosom. That would be an indignity she could do without.

She felt a pang of dread lest the sheets not be stained with a drop of virgin's blood come morning. The whole court would be awash with talk of the ugly princess whose husband could not bring himself to tup her.

"Sir Armand?" she ventured. Was he snoring? Panic forced her to become forthright. She dug her fingers into the thick dark hair at the back of his head and lifted his face from her breasts.

"Wha...?" he asked blearily, looking like he could not quite focus on her.

"Sir Armand, it is our wedding night," she said urgently. "You must do your duty to King and country now."

"Duty?" he echoed with a puzzled frown. Then his gaze seemed to wander down to her breasts and sidetrack him. He sighed. "Gods," he said and licked his lower lip in a distracting manner. "Gimme a taste."

"You've already had a taste!" Una replied shrilly, though her color rose. "You must proceed now to the next step!"

He glanced about them in confusion. "Step? S'not a staircase, love. S'a bedroom."

"Sir Armand!" she said sharply. "You were a soldier were you not? In the late war?"

Sadly, this approach, which had worked well for Una in the past, did not seem at all efficacious with Sir Armand. "Shh," he said. "Too pretty to talk about ugly things."

This astonished Una so much that she was struck dumb for a moment. Of course, he was sotted, she reminded herself when she felt herself blush violently. *Pretty?*

He sighed gustily. "I'm drunk," he said confidingly.

"Yes, you are," she spluttered. He was honest, if nothing else. She bit her lip. "Are you incapable?" she asked forthrightly. He had not actually presented his…well, "manhood," to her. She had felt brushes of something against her thigh. She had thought it must be that, but what did she know?

It was no good just lying here like some shrinking maiden, she thought. He was simply too sotted to take the lead. But from everything she had ever been taught, men were base creatures with essentially two drives ruling them. To fight, and the other. Steeling herself, she wrapped her arms around his broad shoulders and rolled him fully atop her. He grunted and stirred, and she opened her legs to anchor him against her.

"Sir Armand," she panted, out of breath from the exertion, for he was a good deal larger and heavier than she had anticipated. She was tall for a woman and well-built, but he felt like a felled tree against her—if a tree were made of solid muscle. His eyes flickered open as she gripped his hips firmly between her thighs. Something was lying, heavy and hard against her stomach now, wedged between them.

"Mmm," he grunted and moved against her.

Una felt her whole body grow hot. It was happening! Flushed with triumph, she felt a tremor of fear nonetheless, for his manhood felt even larger brushing against her intimately like this. She struggled a moment to think of the right encouragement. What did men like? She had no idea. He had not responded well to reminders of duty. "*Please?*" she ventured timorously.

His head lifted and his eyes focused on her. "You want me, sweetheart?" he asked with a sleepy smile. Una felt a pang. Why did he have to be so good-looking?

30

"Yes," she answered truthfully and saw a flicker of pleased surprise pass over his face. "I really do."

He huffed out a breath. "That's nice," he said thickly, and Una inhaled a breath as one of his big hands caught her under her thigh, urging her to open wider to him, as he moved against her with a breathy sigh. She complied eagerly, suppressing a momentary wobble at how open and vulnerable she felt to him now. He breathed heavily as he bunched the thin material of her shift to her waist and palmed her buttock, stroking something against her most intimate parts.

Una felt a frisson of real panic as he pressed his large shaft between her legs, his eyes closed with concentration as the bulbous end of it nudged insistently against her. Her eyes widened. What had she been thinking? This wasn't going to work. He pressed forward unrelentingly as she bit back the objections her lips started to form. The pressure built as his flesh pressed painfully into her own, until finally, as tears started from her eyes, she felt something give inside her. With a brutal thrust of his hips, he surged forward and he was lodged painfully deep inside her.

Then he startled her by giving a bone-deep groan of his own. "Ah gods, that's good," he moaned.

"Ow!" The objection burst from her lips before she could stop it, not that he paid it any mind. To console herself she slapped a hand against his shoulder blade, sinking her nails into the tanned flesh there.

He grunted and thrust again. "So good," he murmured huskily against her temple, and she felt the brush of his lips there. *Not for me*, thought Una with a wince. She squeezed her eyes shut, trying to remind herself that this was all for the best. After this painful act, no one could dispute that she was a married lady come morning. Lady Una de Bussell, she reminded herself. A princess no longer. She certainly had never felt less like a princess than being swived by this lusty brute, she thought as he labored above her, his movements crude and vigorous. She held her breath and willed for it to be over soon. Even as she thought it, his movements slowed.

"Ugh!" he groaned and collapsed on top of her, breathing hard.

Una lay beneath him, catching her breath. Had he finished? Her cheeks burned. So, too, did the area between her legs. Her thighs were trembling from being held open so wide for the intrusion of his big, heavy body. Something was leaking out of her. Was it blood?

At last, he withdrew and shifted his weight to the one side of her, still caging her in with his big body. He was panting as though he had run one dozen staircases. To her surprise, he lowered his face to hers and kissed her on the mouth. Then he drew back his head, his face flushed and relaxed. Suddenly he gave an exclamation.

"What is it?" she asked, looking up at his expression of surprise.

"How did you make yourself beautiful?" he asked, then collapsed back against the pillows with a snore.

2

Armand woke suddenly with a lurch of his stomach. He groaned and rolled onto his side. Gods, his head pounded. How much had he imbibed? Some urgent memory hovered at the edge of his consciousness, troubling him. Did he owe someone money? Squinting one eye open, he found the room dark and unfamiliar, but that was nothing new. He moved around a lot. More troubling was the way it was spinning. He liked a drink, but he didn't usually drink to such excess as this. For some reason, last night he must have drunk himself into oblivion. He gave a hollow moan and shut his eye again. The sheets beside him rustled.

"Sir Armand?" inquired a voice. A cool hand landed on his shoulder. "Can I get you anything?"

He frowned. Too well-spoken for a tavern wench, though there was a faint accent running through it. Northern, he thought with surprise. You didn't find many northerners in Caer-Lyoness. His eyes opened wide, and he tried to focus on the pale, oval face that now hovered over his with an expression of concern. Fuck. He didn't remember her.

"I'll get you some water," she said and scrambled from the bed. Naked as a jaybird, he noticed with interest, despite his wretchedness. She was tall and well formed, with nice thick thighs, a neat waist, and a curtain of dark auburn hair that hung down to her waist and swished about her in a pleasing fashion. As she crossed the room, her bare feet padding across the floor, he admired her rounded backside, which had dimples on either side of the base of her spine.

Then something more pressing pushed to the forefront of his consciousness. "A basin," he intoned hollowly. "I need a basin." He grimaced, sitting up in alarm. He was going to spew his guts up. She hurried back and thrust a basin into his hands and he retched over it, bringing up a good deal of the strong, sweet wine he'd overindulged in. He would never drink it again, he vowed as his throat burned and a wave of misery and self-pity swept over him.

"Here," said the obliging female, hesitating as he retched again, but there was nothing more for him to bring up. Then he spat, and she wiped his mouth with a damp cloth. "You'll feel better now," she said briskly. "Here, let me take that." The basin was removed from his grasp, and Armand collapsed back against the pillows feeling sick as a dog. "I'm dying," he murmured, squeezing his eyes shut again.

"Drink this water," she said, holding a cup to his lips. Definitely not a tavern wench, who'd have been kicking him out of her bed at this point and cursing him soundly. Armand took a hasty swig of water and then pushed it away. He felt her hand smooth back his hair. Who the fuck was this ministering angel? Tentatively, he squinted up at her again. She had a faintly anxious look on her face. "You must go back to sleep now, Sir Armand," she said politely. "Then wake upon the morrow feeling refreshed, yes?"

He eyed her doubtfully. He liked her optimism, but not the fact she looked so grave. She wasn't his usual type. He liked them on the petite side and saucy, but he could see why he'd picked her alright. She had a sweet, full mouth and a nice round pair of tits with large nipples so dark they resembled autumn berries. He hoped he'd enjoyed her charms fully, because he knew he wasn't going to remember a damn thing in the morning.

With a groan, he rolled toward her, grasping her about her waist and hauling her against him. She gave a faint gasp but did not struggle or pull away as he rested his brow against her soft,

34

deep bosom. She made a damn fine pillow, he thought as his burning eyes drifted shut. After a moment, he felt one hand tentatively stroke his hair. *Nice*, he thought wistfully. He hoped he'd at least given her his mouth the night before, as he doubted he'd been able to stay hard for long considering the amount of liquor coursing through his veins.

*

When next he woke it was daybreak. Someone had thoughtfully kept the shutters closed, but he could see the light that was filtering into the room around the edges.

"Fuck," he groaned, clasping hands to his head and rolling onto his back. "My head." He cast about the room, his thoughts jumbled. Someone should be here with him, he was sure of that much, though the identity of his bedpartner for the moment eluded him.

Slowly, his senses returned to him. He had been competing in that damned fool competition the King had put on as part of the May Day festivities, though everyone knew it was really a ruse to get that ugly cousin of his off his hands. Armand remembered that he and Fulcher had determined he should lose in the very first round, in order to earn the fattest purse, for lately he had been performing well.

Then… His memory faltered. He had been dragged back into the ring and that damned fool jester had given some speech about the man in last place winning the princess. He blinked, and even that seemed to make him feel dizzy. He had won the princess as some sort of twisted consolation prize. They had been swiftly married in the King's private chapel and after that, his memory grew hazy.

There had been a woman jumbled up in it somewhere, a woman with a sweet mouth and a nice pair of thighs, but she was not the princess. What the fuck had he done with the princess? He sat bolt upright and almost immediately wished he had not. His head swam alarmingly. At his groan, someone moved at the opposite end of the room.

"Sir Armand, are you well?"

He turned his head and saw the attractive piece he had spent the night with. She was bent over a basin of water, washing and clad in a scandalous scrap of a translucent fabric that would normally have his full attention, but right now he had more important things on his mind. Where the hells was the fright of a wife he'd just bound his lot to? he wondered with a stab of anxiety. He was no expert on wedded etiquette, but spending the wedding night with another woman did not sound like acceptable behavior from a groom.

The King would likely be after his hide for this. Looking about the room, the fact it was decked out like a flower bower was not lost on him, despite his blunted senses. He turned cold. Had he thrown the bride out of her own bedchamber for a more alluring prospect? What if the princess had gone running to the King to lodge a complaint against him?

"Gods," he uttered in growing panic. "Where is she?"

His companion watched him in consternation. "Where is who?" she inquired as he flung back the covers and lurched from the bed, peering into the adjoining dressing room and then a recessed cupboard. He even stooped to peer under the bed, until he felt his head reel alarmingly.

"Maybe you should lie down, Sir Armand?" the woman suggested, looking concerned.

He recognized her soothing voice, too, from the previous night. "Can't," he gasped, raising a hand to his brow. "Got to think."

"About what, pray?" she asked, crossing the room to gently take his arm and steer him back toward the bed. "Just rest now, you've done everything you ought."

"What did I do with her?" he asked in faint desperation. "I can't remember."

She bit her lip, a pucker appearing between her brows. "With whom may I ask?"

"The princess, of course!" he muttered in anguished tones.

She blinked at him, looking suddenly concerned. "You mean me?" she asked gently.

"You?" He stared at her. "What?"

"Am I the one you're looking for?"

"You? But you're not..."

"I am Una," she said simply. "Your wife."

Armand stared at her. "No," he said uncertainly, then his eye fell on the mattress, where she drew back the covers, and his face fell as he noticed the telltale smear of blood on the sheets.

His eyes leaped to hers, and she colored faintly. "As I said, you did everything you ought," she said in that reassuring manner of hers and gave his arm a small pat. "I will just change the sheets and you must get right back into bed. After a few hours, you'll feel a good deal better. No one will expect us to rise before noon after the excesses of yesterday."

Before he could respond, she stripped the bed in a very methodical, unhurried fashion. He stood like a useless clod while she redressed it and then pulled the top covers back and patted it invitingly. "Come and take your ease now, Sir Armand."

His brains felt too addled to do anything but obey her. He hesitated a moment after sliding under the cool silky sheets. "Come and join me," he said, holding back the covers and moving into the middle of the bed. He watched the surprise flit over her face before she acquiesced. He hoped like hell he had been considerate of her last night, he thought, watching her climb in beside him.

She showed no fear of him, which was something, but he did not trust he had shown the deference or tenderness she would have expected from a bridegroom. Even sober, he knew nothing of bedding virgins, and inebriated, the gods alone knew how he had treated her. He could only wince at the thought of the clumsy coupling she must have suffered.

"I did not recognize you," he said awkwardly as she settled on her back beside him, resting her hands on her stomach. "You look…very different."

"It must be very confusing," Una agreed. "But as I am no longer a princess, I don't have to wear the wig or the costume anymore, you see."

He looked bewildered. "Wig?"

"Yes."

His brows puckered. "Costume?"

"Yes." She sighed. "Your southern royalty does not follow the same practice, but in my family, we were required to don such garb as befitted our station. It showed at a glance, you see, that we were royals. My father wore a wig such as that one his whole life." He cast an uncertain glance at her to find her expression was perfectly serious. "I presume somewhere in the beginning we Blechmarshes must have had very distinctive, fair curly hair. It had advantages on the battlefield, I suppose," she reflected. "Our forces knew to rally round us."

He shrugged at that, forbearing to point out that the north had suffered ignominious defeat four years ago, and rolled onto his side, slinging an arm around her waist. He felt the impulse to rest his aching head against her bosom but suppressed it. If that was what he had done the previous night, she was probably suffering from a lack of decent sleep as much as he was. His eyelids burned as he let them drift shut. He just wanted to wake up and find this had all been a bad dream.

*

When he next woke, his head was admittedly sore, but he found he could string two thoughts together without pain. He reached for a cup of water on the side and gulped it back in a few swallows. The princess was missing again, but he could hear noises from the adjoining dressing room and guessed where she could be found. He lay a moment, feeling sorry for himself. His usual good luck had abandoned him. No one could have foreseen such a fate lay in store for him. Shackled to a wife he could scarcely abandon without reprisal, and from royal quarters at that. Then, with a sigh, he climbed out of bed to face things squarely.

A steaming bath was awaiting him in the far corner of the room. He approached it gingerly. He supposed it must be his. Drying cloths and soap were laid out next to it, and with a shrug Armand stepped into it and gave himself a good wash, though he did not lie and wallow as he usually did when chance afforded him such a fine large tub. Instead he stepped out of it and rubbed himself briskly, first his body and then his freshly washed hair.

His clothes had vanished, but folded neatly on a chair a new suit awaited him, comprising of a burgundy tunic with gold detail on the sleeve and chausses to match. He paused to look at them. One leg was gold and one burgundy. Doubtless, fashionable courtiers would not hesitate to wear such garb, but Armand felt a marked reluctance to do so. Left with little option, he dutifully dressed in the clean clothes. At one point, Una peered out of the dressing room and found him frowning down at his mismatched legs.

"Do you need anything, Sir Armand?" she asked politely, coming back into the room. "Ah, I see you have taken your bath." This morning she was dressed in a burgundy gown with gold sleeves, presumably to match his own ensemble. The gown was elegant in cut, showing her tall, straight figure off to advantage. Admittedly, he had not paid her much attention the previous day, but he was sure she now looked nothing like the peculiar foreign princess who had watched proceedings from the royal box.

Seeing her tip her head to one side, he remembered she had asked him a question. "No, thank you," he replied. He was also surprised by how obliging northern royalty seemed to be. It was almost like she could not do enough for him.

She smiled at him encouragingly. "You look very fine. There is a hat and a cloak to complete the outfit."

Armand winced, but seeing the worried look that stole over her face, he immediately gave her a reassuring smile. "My head," he said ruefully, and she relaxed.

"Oh, of course. These are our going-away outfits," she explained almost shyly, then hesitated. "Do you think you are sufficiently rested and recovered for us to set forth today?" He could see she was anxious about his answer to this, though she was striving to hide the fact. "If not, we could wait until the morrow, of course."

"Gods no, I cannot stay!" He almost shuddered at the thought. "There's a tournament in five days' time I mean to compete in, and it's a good four-day ride from here."

Surprisingly, she seemed more pleased by this than not, for the color rushed to her cheeks and he was surprised to see how different she looked when her eyes lit up. Slowly it dawned on Armand that this royal bride of his had some expectation of his taking her away from court with him, which did not suit him at all. His heart thudded in his chest, and the inquiry he had been about to make died on his lips. Gods, what the hells was he supposed to do with her?

Clearly, she did not expect to be left behind. In vain, he tried to remember the precise terms of the marriage the King had offered with his royal cousin, but in truth he had paid scant attention. He had not intended winning her, after all. He cleared his throat. "What were you doing in there?" he asked, nodding toward the adjoining room, stalling for time for his sluggish brain to think.

"Packing," she told him. "I shall be ready to set forth when you are, Sir Armand."

He blinked. "Princess," he said heavily. "We need to talk."

A look passed over her face, which, if he had not known better, he might have thought was stark terror. The color draining from her face, she walked over to a chair and sat down, folding her hands in her lap. Watching her, Armand wished to the gods he had his full faculties about him. Something seemed "off" to him, though he could not put his finger on what. Why would the princess be so scared of his reactions this morning?

Was she afraid of him? Guilt washed over him again as he faced the foggy memory of his wedding night. Had he been rough with her? At some point, he *had* been confused as to her identity. He hoped to gods he had not confused her willingness. He looked at her so hard his head ached but recalled frustratingly little. She swallowed and lifted her gaze to meet his.

"I am ready," she said, and he could see her hands trembling even from where he stood.

He lowered himself onto the bed and sat facing her. He needed her to think this decision was as much her own as his. It didn't do to piss off royalty. Even disgraced royalty might have the King's ear. "I apologize," he said forthrightly. "But I think we need to be plain with one another." He watched her fingers clutch as he considered how best to proceed.

"Sir Armand," she said, swallowing convulsively again. "I am laboring under no illusions, I promise you. I am well aware that you did not—could not—have expected to win the prize yesterday."

His brows snapped together at that. Clearly the princess did not have the most flattering views of his abilities. He was surprised to find that needled him, considering his livelihood depended on such misapprehensions. He took a steadying breath. "Well, no," he agreed cautiously. "I can't say as I did."

She gave him a direct look. "Can we please be frank with one another?" she asked boldly.

Gods, that was the last thing he wanted! In his experience nothing good ever followed such words. Several unpleasant conversations with his father sprung to mind. He steeled himself for the worst and gave her a grim nod.

"Sir Armand," she said with only the faintest tremor in her voice. "All I want or desire from you is that you take me away from this court and give me the protection of your name. As for the rest of it, I promise I will make no demands on you. I care not if your estate is naught but a tumbledown hut, so long as I can be set down there and left in peace to make it into my shelter. Into my home."

His eyebrows rose at her speech. Though she was striving to make her voice calm and measured, the emotion underneath vibrated through her words. *Peace and shelter?* Not what he had been expecting to hear. For some reason, the words *tumbledown hut* also pricked some sense of family pride he had long thought was dead in his bosom.

"I'm a second son," he answered cautiously. "But my family name is a venerable one. I do have some lands. There is a house my godfather left me." He paused seeing the optimism that had flared in her eyes at his words. Clearly, it was more than she had dared hope for. He needed to extinguish that spark right now.

"Then—"

"Wait," he said, raising a hand. "I am ill prepared for this. I had not thought to take a wife, and the timing is not good for me to take a wife right now," he started. Una's face fell. "I have obligations and they don't involve returning home right away—"

"But that's absolutely not a problem," Una assured him, an edge of desperation to her voice. "I am used to travel; indeed, I am used to uncomfortable quarters and being on the road."

He halted at that as the fact sunk in this was one obligation he was not going to be able to wriggle his way out of. It was all very well saying it was not convenient for him to take a wife, but the fact of the matter remained that he *had* taken one. And ultimately the King must not want her cluttering up his court, or he would not have married her off as a mere consolation prize.

43

"My home will take both time and money to get the place habitable. I cannot simply take you there and leave you to camp out in a…"

"But yes, yes, you can," she urged. "I am not what you think me," she said beseechingly. "I have camped in caves, amidst ruins, and yes, in abandoned, falling-down shacks and outhouses. You forget, I lived a large part of my life being pursued by enemy forces—" She broke off, realizing he had probably once formed a part of the southern army. "If your house is damp, beset by rats, or has no roof even, it will be nothing I have not encountered many times before."

"With a wealth of servants and followers, no doubt," he interrupted dryly. "I keep none. The roof could well have fallen in, for all I know," he warned, realizing his arguments did not hold the weight he had expected. "I am not on good terms with my family," he added, starting to feel like he was swimming against the tide. "They are nearby but would not raise a finger to help you."

"That does not daunt me," she told him quickly. "Indeed, I would be more worried if your family were a doting one, for doubtless they would then resent the fact you were forced to wed me."

Forced? He regarded her blankly. Clearly the princess had no delusions about his willingness to take her to wife. He breathed in then out again slowly. It was no good pitying her. She was a burden he could ill carry. "It can't be done, Una," he said bluntly.

"Please listen." She took a few shallow breaths. "There is treasure," she began haltingly. "Blechmarsh riches I can lead you to. When our forces were taken or surrendered, it was buried at several locations across the border." She wrung her hands, and for a moment he thought there would be tears. She

44

took a gasping breath. "Karadok is one country again now and all can roam freely, so there would be nothing to stop us from retrieving it, is that not so?"

He stared at her, his attention fixed on her face. He did not think she was lying. "Treasure?" he said speculatively.

Una nodded. "Yes, gold and…and many jewels."

He narrowed his eyes. "You would not lie to me about this?"

She shook her head. "No," she said simply.

Treasure? Well, that did put a different complexion on things, he thought, leaning his head back against the wall. He was silent. With wealth he could fix up Lynwode, the estate his godfather had left him, and bring it up to something like a gentleman's residence. And wouldn't his brother Henry just hate that? He dwelt a moment on the idea with a certain grim satisfaction. Yes, that would certainly be one in the eye for old Henry.

Of course, it would mean having to return to Derring, with all its painful associations. He winced. He had not returned since his mother's death. The thought of seeing Anninghurst, the old family home, and his father was as unpalatable as always. Still, he thought, eyeing Una contemplatively, who said getting married, or even settling back in the vicinity, meant he had to heal the breach with his family? Lynwode lay a good seven miles from Anninghurst. They were estranged, and as far as he was concerned, they could continue that way until Doomsday.

"Have you…er…much to take with you?" Gods, was he really contemplating this? The wheels turned slowly in his head. He could hardly go turning up at Tranton Vale with a procession of carts, loaded with her belongings. Tranton Vale was not far from where the border used to lie. They could head for the tournament and then simply take a detour.

"One trunk is all," she told him promptly.

That gave him pause for thought. "One trunk?" he repeated blankly. She nodded. *Oh.* "Do you have a horse?" he asked, thinking practically.

Una shook her head. "The Queen permits me to use the mounts in her stable, but my own horse was confiscated when I was put under house arrest."

"Right," he said slowly. Curse his befuddled wits, for every thought took effort today. "I need to go and seek an acquaintance of mine in the city before I make plans. It shouldn't take me long to run him to ground and then I can return for you—"

"No!" The cry had left her lips before he could finish speaking. She rose jerkily from her chair, almost like a puppet on strings, hurrying over to clasp his hand.

"Please, Sir Armand," she said pleadingly. "I promise you I will not hinder you in any way, but I beg you will not leave me here without you." She squeezed his hand between her own, and he found himself speechless. "If you will only indulge me in this one thing, I promise you I will make you the most amenable wife in the world. I will never go against you, never question your right to hold sway." She gazed at him beseechingly.

What did that mean? He stared at her, trying to unpick her words. Suddenly, it struck him he was being handed the terms for an ideal marriage on a platter. "Let me get this straight," he said. "You are offering to make me a biddable wife and lead me to untold riches and wealth, in exchange for my taking you from the palace with me this day."

She gulped and nodded. "If you could only bring yourself to stand firm in our removal from Caer-Lyoness, I swear I will be profoundly grateful to you, till the end of my days, no matter what happens hereafter."

"You anticipate, then," he said, seeing the flaw in her bargaining at once, "that there will be some resistance to our leaving?"

Una bit her lip. "I fear so," she admitted. "It seems too good to be true that they will simply let me go." She hung her head, and he remembered she had been under house arrest before Wymer had taken her into his court. Maybe even here, she had felt little more than a prisoner.

"I cannot drag you around the city, Princess," he started reasonably, but she shook her head at this.

"No, not Princess," she insisted. "I am simply Lady Una de Bussell now, and yes, you can drag me anywhere, even to hell and back and I will not complain, so long as you take me with you."

Again, he found himself quite bereft of words. "My associate will not be in a respectable part of town—" he started valiantly.

"I do not care."

"Your attendants will surely—"

"I have none," she said swiftly. "Unless you mean to provide me with any."

"None?" he repeated dumbly. That did not seem right. Whenever he saw the King or Queen, they were flanked with attendants on all sides.

"Our marriage means I no longer qualify as royalty," she explained, still clasping his hand. "So, you see, you need not worry about such distinctions."

She was stood before him now with a look of painful inquiry on her face. Could he really say no, and just leave her here to await him in a fever of anxiety, after she had taken such solicitous care of him the previous night? After he had very likely deflowered her with a complete want of consideration? He sighed and shut his eyes for an instant. "Oh, very well," he breathed on an exhale.

Her head snapped up. "Very well?" she echoed.

He nodded. "I'll take you with me."

She seemed to struggle with words for a moment before swallowing and raising his hand to her lips. To his consternation, she pressed his fingers to her lips as fervently as though he were a holy relic. "Thank you," she managed to choke out at last, and to his alarm, he saw her eyes were swimming with tears. Suddenly she released her hold on his hand and turned away, swiping her eyes with her hand. "I will be the easiest traveling companion, I assure you," she said with a brave attempt at a smile.

He stared after her as she darted around the room, picking up a comb and a box of hairpins and snatching up a head veil. He watched as, with minimal fuss, she draped the cloth over her braided head and then pinned it in place. "We'll need to transfer the contents of your trunk into saddlebags," he pointed out grudgingly. "Do you have such a thing?"

She turned to look over her shoulder, but before she could open her mouth, a knock on the door interrupted them. "Come in," she called out.

The door opened and a troop of servants entered bearing food for their midday meal, which Armand was surprised to find he welcomed, and wine, which he did not. A small table was covered with a damask tablecloth and a variety of dishes as Una drew one of the servants to one side for a hurried conversation. Armand was just seating himself when he noticed one of the servants discreetly collect the used bedclothes from where they'd been folded on another chair in the corner.

Una thanked the departing servants and sat opposite him with a bright smile. "Can I pour you some of this ale?" she asked, ignoring the wine, and filling his goblet instead with the far weaker brew. The food was a tantalizing pair of juicy capons served in a thick herb gravy and accompanied by glazed vegetables. Though not yet restored to his usual rude health, Armand found himself doing the meal justice and felt the better for it.

He had barely finished his second plateful when another knock was heard on the door. This time it was not just servants to clear the table, but also a portly young man in sage-green robes with an expression of self-importance on his face. He cleared his throat and closed the door quietly but resolutely behind him as the servants fanned out, clearing away the remains of their meal. "Good afternoon, Sir Armand, Lady Una," he said, bowing to them in turn. "I trust I find you well. My name is Bryce, and I have been sent by my Lord Vawdrey to assist with your plans. It is the King's wish that you both remain here at the palace until your affairs are in order, and messengers sent ahead to prepare your home for your arrival."

"That is very good of His Majesty," Una replied at once. "But I'm afraid we cannot delay and mean to set forth on our journey today."

Bryce's second chin wobbled at this, and he looked a good deal shocked. "My lady, it is not to be expected that—"

"I'm afraid my husband's plans will not permit him to tarry here at the palace," Una interrupted firmly.

Bryce's watery gaze darted from her face to Armand's. "I am persuaded that Sir Armand must be fully sensible to the fact that this cannot be," he said, sounding both shocked and grieved.

"I am sensible of no such thing," Armand said brusquely, picking up his cue. He pulled back his chair and draped an arm along the back of it, assuming a cantankerous look on his face. "As I've always understood it, a wife's duty is to follow the will of her lord and master. Now we have filled our bellies, I am anxious to be off."

Bryce's mouth fell open. He stammered, "The p-princess can hardly—"

Armand raised a hand for silence. "You are speaking now of Lady Una de Bussell," he corrected grandly. "And on matters pertaining to her, I believe my will is the one that must be deferred to."

Una shot him a look of brimming gratification. "Of course, I must do as my husband wishes," she murmured demurely, her eyes downcast.

Bryce looked frankly aghast. "But how are we to make ready for this at such short notice? A trousseau must be prepared for the Lady Una!"

"Such things should have been done weeks ago!" Armand said scathingly, getting a feel for his role. He brought his hand down with a loud smack on the tabletop. The knives and spoons jumped and struck against the empty salvers. The servants leaped back from the tables in alarm, and Bryce's mouth

50

opened and closed. "Was not the sole aim of this competition to wed her off?"

"Aye, but we did not know her bridegroom would be in such indecent haste to leave!" Bryce protested weakly.

"Indecent? Who's to judge whether my haste be decent or not? I am my own man and what's mine is mine and no one else's!"

Armand noticed Una was wide-eyed at this tirade as well as Bryce. As for the servants, they were lapping it up. No doubt, it would be all around court by tomorrow that the poor princess was married to an overbearing ogre of a husband, who meant to rule the roost and bend her to his will.

Indeed, he marveled at his manner himself, for though he fancied he'd always had a talent for play-acting, he'd never imagined himself in the role of domestic tyrant before. He felt positively inspired, though where he was drawing it from, he had no notion. His own father had always been rather aloof and disinterested in his role as head of the family.

"Indeed, good Bryce," Una began placatingly, once the astonished silence had abated. "You need have no worries on that score, for I have packed sufficiently for our journey, and only require some saddlebags in which to convey my things and then I will be most amply provided for."

"And a mount," added Armand smoothly.

Bryce placed a finger and thumb on either side of his nose and breathed deeply a moment. Armand watched him with interest. Finally, he dropped his hand and drew himself up, a picture of quivering indignation. "I will do my best to give satisfaction," he said in outraged tones and backed out of the door in a show of injured pride. "Pray excuse me while I give the orders."

51

"Oh dear, poor Bryce," murmured Una. "I am certain he will go running to Lord Vawdrey, for he is his creature, you know." Armand shrugged. "Perhaps you are not acquainted with Earl Vawdrey?"

"I know his brother better, Sir Roland, the King's Champion."

Una nodded thoughtfully. "You would, of course. From tournament circles."

"Does it matter if he goes running to Vawdrey?" Armand asked.

Una bit her lip, clearly undecided. "I'm not sure," she admitted. "Lord Vawdrey is vastly difficult to anticipate. But in any case, I do not think we could have presented a better front. You were magnificent! Truly. I had not dared to hope you would give so convincing a display."

Armand assumed a modest expression. "I aim to give satisfaction." He almost *felt* modest seeing the look of admiration on her face.

"I could not have hoped for a better partner in the ruse," she assured him warmly. "Indeed, I almost believed you myself!"

He just felt relieved that his new bride was so easily pleased with a bit of bravado and swagger. He had that in abundance, but no doubt she'd soon learn he had precious little else to offer her.

3

Sat atop her new chestnut-brown mare an hour later, Una was ecstatic. Not only had Bryce provided her with a fine horse, but also with one smartly kitted out with saddlebags and panniers and a red leather bridle and saddle to match. He had been ably assisted in this by a fleet of servants who had packed and tied the fastenings, adding a whole host of other things that Una had not even thought to request. When she had been quite needlessly helped up into her saddle, a purse of monies had also been discreetly pressed into her hand.

In truth, she felt quite overwhelmed by it all. When she had humbly thanked Bryce for his offices, she was wholly sincere. She had not looked for such kindness; indeed, she had been expecting displeasure and even censure. To be sent away quite in disgrace, not with this abundance.

For a while, she had feared the King himself would come stomping down the corridor to forbid their flight, which, now she came to think of it, out in the open with a blue sky above her, seemed quite ridiculous. After all, Wymer had heartily wanted to be rid of her! She had known only one wobble, and that was when Bryce had looked up at one of the arched castle windows and she had seen Lord Vawdrey's dark figure stood there like a sinister shadow.

As her heart lurched in her breast, he raised a tentative hand in farewell, and Una caught her breath. He was letting her go! It was perhaps too much to see it as his blessing, but that was how she interpreted it at the end of the day. She had no illusions about where the power truly lay at Wymer's court.

Lord Vawdrey was at the center of everything, and precious little happened without his say-so. Occasionally Wymer got a bee in his bonnet, or Armenal asserted herself to get her own way, but for the most part, it was he who manipulated decisions of import at the royal court. She wondered briefly if the King *would* make him a duke, for engineering her disposal, and then dismissed it completely from her mind.

She had mirrored his wave with her own, and then turned her horse about to follow Sir Armand, who looked a very impressive figure indeed, sat astride his showy-white charger in his new burgundy suit. He wore the matching hat she had sewn, with its gold feather, though the short cloak had been stuffed unceremoniously into a sack. She could not deny it was too warm for a cloak as the late afternoon sun fairly blazed down. Indeed, she had discarded her own, which was now slung across the front of her saddle.

As they crossed through the west gate of the castle, into the bustling city streets, Una felt her spirits soar to quite giddy heights. She was free! Finally free. Only yesterday it had seemed an impossible dream. Not three hours ago she had felt she was fighting for her liberty in the face of a reluctant bridegroom who would be more likely to abandon than aid or abet her.

Armand turned in his saddle. "Stay close to me," he recommended, quite needlessly, for Una had no intention of letting him out of her sight. He led her down a veritable warren of side streets, some so narrow they had to wait until the stream of people subsided before they could ride down them.

Each street seemed to grow darker and less respectable-looking as they went on, and Una felt a twinge of alarm, observing some of the looks they drew from passersby. She fancied she now knew why Armand had looked askance at his new outfit. They did not fit in with the inhabitants of these narrow cobbled streets one bit.

Finally, her husband reined in before a rowdy-looking inn that had a large statue of a crow with an open beak huddled on the roof like a squatting gargoyle. Armand glanced up at the open window where two women, alike enough to be sisters, sat looking down on the street below, clad in somewhat low-cut dresses.

Armand doffed his jaunty feathered hat at them and called up a greeting. Both ladies broke out in simultaneous surprise. "Why, if it isn't Sir Armand. I scarce recognized you, togged out in that regalia."

"Don't you look the proper gentleman!"

"Ladies, I have made my fortune," he responded, beaming. He swept an arm toward Una. "A rich widow has consented to throw her lot in with mine. Behold my good lady wife, the Lady Una."

Both women gaped at Una in open curiosity. "She never!" blurted one, while the other gasped, "Fancy!"

Una rallied at once. "Good day, ladies," she said pleasantly. Neither one seemed disposed to answer her with anything more than a bold, assessing stare.

"Is my man still here?" Armand asked casually. "I rather lost track of him, with all said and done."

"I expect you did," said the first with a toss of her head. "Wiv you up and gettin' leg-shackled and all!"

"He left," put in the other with an indignant huff. "Skipped out on his room wivout paying his board," she said with a sideways glance at Armand.

"Funny," he said with a shrug. "I could have sworn you insisted we paid up front, Bess, my love."

"Well, *you* might," she snapped. "But he never!"

"And we thought you'd skipped out and all when you never returned last night!" the other added spiritedly.

"A most understandable conclusion to make," he agreed sorrowfully. "I shall make reparation, of course, for your inconvenience," he said, soothing their feathers noticeably. "I suppose it's too much to ask that he left my pack in your keeping?"

"He might have left some sundry things what we had to have moved down to the cellars," said one with a shrug. "We didn't have no room to spare for things what got carelessly left behind by folks what skips out wivout paying their bed and board."

"I am most profoundly grateful," Armand said with a small bow, "that you set my things aside for safe-keeping."

The other cocked a speculative eye at Una. "You'll be able to pay for his room, now your fortune's made," she said, and Una thought that Armand had not seen this particular turn of events, though it seemed quite inevitable to her. She could only suppose him lamentably lacking in self-preservation instincts.

"Of course," he agreed cheerfully and swung down from his saddle. "Send out that lad of yours, Dickon, to stand guard here with the horses and I'll come inside and pay my way." One of the women retreated from the window and moments later they heard a side door open. "You'll be alright to remain here while I retrieve my pack and buy some information?" Armand asked Una in low tones.

Una nodded, only thankful he did not expect her to abandon her horse and all its treasures to be robbed. Dickon stumped out, an amiable-looking giant.

"You stand guard now over my wife and horses and you'll be well paid for it, my lad," Armand told him, patting his arm. Dickon nodded and took his horse's bridle. "I won't be long," he added, though Una was not sure if that was for her benefit or Dickon's.

When Armand disappeared into the door, the woman he'd called Bess leaned out of the window again. "Here, love, what did your last man do?" she asked curiously.

Una blinked, but as Bess was falling out of the front of her dress, she did not think that was an unnatural reaction. "He was a glover," she said, recovering herself and hitting on the first profession that sprang to mind.

"Oh yes?" A gleam of interest came into Bess's eyes. "I did hear as an uncommon number of glovers was caught up in that fire last year in Halperton Square. That how you lost your man, was it?"

Una shook her head. "Old age," she improvised. "He was a good deal older than me."

Bess looked unconvinced. "Only I did hear," she continued, "as most of them glovers in Halperton Square lost all their materials and premises in one fell swoop, as well as their lives." She cast a sharp look at Una. "If you was to be a widow to one of them, I doubt you'd be left with much by way of riches."

Una shifted uneasily in her saddle. She wished she'd said her departed husband was a spice merchant now. Noticing her unease, Bess suddenly turned conspiratorial, lowering her voice. "Don't you fret, sweetheart. I ain't going to tell 'im. You gotta make what you can of this life, 'specially us women. Use what the gods gave us. If you hooked 'im, telling 'im you was a rich widow, then more fool 'im, I says."

Una rearranged her expression into one of sorrowful agreement. "It's a hard lot in life for us women," she concurred.

"But I'll give you a piece of advice for nuffink, my love," Bess said with a nod. "First chance you gets, I'd skip out on this one if I was you." She nodded toward Armand's horse. "Before he skips out on you. Depend upon it, that's what he'll do, first chance he gets." A look of disgust passed over her face. "You can't trust men what has a ready, smooth tongue, nor ones wiv a pretty face. And this one you've took up wiv has got both. Clean 'is pockets out, first chance you gets, my darlin'," she urged. "And get yourself another old 'un. They're easier. The older and uglier the better, in my experience."

Dickon guffawed, but Una was spared from having to react by the reappearance of Armand, who was now carrying a pack in one hand and some well-worn saddlebags in the other. Casting a reassuring look in her direction, he strapped these to his horse as Una surreptitiously extracted a coin from the purse that hung from her belt.

Mounting his horse, Armand flipped a coin at Dickon and started forward. Una took the opportunity to turn in her saddle and toss the coin up to Bess. The other woman caught it, a look of surprise on her face. That look deepened when she looked down at the coin in her palm. She let out an exclamation, then hurriedly closed her fingers over the gold gleam. Una smiled when their eyes met and nodded farewell. Bess blew her a kiss. "*Bless you*," she mouthed. "*And good luck*."

There was no opportunity for them to speak for the next twenty minutes, as they navigated their way out of the narrow passages and toward the wider spaces of the main square. Una looked about with interest to see the streets grow clearly more affluent and respectable as they approached the square, with increasingly decorative windows and guild badges and banners displayed on the sides of the buildings. The streets seemed in the main to be named after the livelihoods that dominated them. They went down Saddlers Walk to approach Mason Way and then came out on Tailor Street.

They had now reached the square and could ride abreast of one another.

"What did you give Bess?" Armand asked with interest. "Back at The Stone Crow."

"A coin," she answered, considerably surprised that he had noticed their exchange. His attention had seemed elsewhere at the time. He said nothing, but she could see the faint pucker between his brows. "She was kind enough to give me a piece of advice," she admitted.

His eyebrows rose. "Doesn't sound like Bess."

"Ah, but you're not a fellow woman," she pointed out.

Armand seemed amused. "She has never struck me as a champion of her own sex, I have to say."

Una was silent a moment, pondering this. "Am I to take it she runs a bawdy house?" she asked calmly. Armand went off in a coughing fit. She could see she had stunned him and was instantly contrite. "I'm sorry, have I said something I ought not?"

"Not a bawdy house, no," he spluttered. "It's an inn. She runs it with her sister, Fanny."

"I thought they looked alike," Una observed. "So, she and her sister run a business together. Does it seem unlikely to you, then, that she would be concerned about the fate of another female?"

He appeared to consider this. "Perhaps not," he admitted after a moment. "Do you always tip when someone gives you a piece of advice?"

Una thought about it. "I'm not sure anyone has given me a piece of well-intentioned advice in a long, long time," she confided. "Usually—" She stopped abruptly.

He turned his head. "Usually?" he prompted.

Usually, it will be a veiled threat was what she had been going to say, but she found she did not want to start her new life with dire reflections on her past one. "Usually, people do not imagine I stand in need of it," she improvised lightly. "It made a nice change. I'm sorry if you thought me profligate."

He gave her a sidelong glance. "Not at all," he answered. "And how you spend your money is your own affair."

Una bit her lip at this. Did Sir Armand think she had money of her own? She had better set him straight on that score. "I have only the contents of the purse at my belt," she confessed. "The King did not see fit to provide me with a dowry, I'm afraid." To her relief, he did not seem visibly bothered by this piece of potentially shattering news. She had suspected all along that he had paid scant attention to the terms when he entered the May Day competition.

"We're turning down here," he said, gesturing to another side street that had a series of horseshoes hammered to a post.

"Blacksmiths?" Una ventured.

"Aye, and stabling. We'll leave the horses here awhile, until I run Fulcher to earth." He glanced up at the sky. "I think we'll need to remain one night in the city. There's some honest hostelry to be found here and respectable inns in the next two streets."

60

Una nodded and followed him into a stable yard where a groom immediately ran out to greet them. Una dismounted as Armand went over their needs with the groom. He then approached Una's laden horse and started unbuckling the bags, which he slung over his broad shoulders. Having been assured their needs would be met, he paid his coin up front and gestured for Una to follow him as he made his way back out into the street on foot.

Una lowered her voice as she fell in step beside him. "Would it not be wise for me to take an assumed name whilst we are here?" she asked conspiratorially.

Armand appeared to consider this. "How so?"

"I was thinking of Una being a northern name," she explained painstakingly. "I doubt somehow it is popular in these parts."

"That would doubtless be more remarked upon in the country," he said with a shrug. "You forget Caer-Lyoness is a port and a capital city at that."

"So, my accent would not then draw remark here in the city?"

"Your accent is very faint," he reassured her. "And none would ever recognize you from any public appearance you may have made." He cast her a quick look. "You're scarcely recognizable in truth."

She smiled slightly at that. "Yes, so you demonstrated in the early hours of this morn."

His step slowed. "Did I actually do that?" He groaned. "Search for you under the bed? I was hoping that part was just a dream."

She shook her head. "It's not to be wondered at, I was dressed in full regalia when you married me in the chapel."

He looked at her uncertainly. "Did you pack that headdress with the horns?"

61

"No." She almost laughed again at his look of relief. "In truth, it used to give me a headache. I left it behind, along with the jeweled collars, which were more like breastplates. I doubt very much Queen Armenal will ever wear them, for though valuable, they were both cumbersome and very weighty." She hesitated. "It felt right to leave them at the palace. That is where my ancestors wore them many centuries ago."

He nodded. "They belong in a case on display. No living, breathing woman should have to cart them round like an armored destrier."

She was so relieved that he did not think she should have brought them to be melted down for their gold and precious jewels that for once she did not mind the comparison between herself and a warhorse. "I am certainly not sorry to lose them," she admitted.

They had reached the next street now, which sure enough seemed to be a procession of inns, starting out as large and sprawling and getting humbler and less grand the further along you walked.

"Did they tell you at The Stone Crow where you could find your man?" she asked, hoping she was not overstepping the mark.

He nodded. "Though he is very much his own man, as he will be sure to tell you, if you give him half the chance," he said dryly. "Fulcher usually has a bolt-hole or two he can retreat to. Apparently, his cousin has recently taken rooms in the next street, above a cordwainer's."

They walked about halfway down the cobbled lane before Armand pointed upward at the sign of an improbably colored hog's head. They crossed the road and made for its door. The Blue Boar seemed a clean and pleasant establishment. Armand had no sooner inquired than the landlady assured them a room was at their disposal. He set a handful of coins down and asked for supper to be sent up to their room that evening and then followed the servant up the stairs.

Dumping their bags in the corner of a well-appointed room, he drew Una to one side. "If you will make yourself comfortable now, I will see to my pressing business and be back as soon as I am able." Una nodded and he gave her a searching look.

"Very well," she said, seeing he seemed to expect a vocal response from her.

"Wait!" he called after the retreating servant. He tossed a coin. "Fetch a goblet of wine." He turned back to Una. "Did you want a bath or—"

"No, for I had one this morning," she assured him. "Please don't trouble yourself on my account, I will be quite content to await you here." She gave him a smile, which she hoped was convincing, and watched him disappear out of the door with a sinking heart. Try as she might, she could not rid herself of the fear, however irrational, that it was the last she would see of him.

Of course, she was being ridiculous, she told herself firmly. He was known to the King, and skipping out on his obligation would be no easy thing for him to do. Besides, she had no reason to doubt him, other than his obvious reluctance to take her to wife. Since she had told him about the treasure, he had fallen in with her plans more or less. But oh, how she wished she had not been forced to fall back on the promise of those most ill-gotten gains. She felt a twinge of unease and did her best to dismiss it. But what if others had talked, and the treasure had long since been dug up and carried away?

She had no choice, she reminded herself as she accepted the cup of wine from the returning servant. She had needed to bring something to the table in order to strike their bargain. Her poor self was scant enticement these days. If not, she would scarcely have been offered as a consolation prize. She took a sip of the wine and washed her hands and face, unpinned her braids, and removed her overdress to lie on the bed in her gold-colored kirtle.

She hoped she might take a nap, but alas, sleep did not come. Instead she piled up the cushions behind her back and slowly sipped her wine as she tried not to worry overmuch about what was to become of her. If she could have kept busy, then she could have kept such worries at bay, she thought, but she could not get her sewing out now, not when everything was packed away so neatly and she did not know at what time Sir Armand would return.

It wasn't like she dabbled with a bit of elegant stitchwork like some ladies. Una did not do fancy needlework. Plain sewing was all her nurse had taught her, and she had made her own undergarments and nightgowns for years now, though it might not be considered proper employment for her station. While under house arrest with Lord Mycoft, his housekeeper had taught her how to expand her repertoire to include outer gowns and tunics. Indeed, sewing for her eventual freedom and walking every inch of the grounds of Mycroft Hall had been what got her through those three long years of house arrest.

Her sole pleasure and occupation at court over the past eighteen months, apart from attending the many tedious court events, had been planning and sewing her wardrobe for her eventual freedom. When she had plucked up the courage to ask for materials, she had been sent brocades and satins and velvets enough to make her gasp with delight. Wymer, unlike her father, had not seen anything amiss with such a request. He had made no comments, at least to her face, about making silk purses out of sow's ears.

In the privacy of her own room, she had sewn surcoats and tunics and kirtles aplenty. She had pieced together hats and hose and sleeping caps until she could turn her attention on her future bridegroom's wardrobe. She felt gratified when she remembered the fine figure Sir Armand had cut in the burgundy and gold outfit she had made him. She had never made a garment for a man before and had been a bit worried she had overestimated the proportions. After she had sewn it, she had definitely thought she had cut the tunic on too generous lines, but Armand had no problem filling out the shoulders to perfection.

Her thoughts dwelt on Sir Armand de Bussell a moment with mingled feelings. In some ways she could wish he was a little *less* striking, if truth be told. The contrast between them would be all the clearer when the groom was so handsome. Still, once he had abandoned her on his estate, the difference in their looks would make no odds. Maybe then people would start to finally take her on her own merit.

A knock on the door interrupted her thoughts, and she hurried to answer it to find it was the servant bearing their supper on a tray. Una took it with thanks and explained that she did not know what time her husband would return, so not to bother clearing it until morning. She then set it down on the small table and placed a cloth over it. As for herself, she had no appetite, for her stomach roiled with unease. Besides, she had eaten well at the palace at midday and did not need anything now. Luckily it was good plain fare, a meat pie with bread and cheese. When her husband did return, he could eat it as his leisure.

Una braided her hair into one single plait down her back and undressed to her shift. Climbing into the bed, she left one candle burning and closed her eyes. Finally, she allowed herself to contemplate what action she could take if her husband did *not* return. The most obvious course would be to return to the palace. It would be humiliating, of course, but she had likely suffered worse embarrassments.

Then again, she thought, her pulse picking up, maybe she could just disappear? She wondered how much gold exactly she had left in her purse. Enough to flee Caer-Lyoness doubtless, but was it enough to buy a small place in some obscure corner of the kingdom where she could conceal herself for the rest of her days? She doubted it somehow. She was only four and twenty. There would be years and years she would need to support herself for. Then again, there was her dubious marital status. Could a marriage be so easily overlooked when it had been consummated? She wasn't sure.

Then, just to comfort herself, she allowed herself to imagine a completely unrealistic future where she could support herself by her own wits alone. Perhaps she could stay here, right under King Wymer's nose, in his summer capital? She could return to The Stone Crow tomorrow and ask Bess to advise of cheap quarters where she could set herself up as a seamstress, plying her needle to earn her bread.

A smile curved her lips even as a tear trickled down her cheek. It was a nonsensical dream, but it did give her some respite from the harsh reality of her situation. In her fantasy, there were no guilds or restrictions on women's means of earning a living. There was no prejudice against northerners to drum her out of business. It was a lovely place where everyone would welcome her as a neighbor and a citizen, and she would never be found wanting again.

Her husband woke her in the early hours, hammering on their door. Una, a light sleeper, woke at once and found the candle still burning in its holder. She picked it up and crossed the room to let him in. For a moment, she thought he was drunk again, for his appearance was certainly disreputable in the candlelight. Then she noticed the gash above his eye and the dried blood crusted on his nose. She ushered him inside and bolted the door behind him.

"Are you hurt? What happened?" she asked in concern. He waved these questions aside, making for the basin of water. "Should I ask for more hot water?" she asked, setting the candle down and fetching him clean cloths.

"Nay, this is fine," he said, dunking his split knuckles under the water and wincing. "Ouch."

Una reached around him and submerged one of the cloths in the water. She had experience enough, and that gash needed cleaning. He stood still while she pressed the cold cloth to the wound, lathering up his hands with soap and washing away the dried blood.

"Were you set upon by thieves?" she asked.

He appeared to consider this. "Yes," he said finally. "In a manner of speaking, that is exactly what happened."

Una tutted sympathetically. *Poor Sir Armand!* And all this time she had been thinking quite uncharitably that he had left her in the lurch. "Do not despair," she said, keen to make it up to him in wifely solicitude. "Recollect that I have the purse of gold that Bryce gave into my keeping. All is not lost."

He gave her a sideways look. "I did not say they robbed me."

"Oh. You managed to fight them off, then?" He must be better able to handle himself in a fistfight than he was on the competition field, she thought.

"Yes," he said briefly, drying off his hands.

She noticed he was eyeing her shift and realized it was a bit immodest to walk around in. "Your supper is on the table," she told him, placing the candle there and retreating to huddle under the covers of the bed.

He walked over and peered under the cloth. At the sight of the meal, he seemed to perk up considerably and pulled up a chair to wolf it down. Una watched him in the dull gleam of the candlelight, with her elbows resting on her knees. She wanted to question him but knew full well she had promised nothing but dutiful compliance.

When he had eaten his fill, he sighed, "That's better," then rose to start undressing. Una noticed he had lost his hat, for his dark curls were bare, and there was a long rent up the leg of one of his chausses. She did not mention either as she knew an accommodating wife would not comment on such things.

"Is your business now concluded, so we are at liberty to leave Caer-Lyoness tomorrow?" she asked tentatively.

"We'll leave at first light," he told her with a yawn, and came toward the bed. "Do you not mean to ask me where we are bound?"

"If you are agreeable to tell me, then I would be most interested, of course."

He frowned slightly. "We make for Tranton Vale. It's an annual tournament on the rural circuit."

"I see," she answered politely. "I have never attended one, so it should be a novel experience." He nodded but looked distracted and she felt suddenly uneasy. "But perhaps you do not mean for me to attend?" she said before adding quickly, "I will of course abide by whatever you think best."

"What else do you imagine I mean to do with you?" he asked as he climbed into the bed. "I shan't abandon you on the wayside if that's what you're implying."

She looked across at him in some alarm and was relieved to see she had not offended him. "No, no," she hastened to assure him. "Only that I was not sure if there might be some point en route you might wish to set me down. After all, I do not know in what part of the country your estate lies," she pointed out.

He looked evasive. "It's not on the way," he said shortly, and Una found herself suddenly doubtful he even possessed an estate. She suppressed the small tingle of alarm this gave her, for if he did not, surely that was against the terms of the competition. With an effort, Una forbore to press him further on the matter.

"Tranton Vale lies north," he told her, throwing out a pillow and dragging another under his head. "I've bought a map, and tomorrow we can mark out those treasure sites you spoke of and plan our course of action."

Una's heart sank. Assuredly, they were not heading for her husband's home. Her mind veered away from the risky business of retrieving hidden northern loot. It seemed she would have little choice in the matter, or indeed *any* matter until she had made things worth Sir Armand's time and bother.

4

Armand awoke the next morning feeling a hell of a lot better than he had the previous one. He stretched, then tentatively felt the grazes from his altercation with Fulcher's hired friends. Fulcher had not wanted to give up Armand's sizeable share of their winnings from the previous day. It had taken some persuasion to claim his money. Persuasion provided by Armand's fists.

It seemed his sometime companion thought their gambling racket was now at an end and Armand would turn respectable after his marriage. Fat chance. Still, perhaps the dissolvement of their partnership was timely if he was now to embark on treasure hunting. Fulcher could not be trusted to divvy up their winnings, let alone within a mile of a treasure trove.

He checked his split knuckles, which were healing nicely. Only then did he think to turn his head and check the whereabouts of his wife. In the background, he could dimly hear her moving quietly about the room.

"Do you always rise this early?" he asked blearily, rubbing his eyes.

"Yes," she admitted. "Did I wake you? I'm sorry."

"It wasn't you," he sighed. "Besides, we're making an early start, remember?"

She made no response to this, and from the splashing sounds, he deduced she was washing. He sat up and blinked at the sight of her hunched over the basin, in what he could only suppose was her shift. He had never seen a shift quite like it, for it was fitted to her form to an almost scandalous degree, and the thin material afforded him an enticing view of her backside and those rounded thighs he had admired so much previously.

He cleared his throat and drew his legs up to mask his body's obvious response. Una pressed a drying cloth to her eyes and turned.

"I'm sorry, I did not catch what you said," she admitted, tilting her head to one side in inquiry.

He stared a moment at the bodice, which was just as sheer and just as fitted as the rest of the garment. Just about managing to tear his gaze from her full breasts and those enticingly dark nipples, he swung his legs over the side of the bed. "Nothing of import," he said huskily and reached for a drink of water.

"I'll just get rid of this," she said, carrying the basin over to the window. "And pour you some fresh."

He did not dare watch her progress, or he'd never be able to rise from the bed to wash. At least, not without scaring the daylights out of her. Instead he took a few steadying breaths in and out and tried to think of inane things until his surging ardor cooled. She had taken him by surprise, that was all. He took a deep draught of water before breathing back out again.

Once she'd poured him fresh water and retreated to the far end of the room to dress, he left the modesty of the bedsheets, pulled his braies up over his ass, and made for the basin. He was still hard, but if he presented her with his rear view, hopefully, the princess would remain in total ignorance of the fact.

How typical, he thought wryly, that he would choose this moment to turn weak with lust for her, when she'd lain beside him all last night without arousing so much as a flicker of interest in him. He rubbed the soap flakes through his fingers and gazed down despairingly at his wayward cock, which tented the white linen of his braies, refusing all promptings to go down.

He glanced back over his shoulder and was satisfied Una was occupied shaking out her gown rather than quivering in horror at the evidence of his arousal. He wasn't fooled by her determinedly down-to-earth manner. Her words may be calmly spoken, but her shallow breathing and panicked eyes told a different tale. Una was skittish around him and likely scared of men. Who could blame her? He knew she had not led the easiest of lives.

Stroking his jaw, Armand decided he needed a shave and retrieved his razor. Then he caught sight of his pile of discarded clothing from the night before. Crossing over to it, he reached into the tunic and retrieved the sizeable pouch containing his winnings from his May Day performance. It had taken him a while to wrangle his fair share from Fulcher's grasp. He would miss that devious bastard, he thought with surprise. Who would he talk to now on the road? Who would he plot and scheme with round the campfire? Who would have his back in a barroom brawl? He could hardly expect a princess to make him a decent new business partner.

He should be glad to be rid of his association with the weaselly Fulcher, he told himself sternly. It was tiring how the fellow did not believe the brawn should take the lion's share. He knew full well that Fulcher believed himself to be the brains of their operation, but enough was enough. Hiring four thugs to beat him in an alleyway was not the act of a once-trusted accomplice.

If mourning the loss of his companion achieved something, it was a total quenching of his burgeoning lust. Loosening the strings of his coin purse thoughtfully, he carried it over to the bed and spilled half of its contents onto the blankets. "Here," he said. "You take half."

Una glanced around from where she was fastening her front lacings. Her eyes widened at the gleam of gold coins. "I already have some money that Lord Vawdrey provided," she started, but he waved this aside.

"Just put it in your pack or in your alms purse," he recommended, retying the string of the pouch, and throwing it on the chair next to his tunic. Then he walked back to the basin and soaped up his jaw to shave. After a moment, he heard the chink of coins and realized she was taking his advice.

"I suppose," she said, retrieving her saddlebag, "that it would be as well for me to divide it between my purse and my pack. If our wealth is split between the two of us, and then between our baggage, then we have some safeguard if the one of us was unfortunate enough to be robbed."

He grunted in agreement, dragging the straight blade down his chin.

"Have you ever been robbed before, traveling on the road between tournaments?" she asked.

Armand shook his head. "I ride a massive destrier and carry a sword at my hip," he pointed out dryly, then asked. "Have you?" He watched her in the looking glass as he dunked his razor in the bowl of water. Una hesitated before she shook her head, and he was quick to pick up on it.

It struck him that he might do well to set more store by what she did not say than by what she did. "You've had some experience, I deduce," he said and saw her look up in dismay.

"No, no," she protested weakly. "For I always traveled with a personal guard of at least three men, even when split off from my father's forces."

"A personal guard?" he echoed. "What happened to them when you were captured?"

"They were captured also," she said simply, then caught sight of his expression. "You must not imagine I formed any attachment, for they were very rarely the same men. My father kept them in strict rotation, so no bonds were formed."

Armand frowned. "And why was that?"

Again, she paused before answering. "In case of betrayal or some conspiracy against him."

Armand's eyebrows shot up, but Una was not attending him as she was tucking some money in the foot of one stocking. He still wondered at her stricken expression when he had mentioned thievery, but he did not have time to pursue that right now. Instead he dried off his face and made haste to dress. He avoided the gold and burgundy chausses and opted instead for an old black pair out of his pack.

"If you let me have the torn one, I will mend it for you," Una said, looking around from where she was pinning her veil in the dressing mirror.

"Pardon?"

"The gold legging. I noticed last night it was ripped."

Armand looked down at the chausses he had bunched ready to shove into his bag. "Oh, right," he muttered. Was it? He picked out the gold one and tossed it on the bed next to Una's things. "Thank you," he said, resigning himself to the fact he would likely have to wear odd legs again at some point.

"I can make you a new hat as well, if you like?" she suggested helpfully.

Armand knew for a fact he had managed to lose that damned feather cap at some point last night and had rejoiced in its loss. "I don't usually wear them," he said firmly and saw her silently mouth "*Oh.*"

"Let's make a pact," he said on impulse.

Una turned about and approached him with interest. "A pact?" She gave him a questioning look.

"For our journey. Let's vow to be true companions to one another on our adventure."

He was surprised to see a flush cover Una's cheek and was gratified to see he'd said the right thing. "I'd like that!" she exclaimed, looking pleased, and after a moment's hesitation, she held out her hand to him. He enfolded it in his own and they shook on it.

Armand found he was in a good mood as they made their way to the hostelry to collect their horses. The sun was shining, and something always invariably came along in his experience, even when things looked bleak. *Who knows, maybe this marriage wouldn't be such a bad bargain after all?*

"Do you have that song in the south too?" Una asked with interest as he strapped their baggage to the horses.

"What song?" he asked before realizing he had been whistling a tune.

"'The Wicked Archer of Trusslowe.'"

He shook his head. "We don't call it that. Here it's called 'The Maid of Hamblin's Ruin.'"

"Oh. Either way, I suppose it is always a tragic tale for such a pretty, lilting tune," she commented wistfully.

Armand, thinking of the rather raucous lyrics of "The Maid of Hamblin's Ruin," thought a change of subject might be in order. "Er, yes," he murmured, stepping back. "I think we're all loaded up. Shall we be off?"

They navigated their way out of the city without any mishap, though he noticed Una looked tense as they approached the city wall, which was guarded by soldiers wearing the King's colors of blue and gold. Drawing his horse abreast of hers, Armand shot her a reassuring smile as they passed through without challenge. He saw her visibly exhale with relief when they passed out of the city gates.

Had it been her father, he wondered, who had started those rumors of a warlike princess who espoused the Blechmarsh cause like a true prince of the blood? What a load of bullshit that had turned out to be. He recalled a portrait he had seen of her once, or the remains of it, for it had been slashed and vandalized by southern soldiers running amok in a castle they had taken over the border.

She had been sat astride a horse, brandishing a sword and dressed in breastplate and chainmail above her skirts. From what he could remember, the depiction bore little resemblance to the reality, for all it had suffered so much damage. He felt a coldness pass over him now as he imagined what they might have done to the real woman if they had ever got their hands on her in the aftermath of battle.

She must have seen all manner of horrors and had no doubt seen man in his most bestial and unworthy state. It was little wonder she hadn't thrust him from her screaming, he thought wryly and once again felt uneasy at his dim recollection of their wedding night. He hoped to the gods he had not been a brute with her. He found he did not altogether trust her assurances that he had "acted just as he ought." The gods knew her expectations had probably not been high to begin with.

Shaking his head, he forced himself to focus on the present. "If we take this main road today, we shall be sure to find an inn for our midday meal and also lodging this evening," he remarked cheerfully, and Una smiled back at him.

"Well, that sounds ideal."

And so, it should have been, but over the next few hours, Armand found himself increasingly under the impression they were being followed. He turned in his saddle several times over the morning, but though he saw wagons with goods, peddlers on foot, and wayfarers aplenty, he did not notice any one face featuring particularly among their fellow travelers.

Frowning to himself, he wondered if the main highway might not be the right choice of road they should be taking after all. Or was he just being fanciful? After all, why should anyone choose to follow them out of Caer-Lyoness? While it was true that he and Fulcher had parted ways acrimoniously, he had felt after their dustup the previous night that things were settled.

Then, of course, there was Una. He glanced at her thoughtfully; could there be any reason why she might be pursued? It was hard to imagine that Wymer would set his hounds after them when he had been so keen to rid himself of her in the first place.

"Is anything amiss?" Una asked in a quiet voice, and he bit back the hearty denial he had been about to issue. After all, had they not vowed to be trusty traveling companions?

"I'm not sure," Armand replied instead cagily. "I have had the oddest feeling for the past few hours that we are being followed." He saw her eyes widen and wondered if he should have kept this to himself. "Have you noticed anyone?" She shook her head but looked ill at ease. He paused before asking, "Can you think of any reason why someone might be following us?"

Una paled, looking down at her reins a moment before answering. "It might be my brother, Otho," she said in the manner of one making a painful confession. "He competed at the May Day tournament under an assumed identity."

Armand bit back an oath. "He competed?" he asked carefully.

Una's color rose. "He cannot have been thinking clearly. He was very devoted to the northern cause. I can only imagine that he thought to rescue me." Her shoulders rose and fell in a hopeless manner.

"By marrying you?" Armand asked incredulously.

Una's ears burned red. "It would not have been legal," she pointed out. "I—to be honest, I do not know what could have been running through his head."

Armand thought about this, still a good deal startled. "You are on good terms with him?" he ventured.

"I have not seen him for over four years," she said. "But yes, we were always fond of each other. I liked him best out of all my half siblings."

"How many do you have?"

"My father never counted the girls," she said in an expressionless voice. "But he sired four boys out of wedlock."

He was loath to pry, but if these half-blood siblings might start popping out of the wainscoting, he should be prepared. "Is it a painful subject or…?"

She did not answer for a moment. "Do you have any siblings, Sir Armand?" she asked, and the return to formal address did not go unnoticed by him.

"Two brothers and a twin sister," he admitted.

"A twin? You must be close."

"Not especially." His family was never a thing he voluntarily discussed, but he fully recognized the hypocrisy of expecting her to while he would not. He grimaced. "I have an older brother, Henry, who is my father's heir. He is also a colossal bore," he said damningly. "And his wife's even worse. Then I have a younger brother, Roger, who is also something of a dullard."

"And your sister? Is she also a bore?"

He glanced across and found Una's eyes twinkling. He relaxed at once. "Somewhat," he answered with a laugh. "She didn't used to be, but then she married a bore and became one by association."

She nodded. "So, your family are boring." She sighed. "That must be nice."

He snorted. "Nice?"

She was silent a moment. "Maybe my father had more offspring that I do not know of," she said at last. "But the ones he acknowledged were Forwin, Otho, Umrey, and Waleran. It was a great source of bitterness to him that they were born on the wrong side of the blanket and I his only legitimate issue." She took a deep breath before continuing. "They all served in his army. Had he won the war, my father promised Forwin and Waleran great titles and estates. Their mothers were noblewomen, you see. As for Otho and Umrey, they served as simple soldiers. They were all wholly devoted to his cause."

Armand did not speak, just waited for her to continue. After a moment she did. "Umrey was killed at the battle of Leefold. My father barely acknowledged the loss, for it was in the early part of the campaign and he said we must all be prepared for sacrifices. But when Forwin and Waleran both died at Demoyne he was devastated. I believe he would have legitimized Forwin if his conscience would have permitted it, but he believed too strongly in the divine right of kings to ever formalize a bastard." She lapsed into silence once more and looked sad.

Armand cleared his throat. "Forwin was your father's favorite?"

"Yes, he was his firstborn and older than me by some five years."

"But you did not like him?"

Una colored slightly. "He was too like my father for me to like him," she admitted.

Her lack of filial piety was strangely cheering to him. "I never liked my father either," he admitted bracingly.

Una gasped then coughed. "He was too boring for your tastes?" she asked after a moment.

"He was…very distant," Armand said cheerfully. "Disapproving and aloof. I was my mother's favorite though, and looking back on it now, I can see why my brothers resented me for it." He winced. "She was not a subtle woman."

"Neither was my father," Una added, looking a little guilty. "I never admitted to anyone before that I did not like him."

"How does it feel to say it out loud?"

Una thought about it. "I'm not sure," she said musingly. "In the north, everyone would have it that he was a saint and a martyr. No one would ever dream of breathing a word against him. It feels a little wrong to acknowledge that I held no love for him out loud."

"Give it some time," Armand recommended. "It will get easier." She smiled faintly but made no reply to this. "Tell me about Otho."

Una considered this. "He and I are much the same age. Maybe that is why he was my favorite, I do not know. His mother was a serving maid at my father's castle in Menith. She died when we were both quite small, and my father had Otho fostered out to a knight called Sir Moreland. All my half brothers would be brought to visit on feast days and sit at the high table. Forwin and Waleran came at other times too, but Otho and Umrey were only permitted on special occasions." She lapsed into silence for a moment. "Forwin was always…unkind…to Otho. Umrey too, but it was not so bad for Umrey because he had his mother still and her people, whereas Otho had no one. I suppose, really, it was Forwin's insecurity at his own status that caused him to lash out at them, but it was hard not just to see him as a bully."

"How was Forwin to you?" Armand asked.

"Oh, he never dared to be anything other than scrupulously polite to a princess of the blood," she said in an odd tone.

He wanted to probe further but could tell a dark shadow was being cast over Una to speak of her past. The twinkle from her eye was quite snuffed out and she had turned pale. In the spirit of fair play, he thought he had better volunteer some personal detail. "My mother used to say I was the very image of her own father and favored me over both Henry and Roger," he admitted. "It did not exactly endear me to them."

At length, she asked, "Is your mother dead now?"

"Yes, some four years now."

"What of your father?"

He pulled a face. "Oh, he's still around."

"And he did not play favorites?"

"I'm happy to say he disliked all of us equally," Armand responded with a smirk.

Una lapsed into silence, before rousing herself. "I think you said your siblings are married?" she ventured.

"All save Roger, who is intended for the church. Well, at least he was last time I spoke to him," Armand acknowledged. "Which was a while back."

"I see, and they all settled around your childhood home?"

"Henry and his wife, Muriel, live with my father at Anninghurst. That's the family seat. Henry will inherit, of course."

"They have no children?"

Armand shook his head. "No, and I doubt they will now. Muriel is older than Henry. She was a widow already when he married her and must be nearly fifty if she's a day. My brother Roger has probably left home for the seminary at Upper Derring by now. That was the plan I believe."

"And your sister?"

"She lives about five miles from Anninghurst with her husband."

"And they have children?"

Armand screwed up his eyes. "Boy and a girl, I think." Una blinked at his vagueness. "Pretty sure that's right," he added.

She looked like she wanted to press him further but held herself back. He could only be glad of her forbearance.

"So," he said after a few minutes' silence. "If your brother was to waylay us unexpectedly, what would his motivation be, do you suppose?"

Una looked troubled. "I could not be sure. We have not seen each other since I was taken by Wymer's forces. I was given no news of his whereabouts, or indeed anyone else's while I was under house arrest with Lord Mycroft. I do not know what he has been doing for the past four and a half years," she admitted hopelessly. "He could even have been prisoner for some of that time at least."

"Could it be that he simply wishes to see that you are healthy and happy?" he suggested slowly.

"It could well be," she agreed. "As I said, we were always fond of one another growing up." She chewed her bottom lip.

"What is it?" he asked, idly curious about what was on her mind.

"What if it is not Otho?"

"Who else could it be?"

"Soldiers," she said tensely. "What if they say I did not apply for the King's permission, as is correct?" He saw her knuckles were white where she held the horse's reins.

"His chief advisor was well aware of our plans," he pointed out calmly. "I don't think you need worry on that score. And anyway," he added with a shrug, "if they did, we would simply accompany them back to the palace and *get* the proper permission."

Una's relieved gaze flew to meet his. "Really?" she croaked.

"Of course. What else?" She did not answer, but he saw her relax in the saddle. "What say you to this place?" he asked, nodding to an inn that had just come into view on the horizon. "To take our midday meal."

Una raised a hand to shield her eyes from the sun. "I am agreeable," she said and attempted to throw off the heaviness of their prior conversation with a smile.

He almost wished he had held his tongue, instead of troubling her with it. He stole a look at her as they turned into the courtyard. She was clearly an excellent rider with much experience. It was a pleasure to watch her handle the pretty mare Lord Vawdrey had sent for her use. "Was she one of the Queen's stable?" he asked, directing his gaze at her horse.

"No, I have never seen her before. She's a real beauty. I doubt the Queen would have parted with such a horse without a lively fight."

A groom came out of the stables to meet them and they dismounted, handing the horses over to his charge, after extracting one or two valuable items from the saddlebags.

"Come," said Armand. "Let us see what their table has to offer two hungry travelers." He held his arm out to her and Una took it. Together they strolled into the entrance of The Red Hind, and he saw her seated at a bench by the window as he went in search of some service. He soon found an amiable-looking servant who assured him they would bring out some repast with all due haste.

He was approaching the main chamber again when he heard Una's voice upraised and paused on the threshold.

"Indeed, Otho," he heard Una protesting spiritedly. "You mistake the matter. I was not unwilling in my marriage, and I am here by my own free will."

He could not make out the impassioned words that answered, for the male with her spoke in tones of low urgency.

"No, Otho," Una broke in again. "I will not come with you. I beg you will understand, you are *threatening* my liberty, not aiding it by this action."

Armand stepped into the room. "Ah, good day," he said pleasantly, noting how the man's hand clapped at once to the dagger in his belt. "How do you do? I'm de Bussell and I see you already know my wife." He walked toward them purposefully but slowly, giving the man time to recover his composure. He was a hulking male with close-cropped hair and a strong, stubborn jaw.

"Armand," said Una with relief, and he did not think she had addressed him so familiarly before. "Allow me to introduce you to Otho, who is by way of a kinsman of mine."

Otho straightened up, looking Armand's way with marked reluctance. "How do ye do?" he muttered stiffly.

"But what a pleasant coincidence to run into your kinsman in such a remote spot," Armand commented blandly, coming to a standstill behind Una. He flashed an easy smile as he dropped a propriety hand to rest on her shoulder.

Otho's gaze followed the action with frozen hostility before glancing away. He swallowed before answering. "A minor connection only," he said hoarsely, finding his voice. "From a less venerable branch of the family."

"I see," Armand drawled, swinging a leg over the bench beside Una. "Can I convince you to join us for your midday meal, kinsman Otho? You would be most welcome to share our meal."

Under the table, Una's hand briefly touched his own. He was not sure if it was an unspoken warning or a gesture of support. It didn't really matter; catching hold of it, he raised it above the table and brought it to his lips before folding it firmly between his own two hands. She closed her fingers around his own, grasping him firmly.

"I wish you would, Otho," she said brightly. "It has been too long since I last saw you, and it would be good to hear how you have been."

Otho's jaw worked angrily. "You know I cannot," he muttered.

"Why?" asked Armand politely, though he knew of only one reason for not breaking bread or eating at another man's table. It meant, by the old ways, that you were forbidden from shedding his blood. "You are fasting, Otho," he mused aloud. "Perhaps you are on a pilgrimage? Now I come to think of it, I believe there is a shrine near here to some saint or water nymph, I forget which." The landlord had entered at this point, bearing a platter of fresh bread. "Ah, landlord. Perhaps you can advise us. The shrine near here next to the lake, who is it dedicated to?"

"Why, bless you, my good sir, that shrine is dedicated to Saint Drusis." He set the bread down and leaned his hip against the table. "That there shrine is the reason for most of our trade these days," he chuckled, rocking back on his heels.

"A popular saint?" Armand asked, taking a piece of bread from the plate and tearing it. It was barley bread, fresh and warm. He passed a piece to Una, who took it with thanks.

"I should say he is." The landlord beamed. "Why, newlyweds come from miles around to visit that shrine!"

"Newlyweds?" asked Una gamely. "Then perhaps we should visit it, husband? For we have not yet been wed three days."

The landlord looked from one to the other of them. "Is that so? A happy coincidence! You must make for the shrine as soon as you have taken your meal."

Armand appeared to take this under consideration. "We have been blessed already by a priest," he prevaricated. "Why should we need this additional benediction?"

The landlord seemed to be enjoying a private joke. "Oh ho! You won't want to miss this opportunity, good sir, indeed you won't!" he said, rubbing his hands together. "There is a seat at that shrine, formed naturally in the rock it is. They do say that the saint blessed that seat so whosoever sits in it first, be it husband or wife, will hold sway for the rest of their marriage."

"Indeed?" said Una with raised brows. "It seems too good an opportunity to miss."

"Sounds a very risky business from my point of view," Armand pointed out with a grin. The landlord guffawed and two more maidservants emerged at this point carrying roasted venison, white pea soup, pork pie, and a large flagon of ale.

"This all looks very delicious," Una said to the landlord, who bowed to them and then poured three cups of ale.

"Do not hesitate to hail me should you need anything else," he said, retreating to the kitchens.

"You're sure we can't tempt you to join us?" Armand asked Otho cheerfully, but Una's brother would only glare at the floor and shake his head. "A pity," sighed Armand. "But you can only lead a horse to water." Otho looked up quickly at that, but then flung away from them, slamming the door shut behind him so hard that the hinges rattled.

"He means well by me," Una said unevenly. "Only he does not understand."

Armand reached for the venison and began to carve. "Try not to worry," he said to Una as he placed a slice on her plate. "We won't stop again until nightfall, so you need to eat well now."

"I think he will be dogging our steps," Una replied in the manner of one making a confession. "He has a determined character and will not accept defeat on this so easily."

"Or he will be skulking in the stables waiting for us to finish here," Armand agreed briskly. "But there's little to be gained from worrying about that now."

"Sir Armand," she said earnestly, placing her hand over his. "You must not underestimate Otho. He is very handy with a sword. Indeed, he came out of that May Day tournament as the rightful winner—"

He felt a prickle of annoyance. "Una," he said, turning his hand under hers to capture her fingers. "You must not underestimate me either. I am perfectly capable of handling brother Otho." She looked startled and frankly unconvinced, which was his own fault really for shamming that loss in the first round.

"Was May Day the only event you ever saw me fight?" he asked, releasing her hand and reaching for his ale cup. Was it too much to hope she might have seen one of his more reputable displays in the field?

"The King required my presence at all of the royal tournaments held over these past twelve months," she answered, avoiding his eye.

Armand cast his mind back. Unfortunately, he had found it more profitable to throw all his recent royal performances. He eyed her silently as she picked up her spoon to sample her soup. Gods, she must think her husband totally inept. The thought was strangely bothersome to him. Almost, he hoped her churlish brother was waiting outside for him, so he could vindicate himself by sending him sprawling in the dirt.

"Have some more bread," he said aloud, shrugging off such uncustomary thoughts. After all, what did he care what she thought of him?

He managed to keep the conversation flowing during their meal, ably assisted by Una, who it seemed was an old hand at hiding her unease. Her conversation and dutiful smiles did not show her anxiety. The only thing that gave her away was the way her fingers could not keep still. When they were not plucking at her napkin, they were tearing her bread into small pieces or burying themselves into her skirts.

Armand found himself grudgingly respecting her fortitude. No one could have been pleasanter or smiled wider as she thanked the landlord when he reminded her to visit the shrine and "gain the upper hand." Of course, the landlord did not know that Armand had already wrung a promise from her that she would yield to him in all things. For some reason, that thought was a disquieting one too.

"What piece of advice did Bess give you?" he asked impulsively as he extended his hand to her, helping her up from the bench.

Her smile seemed less forced this time as she took his hand. "She cautioned me against the wiles of a pretty face," she admitted. "And suggested an old man for my next matrimonial prospect."

"Did she, by gods," he laughed, pulling her out of her seat and glad to see the twinkle restored to her eye. "I hear they are easier to handle."

"That always seemed unlikely to me," she admitted. "In my experience old men are stubborn and intractable, and it is almost impossible to change their mind on any point."

He guessed she was speaking of her sire, but not wishing to raise that particular specter right now, he did not voice his suspicion. Instead he led her outside and felt her tense as they approached the stable. The groom, however, fetched their horses without any altercation, and they remounted and were soon back on the road.

The next few hours passed without incident. It was a pleasant ride, the sky was blue, the sun shone, and all seemed right with the world. Whenever he glanced Una's way, she had a smile playing about her lips and was clearly enjoying herself.

Doubtless she was seeing south Karadok at its best, for the trees and hedgerows were in full blossom and the fields full of workers employed in planting out the crops. It must indeed be sweet for her to savor such views, after three years of house arrest with the dour Mycroft family and then a year and a half stuck at court attending stuffy state functions.

"Not long now," he said, catching her eye. "The inn we are making for is The Merry Wayfarer. I know it well and we are assured a good night's rest there."

Such, however, did not prove to be the case. For when they finally arrived at the inn, Armand was most put out to find the landlord who came out to greet them was not familiar to him. It soon transpired The Merry Wayfarer had changed hands. After an indifferent supper, they retired to their room and he drew a map out from his saddlebag and unfolded it.

"Do you think you could mark on this map where you know the northern treasure to be hidden?" he asked, setting it down between them.

Una's expression remained calm, but he thought he felt a ripple of unease from her as she drew the document toward her. Just for the tiniest moment, he wondered if she had lied about the prospect of hidden treasure, but then dismissed the thought. She seemed inherently truthful, if anything.

She frowned over the map, running a finger over its surface. "It still shows the border," she commented with surprise.

"It's an old map."

Her finger hovered over a large area marked by forest, and she looked up. "I can put approximate areas, but the locations are more precisely fixed by markers that are not shown on your map."

He nodded, returning to his saddlebag for quill and ink and a small penknife. "Do so," he said, passing her the items. "You will need to repair the nib. I'm not much of a scholar, or one for writing letters."

Una busied herself inspecting the quill and trimming it to purpose for the next few moments as he sat back in his chair and poured them both another goblet of wine. After this was done, she dipped the pen in the ink and started industriously scratching away at the parchment.

"Tell me about the treasure," Armand said, taking a sip of his drink. The wine was faintly sour and an unpleasant reminder of The Merry Wayfarer's shortcomings.

She was silent, intent on her work. When next she dipped into the ink, she looked across at him. "It is not what you might expect," she said flatly.

He lowered his cup. "How so?"

"There are no crowns or scepters, no royal jewelry."

He thought about this. "Gold?" he asked. "Jewels?"

"Yes," she admitted. "But the majority of the gold or silver is in plates or coins. The jewels will be set for the most part in items of worship."

Items of worship? His eyebrows rose. "The northern cause fell back on ecclesiastical donation in its latter days?" he hazarded.

Una gave him a very direct look. "Donations were accepted from every quarter. The nobles and barons were expected to turn over great reserves of their wealth. When that dried up, the northern cause stripped every house, church, monastery, or abbey that its forces chanced upon."

Armand was silent a moment. "So," he said, "the treasure is not so much a king's ransom as loot."

Una inclined her head. "Yes," she said simply.

"And your father hid some of it?"

Her smile was bitter. "My father was a fanatic. He would envision no future that did not see him set on the throne at Caer-Lyoness and covered in glory. But he had a trusted advisor, a general who was more realistic. He conspired to make caches that could be recovered in time of need."

"And he told you their location?"

She nodded. "He made me memorize them like a catechism, lest I ever had need of them. To rally the cause in the event of disaster."

"And what happened to this general?"

"He was executed after the battle of Kettelbrooke." Her tone was neutral, but he thought he heard a quiver of some emotion there.

"You were fond of him?"

"He was a decent man and always considerate of me."

He set down his sour wine and left her at her task as he went in search of the slovenly maid who had failed to bring their hot water for washing before bed. The inn seemed largely deserted, he thought, descending the stairs without seeing another living soul. Clearly its change of hands had led to a decline in patronage, and he wasn't surprised, if their lackluster supper had been anything to judge them on.

He walked through empty room after room until he was forced to head for the kitchens in search of some service. Crossing the threshold, he found the landlord conferring with the groom, the maid, and someone in a grubby apron, who he could only guess was the cook. They wheeled around in surprise at his entrance, the landlord exclaiming hotly, "We don't receive guests in the kitchen, good sir! My cook is a temperamental man!"

Armand looked at the cook and thought he looked more furtive than bad-tempered. "He does not object to your stable hand's presence, I see," Armand commented blandly, looking at the muddy boots of the groom who had trodden straw all over the flagstones. The landlord puffed out his cheeks and looked set to respond, but Armand forestalled him.

"I am come in search of our hot water," he said sternly. "I was promised it would be brought up to our room after supper, and yet it has failed to make an appearance."

The landlord turned to the sharp-faced maid and berated her roundly for her oversight. "It will be brought up shortly, good sir," he assured Armand, ushering him out of the kitchen.

"Have you no other guests?" Armand asked. "The place seems half-dead."

The other man bridled. "We have a pilgrim lately arrived who is taking his supper in his room," he said indignantly.

Armand's ears pricked up. "Indeed? A devout man would eschew the dining chamber, I suppose. No doubt he took only bread and water, for he would be fasting on his quest."

"No indeed! He partook of a good dinner of roast pork, much like yourself," the landlord said tartly.

Armand did not make the obvious reply that the pork had been lacking in flavor and the vegetables overcooked. Instead, he made his way quickly back up to their room, half anticipating that Una's brother might have ambushed their room without him there.

To his relief, Una seemed quite undisturbed on his return and was in the act of rolling the map back up. "I have marked the five locations," she said. He took it with thanks from her outstretched hand and slipped it into his pack.

"The water is coming," he said apologetically. "This inn has gone to the dogs since last I was here. I will give it a wide berth in future." He hesitated before continuing. "Apparently the only other guest is a pilgrim who has recently arrived. He took his supper in his room."

Una looked up quickly at that. "You think it might be Otho?" she asked.

"It might," he conceded. "We will be sure to lock ourselves in before we go to bed and to be on our guard in the morning."

She nodded and a knock on the door proclaimed the arrival of the maid with the water. She brought it in with ill grace, her unkempt hair escaping from under her cap. After setting the jug down with a thud and sloshing water on the table, she retreated, muttering under her breath.

"I will *not* be leaving a tip," Armand noted, shooting the bolt in the door. He noticed Una folding her lips as she poured the jug's contents into a washing basin.

"Is it cold?" he hazarded.

"Lukewarm," she admitted, and he swore. "We can make do until the morrow," she said placatingly and directed a smile at him. "It was a good day. We should not allow one poor meal to ruffle our composure."

For a moment he debated telling her of the state of the kitchens. But what would that achieve, other than robbing her of her own serenity? "You're right," he rallied. "We'll soon be out of here." He yawned. "Let's turn in."

*

The fire had not been lit in the grate, and though it had been a warm and balmy day, there was now a chill in the air. They both undressed quickly and climbed into bed.

Armand rolled over and blew out his candle before stretching out alongside her. "Are you warm enough?"

"Oh yes, for I found the trick long ago to climbing into a cold bed."

"And what's that?" he asked, sounding curious. The pillow rustled and she wondered if he had turned to face her. If so, he would not be able to clearly make out her features.

"'Tis only to force yourself to relax your limbs. After a few moments, you fool your body, and everything warms up."

"Surely a princess should have her bed warmed as a matter of course," he said, and she heard the slight frown in his voice.

Una paused before replying. "Perhaps in my girlhood, in my father's palace," she replied softly. "But I have not been at Menith now for many years," she said, naming the northern capital. It was a mistake to say its name aloud, for as always it conjured its ghost. The towers of Menith Castle rose in the shadows before her, only to fall away again in ruins.

"How many years?"

Una thought about it. "Some nine or ten at least."

"What's it like?" he asked. "I've never been that far north."

"Cold," she said. "But majestic in its own way. There are mountains and their peaks are always covered in snow. Even in the summer."

"Should you like to go back one day?"

"No," she replied abruptly and shivered. "My life is here now." She squeezed her eyes shut and turned away from him, showing him her back. To her surprise, she felt his arm close about her waist, and he hauled her firmly back against him. Una smothered her exclamation.

"You're not following your own advice," he said dryly. "Relax, Una."

Una? He said it with such easy familiarity that her face flooded with color. No one had ever dared address her with such ease and assurance when she was a princess. It gave her hope for the future. "How far north *have* you been?" she asked, and her voice sounded husky even to her own ears.

"Strethneal," he said shortly.

Oh. She closed her eyes, her stomach lurching as her rising hopes were immediately dashed to the floor. She knew what that meant. Sir Armand had been at the siege of Demoyne, she thought with sudden despair. She had to ask that foolish question, even though she knew it was always a mistake to go down this route. She thought of Lord Mycroft, her grim jailor of three years. His son and heir had died at Demoyne, in the mud and the rain and the misery and pain of that conflict. She remembered the hatred that would flash out of Lady Mycroft's eyes toward her and was glad it was dark and she could not see her husband's face.

She had been foolish to cling to the hope that perhaps Armand de Bussell had not been touched by the evil of Karadok's civil war, but she had always known it was a forlorn one. The whole country was scarred, she thought bleakly, and it would take more than her own lifetime to heal.

He removed his hand from her waist to run up and down her upper arm. "You're trembling," he said, sounding shocked. "Is it me, Una? Is it my touch?"

"No, no, of course not." She wiped a hand over her face in the dark as she strove to make her voice steady.

He swore, sitting up abruptly. "You're crying! Did I hurt you on our wedding night?" His voice had an urgent undertone. "I knew I must have been a clumsy sot, but I never imagined—"

"No, no," she protested, rolling back toward him and reaching out to touch his arm. "It's not that. I'm just being foolish, it's nothing of that sort. Indeed, Sir Armand, you have been nothing but considerate, I assure you."

"Una." He pulled her firmly into his arms, his voice urgent and low. "If that's true, then why are you shaking like a leaf?"

So startled was she by the physical contact that she could not even think to tell him anything but the truth. "It's silly," she said stiltedly, wiping her wet cheeks again. "It's just…talking of the north. Of the war," she forced out.

"We weren't talking of the war."

She looked straight into his face, even though she could not make out his expression in the dark. "You said you had been to Strethneal," she said forthrightly. "I know what that means."

His arms tightened around her a moment in the dark. "You were there?" he asked, and she could hear the incredulity in his voice. "At Demoyne?"

She nodded, unable to speak the words aloud, and his hand was suddenly at the back of her head urging her to rest her wet face against his chest. "Ah, Una, Una, my poor girl," he murmured, along with other soothing nonsense words until she closed her eyes and let the comfort of his warm body soak into her limbs as he rocked her in his embrace.

Even Estrilda had never babied her like this, she thought wonderingly as she took comfort in the press of his warm body and the husky voice in her ear. Her nurse had been a brisk, no-nonsense woman who had shown her affection by the assiduousness of her service rather than affectionate gesture.

"I'm being silly," she mumbled. "Doubtless you had a far worse time there than I."

"They should never have taken you to such a place," he said vehemently. "What can they have been thinking?"

She lay still, not liking to tell him that for those four years, all her life had been nothing *but* a succession of battlefields. She was oddly touched by his indignation. She let herself be weak and relax just for a moment or two before lifting her head. "I'm quite well now," she said quietly but with conviction.

"You're sure?" he asked gruffly.

"Absolutely sure. I must—"

"Don't apologize," he said, guessing her intent and rearranging her so she once more presented her back to him. Then he slipped an arm around her again, quite easily, as though it were something he had done a hundred times before. "Now go to sleep," he recommended. "I'll be waking you in the morning soon enough."

What an extraordinary change in her circumstances, she marveled, that meant she was now lying here in the dark next to this man. Una lay awake long after she heard Armand's breathing even out into sleep. Her thoughts were troubled and gave her no peace. She stared up at the ceiling above her and gave in to the fact she would probably find no sleep this night. It was not unusual for her to be thus deprived. She had lived her whole life on a knife's edge and had often woken to the sound of a soldier's footfall approaching to urge her to dress and flee or even to the sound of clashing swords nearby.

She had been schooled from a young age to never accept wine except from a trusted source, and her father had always employed tasters to sample their every meal. In her old voluminous gowns, it had been easy to tip the contents of a goblet down her wide sleeves. These precautions had to fall by the wayside when she spent three years under Lord Mycroft's household, but in any case, they had been an honorable family, even if they bore no love for her. She could not imagine stiff, autocratic Lord Mycroft lacing her meat with poison, though his wife perhaps might have been sorely tempted.

At the southern palace, her dear Estrilda had insisted on drinking and eating a mouthful of any dish sent to her rooms, and at the public feasts she had eaten but sparingly. Her gowns had grown a good deal looser, and it was hard to remember that in her youth she had been round and plump. Perhaps, she thought folding her hands across her stomach, in old age she could relax enough to grow a little stout. That would be nice.

She was not sure why tonight she had eschewed the wine, although in truth, her husband had pulled such a face at the sip he had taken that it was not to be wondered at. The food, too, had been unappetizing, greasy, and tough, so that could account for why she had pushed her plate away, largely untouched.

If she were truthful though, it could not entirely account for it. In part, her abstinence had been due to her own finely tuned instincts, tingling away and warning her to be on her guard. But why was that? she pondered, turning it over in her mind.

Armand himself had been put out by the fact their hosts were not who he expected. Was that what had triggered her unease? She went over their reception by the smiling landlord who had explained he had taken over the business some twelve months earlier. Could he be an agent of the collapsed north? His accent had not been northern, but that did not rule out such a thing.

She knew only too well that certain factions would like to gain control of her as a figurehead for their planned uprisings and rebellion. Even under house arrest, she had received smuggled messages, which she had been forced to burn, and twice the house had been breached by rebels wanting to free her and incredulous of her disinclination to go with them.

If this did turn out to be some attempt to grab her and spirit her away to some fortress full of loyalists to the Blechmarsh cause, she would resist it with her last breath, she thought with determination. She could imagine nothing worse than returning to that life of hiding and running away, a mere pawn in someone else's game. Especially when freedom had been almost within her grasp.

Was she just being paranoid though? It would not be surprising, she acknowledged, after the life she had led. Quickly she ran over the household in her mind's eye. The groom had been a surly-looking fellow, a hulking great brute who had led their horses to the stables with barely a word.

The maidservant's manner had been decidedly odd. Where the landlord oozed geniality, her gaze had been hostile, and she had tried to mask her malevolence by keeping her gaze low and refusing to meet anyone's eye. It was hard, though, to imagine her a sympathizer to the northern cause. For surely if that had been the case, she would have been more amenable when serving her?

Her ruminations were interrupted by an unexpected squeak from the wood paneling at the foot of the bed. Una looked toward that spot and was alarmed to see movement there. She had been lying with her eyes open, so her vision was already adjusted to the dark. Lifting her head off the pillow, she craned her eyes and fancied it was a portion of the paneling swinging open into their room. She slid her arm along the mattress to grip Armand's upper arm, digging her nails into him cruelly. She felt his breathing hitch, and his head rustled on the pillow as, to her horror, Una realized someone or something was advancing across the floor toward her side of the bed. It was a figure crawling on all fours. Opening her mouth, she screamed loud and high.

Other figures, large and bulky were now coming through the paneling. Pausing to draw breath, Una felt Armand sit upright in the bed, and leaving him to deal with the intruders advancing upon him, she turned to the floor by her side of the bed where a shadowy figure seemed to be rising to its knees. Reaching to the small table by her side of the bed, Una clutched the water jug and brought it down with a heavy swing in a vague approximation of the figure's head.

The jug made contact and shattered, and Una saw the figure reel. Throwing back the covers, she leaped from the bed, and keen to take advantage of her momentary upper hand, she fell upon the figure, seizing its shoulders and bearing it back to the floor. From the size and shape, she rather thought her adversary was a woman. Grabbing her head, Una slammed it back against the floorboards, attempting to stun her further.

Behind her, she heard a scuffle and a bellow and could only hope that Armand was managing to hold his own. His sword, she remembered, was hanging on a chair at the foot of the bed. If she could only reach it, maybe she could help him, for she fancied he was contending with two or three to her one.

Suddenly, the figure beneath her seemed to recover her wits and started struggling wildly. It was all Una could do to remain astride her. She reached for her wrists, but managed to catch hold of only her left, for the right was swinging wildly, and Una realized with a flash that she held some kind of weapon in it, most likely a dagger.

Una redoubled her efforts, but it wasn't easy, for the female had an undoubted wiry strength. "Jeb!" she started screeching. "Get off me, you bitch! I'll kill you!" She slashed wildly at Una, who let go of her left hand to concentrate her efforts on securing the right, which held the real threat.

Dimly, Una heard someone crashing down to the ground behind her. She muttered a prayer that it was not Armand as she finally caught hold of the hand with the knife. The woman beneath her gibbered incoherently with rage as they both exerted all their strength against each other. It was a close-run thing, for Una feared they were very evenly matched in muscle. The dagger was now between their two bodies, and when she felt the blade against her ribs, she felt a new surge of strength born of fear.

Was she really going to end her days in some squalid inn, the victim of what she could only guess was a gang of murderous thieves? She, who had so many times faced death during her short, beleaguered life? Pushing desperately against the other woman's shaking fist, she heard her give a startled grunt, then felt the sickening give as the sharp blade found its mark. Warm blood surged over Una's fingers, and she blinked in the darkness as the other woman turned limp.

There was another crash behind her, and an oath from who she was relieved to discover was Armand. "Una?" he shouted.

"I'm here," she answered shakily.

Then the door burst open and someone stood there with a candle. "Una?"

She recognized Otho's voice before she saw his face and felt a wave of sickness wash over her. *Surely Otho was not at the bottom of this?*

"Halt!" shouted Armand. "Do not come any closer," he warned, "unless you want to suffer their fate." In three strides, he was over the bed and kneeling beside her. He ran his large hands over her arms, feeling her for injuries.

"Nothing ails me," she assured him. "I'm not hurt." He had to help her to rise, for her knees were shaky and felt grazed from the floor. "I killed her," she said numbly.

"Hush, you did well," Armand soothed her.

"Why did they attack us?"

"I don't know yet," he answered grimly, slipping an arm around her waist to support her, and turning back to her brother. "You were also attacked?" he asked, and Una noticed for the first time that Otho was dressed for bed in a nightshirt, which bore splatters of blood across it. It seemed he had hastily pulled on his boots to come in search of them.

"You are hurt, Otho!" she blurted.

"It's nothing," he responded dismissively. "Are they dead?"

Una craned her head over her shoulder to see two bodies lying on the floor on Armand's side of the bed.

"Yes," Armand answered shortly. "How many came for you?"

"The landlord only." Otho shrugged. "It seems they thought you more of a threat than a mere pilgrim."

Armand grunted at that. "Very likely. We need light. I want to see how they gained access to our chamber."

"It was through the paneling there," Una said, pointing to where a panel swung open. Otho came into the room and touched his candle to the wicks of the unlit candles until the room was illuminated in a yellow glow.

Armand pulled on his breeches and boots and grabbed a blanket from the bed to drape it about her. "Here," he said, and Una noticed she was clad only in her thin shift. Her surge of fear had inured her to the cold. "Take a seat here, Una, in this chair,

104

while I take a look." Picking up a candle, he advanced on the open paneling and lifted it high to peer in.

Una turned to her brother, who was examining the bodies, turning them over with his foot. "This one's the stable hand," he pronounced, moving on to the other fellow. "But I don't know this one."

"It's the cook," Armand said, his voice drifting back to them as he stepped inside the paneling.

"Be careful, in case there should be any more of them concealed there," Una called anxiously.

"If this is the maidservant," Otho said, walking over to the dead female, "then this is likely the entire household." He peered down. "It is she."

Una took one look at the knife handle protruding from her chest and had to look away.

"You did well, sister," Otho said gruffly, and Una looked up in surprise. Otho had not permitted her to call him brother for many years, not since they were children and he decided it was unfit for a princess to acknowledge her bastard-born sibling.

"You too, brother," she replied. "Thank you for coming to our aid."

"That was for your sake alone," he answered, his lips flattening into a thin line.

"I am aware." She had started to shiver now, and noticing it, Otho exclaimed.

"I should find you some brandywine," he muttered. "But I don't like to leave you alone in this chamber of death."

"I confess, I do feel a little shaken, but I would be happy to sit here and wait for your return."

He hesitated. "You're certain?"

"Oh yes."

He looked grimly satisfied. "You're stout of heart, Una. The Blechmarsh dragon is strong in you."

She gave him a wan smile. "And in you, Otho."

He smiled a little at that, and then turned and left the room in quick strides. She sat alone for five minutes or so, her eyes fixed on the paneling and away from the grisly remains before she heard Otho's stride along the passage outside. He reappeared carrying a stoppered bottle and two cups.

"Here," he said, pouring some out for her. "This will restore some color to your cheeks." She accepted it gratefully, and he poured himself a liberal measure and crouched down beside her. "He should not leave you alone like this," he muttered. "Not after the upset you just suffered."

"I am not alone," she pointed out. "For you are here."

"He does not take care of you as he should. As a northerner would," he insisted.

"Being treated as a princess is the last thing I want," she said in a low, steely voice. "For I am no longer one."

"In the north you will always be the last of the Blechmarshes!" Otho said hoarsely.

She looked at him in despair. "None of you ever listen to me or what I want," she said bitterly. "Why can I not just be your sister, Otho? Why must you insist that I occupy some exalted

106

position I do not want? Am I not good enough, if I am not royal?"

He looked startled by her words, his mouth falling open. "Where has this kind of speech come from?" he spluttered. "Have those southerners indoctrinated you into their false beliefs?"

"Otho, please listen to me. I do not want a crown; I never have. I know you all looked up to our father as some godlike figure, but to me, he was a tyrant and a cruel, unfeeling man."

He stared at her. "Una, this is treason!"

"Never did he give us one scrap of fatherly affection. I feel no loyalty to him, Otho. None whatsoever."

He looked pale and distressed. "You do not know what you are saying," he said shakily.

"For the first time in my life, I am speaking what is in my heart," she said simply. "I bore no love for the northern king. Every day I spent in his household was one of misery for me. It seems," she continued sadly, "that you do not really care for me as your sister, Otho. Like all those other poor fools who followed his banner, you just see me as a figurehead for our father's cause."

He staggered to his feet. "That is not true," he said, passing a hand over his brow.

"If that is so, then you will not keep trying to divert me from my current course. I am a married woman now. My name is Una de Bussell. If you can't accept these facts, then I must ask you to part company from us on the morrow," she said gravely.

He swallowed and opened his mouth, but quick footsteps approaching made him close it with a snap and he reached for his sword.

"Hold!" Una said sternly. "It is my husband who approaches."

He lowered his hand with some reluctance, and Armand appeared, climbing out of the paneling. "Our fortunes are made." He grinned, pointing his thumb over his shoulder. "It's a labyrinth back there, but there's plenty of gold!"

Otho grunted. "Ill-gotten gains," he grumbled. "Anyone who touches it will be stained with the blood of their victims!"

"I'm not fussy," Armand answered, rubbing his hands together. "Better we benefit from it than they." He nodded at the corpses littering the floor. "What I suggest is this. We split it three ways, cart the loot out and load our horses with it, and clear out before first light. With a bit of luck, there will be a couple of nags in the stables we can use as pack horses."

"So now we steal their horses too?" Otho said sourly. "What about giving the bodies a proper burial and alerting the authorities?"

Armand shrugged. "Why cause ourselves a lot of unnecessary bother? I don't mean to be insensitive, but this is a rural area and sure to have a lot of prejudice."

"You mean the word of two northerners would not stand for much?" Una interjected, and Armand pulled a face.

"Exactly. We could be stuck here for days protesting our innocence."

Otho nodded, his expression grim. "There is something in what you say," he admitted grudgingly.

"There! I knew you would see sense!" Armand replied, his eyes gleaming.

"I'll help you load up the horses, but I want no part of the treasure," Otho said staunchly. "I ask only that you take me into your service so that I may serve my prin—" He broke off his words awkwardly. "So that I may serve the Lady Una."

Armand's eyebrows rose. "Una?" he asked, turning to her. "What say you to this handsome offer?"

Una hesitated, but after all it was the first time her brother had addressed her as "Lady Una." "If Otho wants to journey with us until he is satisfied that I am comfortably situated, then I am agreeable."

"Well, there you are, then." He turned to Otho. "Follow me. We'll start hauling it out. Una, you get dressed now, there's a good girl."

She nodded, though she could see Otho was rattled by Armand's informal address. She watched them both disappear into the wall as she stepped over the dead maid to retrieve her clothes. She dressed in a hurry, pinned her hair up and added her veil, and then started packing her things up. Then she set Armand's tunic on the chair and packed his things, which, admittedly, were not much. Then, not feeling she could stand another minute in the same room with the bodies, she carried her own things out and down the stairs.

Setting her pack down on a long table in the dining chamber, she wandered through to the kitchen in search of some food to take with them on their journey. The room was filthy, and she wrinkled her nose as she stepped across the dirty floor to reach the pantry. Inside she found two loaves of bread and the remains of the roast pork from the night before. Extracting these, she took them over to the table and then went back to find the butter.

By the time Otho came hurriedly into the room, she had washed the table down with water and soap leaves she had found and sliced the pork and picked out the choicest cuts. She had then added the meat with the loaves and the butter into a clean sack she had found along with an untouched wheel of cheese.

"There you are!" He breathed a sigh of relief. "We came out of the passage to find you missing!"

"Hardly that, Otho. I merely did not wish to remain in that room with a pile of corpses. Can you blame me?"

He murmured at that and turned to survey the room with a disgusted expression. "This room isn't much better," he pointed out.

"Well, true," Una agreed. "Now I have packed us some victuals, I will come and wait for you in the dining chamber. Have you gathered the spoils now?"

"Nay, for there is a good deal of it," he said, shaking his head. "Your husband is still dragging out sacks even now."

"That much?" said Una, a good deal startled.

"The villains must have benefitted from the previous good name of the place," he said. "Here, let me carry that." Una passed over the bag of food and led the way through into the next room.

"You did not bring down your brandywine," Otho remarked. "Shall I fetch it for you?"

"No, brother, for it makes my head swim. A few sips sufficed."

Otho looked troubled. "You should not call me that, you know. I am aware I slipped first, but that was in the heat of the moment. Now I am to be your attendant, you must not address me as such."

"Otho—"

"If you hold any regard for me, you will respect my wishes, Lady Una," he said with emphasis.

She sighed. "You were the only one of my siblings I held any affection for. It seems very hard that I am now expected to deny the bond."

He looked shocked. "What of Forwin?" he spluttered, mentioning their older brother.

"I heartily detested Forwin. He was a vile bully, the most like our father out of all of us."

Otho's color drained. "You should not speak thus, Una. It is not right."

"We both know it to be the truth. He was cruelest of all to you and Umrey." He flushed at this. "I'm sorry, Otho," she said gently. "But I will no longer mince my words and pander to lies and blatant falsehoods." She paused, but he did not speak. "If you wish to join our household, you had better get used to how things now stand."

He pursed his lips and ran his fingers through his close-cropped hair. "Aye," he said throatily. He glanced her way, meeting her eyes squarely. "It does not bother you, how this husband of yours besports himself above? The light of avarice burns in his eyes. He cares not how evilly this treasure was amassed. He means to have it."

111

Una faced him squarely. "Otho," she said seriously. "You were a soldier in our late army. You know how that army was supported in the last stages of the war. The looting of churches and the stripping of shrines—"

"That was done for pure necessity sake!" he burst out, turning bright red. "Not for personal gain."

"I doubt that mattered much to the poor friars and abbots who were thrown to the ground and trampled."

"No men under my command—"

"Maybe not, but you forget that I also was dragged around with our father's forces, and let me assure you, I saw many atrocities. It was not merely holy places that were sacked. Crop stores were also stolen from villagers. I saw the deaths of many men merely trying to defend their livelihoods and feed their families."

Otho looked away, swallowing painfully. "You should not have been subjected to such sights."

"I? And what of the wives who were left to pick their dead husbands out of the mud? I think they suffered more than I did."

"Don't, Una," he burst out. "In times of war, many wicked things happen that would never occur in times of peace and plenty."

"Peace and plenty," Una said bitterly. "Our father did not care one whit for his subjects' well-being, and you know it. All he cared about was conquest and fame. If he had been content to sit in his throne at Menith, his people would have known peace and plenty, but that was not good enough for him. He wanted the south."

"He wanted to unify all Karadok," Otho corrected her.

"Well, it is now unified," she told him lightly. "So, in a way his greatest wish was granted."

"Under the Argent King's standard!" Otho burst out.

"Yes, indeed. King Wymer's golden lion defeated the green wyvern, and the sooner you accept that, Otho, the better your life will be."

"Is that how you really feel?" he asked incredulously.

"It is."

He shook his head slightly. "It was me, not this fine husband of yours, who came in search of you, does that not tell you all you need to know about his motivation?"

"It tells me you still believe me some cosseted princess in need of coddling," she answered dryly. "Despite the fact I have not been so since I was fourteen and forced out of the palace. As for Armand…" She shrugged. "We have total frankness between us, which I find refreshing."

"What does that mean?"

"It means, broth—" She corrected herself. "Otho…that we have vowed to be ideal traveling companions together on our adventure. I am fulfilling my end of the bargain," she said, gesturing to the sack of food. "If our marriage continues on these lines, I will be vastly satisfied with it." Seeing her brother's troubled expression, she added lightly, "He did not expect to win that tournament, Otho, or take a wife that evening."

He snorted. "From what I saw, he could win precious little glory in the field." He sighed. "He is not a fit husband for you, but at least he bested those two last night. After seeing his woeful performance on May Day, I would not have thought him capable."

Una winced. "He was beset by robbers the day after we were married and fought them off with aplomb. I think perhaps he is better in a brawl than in a formal match."

Otho shrugged. "Curious for a knight, but if you say 'tis so, then I will accept it."

She regarded her brother thoughtfully. "Otho, what were you planning to do after you had won that competition? You took such a risk. If your imposture had been found out, I do not like to contemplate what your fate would have been."

He flushed and would not answer for a moment. "There is a convent near Woodcote, with a monastery at the foot of the hill. I thought I could take you to the abbey and I would enroll with the holy brethren nearby. You would be safe, and though we would not be together, we would be close by always."

Una felt oddly touched. She reached out and lay a hand fleetingly on his sleeve. "That was sweet of you, but I have never aspired to be a holy sister, Otho," she said gently. "I want children and a home of my own."

"You think de Bussell can give you that?"

"Yes," she answered simply. "He has a pleasant personality, open and genial. I think with time he will grow accustomed to the fact he has a wife not of his choosing. He bears no grudges that he was forced into marriage with me."

"No grudges!" spluttered Otho. "It is an honor he does not deserve!"

"There we must agree to disagree," she said with a wry smile. "But I think all will work itself out. For the first time in my life,

I feel optimistic about my future, Otho. You have no idea how freeing that feels."

Her brother looked hard at her and then turned away. "I'd better go back and help him," he growled. "We only have an hour at most before dawn."

Una nodded. "I will be perfectly fine down here by myself," she assured him. "Unless you think I should come up and help?"

He looked appalled at the notion. "Take your ease while you can," he recommended sternly. "You've not had a full night's sleep and you'll be flagging by noon." He hesitated. "Do you think you could get your head down for an hour's sleep?"

She shook her head. "Absolutely not. I will just sit here quietly and await you."

He left her with a nod, and she heard his quick step on the stairs. It was only then that she caught sight of a pair of shiny eyes under the table, peering up at her. Una started and then realized it was a tiny little dog, shivering in the shadows.

"Hello there," she said in a kindly voice. "Where did you come from?"

The animal cringed away from her, looking frankly terrified. He was a malnourished little thing, his every rib sticking out, his gray fur matted and tangled in tufts.

"Come here, I won't hurt you," she promised him softly, but he could not be persuaded. Thoughtfully, Una stood up from the bench and walked through to the kitchen where the remains of the pork joint were on the side. It had not been cooked with any spices or seasoning, so she fancied it would be bland enough for the dog's palate. Cutting some nonfatty pieces, she placed them in a napkin and walked back through, reseating herself on the bench and setting the napkin on the table.

Selecting one piece, she threw it under the table. "Here, boy," she crooned, though in truth she had no idea if it was a boy or a girl. The little dog hesitated and then darted for the meat, gobbling it down as if he had not been fed in a month. She took another piece and dropped it at her feet. He stared at it awhile before dragging himself over to retrieve it and then scurrying back to eat it at a safe distance.

Una dropped another piece at her feet, and the little dog was quicker to come forward this time and did not retreat as far back to wolf it down. "Good boy," Una told him approvingly. "You can see you need not fear me, for I am your friend." She dropped another piece, and this he ate at her feet, looking up at her hopefully. "Yes, there is more," Una assured him.

By the time Armand and Otho started carting the sacks of ill-gotten gains down the staircase, the little dog was eating from her hand.

"Who's this? Found a friend?" Armand asked with a grin. "He's a poor little scrap."

"He's half-starved," Una corrected him. "And has been most cruelly treated for he has cuts and bruises all over his poor little body. I'm sure that with good food and nourishment he will fill out nicely."

Otho snorted, but Armand seemed resigned. "If you're bringing him with us, you'll need to wash him. I can smell him from here."

Una looked down at the little shaking dog. The men's voices seemed to have set him in a new quake. "There's nothing to fear," she soothed him. "You're among friends now." To her surprise he suddenly sprang up and placed his two paws against her skirts, asking to be taken up.

Una reached down tentatively, not wanting to touch him anywhere he was sore. Picking him up, she placed him on her lap and he cowered there, leaning against her, in what she could only guess was an appeal for protection. Folding her arms around him, she drew the shivering dog into a gentle embrace. "Yes," she said with decision. "Abelard will be coming with us."

"Abelard!" echoed Otho, looking critically at the animal. "He hardly seems to embody noble strength!"

"A lofty name for so timid an animal," observed Armand.

"It took great strength to survive in such a household as this," Una said coolly. "Have you not many more sacks to carry down?" She saw Armand smother a laugh at her pointed words. Standing up with the animal cradled in her arms, she announced her plans with dignity. "I shall wash him in the kitchen. There were some soap flakes there, though they cannot have been often used." Then she stalked out of the room.

*

It had taken them a good deal of time to get the horses loaded up with their booty. They found three horses in the stables that they appropriated for their needs. Otho proved himself a very able hand as he carted the sacks out and strapped them securely to the beasts.

Armand wondered that Una's brother had foresworn his share of the loot. From what Una had told him, he had nothing but the clothes on his back and the sword at his hip. You would think he would have jumped at the chance to set himself up with some security for the future.

Armand eyed him as he helped Una up into her saddle. Then again, he could be playing a deep game. After all, his intent could be to take off with both treasure and the princess and leave Armand in the dust. He would have to keep his eye on Master Otho.

It was still dark when he eventually led the way out of the courtyard. Seeing the three loaded horses and the bulging sacks, he had soon changed his mind about the tournament at Tranton Vale. He could hardly put up in a pavilion with all these valuables to guard. With some reluctance, he came to the conclusion that the only thing for it was to head for his own estate, Lynwode. He saw the light spring to Una's eyes when he announced this and winced.

He had not seen the place in five years, and even then it had been a shambles. The only resident had been a deaf housekeeper on her last legs. He sent the odd bag of coins her way every once in a while, when he was flush and in funds, but she never wrote to him, and indeed he had never expected her to. Most likely the old woman was illiterate. She could have dropped dead in the place for all he knew, which would mean introducing his wife to yet another corpse! Then there was his family to consider, he thought darkly. If they caught wind he was in residence, there would be hell to pay and he would have no peace whatsoever.

Still, there was nothing he could do about it now. He had little choice in the matter, and in truth, he had enjoyed five years of giddy freedom doing as he pleased and never once thinking about his duties back home. He should be rejoicing at the large fortune that had fallen into his lap, however grisly the circumstances. Wymer had not seen fit to dower Una, so he would simply view this as its equivalent. If his family questioned his newfound wealth, he would tell them his bride came heavily dowered. Neither his father nor brothers had any connections at court, so it wasn't like they would ever learn otherwise.

118

He glanced over at Una now, with the little dog swaddled against her breast like a baby. He had tried to object, pointing out the little cur might piddle all over her gown, but she had been resolute, insisting she would wrap her mantle about her shoulders and secure him to her.

In the end, he had glanced at Otho, who had merely shrugged, and let her have her way. The dog's eyes were closed, and he seemed to be enjoying the proximity. Armand couldn't really say he blamed him, as Una did have a fine pair of breasts. It was one of the first things he'd noticed about her. Suddenly, a memory came back to him of lying against Una's naked bosom. He sat up in his saddle. She had stroked his hair. Was he reading too much into this, or could it mean he hadn't been too contemptible a bed partner for a sheltered virgin? He felt a rush of relief and was encouraged to hope that was the case. Thank the gods that he had not remembered her crying or trying to push him away.

At least he now knew why she had looked so stricken when he had asked if she had ever been set about by robbers. She must have seen a good deal of brutality in her time. Of course, soldiers sacking unprotected communities was nothing new and was done on all sides, but he had not thought such facts would console her.

His eyes traveled over her critically, now some light was creeping into the sky. In truth, she was not a bad-looking woman. Her build was not diminutive as he had always preferred, but her tall, upright bearing was admirable in its own way. Her face would not be displeasing if only her expression was not so grave and weighty all the time, as though she had too many cares.

He did not think he had heard her really laugh, but when she smiled, it often lit her up in a pleasing way. Her eyes, which were in truth more gray than blue, were not at all watery like in that ghastly portrait of her everyone knew. They must have modeled the likeness to that of her sire, he supposed, to show she was a chip off the old block. Any woman he knew would have thrown a fit if they had been so misrepresented on canvas.

Then again, she had been going about in that awful yellow frizzed wig and wearing that peculiar gown that stole any womanly shape from her body, so mayhap she had wanted to conceal her comeliness. He knew from experience that she had ample charms when her clothes were off. He shifted in his saddle and forced himself to think of other things.

On reflection, he rather thought it was the right decision to take her to Lynwode and establish her there. Though the place was in considerable disrepair, maybe he could set this wife of his to its renovation? She seemed capable enough in her own quiet way. His thoughts brightened. Maybe then, once he had given her time to adjust and made the necessary introductions, he could be off again, living his merry, touring life?

The idea appealed to him. Perhaps by supposedly taking a rich wife, even his family would think he was taking his duties seriously for once? A smile twisted his lips as he anticipated their stunned reaction to the news that he was married. He was in no hurry to impart such tidings, but it would have to be done even if it meant them all converging on him.

The thought of his disapproving father and two joyless brothers soon wiped the smile from his face. No doubt Henry was as penny-pinching a miser as ever and Roger the same old sober bore he had been since childhood. As for his twin sister, Armand had not felt close to her for years, if ever. Anne had married a wearisome country squire and then produced what he was sure would be a pair of equally tedious, fractious children. He sighed. Family was the devil.

They kept riding till noon, without much event, then left the path for a rest in a shady orchard. Una produced a bag of provisions. As neither he nor Otho fancied the tasteless pork, she fed it to her little mutt, and they all had bread and cheese. Otho watered the horses and then leaned his shoulders against a nearby tree. Armand lowered himself onto a fallen trunk where Una sat.

"How are you feeling? Tired?" he asked in a low voice.

She looked across at him quickly. "You must not worry about me, Sir Armand. I am used to long hours in the saddle."

"Armand," he corrected her, and she flushed.

"Yes, of course," she said hastily and fed her dog another piece of meat. He had been freed from her mantle and was now at her feet.

"I know we have not yet had much time to get acquainted," Armand continued. "But hopefully once we are at Lynwode, we will have time for that."

"I'm very much looking forward to seeing it," she replied warmly.

"I should probably warn you that the place will be in need of a good deal of work, I have not seen it in some five years now…"

She nodded, still looking keen. "That does not daunt me, I look forward to setting to work."

"Do you speak true?" he asked, a smile quirking his lips. "Or is this merely part of your promise to be amenable in all things?"

"Oh no!" she protested. "Indeed, I am entirely sincere, I assure you."

"My family, too, will not be far from us," he told her glumly. "I am sure they will come poking and prying before long."

"I look forward to meeting them also," she said with a twinkle in her eye. "For I feel sure they cannot *all* be as dull as you describe them."

He laughed and saw Otho scowl at their cozy conversation. "Your brother still does not seem reconciled to me," he said in a low voice. "He's a good deal squeamish for a soldier, isn't he?" When she frowned, he added, "Refusing his share of the treasure. Which seems strange after what you told me of your own soldiers' looting and sacking."

Her brow cleared. "Otho's an idealist," she replied. "Even in the face of the starkest evidence to the contrary, he still retains his beliefs." She hesitated. "He had a hard upbringing and had little to cling to. What little he did have, he refuses to let go of."

"You think I can trust him not to plunge a knife in my ribs at the first opportunity?" Armand asked dryly.

"Oh yes," she said quickly. "He has always been very honorable. Once he gives his word, he would never go back on it."

He nodded, squinting his eyes against the sun as he gazed the length of the blossom-filled orchard. "I did not thank you for waking me so precipitously in the early hours." He gave her a swift glance.

"Did my nails leave a mark on your arm?" she asked ruefully.

"If they did, it's of no matter and infinitely preferable to a dagger wound. To my regret I am a heavy sleeper—always have been."

"That has caused you inconvenience in the past?" she asked lightly.

He grinned. "Aye. As boys we used to play all manner of tricks on one another. My fellow squires soon learned the best time to take revenge on me was at night. I often woke to a bedful of frogs or slugs."

Una wrinkled her nose. "I notice you say *revenge*," she remarked. "And deduce you were the initial culprit."

Again, he laughed. "I was a mischievous boy," he admitted with a shrug.

She looked at him thoughtfully. "I can well believe it. Who were you squire to? Your father?"

"Gods no, my father has no love for knights. I was squire to Sir Jesmond Chevenix over at Greater Derring. He had two sons and a nephew, so there were always plenty of us racketing about the place."

"You mentioned Derring before, I think in connection to your younger brother attending a religious seminary there?"

"That was Upper Derring, but they are less than an hour or so's ride from each other."

"And close to your home?"

"Yes. Lynwode is just outside Little Derring. My father's place is over at Derring Lacey. They are all within easy distance of each other." His mouth twisted. "Vastly cozy."

Otho cleared his throat. "Should we not get back on the road?" he rumbled. "This isn't the time for confidences. We need to put as much distance as we can between ourselves and that accursed inn."

Armand felt a twinge of annoyance at the interruption, but in fact the surly fellow spoke no more than the truth. He stood and held his hand out to Una, who took it, and he pulled her to her feet.

"Has that dog—" Otho started, then bit off what he had been about to say.

Armand nearly laughed. "Relieved himself?" he suggested. "And yes, he has. I saw him piss up that tree you're leaning against," he answered straight-faced.

Otho loosed an oath, whipping around to gaze at the trunk with disgust.

"He's jesting, Otho," Una assured him. "Abelard would not stray so far from me. Indeed, he piddled on this very log. I think 'twas where Armand was sat." Armand chuckled at this, leading her over to her horse, where she set about arranging her mantle in a sling for the little dog. This time it was he who helped her up into her saddle.

They carried on their way late into the afternoon when Armand let his horse drop back to draw level with Otho. "What do you say to riding through the night?" he asked quietly. "If we rode through, we could reach Little Derring before noon tomorrow."

Otho glanced back at Una and the pack animals. "If we take adequate breaks, I think it could be done," he replied.

Armand dropped back further to pull abreast with Una. "If we ride through the night, we could reach home by noon tomorrow," he said. "I'm aware that probably doesn't sound very appealing, but it might be for the best, all things considered."

"I quite agree," Una answered with a bright smile. "You must not think I am fatigued, for I have done such things before."

He paused at that. Of course she had. "We'll press on, then," he answered, and she nodded.

It was a hard slog. Even Armand found his eyelids drooping, and he could hear Otho's smothered yawns behind him. It was as well that he was familiar with the way or they might well have stumbled or taken a wrong turn in the dark.

They stopped at intervals, giving water to the horses, and finishing off Una's bread and cheese. The little dog gobbled down the last of the pork. They met no one after night had fallen, and though Otho scanned behind them frequently in case of pursuers, there were none to be seen.

By the time dawn broke, they were a weary bunch indeed, though the rising sun cheered their party greatly. Armand turned in his saddle. "We've made good progress and covered more ground than I thought we would. It should only be a couple of hours till we reach Lynwode."

Una looked relieved. "Oh, that's wonderful news," she responded with a tired smile.

"Should we stop again?" he asked, giving her a shrewd look.

"Let's keep going," Otho growled. "She needs sleep, not to sit on the grass." Armand kept his gaze trained on Una.

"I'll be fine," she assured him. "I just want to reach home." She flushed slightly after saying the word *home*, and Armand started to get an inkling of how much the idea meant to her. He spurred on his horse and they carried on apace.

It felt an age later as they rode through the small village of Little Derring. People were just starting to go about their day, and the procession of horses incurred considerable excitement. Folk stopped what they were about and stared. Small boys ran alongside them with round eyes. Armand dug in his purse for

125

any small coins he could find and flipped them in the air to accompanying whoops of delight as they were caught by eager hands.

"Where be you headed for, sir?" shouted the boldest of the bunch.

"Lynwode," he called back. "Let it be known Sir Armand de Bussell and his lady have returned home."

This produced another burst of excitement and much jostling of elbows. He glanced back to see Una nodding and smiling at the gathering crowd. Otho had a face like thunder, but Armand ignored him.

The same boy pointed at Otho. "Is it 'im?" he asked Armand.

Armand's eyebrows rose. "Certainly not. *I* am Sir Armand, and this is my good wife, the Lady Una." He swept his arm in her direction.

Another boy encouraged by this exchange shouted, "Welcome home, good sir and your lady too."

They had soon passed through the village and after another five minutes had reached the turning for Lynwode. They rode past the unoccupied lodge house and rounded the bend which revealed the gray stone edifice of the house, with its four gables of differing heights and its large arched doorway.

He eyed the house critically, trying to imagine he was looking at it for the first time, as Una was. The tall, gothic windows with their curved masonry cunningly wrought into petal and trefoil shapes were probably the most impressive feature of the house. He could not deny that it was a handsome pile in all, with its gray brick mellowing to a pleasant yellow. Although not as sprawling as Anninghurst, his father's house, it was large enough and the green creepers encroaching over the stone perhaps made it even more appealing in the morning light.

"Oh, it's beautiful," Una breathed. "From the way you spoke, I was not expecting anything so lovely!"

Armand felt a slight swell of pride and wondered at it, for he had never more than visited the place since his godfather had left it to him. Still he heard himself ask her if she liked it and received her enthusiastic response as if it were his due.

"Trees need pruning," Otho said shortly. "Where's the stables?"

"Around the back, along with the vegetable gardens and fruit orchards. We can secure the horses out front until we've found the housekeeper. I suppose I'll need to employ a groom."

"Well, you should be able to afford one now," Otho pointed out.

Armand rolled his eyes, dismounting and holding his hand out to Una to help her down. They were all stiff and sore, and after tethering the horses, Armand knocked at the door. He turned back to the others. "Mrs. Challacombe is a little deaf," he said, then noticing the door was not locked but ajar, he gave it a push. It fell open with a creak, disclosing a very strange sight.

There in the hallway was a young woman twirling around and around so the skirts of her rose-pink gown flew wide and her flaxen hair spun around her in a cloud. The light from the window was shining down on her, so she looked like some ethereal vision, and she was singing to herself in a sweet, lilting voice.

Armand stared at her in bewilderment. Who the hells was this? Suddenly, she dropped into a very low, graceful curtsey, not in their direction, but facing the opposite wall, as though to some

127

object of her fancy. Then she straightened up and turned toward them still humming the snatches of her tune.

Catching sight of them, she gave a high-pitched scream and dropped the bouquet of meadow flowers she had been holding, scattering them all over the dusty floor. Her wide blue eyes stared at them in dismay.

Armand could feel Otho's accusing gaze burning into him at this point. "I thought you said she was old and deaf," he said ominously.

Armand ignored him. "Who the devil are you?" he demanded. "And what are you doing in my house?" His abruptness seemed to send the girl into a frightened confusion. She gasped and shrank back with a cry, flattening herself against the nearest wall, as though he had drawn a blade on her.

"Armand," Una muttered reproachfully, advancing into the hall. "You're frightening her."

Armand passed a hand over his eyes. "I'm tired, in need of hot water and a clean bed. Can you point us to someone who can help us with these things?" he asked of the girl, but again was met with nothing but a stunned gaze.

Una stepped past him. "Perhaps you can help us?" she said in a soothing voice. "My husband here is Sir Armand de Bussell, and this is his home. He was expecting to find a Mrs. Challacombe in residence as custodian. Perhaps you know what has become of her?"

The girl gulped. "Good sirs, she died some twelve months past." She dropped again into an elegant curtsey. "I am her granddaughter, Rose, and have been filling the post since then."

Armand snorted, looking about at the cobwebs and dust, but Una laid a restraining hand on his arm.

128

"So then, you are acting housekeeper here at Lynwode?" she asked gently. The girl nodded her head uncertainly. "Well then, that is fine," Una said, smiling. "We are all vastly tired from traveling and desire to wash and take our rest. Do you have bedchambers fit for our purpose?"

"I'll require one in the servants' quarters," Otto growled, and the girl stared at him with undisguised terror.

Armand felt himself lose all patience. The girl was either half-witted or being deliberately obtuse. "My wife and I require the master bedchamber to be made ready," he said in a clipped voice. "Kindly see to it forthwith."

That was when the wretched girl began to sob, great fat tears rolling down her cheeks as unrestrainedly as a child. He glared at her, threw up his hands, and leaving Una to deal with the creature, he strode in what he remembered was the direction of the kitchens.

His progress through a faded great hall full of dirty tapestries and filmy windows did nothing to mitigate his poor impression of Mrs. Challacombe's granddaughter. If she spent all her time dancing and picking flowers, he thought with disgust, then it was no wonder the house was filthy.

When he reached the kitchen, he paused on the threshold with an oath. It was a complete shambles. Pots and pans littered the central table and the shelves were cluttered and untidy. The large fireplace was filled with a great heap of ashes, which did not look like they had been swept out in a twelvemonth. His mouth tightened.

One might expect the girl to be unable to maintain so large a house with no other help, but the kitchen at least should have been kept in some semblance of order. He heard the clatter of

Otho's boots behind him and moved away from the door to let the other man see the chaotic room.

Otho swore. Walking forward, he peered into one of the pots on the table. "There's a nest of mice living in this one," he announced without expression.

Armand groaned and massaged his temples a moment.

Otho turned and looked him full in the face. "You claim you do not know this woman?"

"I haven't been in this house in five years," Armand retorted scathingly. "The last time I came home was to my father's house to visit my mother's deathbed. I came nowhere near Lynwode on that occasion. I've never seen that girl before in my life, and if it's up to me, she'll be out on her ass as soon as can be managed."

Otho still looked suspicious but gave a shrug. "You can't blame me for asking."

"She's not at all the type I admire," Armand said shortly, which was nothing less than the truth. He liked them womanly and bold, not slender, and away with the faeries. "Gods," he sighed. "I dread to think what state the bedrooms are in. If you go out and make the stables ready, then I'll rake this fire to heat some water."

Otho nodded and headed for the door leading out to the back, and Armand turned his attention to the fire.

5

Una was dog-tired, but she turned to the nervous Rose and fixed a smile upon her face. "Rose, if you show me up to the master chamber then you and I can make it ready together."

Rose perked right up at this suggestion. "Yes, milady, this way, milady." At least she was obliging, thought Una as she mounted the unswept staircase, if nothing else. Beside her, Abelard gamely kept up, unwilling to let her out of his sight. Una dusted the cobwebs off her shoulder as they reached the first floor, then when Rose threw open a door for her, she wished she hadn't bothered. The room was simply under layers of dust. Everything looked quite gray.

"Perhaps putting the furniture under sheets would have helped, Rose," she said faintly, looking about her with growing dismay.

"I didn't think of that, milady."

Una turned back to her despairingly. "How were you employed before you became housekeeper here?" she asked with curiosity.

"I was personal maid to old Mrs. Gaventree over at Upper Derring for six years until she died, poor thing. She taught me how to embroider and play the harp," said Rose proudly.

Una deduced Rose had been the old lady's pet most likely. No wonder she was unfit for practical purposes! "I take it Mrs. Gaventree had no children of her own."

"No, milady, but how did you guess?" Rose marveled. "This is a fine big room, is it not?" she said, turning full circle to take in its size.

"It is," Una agreed. There was a beautiful wide arched window with three stained-glass panels casting colored lights into the room and a window seat beneath it, which would be inviting, if it were not so dirty. She could not make out the color of the upholstery in its current state but would be interested to see what it turned out to be.

The ceiling was a vaulted timber frame with dark wooden beams that made the room seem even more spacious, and Una could see it was a well-proportioned and handsome room. The bed was a large wooden affair, set on a raised platform with a canopy suspended from the ceiling from which hung filthy curtains.

On the opposite side of the room was a large dresser, also very decorative, with a large looking glass hanging above it, though you could see precious little in its reflection at present. A tall cabinet, a large chest, a carved table, two chairs, and a footstool were the remaining furniture, and Una looked forward to seeing them without their coating of grime. Abelard, who was timidly peering under the dresser, sneezed before creeping under it to hide.

Una squared her shoulders. "Is there any clean linen for us to remake the bed?" she asked, turning resolutely to Rose. The girl blinked, looking uncertain. "There is no linen cabinet in the house?" Una said with surprise.

Rose hung her head and drew her slippered toe through the dust on the floorboard. "I don't know, milady," she whispered.

Una was left to conclude that Rose had never done an inventory of the house. "Never mind," she said briskly. "Let us get these curtains down first. Fetch a chair to stand on, and you start this side and I'll start the other."

Rose nodded and ran to fetch a chair. *Yes*, thought Una, *she is willing, just badly in need of someone to give her orders.* After they had taken down the curtains, they stripped the bed of its coverings and then bundled them into a large pile for washing. Una was just dragging this to one corner when Armand came into the room.

He stood for a moment, looking about him with a jaundiced eye, sent a withering look in Rose's direction, and then addressed Una. "I've lit the kitchen fire," he said. "Water's on to boil."

"Wonderful. We are just setting things to rights in here," Una said quickly, hoping to forestall any remark he might make to send Rose in a quake again. "We need clean bedclothes and dusters. I don't suppose you have come across such things in your wanderings?"

Armand closed his eyes briefly, as though mustering strength. "Surely to gods—"

"No, she doesn't," Una said swiftly, and Armand drew in a sharp breath before speaking again.

"I'll undertake to find one," he said through gritted teeth. He turned sharply on his heel and left the room.

Rose's bottom lip trembled. "I don't think the master likes me," she said in a woebegone voice.

Prudently, Una did not comment on this but asked the girl to fetch a basin of clean water and some soap if she had it. Rose trailed off, casting mournful glances over her shoulder. Una suspected she did not want to encounter Otho below stairs, who had looked rather fierce.

When Armand reappeared moments later with cloths and a pile of sheets and blankets, Una welcomed him thankfully.

"The sheets smell a little musty," he admitted. "They've probably sat in that cupboard since Mrs. Challacombe died."

"Very likely," Una agree with a tired smile. "We'll need the mattress restuffed."

Armand suppressed a sigh. "I'll see what can be done."

He had no sooner hauled the mattress from the room than Rose reappeared with a jug, a basin of water, and a hard cake of soap under her arm. She retrieved it and held it out to Una. "I've never used it, as I don't like the smell."

Una took a sniff. "That's because it's lye. It cuts through grease and dirt, but it's very harsh on the skin." Rose looked down at her rosy fingers in concern. "It has to be done, I'm afraid," Una told her bracingly. "All the furniture needs washing down. We'll do it together."

They then set about it with gusto, and even Rose put her back into it. To her delight, Una found the dresser was carved charmingly with intertwining leaves and flowers that were replicated on the matching trunk. The cabinet had beautifully painted doors with scenes of ladies walking beneath trees and embracing unicorns.

"Isn't it lovely!" Rose had cried. "Why, I don't remember ever seeing this before, though I suppose Granny must have shown it to me."

"Where is your room, Rose?" Una asked.

"I took over my grandmother's room in the servants' quarters," Rose told her happily. "It's very comfortable, though not fancy like this one." Una privately reflected that the housekeeper likely would have the best of the servants' rooms, save perhaps for the steward.

134

"Do your parents live locally, Rose?"

Rose shook her head. "My mother and father died of a fever sickness when I was fifteen. I was only spared because I had left four weeks before to take up my post with Mrs. Gaventree. I have no one left now to me in all the world."

When the mattress reappeared an hour or so later, it had been restuffed, and they set it on the bed and dressed it in the clean sheets. It looked so inviting to Una at this point that she was tempted to simply fall onto it. Instead she sent Rose in search of a broom, and the twiggy threadbare thing she returned with was just about fit to sweep the mounds of dust out of the door and into the hallway.

Abelard was very disturbed by the appearance of the broom and Rose had to coax him out from under the dresser. "Poor little creature!" she exclaimed. "Why, he's trembling."

"He has been very cruelly treated by his former owner, I'm afraid. He may likely have been struck with a broom," Una reflected. "Perhaps you should take him up in your arms while I do this?"

Rose was happy to oblige and cooed and fussed over Abelard while Una finished sweeping. She had just finished when Armand strode back into the room carrying a steaming jug and basin, which he set down on the dresser.

"You, out," Armand said briefly to Rose. "You can get down to the kitchen and start washing those pots." Rose's face crumpled, but she set Abelard down and fled after a quick curtsey in Una's direction. "Well, you've worked miracles," he said. "But now it's time to wash and sleep."

Una was frankly too tired to even think about disagreeing. When she fumbled with her lacing, he came over and helped her with an efficiency that made her wonder if it was not the first time he had helped a woman undress. She did not ponder it for long, however, as the hot water was too appealing. She washed with a thankful sigh, then crossed to climb into the high bed.

Abelard had curled up under one of the tall-back chairs and looked as comfortable as the nervous little dog ever did. She would have to make him a little blanket of his own, she thought as she drew the covers up to her chin. Another item on her long list of things that needed to be done. Armand was now stripping, and she meant to wait for him to finish washing to inquire after Otho, but her head had no sooner hit the pillow than she fell into a deep sleep.

When she woke, it was to the sight of Armand's profile on the pillow next to her. He was fast asleep, his face relaxed in repose. Without his twinkling eyes on display and the smile that so frequently played about his mouth, he looked a good deal more daunting, despite his slumber. His jaw was firm and determined and covered now in dark stubble, for he had not bothered to shave. His brows were black and straight, and Una wondered that she had not noticed these more formidable features before.

She suspected she had been distracted by those pretty eyes, which were some shifting shade between green and blue, like the ocean when the sun hit it on a summer's day. Then, too, there was that laughing mouth, she reflected, and the teasing quick words. When they were not in evidence, you noticed other things. Her gaze traveled over the expanse of his broad chest and the bulging muscles in those arms, one of which was tucked behind his head, the other resting beside her.

King Wymer had been right in thinking he was a fine figure of a man. She sighed and rolled onto her back, looking up at the arched beams above her. Lynwode was a beautiful house, well-proportioned and spacious. For the first time in her life, the dice had rolled, and she had been revealed as a winner. True, the house needed a thorough going-over, but she liked to be kept busy. Her three years under house arrest was the longest time she had been kept idle, and even then, she had made it bearable by plying her needle.

She glanced toward the window, but stained glass was not the best type for enjoying the view. Sitting up, she drew back the covers to climb out when Armand's arm wrapped around her waist.

"Where are you going?" he murmured. Glancing back at him, she saw his eyes were still closed and wondered if he was still half-asleep.

"I was just going to look out of the window and determine what o'clock it is."

"Does it matter?" He frowned without opening his eyes.

"Well…"

He tugged at her waist and Una relented, lying back down beside him. Did he even realize who his current bedpartner was? He shifted closer with a gusty sigh until the length of his body was pressed fully against her, his arm holding her close.

"You can't be fully rested, so go back to sleep," he recommended grumpily. Una held her tongue, too surprised to point out that she usually slept poorly in unfamiliar places, and also because apparently, he knew full well who she was. After a few minutes, his steady breathing and big solid body lulled her into relaxation and she felt herself drifting back to sleep.

When next her eyes opened, it was much later, for the room was in complete darkness except for the glow of the fire in the grate, and she was alone. She lay a moment, getting her bearings, and then sat up, hugging her knees. Someone must have laid that fire, she realized, for it had not been lit when they went to bed. Then she noticed little Abelard's scrawny body stretched out before it, bathing in the warmth. He must have crept out from beneath his chair, she thought with a smile.

The door creaked open, and from the size and shape of the shadowy form entering, she deduced it was Armand. As he drew closer, she saw he was carrying a tray bearing two lighted candles and sundry other objects. "How long have you been awake?" he asked, setting it down on the table. Una was gratified to see the first thing he took from the tray was a bowl of water for the little dog, who had rolled to his side at the sound of Armand's voice and was poised for flight.

Setting it down beside Abelard, he murmured something soothing to the little dog and then took two goblets of wine from the tray. He approached and handed one to Una and then sat down beside her on the bed. "You slept well?" he asked, his eyes flitting over her. He took a hasty gulp of wine.

"Yes, I did, thank you." He narrowed his eyes at her, as if he knew full well that she had been about to slip and call him Sir Armand again. But he couldn't possibly know that, she told herself uneasily, and raised the blanket to cover her thin shift. She had thought in the candlelight it would not be too immodest, but the direction of Sir Armand's gaze told her that more of her was on display than she had realized.

He pulled a face and drained his cup. "Hungry?" he asked. "There's bread and butter and a sort of pottage your brother made. Sadly, the pantry is otherwise empty. The gods alone know what that wretched girl has been existing on."

Remembering Rose's slight frame, Una guessed she probably ate like a bird. "Pottage is fine, and I am very fond of bread and butter."

He nodded, set his goblet down, and rose to his feet, with some reluctance it seemed, though she could not understand why. Then he moved to the table, transferring the contents of the tray onto it. "Come and sit down," he said, dragging the chairs up to the small table. When she slid from the bed, he added, "Don't bother dressing."

"I have not unpacked my robe."

"You can sit in this chair, closest to the fire. Or in my lap," he added thoughtfully. "If you think you may grow cold."

Una could only suppose he was joking and slipped into the chair he'd indicated as he passed her a bowl and spoon and cut her a piece of bread. The pottage was in a large dish, and Una helped herself to a decent helping and tucked in. There was no meat or fish, but the vegetables and grains were tasty and filling enough, and she had eaten far worse in her time.

Armand grimaced when he sampled his, but then proceeded to demolish three bowlfuls and half a loaf, before pouring them both another cup of wine and sitting back in his chair. She was just watching Abelard get up from the fire and retreat under the dresser when Armand cleared his throat.

"Una, I think it's time we discuss our wedding night," he said heavily.

Una almost dropped her piece of bread with surprise. "Must we discuss it?" she asked in a strangled voice once she could finally muster a breath. "What is done is done." Her brain raced. Was he going to question the consummation simply because he could not remember it? Her mouth turned dry with apprehension.

He eyed her gravely. "Because I've a notion I did not treat you as a princess might expect," he said slowly.

"Well, I was no longer a princess by then," she pointed out in what she hoped was an even tone, though her heart was hammering wildly. Just when the fates were smiling down upon her, she thought despairingly.

"I know it's probably indelicate as hell, my wanting to talk about this, but you don't need to look quite so terrified," he said impatiently. "I'm not about to force myself on you."

Una took a sip of wine while her brain raced to grasp what he was saying. "I'm terrified because I'm scared you want to deny our marriage's validity," she said frankly. "Not because of anything you did or didn't do and not because I'm scared of you, Sir—" She broke off in confusion. "I mean, Armand."

A heavy silence hung between them. "I'm not about to deny the consummation," he said shortly. "I don't know where you got that impression." She let out an audible sigh of relief and slumped back in her seat, feeling quite limp.

He frowned. "Just because I don't precisely remember it doesn't mean—" He gave up abruptly before starting again. "I do have some confused memories of us…" His words trailed off. "In any case, a man can tell when he's, ah…"

Seeing his confusion, she set down her cup and said soothingly, "You did everything that is expected of a bridegroom on his wedding night, I assure you."

"It's the things I probably didn't do that worry me."

"But there wasn't anything," she said, frowning. "In truth," she started hesitantly, deciding that perfect frankness was the best course of action. Taking a deep breath, she plunged on. "You would simply have slept right through if I had not insisted you did your duty." She felt herself turn a deep dark red at this confession.

Armand stared at her. Then he rubbed his brow distractedly. "You insisted I did my duty and bed you?"

"Of course. You must understand," she said appealingly, "I was quite desperate to legitimize our marriage." His expression grew grim, so she hurried on. "You were very sleepy and I—I simply rolled you on top of me." Her face was on fire at the admission.

"That's it?" he asked incredulously.

She nodded. "Yes."

"I did not ready you in any way?"

Una hesitated. "You kissed me and touched my bosom."

He looked away, avoiding her eyes. "Between your legs, I mean."

"No," she admitted in bewilderment, casting her mind back.

He closed his eyes an instant. "How you can say that I did everything I ought when I clearly did not is beyond me." When she sat in confused silence, he took another liberal swig of wine. "If I said I wanted to do it again, would you find the thought distasteful? This time, I can promise you, will be different."

Una lowered her goblet and stared at him. "Oh!" she said lamely. Wherever she had thought he was going with this conversation, she had not expected this. She made a valiant

141

attempt to gather her scattered wits. "Well, of course, you are perfectly entitled. That is your husbandly right." As soon as she had said it, she could see he was not happy with her choice of words. "I mean I should be most happy to accommodate you," she said, flushing hotly.

He plunked his cup down on the table and muttered something under his breath.

"I wish you would tell me what you would prefer I should say," Una said with perfect truth. "I'm afraid I don't have any experience to draw on."

He gazed at her a moment. "Sometimes actions speak louder than words." Una's eyes darted uncertainly over to the bed. Did he mean she should simply climb into bed to await his pleasure? As if guessing the way her mind was working, he said softly, "Come and sit on my lap, Una."

She pushed back her chair at once and rounded the table. Once she had sat square in his lap, his arms came around her and he looked full into her rather hot face.

"I like this shift," he said, his eyes dwelling on the tops of her breasts. "It shows off your womanly form to perfection." He paused. "And I can see the outline of your pretty, dark nipples underneath."

"Northern shifts are more fitted than southern ones I find," she answered, dimly aware her words had not precisely struck the same chord as his.

"You weren't wearing a shift when I woke that first night and you had to fetch me a basin," he continued smoothly. "You were entirely naked. I noticed it particularly."

"I was wearing one when I was put to bed," she answered awkwardly. "But you—"

"Yes?"

How could she possibly say out loud that he had wanted to fondle her breasts? She stared at him, tongue-tied and miserable.

"Just say it," he recommended, his hand hot and heavy where it rested on her thigh. "I like a woman with a bold tongue in her head." He squeezed her thigh. Then a sudden cloud passed over his expression. "Unless you're about to say I ripped it off you," he said, looking suddenly apprehensive.

"Nothing of the sort!" she hastened to assure him. "I pulled my straps down for you, you see…" She was breathless now and anxious to dispel his fears. "You wanted…um…that is you seemed to want…" She shut her eyes so she could no longer see his expression. "I was under the impression you wanted to touch my breasts."

"I'm sure I did," he rumbled back. "So, you pulled your straps down for me, did you, sweetheart? I wish you would do so again."

Una's eyes sprang open. Far from looking annoyed or bored with her, Armand's gaze was fixed on her with searing intensity. She reached for her straps and pulled them down, peeling the filmy material from her generous breasts, so the shift bunched at her waist. Armand made a growling sound deep in his throat, and Una's gaze darted to his for reassurance.

His eyes were hooded now, and she would think him sleepy if they did not gleam so. "What did I do last time?" he asked huskily. "Tell me."

Una swallowed. To her memory he had pawed and slurped at her bosom before practically falling asleep face-first in it. However, she had a strong suspicion this would not go down

143

well. "You…er…said you wanted a taste," she admitted, scarlet-faced.

Again, he made the growling noise in his throat, and Una felt something stirring beneath her bottom. "I bet I did," he said thickly. "What about you, did you like it?"

Una cast her mind back. "Yes," she admitted with slight surprise. That part she had not minded at all.

Suddenly one big hand was cupping her left breast, lightly squeezing it. "You've a fine pair of…breasts, Princess," he said in a gravelly tone. She guessed he had been about to use a ruder term, and then gave a gasp when it dawned on her what he had called her.

"You must not call me that, Sir Armand," she blurted as he lowered his head to her breast.

"Ah, but you keep calling me Sir Armand, and I have to cure you somehow," he answered with a wink.

She had just drawn in a breath to point out that her words were not considered high treason when he sucked her nipple into his hot, wet mouth, and her mind turned blank. His other hand slid from her outer thigh to her inner and then considerably higher, until Una whimpered to feel his fingers slipping through her nether curls, to that which they concealed.

He released her breast with a lascivious lick. "Delicious. Did I not touch you here before, Princess?" he asked and though his tone was teasing, she could hear a thread of real concern running through his voice as he ran his thumb gently up and down her slit. She bit her lip and shook her head, and he cursed softly. "Draw your knees up, Una. There's room on this chair. Rest them against the arms."

144

Una regarded him aghast for a minute that he would expect her to splay her legs open in such a fashion. When he continued to wait expectantly, she drew up her legs and rested her bare feet on the edge of the seat.

"Good girl," he praised her again, bunching up the skirt of her shift and urging her back against his front. "Now spread your legs for me, Princess." His other hand cupped her right breast, kneading and squeezing it until her nipple ached. Slowly, Una did as he asked and rested her legs against the arms of the chair.

Armand groaned. "I wish we had a long mirror against that wall," he said throatily. "So I could enjoy the view." Una gasped as her mind reeled at such a lewd idea. His fingers had dipped right inside her now and were tracing so very lightly over her private places that when he pinched hard on her right nipple, she bit back a cry at the contrast.

To her surprise, she felt an answering pulse in her core, and suddenly Armand's fingers felt slippery and wet as they delved and toyed with increasing boldness into her most secret feminine place.

"Ah, Una," he whispered. "This is how I should have treated you that night, how a princess deserves."

His words were complete nonsense, but for some reason she was shifting in his lap now, restless and biting her lip to stop from sobbing. She knew for definite now what was pressed so firmly against her bottom, but she didn't care. Parts of her body that had felt purely functional before, were now quivering with new awakened life that astonished her. He released her right breast and returned to her left, plucking that nipple, too, in a manner that made her writhe against his hardness.

145

"Such a pretty color," he muttered. "Like ripe berries. That's right, show me where you like to be touched," he murmured. "Sweet Una."

Suddenly his thumb between her legs passed over something that made her lose all the breath from her body and stiffen in his lap. He did it again and Una cried out incoherently. "That's it," he praised her, now circling his thumb over the same spot in a sweet, agonizing torment. "Keep your legs open, don't fret. I won't stop until you're there."

Again, his words meant nothing to Una, but she realized her shaking legs were trying to close over his hand. Not to stop him, she realized with dim shock, but to keep his wicked hand where she wanted it. With an effort, she widened her knees again. Her breasts heaved from the sheer force of effort, and he rewarded her exertions by squeezing each of the full globes firmly in turn.

This last was too much. The pleasure building inside her suddenly burst; she managed to half choke out his name and then collapsed in his arms, legs akimbo. She wasn't sure how much later it was that she came out of her daze to find Armand kissing her neck, at least two of his fingers buried deep inside her. It was only then that she realized how ragged his own breathing was and how insistent the hard thrust of his arousal was underneath her.

"How do my fingers feel?" he asked gruffly, and Una was hard put to know how to answer such a question.

"Deep," she answered truthfully.

His breathing hitched. "I really want to bury my cock, I mean *myself* inside you right now, Una. I swear I'll be gentle this time, Princess."

She was oddly touched that he kept trying to moderate his speech even in such moments, though she really would have to speak to him about the "princess" thing. "Yes," she agreed. "I mean, of course."

The words were no sooner out of her mouth than she was swept up into his arms and carried over to the bed. He lay her down on the mattress widthways rather than lengthways, and while she lay there catching her breath, she heard him swiftly stripping off his braies. The next thing she knew, his naked body was above hers, though he kept his weight off her with his arms.

"You did that last time too," she said in a rush of confidences. "You were careful not to crush me, I mean." At least until after he'd had his way, Una remembered, when he'd collapsed on top of her like a fallen oak.

"Well, that's something," he muttered. "Open your legs now, sweetheart." She did so, admittedly with some trepidation. Still, it felt different this time. Armand's fingers were between her legs again. "You're so nice and wet, Princess," he whispered. "I can't wait."

"You—you said it was good last time," she blurted.

His eyes met hers. "I did? When I was inside you?"

She nodded and his nostrils flared. "This time I'll make it good for you too," he vowed. Again, she nodded, and then he was reaching between them to place his manhood at her entrance. His eyes sought hers again. "I'm ready," she said bravely, and he started to push his way into her in an insistent, but not uncomfortable, slide. She could only suppose her wetness was facilitating his entrance this time.

When he was halfway in, Una braced herself for the brutal thrust that caused so much pain, but to her surprise, when it did come, it was not met with a blast of discomfort. Feeling her stiffen, Armand stopped at once.

"It hurts?" he asked.

"No, not at all." He looked relieved and then thrust again twice more, until his eyes closed, and he gritted his teeth.

"What's wrong?" Una asked in alarm.

"Nothing," he grunted. "It just feels really good."

"Oh." She gave a slight wriggle to check nothing pinched, but other than the peculiar sensation of fullness, she felt no ill effects.

Armand, however, gave a deep groan. "Una! For the Lord's sake, I'm hanging on here by a thread."

Una paused. "What does that mean?"

"It means—uhhhh, gods." His hips gave what looked to be an involuntary thrust and he braced his hands by her shoulders. "I want to do this, and this, and this," he groaned, punctuating each phrase with increasingly harder thrusts of his hips. "Until I come. I don't know how much longer I can hold back. Should I pull out?"

"Pull out?" Una gazed up at him doubtfully. "Last time you just thrust until you collapsed on top of me."

He blinked at that. "I bet I fucking did," he said, looking pained. "Wait a minute, I'll just—"

"No!" Una placed her hands on his shoulders. "All's well." She gave him a reassuring smile.

He hesitated. "You're certain?"

"I am."

He gave a relieved groan and labored over her, his movements crude and brisk. Una held him tightly, huffing her breath against his throat. She was not precisely disliking it, but it also felt extremely strange. Suddenly, she felt his thumb between her legs, landing on that self-same spot he had lavished with such attention earlier. Una's closed eyes sprang open. "Oh!" she gasped with surprise.

He gave a satisfied rumble in his throat. "Bring your legs higher. Wrap them around me. Tight."

Una lifted her legs and crossed them behind Armand's back. His breathing hitched. "Damn it," he swore, closing his eyes a second.

"Is that too tight?"

"No," he grunted. "It's good. Too good." She felt him begin to pulse and jerk inside her and then he was slamming his hips against hers again with increasing urgency.

"Ah gods, Una," he groaned. "Next time, my love. I swear it."

Next time what? she wondered as he thrust to his completion and once again collapsed on top of her with a harsh bellow.

6

When Armand woke the next morning, he felt drowsy and happy. This feeling diminished slightly when he found himself alone in the bed, but a sound at the door heralded Una's arrival with hot water and a cheerful smile. She was dressed in a gown he had not seen before of deep blue with a red underrobe that showed through at the sleeves and neckline, her auburn hair neatly braided and pinned.

"Good morning," he said, clearing his throat. "How long have you been about?"

"An hour or so," she said, setting the steaming jug down on the table. "Here's clean cloths for you," she said, placing them down next to the basin.

He frowned. "Why are you fetching and carrying?" He could see their bags had been brought up. "I hope you did not cart those up the stairs."

Una followed his gaze to where the saddlebags were piled up. "I did not want you to be disturbed; you were sleeping so soundly," she admitted and colored faintly.

He took that as confirmation that she had indeed carried their things upstairs, and he felt a faint stab of something close to guilt. Then again, it wasn't his fault she always rose so damn early! He rolled onto his side.

"That gown becomes you," he said. "But I prefer your hair down."

Una gazed at him as though unsure how to respond. "Thank you," she said after a moment's pause.

"If you say Sir Armand, I warn you I will drag you back in this bed," he said thickly.

"I wasn't going to," she said reproachfully, her blush deepening.

A shame, he thought, as the idea had definite merit. He sighed. He would have to climb out of bed, he supposed, and face the never-ending list of tasks that would be needed to set the house to rights. The idea was not an appealing one. He eyed Una as she opened a large trunk and placed something inside it. The patter of feet told him her ever-present little dog was still at her heels.

"What is Otho up to?" he asked grudgingly, rubbing his eyes.

"Patching the stables, so the roof does not leak on our poor horses in the event of rain," she responded promptly. "He has carried all of your sacks from The Merry Wayfarer inside and put them in the attic. There is a room there that locks and seems to have been used as some sort of stronghold previously." She lifted something from the belt of her waist to show him, and he was amused to see she already carried a bunch of keys to the house. No doubt they were much safer in her clutches than those of that incompetent girl. "Shall I give you the key to it now?"

He waved a hand. "Leave it on the side." He could not be bothered with it now and it was hardly urgent in any case. He was still plump in the pocket from his winnings on May Day. "What of that appalling girl?" he asked irritably. "Is she still on the premises or have you thrown her out on her ear?"

Una looked startled. "Rose? Indeed, I have not. Otho kept her up until all hours last night and the poor girl is exhausted this morning."

151

Armand, who had been taking a sip of water, choked. "Did he? By gods, I would not have thought he had it in him."

Una gazed at him a moment, before continuing painstakingly. "Not only did he make her scour every pot and pan in the place, but he also had her scrub the kitchen from top to bottom before he would let her retire. By all accounts, she is not used to scullery work at all."

Armand set his cup down with a thud. "And what is she used to, pray?" he demanded with sudden irritation. "Does anyone know? I have been sending coins back here to cover the expenses of a housekeeper. Admittedly, the payments have been irregular, but I would like to know how they have been spent if she has not done any of the work these past twelve months!"

His outburst surprised him, more than it did his wife. Gods, he already sounded like an irate householder, he thought. Maybe he would wind up as petty and penny-pinching as his brother Henry!

"Otho has already discovered three of those purses on shelves or in cupboards," Una said apologetically. "They are practically full. From what I can make out, Rose's only expense has been a loaf of bread and the odd sack of grain from the village. She has been remiss in her duties, it is true," Una continued soothingly. "But she has barely touched the money and—"

"What of that fancy gown she was swanning around in?" Armand interrupted cuttingly. "That would have cost a pretty penny and is hardly the garb of a servant."

"No, but you see her previous position was as a sort of pet to a rich merchant's widow. She indulged her, buying her pretty gowns and teaching her genteel occupations like needlework and music. Poor Rose has not received any instruction—"

152

"Poor Rose!" Armand burst out indignantly, flinging back the covers and climbing from the bed. He was not sure why he was so annoyed, for usually he could not be bothered with household matters at all. If anything, he should be more concerned about checking on his new treasure trove, but for some reason, his priorities seemed all over the place this morn.

He strode across the room for the jug and basin, noticing Una looked hurriedly away at his nudity. This fact alone went some way to restoring a measure of his good humor. So, she was not so immune to him as she pretended, looking all polite and meek-faced this morning after their oh-so-satisfying tryst of the previous night.

That was why he was out of sorts, he realized suddenly. She was acting as if that whole encounter had not happened! Also, why was she not jumping at the chance to get this Rose off the scene? he wondered, aggrieved. It was an insult to his potent masculinity that she was not jealously guarding her property!

"I find you very remiss this morning, wife," he said, lathering the soap flakes between his hand and sloshing the water about as he washed his face and neck.

"Remiss?" Una closed the cabinet doors and looked at him inquiringly.

"Aye, for you have not fulfilled your obligations this morn."

"Which ones?" she asked, clearly puzzled.

He turned to face her, and she straightened up, her face fixed respectfully to his and not his nakedness below. He dabbed a drying cloth at his neck. "You have not kissed me," he said simply. "Here in the south, it is customary for a wife to greet her husband every day with a kiss."

"Oh," she said, taken aback. "I had not realized."

153

"You should probably remedy it at once," he recommended. "Lest I take offense."

She sent him a level look at that, as though suddenly suspicious he was teasing her, but there wasn't even a glimmer of amusement in his eyes for he was in deadly earnest. Even he was slightly surprised about the fact.

Straightening up, she walked over to him, placed her hands over his ears, angled his head, and placed a smacker on his lips. "Good morning, husband," she said, drawing back. Armand had been so startled, he had not much time to do anything other than pucker his lips to meet hers. Her height meant she had only to rise on her toes to bring her face to his, and he had not had to stoop at all, meaning he had been unprepared for her kiss.

"One moment," he said, lifting a finger as she beat a hasty retreat. "That is not all."

Una turned slowly toward him. "What else?" she asked, glancing down at Abelard, who was now once more retreating under the dresser.

"If a husband has given a wife pleasure," he said, cocking his head to one side, "then she must shower him with kisses in recompense."

She definitely checked at that one, sending him a look eloquent of disbelief. "Every time?"

"Without fail," he agreed, and crossed over toward the bed, sitting on the edge.

"Shall I wait for you to dress?" she asked, clearing her throat.

"That won't be necessary." He lay back on the bed, his arms folded behind his head. He could feel her gaze on him but waited patiently until he heard her feet head toward him. He patted the bed. "Don't be shy."

"I'm fully dressed!" Una objected, coming to a halt beside the bed.

"I'm not asking you to get in it." *Not yet anyway.*

"Sir Armand—" she began, her voice betraying some exasperation, and then she broke off, realizing her mistake. "I mean—"

"Now, you know what I am going to do every time you make that slip, don't you, Princess?" he said reproachfully. Though in truth, he found he liked calling her princess. In the bedchamber anyway.

"I really wish you would not," she muttered as she climbed onto the bed beside him, bracing her hands on either side of his head and then lowering her face to his. When she lightly peppered his brow with soft, chaste kisses, Armand stilled and lay very quiet. She repeated the process over his cheeks and then drew back. "Like that?" she asked with just a hint of uncertainty.

He huffed out a breath he hadn't realized he was holding. "Yes," he found himself answering, though in truth, he had intended something quite different. "Just like that."

*

When he made his way downstairs half an hour later, Armand told himself he had shaken off the strange mood that had overtaken him. Una had asked him to act the role of proprietary husband back at Caer-Lyoness, and this morning he had slipped into the part as though it were perfectly natural to him! He would have to watch his step, or the gods alone knew how he would end up.

He was frowning abstractedly when he came across Otho, who was carrying his own saddlebags into the house. "Morning," he said. "Sorted yourself a room out, have you?"

Otho halted, looking surprised to be hailed by him. "Yes," he said, then seemed at a loss how to continue.

"We'll need more staff if we're to set this place to rights," Armand said briskly. "You feel up to the job of steward?"

Otho flushed. "I could do it," he said cautiously. "I was thinking of riding into the village later for provisions. I could put the word out we're looking for servants."

Armand nodded. "Kitchen staff are the most pressing, I'd say."

Otho murmured in agreement. "And garden. It's overgrown and ill tended. She kept the herb bed in order and precious little else."

By "she," Armand deduced he was speaking of Rose. He rolled his eyes. "I'm surprised she managed that much," he said sourly, and Otho grunted in agreement. "Una wants to keep her on," he admitted grudgingly.

Otho looked disgusted. "Why?"

"I can't possibly be expected to repeat her line of reasoning on an empty stomach, but mayhap you could dissuade her on the matter."

Otho seemed skeptical. "She's a mind of her own, for all she seems so reasonable."

"You can try at least." Otho shot him a narrow look, and Armand realized that Una's brother still harbored suspicions that Rose might be some castoff from his past. "Never mind, you will do as you see fit, I'm sure," he said, passing on and walking to the kitchen in search of sustenance.

156

It looked a good deal cleaner and tidier this morning, though very bare, with none of the paraphernalia of a functioning kitchen he had ever seen. There were no herbs hanging from the rafters, no smell of dough or waft of spices. Still, at least it no longer looked like a filthy hovel.

He crossed to the empty pantry and observed the half-empty sack of grain with disfavor. Above it on a shelf was the end of a loaf of bread. That would have to do. He took this and slathered it liberally with butter and let himself out of the kitchen door and into the gardens at the back of the house.

Otho had not exaggerated. Armand's eyes roved over the extensive kitchen gardens, which were full of untidy plants that had either bolted or gone to seed. He walked down the overgrown walkways, eating his bread, and taking in the abundant signs of neglect about the place. He could not blame it all on Rose, he reflected fairly. For in truth, there was no way that one woman could maintain such a large property. He had been the one who had neglected Lynwode ever since his godfather, Sir Adrian, had died.

At the bottom of the garden, marking the end of his land, was an extensive ruin in gray stone of a much earlier property. So occupied was he in gazing at what was left of it that he did not hear Una coming up the garden behind him and was only aware of her when she stopped at his elbow.

"It is a very picturesque view, is it not?" she murmured, standing beside him.

"You think so?" He turned to look at her as she stood gazing steadily at the remains. Her little dog sat at her feet, staring up at Una rather than the ruin.

"Oh yes. It must have been a sizeable property indeed, for look." She pointed. "That looks like the remains of a rampart and that tower looks almost intact with its little arched window at the top."

"It has barely three walls, and you are not to go near it," Armand heard himself reply sternly. "When we were boys, my brother Henry dared me to climb that tower and I nearly broke my neck. The steps are crumbling, and several have eroded. I can't imagine it has grown any safer in the past twenty years."

"I did not intend to climb it," she answered, looking at him rather oddly.

He strove for a lighter tone. "A good deal of the stone from it was used to build Lynwode," he said, turning back to look at the house.

Una followed his example and gazed up at it appraisingly. "It is a lovely house," she said softly. "You must be very proud of it."

Was he? In truth, he'd barely given the place a second thought, save for basking in the satisfaction that Henry had been seething to see him land such a large inheritance. Poor Henry, whose only distinction had been the fact he was born first. As though aware of his thoughts, Una asked, "Why did your brother dare you to climb it? Were you very competitive growing up?"

Armand laughed. "Hardly. Henry's a poor creature." He offered Una his arm and they proceeded toward the ruin, followed closely by a trotting Abelard. "When I say he challenged me, what I really mean is he claimed it was impossible to climb the tower. A miserable worm like Henry would never even make the attempt. He disdained archery, riding, wrestling, and swordplay. Henry would only ever sit bent over his books and his music on even the sunniest of days."

Una pursed her lips. "Not everyone has the aptitude for outdoor pursuits," she pointed out mildly. "That is no reason to despise your older brother any more than he should look down on you for enjoying more physical occupations."

Armand was startled. "Well," he rallied, "he certainly did look down his nose at me for my neglect of book-learning, so I suppose we were even with one another."

"Did your parents never attempt to encourage some accord between you?" Una asked as they came to a halt before the ruin.

Armand shook his head ruefully. "I was my mother's favorite," he admitted. "I think I mentioned it before?" Una nodded. "She lauded my every accomplishment and lambasted Henry as a poor dog by comparison." He shrugged. "Now I am older, I see of course, poor Henry must have squirmed, but at the time I reveled in it."

He hesitated. "Henry sought my father's approval, I think, but Father was often from home, and even when he was there, he did not seem very interested in any of us. His heir was no exception." He took a deep breath. "But likely he has my father's attention now, for they live under the same roof together and my mother is long since dead." He shrugged. "In any case, it's all water under the bridge."

"How much older is Henry than you?"

"Some five years."

"So, he is a young man still."

"He must be five and thirty now," Armand replied. "But Henry has never seemed young. He married a widow from Great Derring, which just added to his old-womanish ways. She was in her mid-forties when he met her, and she has at least a good ten years on him, if not more."

Una nodded. "And who is your younger brother more like? You or Henry?"

"Roger?" Armand considered. "I scarcely know. He was so much younger than the rest of us, and I had gone away to squire while he was still in leading strings. Still…" His frown cleared. "He was studying for the priesthood last time I heard, so we can hardly be kindred spirits."

They had walked about the ruin now and were contemplating the winding staircase that was exposed to their gaze, for a good deal of the outer wall of the tower had worn away. Funnily enough, Abelard chose this moment to show some independence of mind and trotted over to it sniffing at the bottom step. Una called him away.

"It does look dangerous," she admitted as the dog returned to her. "Did you really climb it? Right to the top?"

Armand nodded. "And waved my hat out of the window to prove the feat. My godfather whipped me soundly afterward with a switch."

Una shivered. "He was probably a good deal frightened. That top chamber looks balanced so perilously up there. One day it will probably come crashing to the ground."

Armand murmured in agreement, looking up. "Aye, more than likely. That's why it's best if you stay away from this spot altogether."

*

After they had returned to the house, Una set about viewing the rooms and making her plans while Rose and Abelard trailed after her, the very picture of two faithful companions.

Otho returned from the village with a strapping laborer called Peter who didn't have much to say for himself but had plenty of muscles. Armand was in the stable seeing to his horse when Otho confronted him with a rather defiant air. "He can start right away, and we don't need to put him up at the house for he lives in the village with his widowed mother."

Armand glanced the bashful lad over. Peter hung back in the shadows, as if embarrassed by his own size. He looked no more than one and twenty at the most. "If you think he's suitable, then set him to work," he answered with a touch of impatience, for he was brushing down Arturo, who expected a good deal more attention than he had received the previous day. "I put you in charge of the hiring, Otho."

"I can help out in the stables too," Peter piped up unexpectedly. "My father was a blacksmith, so I'm used to being around horses."

Armand glanced up. "Well, then that's fine," he said, directing a look at Otho. "Well done."

Otho's face relaxed, and he sent Peter outside to start on tidying the kitchen garden at once. "I also found a possible cook," he started, folding his arms and jutting his chin out. Armand wondered if every conversation with Una's brother was going to be as confrontational as this one.

"Yes," he answered, striving for patience. "Well, that's good, isn't it?"

Otho's lips thinned. "He has a somewhat checkered history," he admitted cautiously.

Armand straightened up. "What does that mean?"

161

"He used to be a successful baker in a city about ten miles from here, but he's had to move in with his wife's family in Little Derring."

"Why is that?" asked Armand, reaching for a brush.

"He burned his premises down."

Armand lowered the brush. "He burned it down?" he repeated slowly as Otho stared resolutely back at him. "Some kind of whim or fancy took him?" he hazarded.

Otho's expression grew stony. "By all accounts, he used to have a problem with the drink, but he's abstinent now so…"

Armand sighed. "It's your decision, Otho," he said, applying the brush to Arturo's long back. "If you say the man is reformed, then by all means give him a trial."

"We needn't furnish him with lodgings, for he has a wife and child at the family home to return to."

Armand nodded. "By the way, how many servant bedchambers are there?"

"Four," said Otho, looking scandalized that Armand had to ask. "But there's room for more than one bed in all of them."

"If you keep employing villagers, we won't need to double them up," Armand observed sagely. He crouched beside Arturo's great legs then realized Otho was still lingering. "Is there anything else?" he asked, looking up.

"That girl," Otho said, not meeting his eye.

Armand gritted his teeth. Otho's attitude over Rose was starting to seriously annoy him. "Well, what about her?"

"If Una wishes to keep her around, she'll need demoting. She's not fit for a housekeeper."

"Agreed."

"She needs moving out of the housekeeper's room into a smaller one." His jaw hardened. "You should see the state of it."

Armand's eyebrows rose. "Is it dirty?"

"It's not that," said Otho in clipped tones. "It's crammed full of wildflowers! Looks more like a meadow than a bedchamber."

"Well, I suggest you cross that bridge when you've found a new housekeeper," Armand observed dryly. "Otherwise she'll be spouting tears for the next week, and it is your sister who will suffer for it."

Otho rocked back on his heels, looking much struck by this argument. "There is something in what you say," he admitted grudgingly.

"So good of you to say so," Armand muttered as Otho strode purposefully out of the stable. Arturo whickered as though in sympathy. He patted his horse. "Exactly so. I'm glad I may depend on you at least."

Their midday meal was another haphazard affair. Armand made his way into the great hall without great hopes of sustenance, but it seemed that word had spread in the village of Lynwode's occupation. Several tradesmen had presented themselves at the kitchen door that morning, and Una had purchased a keg of ale, a baked ham, and three loaves of bread.

He and Una sat at the head of the freshly scrubbed table, on a raised dais, under a high vaulted ceiling and a minstrel's gallery and ate their simple meal with relish. If it seemed incongruous

163

to be sat eating bread and ham in such an impressive setting, neither of them saw fit to mention the fact.

It appeared Una did not pass as many morsels of ham down to her little dog as he would like, for at one point, he timidly cast a glance in Armand's direction, smacking his lips. Discreetly, Armand dropped some meat at his own feet and the dog darted forward to retrieve it before returning to his mistress.

Once Abelard had settled again at Una's feet, Armand let his eyes travel up her skirts appraisingly until he reached her face. She was gazing at the decorated wooden screen that concealed the three doorways to the kitchen, pantry, and buttery, no doubt thinking about furniture polish or some such thing. Armand found his thoughts wandering to less practical matters.

He rather liked her height, he decided with surprise. He certainly appreciated her long legs when they were wrapped around him last night, and he liked that she could kiss him like she had that morning without struggling to reach his lips.

"I wonder that the others do not join us." Una frowned. "Is that not something that is done in the south?"

"What's that?" asked Armand, who had been distracted with his inventory of her charms.

"In the north, the servants join their masters at table for their meals, only we would sit at the head and they would be further down. Is it not the same here in the south?"

Armand shrugged. "Depends on the household. If that's what you want, then I'm agreeable. You may have to run it past your brother first though," he added.

Una looked surprised. "Why do you say that?"

"Otho seems to think some order needs to be restored at Lynwode," he answered. For a moment he debated telling her of Otho's plans to oust Rose from the housekeeper's quarters, then realized he could not be bothered. "Has he told you he thinks he has found us a cook?" he asked, sticking to important matters.

"He mentioned giving someone called Mr. Beverley a trial in the kitchen for tonight's supper," she said. "Though at present there is precious little for him to work with."

"Maybe you'll receive more visitors plying their wares this afternoon?" Armand replied.

"I hope so. What a good thing it was that you announced our arrival yesterday." She smiled at him, and Armand was tempted to bask in her approval awhile. He suppressed the impulse, but it was a struggle.

7

Armand retrieved the attic key from their room after they'd done eating and headed up to peruse his newfound wealth at his leisure. Meanwhile, Una walked through to the kitchen and found Otho, Rose, and a large young man sat around the kitchen table partaking of the same simple meal she and Armand had shared. When the young man went to pull back his chair and hastily stand, Una begged him not to trouble himself in the midst of eating.

"This is Peter. He'll tend the garden and help out in the stables," Otho said, swiftly glancing up.

"I am pleased to meet you," Una said. "In future, Sir Armand and I would like the household to take our meals together in the great hall," she asserted, though Otho scowled and Peter looked terrified at the notion.

Abelard danced up to Rose and pawed her knee with a familiarity that astonished Una. Rose smiled at him and promptly gave him the entire portion of ham from her plate. When Otho opened his mouth to reprove her, Una gave him a stern look, and he bit back his words unspoken.

"Would you like some more ham, Rose?" Una asked her as the girl watched Abelard fall upon the bounty with enthusiasm.

"Oh, no thank you, milady," she said with a shake of her head. "In truth, I do not care to eat the flesh of animals at all."

Otho lowered his knife and looked at her with even more disapproval, if that were possible, but to Una it explained perfectly the mystery of the empty pantry. She nodded and left the kitchen to inspect the buttery, which she had overlooked so far. To her surprise there were several dusty casks of what looked like wine, but the only barrel of ale was the one she had purchased that morning. They would certainly need more delivered, she thought as she pulled back a piece of sacking and discovered a supply of candles.

Wondering if the wine would be quite sour by now, she left the buttery and returned to the kitchen. "We need more ale delivered," she told Otho. "As soon as possible now our household is expanding." She turned curiously to Rose. "What did you drink throughout the day, Rose?"

"Water, milady," Rose answered absently.

"Water!" Otho burst forth disgustedly.

Rose nodded. "It's clean and fresh from the well."

Otho looked forbidding as the girl rose to her feet. "You needn't think you're prancing off now," he said witheringly. "You can wash these dishes before you run after your mistress."

Rose looked crestfallen but started collecting the empty platters obediently enough.

"Have you found any suitable kitchen maids?" Una asked in a low voice as Peter, too, rose from the table and let himself back out into the kitchen garden with all haste.

"There's a girl coming for me to look her over this afternoon. And a prospective housekeeper," he added loudly, presumably for Rose's benefit.

Una frowned at him, but he ignored her. "There's no need to be harsh to her, Otho," she hissed as she glanced at Rose, who was lathering the lye soap and looking thoroughly miserable.

"There is every need," he contradicted, his lips set in a firm, straight line. "De Bussell has given me sway over these matters and I mean to take my duties seriously."

Somewhat taken aback, Una retreated to inspect the faded cushions and flick a dusting cloth over the furniture in the solar, a room that she had so far neglected. The tapestries that hung there were so dirty and faded that Una could not make out their decoration, but the collection of books looked delightful. When she opened their pages, the ink was still strong and vibrant, and she looked forward to spending an hour or two with them when the place was set to rights.

On one side of the solar was a wide oriel window protruding outward, which afforded a lovely view from the front of the house. Una appreciated this for a moment before turning to inspect the carved chairs and small, cunningly wrought tables dotted about. They would be perfect for sewing, embroidery, and quiet reading. In one corner stood a harp that was not as dusty as the rest of the items and Una wondered if Rose perhaps played it.

It was a charming room, and she was sure she would spend many pleasurable hours in it. It just needed sprucing up, that was all. She spent a good while setting things to rights before it crossed her mind that Otho must now be meeting with the prospective housekeeper.

Unable to suppress her curiosity, Una descended to the great hall, tempted to interrupt the interview for a glimpse of the woman. However, something about her brother's expression when he said Armand had entrusted the task to him stopped her. Instead she vowed to wait for Otho to bring the woman to her and instead plied a cloth over the wooden screen until it gleamed.

From the snatches of conversation she could catch, it seemed Mrs. Brickenden was a local woman with two grown daughters now settled in their own households. She sounded of middling years and eminently respectable. Una felt sure Otho would hire her and was not surprised when she heard him confirm this aloud. Mrs. Brickenden evinced no great surprise or enthusiasm toward her engagement, and Una hastily retreated to the other side of the hall to await her introduction. To her surprise and perturbation, she heard the outside door slam some minutes later and realized the thought must not have occurred to her brother.

She crossed the hall into the kitchen and found Otho alone and looking pleased with himself.

"Well? Did you hire someone?" Una demanded, plunking her hands on her hips.

He nodded. "Aye, a very capable woman by the name of Brickenden."

"And where, pray, is my introduction?"

Otho opened his mouth and then closed it again. Then he scratched the back of his head, looking abashed. "I did not think."

"I would have thought Mrs. Brickenden would have wished to meet her mistress," she responded indignantly. "Indeed, I think it most peculiar of her that she did not request such a thing."

Otho looked alarmed. "Nay, Una, don't take on. It isn't like you to cause a commotion over so little a thing."

"So little a thing?" she cried. "This is of the greatest import to me, Otho!" She turned away from him until she had mastered her sudden rush of feeling. "You must understand that I have had no say in the people I have been surrounded with since…since I can remember!" She took a steadying breath. "You seem to forget, brother, that I have been under house arrest for three years! Surrounded by people who were hostile toward me!" She gave him a very level look. "Did you tell this woman that her mistress will be a northerner?"

Otho blinked. "What does that signify in these times?" he rumbled awkwardly. "If any of these servants even look at you askance, you can just dismiss them after all. You must not attach too much significance to them. They will be beneath your notice in any case."

"They most certainly will not, Otho!" she retorted hotly. Lowering her voice, she added with spirit. "You keep forgetting I am no longer a princess, but the mistress of her own home! How can the members of my household be beneath me? Such a notion is ridiculous!"

Seeing her evident distress, he hastened to her side and placed a conciliatory hand on her arm. "Una, I did not think. That is, I did not realize you felt this way. You must forgive me."

She unclutched her fists at her side and took a deep breath. Outbursts of emotion were not common to her, and she always felt wretched rather than relieved in the aftermath. Otho pulled out a chair for her, and she sat down as he poured her a cup of the weak ale.

"The girl who wants to be maidservant should be arriving here shortly," he said awkwardly. "We will see her together, shall we? How would that be?" Una nodded and sipped her ale as she calmed down. "Should we move into the great hall?" he asked. "It's hardly fitting for you to receive her here in the kitchen—" he started, but Una shook her head, bringing her palm down on the table sharply.

"In here will be just fine, Otho." It trembled on the tip of her tongue to point out once again, she was no longer royalty, but she had probably subjected him to enough reproaches for one

170

day. Instead she concentrated on getting her breathing back to normal and letting the flush retreat from her overheated face.

She had no sooner drained her cup than a loud knock was heard on the door. Otho opened it to greet a buxom young woman who sailed in, looking to the left and right of her with great interest.

She was dressed very plainly in a sage-green wool gown with her dark hair scraped back and braided closely to her head, but the few tendrils escaping at her neck and temples were very curly. She was a plain girl of stocky build, but her eyes were lively and bright, and when they alighted on Una, they gleamed with satisfaction.

"Milady." She curtsied briefly.

"I'm very pleased to meet you," Una replied truthfully. "Your name is Janet?"

"That's right, milady. Janet Frampton. My father runs the mill just outside the village."

"Does he really?" Una gestured for Janet to take a seat at the kitchen table, and she happily complied as Otho hurried over to join them.

"Yes, milady. For twenty years now. He runs it with my three brothers. Our mother died ten years ago, so I've picked up all her duties about the place."

"I see," Una replied. "How do you think he will manage without you at the mill, Janet? Did you tell him you were coming along today?"

Janet snorted. "Not likely!"

Otho coughed. "How old are you, Janet?" he interrupted loudly.

"Twenty," she answered promptly. "And not the smallest push has my father made to find me a husband!" she added, a light kindling in her eye. "An unpaid drudge, that's what I am," she said darkly. "Taken for granted and expected to pick up after those three oafs who call themselves my brothers!"

"I expect it's far too convenient for your father to keep you at home," Una commented sympathetically.

"That's what I says! And what does my aunt Matthews say, but that I must be patient and do my duty by my family." She pressed her lips together. "And I says, what have I been doing these past twenty years, that's what I should like to know! If I don't look sharp, I shall be in the same place in another twenty years and end up an old maid!"

"A young woman does need to plan for her future," Una agreed as Otho looked increasingly annoyed that the formal interview he had planned was turning into an exchange of female confidences.

"Now, what I wants to know is this," said Janet, leaning forward in her seat. "Is bed and board included, as there's sure to be a ruckus when Pa finds I'm jumping ship."

Otho opened his mouth, a disagreeable expression on his face.

"Certainly there is," Una responded, forestalling her brother smoothly. "Though there is the likelihood you may need to share a bedchamber with another maid."

"Lord, I won't fret about that," Janet said, settling back in her seat, looking vastly contented.

"How soon can you join us here at Lynwode?" Una asked.

"Lord bless you, milady, I only needs to throw a few things in a sack, and I can be with you this very evening!"

Otho collapsed back in his seat, looking defeated.

*

She did not see Armand until before supper, when they met in their bedchamber. Una, who had just changed her dress, looked back over her shoulder to see him looking dusty and cobweb strewn, and guessed he had only just emerged from the attics. "There's clean water on the side," she told him, and he headed for it immediately to wash. "It must be dirty in those attics."

He grunted in agreement. "Extremely."

"Shall I lay out a clean suit of clothes for you?" she asked, turning to look at him critically.

He looked down at himself in surprise. "I'll just dust myself off," he said, then looked at her with dawning suspicion. "Are we expecting guests for supper?"

"No, no," she hastened to assure him. "'Tis only…" Her words trailed off.

"What?" he asked. "Tell me."

"Well…" Una fussed with the pleats at her beaded waistband. "'Tis only that tonight will be the first night that we take supper with our whole household in the great chamber."

"Whole household?" Armand asked with a lift of his eyebrows.

"Otho hired Peter, Mr. Beverley, Mrs. Brickenden, and Janet today."

"I have met Peter," Armand said, "but who are the others?"

"Mr. Beverley is the cook."

"Ah yes, I have heard of him," Armand said dryly, turning back to the basin of water and scrubbing his neck with a cloth. "His reputation precedes him. Or should I say ill fame?"

"He is cooking for us tonight in any case," Una informed him. "Mrs. Brickenden apparently will not be joining us until the end of the week, but Janet, our new maid, will be there."

"Oh yes?" Armand did not sound particularly interested. "So, I am expected to put on a clean outfit to impress our servants, am I?" Una did not answer, and after a moment, he turned to survey her. "Una?"

"No, of course not," she said quietly and started to walk toward the door. She wasn't sure how it happened, but somehow, suddenly, Armand was stood in front of her, blocking her way. She blinked at him with surprise, for he moved with surprising rapidity for such a large male. He caught her wrist and held her arm out, surveying her dress of rich gold brocade.

Suddenly, Una felt foolish for putting on such a fancy gown. Was she making a spectacle of herself? She couldn't quite meet his eye.

"Very nice," he said slowly. "Well, if my wife is to be so fine, I can hardly appear below stairs in these old things, now can I?" She caught her breath and raised her gaze to his. He smiled. "Whatever you want me to wear, I will wear it."

Una felt a rush of gratitude so strong, she could have kissed him. Then it flashed into her head that after what he had said that morning, she very likely should. Before she could change her mind, she surged forward and bestowed an impulsive peck on his lips, then stepped back and would have hurried to fetch him a clean tunic before realizing he still had a firm hold of her.

Una looked toward him questioningly, and he tugged her toward him. "Just a minute," he said, drawing her closer and lightly clasping her waist. "I don't want to get you dusty, but I need to know what that was for?"

"For…for giving me pleasure," Una stammered, feeling she was on uncertain ground. "Is that not what you said I ought to do?"

He stared at her enigmatically a moment before clearing his throat. "I suppose it was," he said, sounding a little unsure himself.

"What about the burgundy tunic I made you?" Una asked eagerly. "With the matching chausses?" For a moment, she thought a look of displeasure flashed across his face, but it was gone so fast, she thought she must have been mistaken.

"Was not the gold legging ripped of that pair?" he asked.

"I mended it this afternoon."

"Oh." He swallowed. "Then yes, of course." He smiled and Una felt reassured. He released her with a show of reluctance that was highly flattering and then started stripping off his black tunic and breeches.

Una crossed to the trunk and retrieved her handiwork, laying it lovingly on the bed for him, then hurried downstairs to see that Rose had set out the candlesticks they had retrieved from storage as she had bade her.

She need not have worried, for Rose seemed fully aware of the momentous occasion, or perhaps she just liked to see the room illuminated by candlelight, for by the time Una descended the staircase, the great hall had a blazing fire in its grate and at least fifty candles lit along the high table.

"Oh, you look beautiful," Rose breathed, coming toward her and taking her hands in what was no doubt a breach of etiquette. But Una found she did not mind at all. "What a lovely, lovely gown."

"I made it myself," Una told her, and Rose gasped with gratifying astonishment, encouraging her to turn full circle. Una happily complied.

"I so admire the sleeves," Rose marveled, gazing at the long tips, which extended down to her knees. "And the matching cap. It all drapes so beautifully to show your figure to advantage. You must be extraordinarily talented with a needle."

Una reached up to touch the small beaded cap that sat atop her coiled auburn braids. Though the fabric was rich and beautiful indeed, the gown itself still felt wonderfully elegant and fuss-free to Una, who was so accustomed to wearing padding and rolls and panniers. Perhaps she had a distorted view of what was considered formal wear?

The only aspect she found a little daunting was the neckline, which was cut in a square as fashionable ladies wore and showed rather more shoulder and skin than Una was used to. She had not dared to go as low as the Queen, who was graceful and slender and a good deal less endowed in the bosom area than Una. She knew full well that what looked refined and stylish on Armenal would look vastly indecent on herself!

They both heard a footfall on the staircase, and Rose hurriedly retreated to the kitchen to let everyone know the master and mistress were in place. Una walked to the foot of the stairs and felt her heart almost burst with pride when she saw Armand coming toward her in the outfit she had made him.

Seeing him wearing it hurtled her right back to that first time she had seen him in it. She felt the emotion welling up that she

176

had felt on that day she had escaped from the palace at his side. The tunic truly fit him to perfection, and the burgundy and gold chausses made him look as fashionable as any courtier in the southern court. She mourned the loss of the matching cap but knew she had not been mistaken in thinking he had not liked it, so she could stand its omission.

When he reached the foot of the stairs, he held his arm out to her and she took it, and they made their way into the great hall and mounted the dais as Otho came hurrying through from the kitchen, carrying a large flagon of wine and a tray of cups. Peter followed him with a large platter of three loaves of freshly baked bread and a dish of butter.

"The bread smells wonderful," Una commented as Armand pulled her chair back for her. He sat beside her as Otho plunked down the wine before them.

"I sampled the wine, and it tastes alright to me, but I'm no connoisseur," Otho said with a shrug. "I don't know how long it's lain in the buttery."

Armand poured two cups and passed one to Una, then passed the flagon back to Otho, who poured it into the remaining cups. Una took a sip.

"It tastes fine to me."

Rose entered the room, gracefully carrying two large dishes, one holding glazed root vegetables and the other of fresh peas with parsley, butter, and mint. Following her bounced Janet, proudly bearing a side of roasted beef covered with mushrooms and gravy. Last but not least, came the cook himself, a small man with large moustaches, carrying a large, decorative golden pie. He set this down with a flourish. "Roasted chicken, cooked in wine with saffron and served in a herb-crusted pie," he announced.

"It's a very beautiful pie," Una said, gazing on its magnificence. Not to mention its enormous size. They would be feasting off such a pie for a week! Doubtless, Mr. Beverley was exerting his every effort to impress them with his culinary skills.

He executed a bow and hurried down the table to take his seat opposite Rose. Peter sat opposite Janet, and Otho sat himself squarely between themselves and the servants as a sort of barrier.

"I wish Otho would come and sit next to me," Una murmured to Armand. "Why must he sit there in the middle on his own like that?"

Armand opened his mouth, either to reply to her or summon Otho closer, she could never be sure, because at that instant came the sound of a loud rapping, presumably from the front entrance. Conversation fell away as everyone looked from one to other in consternation. No one was invited for supper, yet only guests would come to the front door.

Armand and Otho exchanged a look, and Otho sprang to his feet. "Peter, come with me," he said and strode out of the great hall, closely followed by the brawny young man.

Una's heart raced as she was suddenly filled with an irrational fear that whoever it was had come for her. As though he picked up on her inner turmoil, Armand's warm hand covered hers. "It'll be nothing," he said calmly, but Una could already hear raised voices in the passage outside. *Soldiers*, she thought, turning dizzy as her stomach pitched and rolled. *They've come to drag me away.*

She saw Armand's head turn quickly, and then the door was flung back and Otho was leading a small party into the great hall. They were not soldiers, Una saw, forcing herself to draw a pained breath. Just three men and a woman.

"Oh gods," muttered Armand under his breath. "Brace yourself. It's my bloody family." He dragged his chair back, plastering a smile onto his face. "Welcome! Father! Brothers! All!"

*

After that came a round of confused introductions that Una unfortunately felt completely removed from. Her head swam and she still felt quite sick with the dread that had overtaken her at the unexpected interruption.

Desperately, Una tried to focus on the tall flinty-eyed stranger who she was sure Armand had introduced as his father, Sir Hugo de Bussell, and then the other two males who curiously did not resemble her husband at all. They must be Henry and Roger, she realized after they had been persuaded to sit themselves down and been given trenchers and plied with wine and bread.

The younger one's eyes nearly fell out of his head when Rose passed him his goblet of wine, and Una frowned, for had not Armand said his youngest brother was bound for the clergy? Everything seemed to have got muddled up in her head, and she gave herself a slight shake to try to rouse herself from her stupor.

Armand turned away from the hearty conversation he was conducting toward the menfolk of his family and refilled her goblet. "Drink this," he muttered, passing an arm around her back. "Are you going to faint?"

"I—I don't think so," Una gasped out. "Not now." She swallowed down half the cup of wine. "I don't know what's come over me," she said miserably.

His hand at her waist squeezed comfortingly. "A perfectly natural reaction, I assure you," he said staunchly. "I told you they were a parcel of frights."

Una gave a choked laugh. "Nothing of the sort," she said weakly.

Just then, a woman's querulous voice rose above the hubbub of conversation. "Two kinds of meat at one sitting, Henry, mark you," she said in a thin, reedy voice. "I hope you could never accuse me of such folly, even in the early days of our marriage."

"Such extravagance would bankrupt me within a twelvemonth," replied Henry sourly. "But it seems my brother is above such considerations."

Una glanced down and saw the other woman eyeing her gold gown with a scandalized expression. She was clad respectably, if shabbily, in a velvet robe of navy blue, which looked a little threadbare at the elbows and hems.

"Ah, but we are newlyweds, my dear Muriel," Armand boomed. "You must allow us our homecoming feast." He gave them a beaming smile. The woman sniffed, her long nose quivering. Una thought she muttered something about the extravagant use of candles, and the harassed-looking Henry tutted.

"Roger!" Sir Hugo barked suddenly, and Armand's younger brother was forced to divert his rapt attention from the fair Rose and back to his supper plate.

"Sorry, Father," he mumbled.

Una turned her head to Armand's ear and murmured, "I'm so sorry, but I did not perfectly take it in, that lady is your—"

"My sister-in-law, the sainted Muriel," Armand supplied, then a look of horror passed over his handsome face. "Please don't say you mistook her for my twin sister!"

Una leaned against him heavily. "No, no," she said and, glancing at her plate, realized she was not going to be able to eat even a morsel of her food. "Oh dear, I do hope Mr. Beverley won't be offended."

Armand gave her a shrewd look, then reached over and stabbed a piece of beef from her plate and ate it. For the rest of the meal, he ate alternately from their plates, so it appeared Una had cleared hers. No one seemed to notice, though she was sure people must think it strange that he kept her clamped to his side in such an odd fashion.

"I won't fall over," she whispered at one point, and he smirked.

"Ah, but what you don't realize is that *I'm* the one clinging on to *you*. For moral support," he added with a wink.

Una could only give thanks once again that the fates had blessed her with so good-natured a husband.

Toward the end of the meal, he raised a toast to his "good lady wife," which was echoed heartily by the servants and faintly by her mealy-mouthed in-laws, and then the meal was over and done with.

After supper, the servants started to industriously tidy away. Una managed to tell Mr. Beverley that he had surpassed himself, and Armand's family trooped up to the solar.

Armand cast his eyes heavenward. "We're not done yet," he murmured, and led her up the stairs to join them there.

As Una stepped over the threshold, she heard Muriel making disparaging comments about the state of the tapestries, and she winced inwardly, for though she and Rose had shaken and beaten them, it had not improved their murky green appearance one bit.

"Oh," said Armand nonchalantly. "You needn't worry about those old things, for we mean to tear them down and consign them to a dung heap. We'll have new tapestries all round," he announced to the sharply indrawn breaths of Henry and Muriel.

Una could only suppose that he was deliberately baiting them, for now she came to think of it, she was sure that he had previously described Henry as a miser, and clearly his wife also had something of a mania for economy.

Armand led her to a two-seated bench and drew her down beside him, his arm sliding about her waist once more. "And now, music," he said extravagantly. "Will you entertain us, dear sister-in-law, with a song?" Muriel pressed her pale lips together and folded her thin hands in her lap. She was dressed in the fashion of at least a decade ago, with a large pointed wimple and velvet hood that covered her hair completely. Her little face looked quite swamped beneath the huge headdress.

"No?" continued Armand in mock disappointment. "Well then, I suppose we must not be greedy. After all you have been entertaining us with your voice all evening."

Roger let out a guffaw, which he hastily stifled by pressing the back of his hand to his mouth.

"Armand," said his father warningly.

"I could ask Rose to come up and play the harp for our entertainment," Una suggested. "She is a most obliging girl and—"

"I think not," said Sir Hugo, cutting across her words coldly.

182

"Father," Armand said in the same warning tone his sire had used only moments before. They stared at one another.

"I apologize," said Sir Hugo stiffly. "I forgot where I was for a moment." He rose jerkily from his seat. "I think it is high time that we departed. Henry, Roger." The other two rose and Henry crossed to where his wife sat rigid-backed to offer her his hand before hauling her out of the chair.

"Thank the gods for small mercies," Armand murmured before wishing them a cheery good night.

8

"Do you suppose Henry's wife has a bad back?" Una asked later as she sat on the edge of the bed and braided her hair.

"What's that?" Armand lowered his razor and glanced over at her. He had been reflecting on the fact their bedroom fire had not been lit, despite the evening going off cold.

"I just wondered…" She trailed off. "I suppose they must have heard from someone in the village that you were home." Suddenly, she gave a suppressed wail and dropped her face into her hands.

"What is it?" he asked with alarm.

"I wish I had not made such a horrible impression on your family!" she said through her fingers. "I was awful!"

Armand gave a soft laugh. "You weren't anywhere near as bad as they were." He set down his razor and wiped his face. "How are you feeling now?" he asked, blowing out the candle on the table and approaching the bed.

"A lot better," she sighed.

"Good." He pulled back the bedcovers and climbed in, eying her back as she tied the ribbon at the end of her braid. Then she swung it over her back and blew out her candle, joining him in the bed.

They were both silent lying side by side, the only sound their breathing, except for some scuffling under the cabinet, which he hoped was her dog and not a rat. "Are you doing your trick to take the edge off a cold bed?" he asked casually.

He heard her turn her head toward him. "Are you cold? I did not think to remind Rose to light the fires," she said regretfully.

He grunted. "It will be a good thing when that new housekeeper starts. Maybe she can keep her in line."

Una was silent at this, and he found himself going over the evening in his mind's eye. His father hadn't changed one bit, still a stiff-rumped, disapproving old buzzard. The least said about Henry and his ghastly wife the better, and it seemed Roger had *not* gone off to his religious seminary after all. He wondered vaguely what his father was planning to do with the feckless idiot now he had no clear path in life.

After dismissing his family from his thoughts, he dwelt instead on his wife, who had unexpectedly been sent into a blind panic at the prospect of unannounced visitors. He didn't think he'd seen her flurried before. Except perhaps that morning after their wedding when he'd planned on leaving her at the palace. That had sent her into something of a spin. Still, it hadn't been a glazed-eyed, pale as a ghost, cold sweat sort of panic. Not even after they had so nearly been murdered in their beds in that second inn.

No, she had been shaken that night, but not sick with dread and fear. He considered this a moment in frowning concentration. He had a strong notion it had been the knocking on the door that had set Una into a panic, and he remembered vividly how she had wept in his arms at that first inn, the night they had spoken of Strethneal. He had known then that Una hadn't really laid her ghosts to rest from the war but hadn't wanted to dwell on the matter.

After all, it was no business of his, or so he had reasoned at the time. Now he found himself wondering if there had been a knock at the door when Wymer's forces had arrested her. He would never ask, of course. Forcing a confidence from her might make her believe him willing to take on more than he intended.

Also, he did not mean to reopen any old wounds if he could help it. Una's scars were not visible, but clearly, they ran deep. If not, they could not make her lose her appetite and send her into a frenzy even now, years later, simply by a knock at the door.

In any case, what could he possibly do to lighten her burden? She was obviously used to shouldering it alone and simply putting on a brave face. For some reason, that thought didn't sit quite right with him. He reached out for her in the dark and drew her closer to him. "How's your stomach now?" He placed his palm carefully over the slight swell of her belly. "Still queasy?"

"It's not turning over anymore," she assured him.

"You're not hungry?"

"No."

"A pity," he sighed. "Mr. Beverley's pie will probably last us a sennight as it is."

She gave a soft chuckle at that. "Did you tell Otho to hire him?"

"Not in so many words."

"You may have to," she said, and he heard the pillow rustle as she turned her head to look over her shoulder at him. "Otho's far too harsh a judge of character."

He grunted. "You don't need to tell me that. He's still looking at me as though deciding where to dispose of my body." He could almost feel her frowning in the dark. "That was in jest. I usually am...joking, I mean."

186

"Yes, I know," she agreed absently, and he wasn't sure whether to be annoyed or not. "Your brothers aren't very like you, are they?"

"No," he agreed. "I did tell you so."

"Yes, but you also told me your younger brother was entering the priesthood," she pointed out. "He certainly seems very ill suited for such a vocation."

"Yes, I think that plan must have fallen by the wayside," he murmured in agreement. "Noticed that about Roger, did you?"

"His tongue was practically hanging out across the table," she said dryly, and Armand laughed. "I don't think Rose even noticed," she mused. "She's a very pure-hearted girl."

Privately Armand thought Rose was something of a simpleton, but he gave a murmur that could be taken for agreement. "You will admit I am right about Henry being chicken-hearted at all events," he said. "And presumably your heart no longer bleeds for him after my cruel treatment of him in boyhood."

"When did I say—"

"When we were at the tower," Armand retorted. "You read me a lesson on proper brotherly feeling."

"Well," she said after a moment's pause, "that sounds very tiresome of me and I apologize."

He retreated into surprised silence. "If you're going to be so reasonable about it, I have little choice other than to accept your apology," he said humorously and yawned, rolling onto his back. "In any event, you will admit, I sketched my sister-in-law to perfection. Did you hear her carrying on?" He shuddered. "Only Henry would put up with her. She's a face like a withered apple too."

"Armand!"

"It's true!"

"I'm sure she has many admirable qualities," she said, and Armand laughed again, this time with a derisive edge.

"No, you're not," he retorted.

Una was silent a moment. "Very well, I confess she did not look to advantage under that cumbersome wimple, but I know myself how such trappings can make you look your worst." She hesitated. "When I was at court, you know, they called me several names due to my own appearance. It was hurtful."

"Names?" he asked. "What names?"

"Not to my face," she said quickly. "Except for that court jester. He can insult even the King to his face without fear. As for what names, they were mostly equine in nature."

Armand felt like he was really floundering now. He had vague recollections of the jester from May Day, but nothing certain. "Equine?"

"Such as…the northern mare, that sort of thing."

That did ring a vague bell. "It was doubtless just a foolish way to disparage you," Armand said dismissively. "You don't look anything like a horse. If you want," he offered casually, "I'll knock that jester down next time I see him."

"That won't be necessary," she answered, and he could hear the quiver of amusement in her voice.

"Shuffle closer," he told her, "and put your arm around my waist. I'm cold."

"Anything else?" she asked with a hint of wryness as she looped her arm about his waist.

"Yes, throw your leg over mine."

She hesitated before doing that. "Is this truly comfortable for you?" she asked doubtfully.

"Yes," he answered, folding his arms behind his head. "Now stay close until I fall asleep." He closed his eyes, secure in the knowledge that only he would ever know he wasn't actually cold at this point at all.

*

Armand woke early the next morning feeling overly warm. Finding Una still lying half atop him, he flung back the covers and dispensed with them instead. If given a choice, he'd take a nice, warm woman over a blanket any day. He palmed her delightfully rounded backside and debated rolling her onto her back and waking her with his cock, which was already perking up with interest. That enticingly close-fitting shift of hers had ridden up in the night, and he could feel her soft inner thigh lying against his own. It was extremely stimulating.

After a moment's consideration, he regretfully decided against it. She had not had the easiest of evenings, thanks to his godsawful family dropping in on them. Instead, she'd been reduced to hollow-eyed panic and nausea. Only the most inconsiderate of husbands would now insist on a round between the sheets when she might still be feeling the aftereffects.

Besides, he needed to find a way to coax her out of her reservations when it came to the bedchamber. Armand was as lusty and playful there as he was in every other area of his life. He liked a bit of spice and plenty of sauce when it came to bed sport. A straightforward coupling was all very well when nothing else was on offer, but he favored a bit of slap and tickle where he could get it.

Was one supposed to get it from one's wife though? he wondered vaguely. He'd never really considered the matter previously, but the fact remained, Una was a royal princess and hardly raised to romping in the sheets with the likes of him. He thought about those grave eyes and how they regarded him so seriously when he said something flippant or offhand.

She'd practically ticked him off for pointing out his sister-in-law looked like a windfall last night, he thought ruefully. Still, it was small wonder she was sensitive about such things, after the horse shit she'd had to put up with at court. Spiteful bastards courtiers could be sometimes, he reflected with a frown.

Flirting with her at the moment seemed entirely a lost cause. She either colored up and refused to rise to the bait or else gave him a hard stare and took whatever he'd said quite literally. It had been as arousing as a bucket of cold water when she'd spoken of his rights and entitlements, he thought with a wry twist of his lips. He liked a wench to be keen and fully participate in the pursuit of pleasure. Not enduring his touch stoically like some kind of martyr.

Then again, Una was not a statue precisely. She'd been willing alright after he'd spent the time getting her worked up with his fingers. Maybe she'd lighten up eventually and even learn to crack a spontaneous smile once in a while.

She was not without a sense of humor, he reflected. He'd seen glimmers of it flash out at him in the quiver of her lip, the way her eyes would sometimes lighten, and a sort of lilting quality to her voice. Still, he thought with dissatisfaction, he hadn't actually seen her throw back her head and laugh. Not an honest to gods, outright laugh.

What would it take to hear that? he wondered, his fingers lightly tracing the swell and curve of her buttock. "Are you ticklish?" he asked, moments later, when her head lifted off his chest to regard him blearily.

"I'm sorry?" she asked in confusion. "What did you say?"

"I asked if you, Princess Una, are ticklish?" he repeated huskily.

She regarded him blankly, and for a moment he wondered if she was still asleep. "I don't know," she answered with surprise. "Why do you ask?"

"I'm curious," he admitted. "Let's find out." He slid his hand up to where her waist dipped in and pinched her there, making her exhale and flinch against him in surprise. Then he was tracing her sides, lightly at first and then, when she squeaked, with increasing firmness.

"A-Armand!" she protested, trying to lift off him.

"Yes?" he answered, holding her in place.

"Oh!" she squawked and struggled against him. "Oh, don't!"

"Why? Does it tickle?"

"It—yes, it does!" she answered breathlessly. "Please stop!"

By this point, he was so entranced by the way she was wriggling against his hard cock that he didn't even mind that he didn't get the belly laugh he'd wanted. "I'll stop if you let me tickle you somewhere else," he said thickly and rolled her onto her back. *And with something else*, he thought, his eyes roving over her heaving bosom and flushed face. "Fuck, Una," he groaned. "Do you still feel sick this morning?"

"No, no I'm quite well," she assured him. Then she hesitated, just the smallest instant before letting her legs fall open for him.

191

"That's where you meant, isn't it?" she asked with just the smallest hint of uncertainty.

"Yes," he agreed, feeling a surprising surge of something else as well as lust wash over him. He wasn't entirely sure, but he thought it might just be tenderness. "That's exactly where I meant."

*

Armand made his way downstairs sometime later feeling refreshed and invigorated. Their morning tryst had been most pleasurable, and while Una had not exactly been tearing his braies off, she had at least welcomed his advances and not started bleating about it being daylight or any other such nonsense he assumed respectably married women bothered their heads about.

Of course, he hadn't really cut loose. It was still early days, and he hadn't thought yet of a way to encourage her enthusiastic participation just yet—but he would. He just had to hit on the right method. Maybe next time he should give her his tongue? It would shock the holy hells out of her, but once that was out of the way, he had a feeling she would respond as sweetly to that as everything else he had cautiously introduced her to.

On reaching the great hall, his good mood was rapidly suspended. The tables were piled high with tarnished silver candlesticks and salvers and jugs and he knew not what. They must have stripped the house from top to bottom of all its plate. Rose and that new somewhat garrulous maid were huddled over the great mounds with polishing cloths, conversing conspiratorially.

"Morning, sir," the dark one piped up loudly as soon as she saw him, and Rose broke off what she was saying with a start.

Armand had the sudden, uncomfortable suspicion they had been talking about him. He cleared his throat. "Your mistress requires a bath," he said shortly. "Kindly have one taken up to her as soon as possible."

"Yes, sir, right away," she answered cheerily and bounced up from her seat to run through to the kitchen.

At least this one didn't stare at him blankly after every order. He turned to Rose. "What was her name again?"

"Janet," she mumbled and returned to polishing a silver tankard with fervor.

Armand carried on to the kitchen and surprised Janet staring out of the window at Peter, who was weeding the overgrown vegetable patch.

"I've just put the water on to boil," she muttered guiltily and unhooked the bathtub from where it hung against the wall.

Armand refrained from comment, helped himself to bread and butter out of the pantry, and let himself out of the kitchen door, wandering down to the stables. He leaned against Arturo's stall as he finished his snack, contemplating what to do with himself for the day. He thought he'd take his horse out for a ride over the countryside and stretch his legs.

He was looking over the indifferent nags they had helped themselves to from The Merry Wayfarer, all ensconced in stalls of their own, when Otho entered the stables with a sack of fodder over his shoulder, which he set down in one corner. He gave a start on seeing Armand, then recovered, straightening up and growling something that could have been a greeting.

Armand decided to interpret it as such. "Good morning to you too," he responded affably.

"Did you know there are three tenant farmers on your estate?" Otho demanded abruptly.

Armand brushed the crumbs from his tunic. "Three?" He frowned. "I knew there were one or two farms outlying on the edge of the grounds," he said vaguely.

"There's three," Otho corrected him heavily. "And I have seen nothing to indicate they have paid you any dues for the past four years."

Armand shrugged. "I daresay they haven't, after all, who would have collected it?"

Otho regarded him thunderously. "You should have appointed a steward in your absence," he said cuttingly. "That is what a responsible landowner would have done."

"I daresay," Armand agreed. "But I didn't, and I'm not, so that's neither here nor there at this point."

Otho stared at him. "What happened to Sir Adrian's steward?" he asked in exasperation.

"Old Haines? He dropped dead about three months before my godfather. By all accounts, he simply keeled over, face-first into the account books."

Otho's expression darkened. "I can well believe someone died between the pages of that book," he said damningly. "It's a messy scrawl and barely legible."

Armand pulled a face. "Well, he was very old," he muttered.

"We'll ride over and visit with them later," Otho said decisively. "You and I."

"Visit with whom?" Armand asked, still thinking of Haines, who had been an old bachelor and left neither kith nor kin behind him.

"Your tenant farmers," gritted out Otho with narrowed eyes. "And you're not weaseling out of it."

Armand sighed. His new brother-in-law, while useful in his own way, was also something of a despot. "What do you do for pleasure, Otho?" he asked, suddenly curious.

"What?"

"Wine, women, or song? Which do you favor?"

Otho glared at him. "None of them. I've better things to occupy my time with."

"Better things?" Armand repeated, but just then, Peter appeared framed in the stable doorway.

"Sir Armand, you've visitors in the house," he puffed. "Janet bade me fetch you."

"Visitors?" His heart quailed. "Not the same ones as last night?" he asked with sudden misgiving.

Peter shook his head. "They'm new ones, Janet said."

"Oh, very well," Armand said, straightening up. "Hold that thought, Otho," he said sternly. "We will revisit that topic again. Oh, and now I come to think of it, make sure you hire that drunken baker. What's his name?"

"Beverley," Otho ground out. "But I don't think—"

"Hire him!" Armand yelled back over his shoulder as he exited the stable, and Otho's obvious chagrin restored the smile back on his lips. He was whistling "The Maid of Hamblin's Ruin" as he made his way back up to the house. Or what was it Una had said it was called in the north? Something about a wicked archer? He'd have to ask her.

As he opened the door, Janet greeted him with wide eyes. "The mistress is still in her bath," she blurted. "And Rose is helping her to wash her hair."

Armand checked on the threshold. "Very good," he said, at something of a loss as to Janet's breathless manner. "Where are the visitors?"

"Awaiting you in the great hall, sir. I didn't like to take them up to the solar without your say-so."

Even before he reached the great hall, Armand recognized the strident female tones emanating out of it.

"Now, Toby, you put that down!" she scolded. "This is your uncle's house and everything in it belongs to him." There was a sudden clatter as if Toby had dropped whatever the item was to the ground. "Oh, Toby! Now you have put a dent in it!"

Armand groaned. Now his bloody sister and her offspring had descended on them! He passed into the room and regarded his sister warily. Anne was tall and dark like him and a handsome woman, despite her determined jaw. "Anne," he said. "Well met. And my nephew and…" His eyes passed over the other small person regarding him through rounded eyes. "Niece."

"Very good," his sister said sarcastically. "Now demonstrate to me if you can remember their names?"

"Of course I can," he said glibly and placed a hand on the boy's head. "Let me see." He tapped a finger on his chin, sizing up the little girl who must have been about five or six. "My niece's name is Currant Bun," he said ruminatively as the little girl giggled.

196

"S'not! It's Joan!"

"And my nephew's name is Jam Tart."

"S'not!" his nephew roared lustily. "S'not Jam Tart!"

"I was joking, of course," he said, turning back to Anne. "Their names are, of course, Joan and Toby. Satisfied?"

"Still think fast and land on your feet, I see." His sister smirked. "That much hasn't changed."

Armand came forward and he brushed her cheek dutifully with his own. He had always thought his sister tall for a female, but Una had at least two inches on her. "Anne," he said in cautious greeting. "You are very welcome. How are you?" He looked around at the chaos of brass and silver strewn all over the tables. "I would offer you a seat, but…"

"The benches at least are clear," she said, sinking down onto the nearest one.

Armand, following her example, sat opposite her. He watched distractedly as Joan darted underneath one of the tables closely followed by a waddling Toby. "Have they no nurse?"

"I married a farmer," Anne replied shortly.

"A wealthy farmer."

She brushed this aside. "I thought you might want to see them," she said in a faintly accusatory tone.

"Did you?" Armand's brow puckered. *What strange notions women did get into their heads.*

"You haven't even met Toby before," she said waspishly.

Armand cast a dutiful eye over the child. "He seems very short."

197

"He isn't yet three years old!"

"That would explain it."

"Is that it?" Anne demanded, struggling to find words. She huffed out a breath. "I see you're still devoid of every proper feeling."

Armand stretched out his long legs and leaned back on the table, elbowing a large embellished butter dish out of the way. "Did you imagine I might have undergone some kind of change?" he asked lazily. "Sorry to disenchant you."

"Well, I did hear you're now married," she pointed out. "You may imagine how I felt being informed of the fact by Muriel!" she said bitterly.

"Why should that rankle?"

"I'm your twin! Yet I have to hear this news through our sister-in-law." Armand shrugged. This was nothing new. Anne was always flying up into the boughs about something. "Where is she, then?" she asked irritably. "Am I not even to be dignified with an appearance?"

Armand's attitude of indolence disappeared at once as he straightened up. "She's at her bath," he said, narrowing his eyes. "And you're not to start in on her with that shrewish tongue of yours."

Anne opened her mouth to hiss back at him, but Janet chose this moment to come sailing in from the kitchen with a tray of ale and milk for the children. Anne swallowed her words as Janet set their refreshment down in the midst of a suit of armor, curtseyed, and then retreated back to the kitchen.

"At least *someone* here knows what's due to a guest!" Anne snapped, reaching for the milk jug. "Toby! Joan! Come and

198

take some milk!" Once the children had dribbled milk all over themselves and the floor, they returned to their game under the table. His sister poured out ale for the two of them and regarded Armand thoughtfully over the rim of her cup.

"Muriel told me that you were pawing and fondling your bride the entire meal, in such a fawning manner it quite turned their stomachs."

Armand nearly spat out his ale but managed to gulp it down before going off in a coughing fit. Gods, Muriel must have the most uptight views that he had ever heard of! He almost pitied Henry. "They burst in on us, unannounced," he answered with as much dignity as he could muster, wiping his mouth with his sleeve. "And we *are* newly wed."

Anne regarded him with interest. "So, it's a love match, is it?" she said smugly. "I knew you'd go off the deep end one of these days. It was bound to happen. Muriel said she's wildly extravagant, without a practical thought in her head. Says she'll bankrupt you within a twelvemonth."

"Oh, Muriel said that, did she?" he rallied. "Well, Muriel's wrong."

"Well, well, look at you springing to her defense, brother. I never thought I'd see the day! Armand de Bussell rushing to defend a lady's reputation."

"So glad I can afford you some entertainment," he muttered through slightly clenched teeth.

"Roger said you were done up like a regular coxcomb to impress her. Parading round in gold chausses like a courtier."

"Only one leg was gold," Armand corrected her testily before realizing that didn't sound much better.

Anne's eyebrow rose. "Who is she? Some squire's daughter from those barbarous tournaments you will insist on frequenting? Or did you finally get caught in the parson's trap by a designing widow?"

"That's enough, Anne—" he started when they both heard a step on the stair. He held up his hand for silence, and at that moment a cascade of falling silver salvers rang out, deafening them all for several seconds. When the ring of metal faded, a child's loud wails started up in the far corner, causing even more of a din. Anne jumped up from her seat and went flying across the room in search of her progeny.

Armand closed his eyes an instant, then looked up and saw Una stood in the entrance of the room, wearing a becoming gown of blue silk with a simple fitted bodice and elaborate sleeves, slashed to show the crisp white of her underrobe.

Her hair was only loosely braided and looped over her shoulder, he guessed because it was still damp, but it made her look quite girlish without its usual arrangement. When her eyes sought him out, he smiled at her and extended his hand without thinking. She came to him immediately, and as he drew her down beside him, surprised him by leaning forward to press her lush mouth to his.

That was when he felt that strange sensation again, like a surge of blood rushing through his chest. Immediately, he forgot all about Anne's irritating visit and found himself seeking a second touch of those sweet lips against his. He even closed his eyes for a few seconds to savor it. Then another child started bawling, and he returned to earth with a bump, quickly turning his head to find his sister staring at him from the other end of the room, one infant on her hip and another clutching at her skirts.

"Anne," he said unevenly. "This is my wife, Una. Una, this is my sister, Anne, and her delightful children," he added dryly, "who seem determined to put dents in all our plates."

Una stood up immediately. "I'm delighted to meet you, Anne," she said with a brief curtsey. "I've very much looked forward to meeting Armand's twin."

A look of surprise crossed over Anne's face as she returned the gesture. "Oh, he's told you about me, has he? Good of him!" Armand could see her eyes appraising Una with open speculation, and he felt a stab of something unpleasant and unfamiliar jolt him to his core. He wondered for a moment what it even was. He struggled to put a name to it, he felt so wholly unaccustomed to it. A sort of anxiousness or trepidation was the closest he could come to it.

He sent a look of dark warning in Anne's direction as he circled an arm about Una's waist. There was no way in hells he was leaving Una alone with his meddlesome sister.

"Is that your dear little boy?" Una was asking. "Armand told me he was an uncle. It looks like he has bumped his head. Can we get him something from the kitchens to help with the swelling?" She would have taken a step forward, but Armand's restraining arm prevented her.

"This is my son, Toby," Anne admitted grudgingly. "And this my daughter, Joan."

"I'm very pleased to make their acquaintance," Una said, smiling encouragingly at the two children, who were now subdued after the commotion they had caused and giving an entirely false impression of shyness.

"Perhaps we could get them some fruit from the garden," Una said doubtfully. "I'm afraid we don't have any comfits or treats at present, as we have only just engaged a cook."

"They've had milk," Armand pointed out. He privately thought neither child deserving of reward.

"How kind of you," his sister said suddenly with an ingratiating smile that immediately put Armand on his guard. "Are you fond of children, Una?"

"I…that is, yes," Una answered, flushing slightly. Armand's head turned sharply to look at her. Was she?

"Come now, Toby," his sister wheedled. "Would you not like to go and greet your aunt Una and welcome her into the family?"

"No! No!" Toby yelled, burying his head in his mother's shoulder.

"I will," piped up Joan, tripping forward with a gummy smile. Surely, she should have teeth by now? Armand thought, noticing the child had nothing but bare gums at the front. When she reached Una, she angled up her head and screwed up her face. Armand regarded her with bewilderment, but Una seemed to realize what was due and bent down to kiss the child on the cheek.

Joan turned back to send a smug look at her brother over her shoulder. "You see, Toby, *I* can do it," she caroled. "*I'm* a good girl."

"No! No!" screamed Toby, kicking his legs. "Not Joan! Not Joan!" Anne set his wriggling body down, and he stomped up over to Una with a fierce scowl and tears still glittering in his eyes before he repeated the same action. Again, Una bent down and kissed his cheek. His bottom lip quivered as though he were still debating throwing back his head and screeching.

Armand blanched and braced himself, but Una's calm voice suggested they repair to the solar where they could sit in less cluttered surroundings. Armand half expected his sister to refuse the offer—she had been so prickly at the outset—but to his surprise, she almost jumped at the chance, sending a gloating expression his way as she mounted the stairs behind Una.

He wasn't quite sure how it was, but Armand found himself carrying up the children one on each arm. At such close quarters, their penetrating stares were somewhat unnerving.

"Why haven't you got a beard?" Joan asked in her high, carrying voice. "Fathers always have beards."

"I'm not a father," Armand said shortly. "And if it comes to that, where are your teeth?"

Joan giggled. "They keep falling out," she confided. "I bit into an apple and my front one came out. This one," she said, pulling down her lip to show him the gap.

Armand felt both impressed and faintly revolted. "Maybe you should stop eating apples," he suggested.

"I gotter napple," Toby interrupted, keen to prevent Joan from gathering all the glory. He breathed in and out excitedly as Armand wondered if this was the full extent of his contribution. "I hided it."

"No, you did not you storyteller!" Joan burst out indignantly. "Mother! Tell Toby to stop telling lies!"

"I not!" screamed Toby.

Armand only managed to stick half an hour with them in the solar before he was forced to go in search of Otho for some respite. Even visiting tenant farmers was preferable to spending time with his family. If Anne thought she could blacken his name to Una while her hideous children were in tow, running circles around them and upsetting tables, then good luck to her was all he could say!

9

Una picked up the small table and set the book back on top of it for the third time as Anne scooped Toby up and remonstrated with him.

"He's tired," she said, shooting a defensive look at Una.

"Well, he's only little," Una murmured tactfully. Poor Abelard had retreated shaking under a wooden bench. New faces apparently set him back considerably in his recovery, and the noisy children seemed to be his limit. Una had expected him to slope off to her bedchamber, but he wasn't quite willing to let her out of his sight just yet.

Joan, who had initially wanted to play with the little dog, was finally sat quietly in the window seat, having a whispered conversation with a faded cushion she insisted on calling Ida.

Anne pulled a face and lowered her voice. "Ida was a girl we had at the farm last year for a while. Very taken with her the children were, but they weren't the only ones, so I had to get rid of her," she said significantly. "If you catch my meaning. If you will take my advice, you won't spare any time doing likewise with that girl Rose you've got under your roof."

Rose had brought them up more drinks earlier. "Rose is a very obliging girl," Una replied mildly, and Anne gave her a pitying look.

"Those are the ones you need to look out for, my dear. I know you're new to this, but it's never too early to nip these things in the bud. My John has never had a roving eye, unlike Armand, but I make sure never to dangle a tempting morsel beneath his nose like that. You're setting him up for a fall."

"Does Armand have a roving eye?" Una asked, not particularly surprised, for she had seen enough of those easy manners and charming smiles to guess as much.

"Well, let me put it this way, he had always had a lively appreciation of women," said Anne with feeling.

"I see," Una said slowly. "Well, Rose *is* exceedingly pretty, but she is also a modest and virtuous girl. Even if she did catch his eye, I do not think he would willfully seduce an innocent young woman under his own roof."

Anne grimaced. "Maybe not, but he has a smooth tongue and a handsome face. He never lacked for feminine attention, I assure you, even at sixteen. I remember one time our father was forced to intercede in an entanglement he got himself into—" She hesitated. "But perhaps that is not a suitable story for me to tell."

Una smiled at her reassuringly. "I am aware that my husband was not a monk before he met me," she responded calmly.

Anne set down her cup and jiggled Toby on her shoulder. The child's breathing was noisy and regular, and he seemed to have finally fallen asleep. "You're not what I was led to expect," she said frankly. "Muriel has many faults, but she's usually a decent judge of character. I can't think why she was so mistaken about you."

Una winced. "In truth I was not quite feeling well last night. I fear I made a poor impression."

Anne looked intrigued. "You're not…?" Una looked back at her expectantly. "With child?" she suggested, lowering her voice confidentially.

"I shouldn't think so," Una answered truthfully. "It's such early days."

Anne looked coy. "You never know," she said vaguely. "It might explain—" She bit off her words with dismay. "I mean, it would probably be good for Armand. Teach him some responsibility and encourage him to be a little less selfish. Of course, it would thoroughly dash my own son's chances of inheriting Anninghurst," she said with a regretful sigh. "But then, John always said the chances were never that high anyway. Not with Roger forswearing the religious life like he did."

Una lowered her own cup. "Anninghurst is your father's seat, I think?"

"Oh yes, and there's not the smallest chance of Henry ever having issue now. Muriel must be well past child-bearing years," Anne continued blithely. "But I never would have foreseen Armand settling down for another good ten years or so," she admitted. "Which all just goes to show you should never count your chicks before the eggs hatch," she said with a philosophical shrug.

"As I understand it," Una said, refilling their cups, "you have not seen Armand in a few years."

Anne reached for a cup with a snort. "That's an understatement. He avoids Derring like the plague." She shot a sideways glance at Una. "Has he spoken to you of his upbringing?" Una opened her mouth, but Anne did not let her continue. "He was our mother's favored child, you know. She spoiled him to the exclusion of the rest of us. She always used to say he took after her own father and never had a good word to say about Henry or Roger. It was all Armand, Armand, Armand." Anne's lips thinned with displeasure. "Of course, now I'm a mother myself, I see just how bad it was."

Una bit her lip. "He may have mentioned something of the kind," she admitted.

207

Anne looked surprised. "He has? I wonder." She took a sip of ale.

"What are you wondering?"

"If you're enough to lure him to spend a bit more time at home," Anne said bracingly. "He's spent precious little time seeing to his affairs here." Her features assumed a slightly wistful air. "I was encouraged to hear him say he is visiting his farms this afternoon. Perhaps that is down to you? John says he has not a head for honest—" She broke off her words hastily.

"What I mean to say is," she started again painstakingly. "I do hope you will be able to exert a beneficial influence over Armand. If you could only stop him from attending those awful tournaments and making a show of himself to the crowds there that would be a start."

Una frowned uncomprehendingly. "But I understood that even the highest knights in the land sometimes compete at the rural tournaments?" she said. "There is no dishonor in it surely?

Anne shook her head. "You do not understand. My husband went to watch him once and he said he was embarrassed to see a brother-in-law of his indulging in such artful fakery and squandering his talents the way he does." She shook her head. "He wasn't raised to keep low company and cheat people. For that's what he's doing, make no mistake."

Una blinked. "You mean—"

"Don't make me say it any plainer," Anne begged. "It's bad enough coming as close to it as I am. I'm sure you take my meaning. Your understanding seems sound enough, whatever Muriel says."

Una nodded thoughtfully as she mulled the idea over that Armand was rather more of a scoundrel than she had initially realized. From what she had seen of the royal tournaments, the knights were fiercely competitive and hated to lose. The idea that Armand played fast and loose with his wins and losses was a difficult one to contemplate.

She accompanied Anne downstairs, as her sister-in-law needed help carrying her children, who by now were both fast asleep. She had a farmhand stood waiting for her outside in a cart, so Una passed up the sleeping Joan once Anne was sat securely on the bench.

"I'm sure we will meet again soon," Anne said, arranging her daughter onto the seat. "Perhaps at Anninghurst?"

"Perhaps," Una replied with a smile, not pointing out Muriel had issued no such invitation. She waved them off and then proceeded to walk slowly around the side of the house with Abelard on her heels. So deep in thought was she that she almost collided with someone skulking among the bushes there.

"Oh!" Una exclaimed, drawing back in alarm. "Your pardon, I did not see you there." She regarded him with sudden misgiving, for the man was a total stranger to her. He had a narrow face and wore a disreputable-looking hat on his head underneath which greasy straggles of his hair showed.

He nodded and cast a rather furtive glance around. "How do."

"May I ask your business here at Lynwode?" Una asked coolly, wondering if she could turn and run if the occasion demanded it. He was a thin man of middling height and probably possessed more strength than you might anticipate, as so many of that wiry build did.

He sniffed. "I could have sworn I saw someone lurking in those trees," he said, waving a vague hand in the direction of the orchard. "So, I thought I'd better investigate, Your Highness," he added with a smirk.

Una reared back as though he had struck her. She heard Abelard set up a hysterical yapping and took to her heels with a low cry.

"Hey!" he shouted after her. "Where are you…? Ouch!"

She didn't stop to hear the rest of his words but instead flew back around the front of the house as though the hounds of hell were on her heels. She never knew she could run so fast. She rounded the bend to the sound of approaching horse's hooves and knew a moment's terror that her attacker likely had accomplices ready to carry her away.

"Una!" Armand's shouted greeting abruptly snapped her out of her panic-stricken state. With a grateful sob, she ran directly toward him as he slid out of his saddle and down to the ground to catch her. She practically collapsed in his arms. "What is it?" he demanded. "What's happened?"

"A man!" she sobbed. "There's a man!" She pointed shakily to the side of the house and saw Abelard come bolting around the corner after her with his tail between his legs. Otho, who was with Armand, quickly dismounted and made in the direction she'd indicated.

Una shuddered. "He—he called me Your Highness," she said, catching her breath. "He *knew*!"

"Did he, by gods?" Armand's arms were tight about her. "Let's get you into the house and I'll go and take a look." Una nodded, but clutched even harder at his tunic. "Come on," he coaxed her, rubbing a hand over her back. "You're safe, I have you. You're not going anywhere. This is your home."

She looked up sharply at that and fixed her eyes on him intently a moment. *How did he know the right thing to say?* She felt herself relax, and immediately he scooped her up in his arms as though she weighed next to nothing, instead of being the substantially built woman she knew herself to be. He carried her into the front of the house and through to the great hall where Janet and Rose sprang up from their polishing.

"Whatever's happened?" Rose cried.

"Your mistress has had a fright, now go and fetch her some refreshment and don't go causing a scene!" Armand retorted sharply. "If the Lady Una managed to keep herself calm and contained then the least you can do is try and emulate her!"

Rose stood wringing her hands and looking stricken, but Janet immediately ran for the doorway that led to the kitchen.

"She'll tell everyone," Una agonized as Armand set her down on the bench and knelt beside her. "Armand, go after her—"

"It little signifies," he shushed her. "Stop fretting."

At that point, Una noticed with horror that a trickle of blood was on Abelard's muzzle. "He's hurt my dog!" she burst out angrily, scooping him up in his arms, comforting him. "He must have kicked him in the face! Oh, Abelard!"

They both turned their heads sharply when they heard footsteps approaching. Seconds later, a grim-faced Otho marched in the man who had accosted her outside. Una gasped, felt her color drain, and sat up straighter. He looked a villain, even now her fear had receded into cold anger.

Armand groaned. "What the hells are you doing here, Fulcher?" he demanded, standing up. "And what the devil do you mean by frightening the wits out of my wife?"

*

211

Una was not reconciled to Fulcher's presence at their supper table that evening until she saw his bloodied cuff and the fact he'd ripped some fabric away from his sleeve to bind what was clearly a wound.

"Did Abelard bite you?" she blurted in astonishment, breaking her cold silence.

Fulcher sniffed and held up the affected hand. "Bite me?" he said in aggrieved accents. "I should say he nearly tore my fingers clean off!"

Armand snorted. "He'd be hard-pressed to fit even one of your fat fingers in his tiny mouth."

"My fingers ain't fat!" Fulcher objected, looking offended. Una noticed with horror just how black his fingernails were. She hoped Abelard would not suffer any ill effects.

"Valiant Abelard!" Rose said loudly from the other end of the table. "He certainly deserves the bones this night, instead of the stockpot." Otho sent her a stern look, and she returned crestfallen to her meal.

Una picked up a large piece of beef off her plate and passed it down to where the little dog was leaning against her ankles. He smacked his lips and tucked in at once. Now that she knew Armand's strange acquaintance had not assaulted her dog, she could let her frosty manner drop, though she still thought he looked a thoroughly bad lot.

She let her eyes wander over him with a sort of fascinated horror. That awful hat, which he still wore on his head at such a rakish angle. A bit of bedraggled feather hung from the top of it, somehow making its appearance even worse. Under the layers of grime and grease, it must once have been brightly colored, she thought, and then let out a gasp, for she recognized it!

Surely that was the hat she made Armand for a wedding gift to match his burgundy and gold suit! Her eyes widened as she stared and then turned slowly to look at Armand's profile. He was tucking into his meal, and quite oblivious to her scrutiny. *This* must have been the man who Armand had left her on that second night to meet with. She recalled that Armand had returned from the encounter with a cut lip and a grazed face. And without his hat.

Her gaze narrowed. What sort of acquaintance, she pondered, would steal a man's hat? Could it have been he who had attacked Armand? She dismissed the idea almost as soon as it occurred to her. Mr. Fulcher was so much spindlier in build that the idea seemed absurd. Armand had said it was thieves with cudgels who had wanted to rob him. But assuredly, this Fulcher *had* stolen his hat.

"Are you staying long in the area, Mr. Fulcher?" Una roused herself to ask. He stopped chewing and a wary look entered his eye.

"As to that, I really couldn't say as yet, Your—" He broke off his words. "*My lady*," he said with exaggerated stress and then sent her a leering wink. Una saw Otho stiffen and send him a glare, but Armand seemed entirely unruffled.

She cleared her throat. "You have business that brought you to Derring?"

"You could say that, in a manner of speaking," he said with a forced casualness that made the hairs on the back of Una's neck rise with foreboding. She had heard men speak in such tones before. He spoke with the studied indifference of a man who

213

utters a veiled threat. Or that of a blackmailer. But what could he possibly be hoping to blackmail them with? she wondered.

Surely not the fact she was a princess? It occurred to her, as she picked up her wine goblet, that Armand had not seen fit to inform anyone in Derring of the fact, and with sudden clarity she remembered the King telling her that the de Bussell family had always been loyal to the Argent cause.

She set down her wine unsampled. Very likely his father *would* be horrified at the news, she thought hollowly. And they barely seemed to be on amicable terms as it was, quite apart from this fresh blow. She bit her lip and noticed that Otho was regarding Fulcher through narrowed eyes, as if he, too, harbored suspicions as to the man's motivations in turning up at Lynwode like this.

After supper, Armand announced he and Fulcher had some private business to discuss, so Una retired upstairs to the solar alone for an hour or so. She could not settle and instead made a mental list of the fabrics they would need to refurbish faded household items and tried not to dwell upon whatever business her husband could have with the nefarious-looking Fulcher.

Hearing a tread on the stairs, she looked up quickly, but it was only Rose, offering to play for her entertainment on the harp. Una declined, fearing it would only set her feelings further on edge, and Rose looked disappointed.

"I expect you played for your former mistress every night?" Una guessed, watching Abelard emerge from her skirts to approach Rose for a fuss.

"Oh yes, milady." She beamed, stooping down to pet the little dog. "She said it soothed her nerves as well as any tonic."

"I'm sure it did. How are all the new servants getting along? I expect it must be a big change for you to adjust to."

"Oh, they have all been vastly busy. I have scarcely had speech with any of them apart from Janet. She says we should finish polishing the plates by tomorrow evening." Rose looked a little doubtful.

"I think that new housekeeper starts with us tomorrow," Una commented, and Rose colored hotly, bending over Abelard to hide her face. "Do you know her, Rose?"

Rose shook her head. "I scarcely know anyone in the village, milady."

Looking at her dejected attitude, Una thought it better to let the subject drop. "I wonder if you could have some hot water sent up to my bedchamber, Rose. I believe I will retire early tonight."

Rose looked grateful for the excuse to flee and ran off immediately. Una made her way along to her bedchamber holding her candle before her, while her dog followed along behind. She paused at one point, hearing footsteps above. She glanced up, but of course, could see nothing. *Could Armand have taken his guest up to the attics? And if so, why?*

It was about an hour later that he came to bed, carrying his own jug of washing water with him. Una lay quiet as he hurriedly stripped and washed and then climbed under the covers beside her, blowing out his candle.

"Are you asleep?" he asked quietly.

"No," Una admitted, rolling onto her side to face him. "Is everything well?"

"Of course." She heard the frown in his voice. "Why would it not be?"

She hesitated. "Did you…show Mr. Fulcher your strong room?"

She heard the rustle of Armand's pillow as though he'd raised his head. "Why do you ask?" His words sounded rather brisk, and Una bit her lip, hoping she'd not offended him. "It's just that, I hope you do not trust this man overmuch, Armand. Mr. Fulcher seems a very wily sort, and you have such a sweet and sunny disposition. I do not want him to take advantage of you."

A stunned silence met her words. Una peered anxiously into the darkness. She had offended him, she thought with a pang. She knew men could be rather sensitive about any perceived weaknesses. "You must understand that I do not say this as a reflection on your judgment," she carried on quickly. "I just think you have a lovely nature and need to be on your guard."

Again, she was met with blank silence. "Armand?"

"Una," he groaned.

"I did not mean to imply—"

"Please don't say any more," he begged. "I don't know if my self-esteem could stand it."

Una shifted toward him in alarm and reached out her hand to his face. "I have upset you," she said, immediately contrite. She stroked his cheek. "Indeed, I meant no offense. You have been the best of husbands to me. I am sure you have known this Fulcher a good while and that he must have earned your trust somehow…" Her words trailed off as she thought of that shifty, untrustworthy face. "Perhaps I speak out of turn, 'tis only that I wish to urge caution, for I have come across men of Fulcher's ilk and I do not think you appreciate—"

216

Armand caught her fingers against his face and held them there. "Una," he said in a comfortably reassuring voice. "I am fully aware of the kind of man Fulcher is."

He hesitated, and Una found herself blurting out: "He stole your hat!"

"My hat?" She could hear the bewilderment in his voice at the turn the conversation had taken.

"The night you were attacked in Caer-Lyoness, do you remember? You lost the hat I made you. Your friend Fulcher is wearing it, bold as brass!"

Armand was silent a moment. "I don't think that can be the same hat," he said, rallying. "It looks nothing like I remember it."

"Armand, I recognize my own handiwork! That is your hat and he sat through supper wearing it, at your own table. Quite shamelessly!" When he was silent, Una continued, aggrieved. "I do not mean to imply he was in league with those ruffians who set upon you, but you must admit that it looks very suspicious." Was it her imagination or did Armand's shoulders shake slightly?

"My love," he said, and she was sure she could hear a thread of amusement running through his voice. "You are accusing an old and valued acquaintance of mine of being a hat thief."

"Yes, I am!" Una flung at him. "Though, I wish I had not become diverted down this particular sidetrack, for 'tis a minor issue compared to my general misgivings about the man! In truth, I do not think you are at all wise to trust him with your secrets!"

Feeling flustered, Una struggled in vain to put some space between herself and Armand, but his arms closed about her to keep her where she was. Had he just called her his love?

"Shh, now, Una, I won't tease," he said. "Let me be frank with you." She stilled at once. "Sensible girl," he said. "Now trust *me* to have some sense also. You are right. Fulcher has certain associations that would not bear up to close inspection. However, in this instance I mean to use that to my advantage." Una's ears pricked up, and she waited patiently for his next words. "As you know, our fortune is ill-gotten. I have no doubt that several pieces could be traced back to their original owners. Selling them on will be difficult for us. It could even bring down the law on us as suspected murderers or thieves. I do not want any trail leading back to Lynwode or to us." He waited expectantly.

"You mean to use Fulcher's connections," she said hesitantly, "to offload the stolen treasure?"

"And convert it into nice gold coins for us. Yes. Fulcher has dubious acquaintances in every city in Karadok. I can send him off with a sack of treasure and he will return in a month with however many bags of gold he received for them."

Una considered this in silence. "He will, of course, demand a share of the profits."

"That is only fair. He will be taking considerable risk after all," he pointed out.

"How do you know he will not cheat you by bringing back three bags when he received four?"

Armand pinched her backside. "I have already taken that into account when I negotiated his share. He is an excellent negotiator and will likely extract a far higher price for many pieces even than they deserve. No one ever gets the better of Fulcher in a deal," he said dryly. "I know him of old, you see."

Una considered this. "Yet, you are fond of this man," she said, faint accusation in her voice.

"Yes," he admitted. "I am."

"Even though you know him to be a rogue and a cheat?"

He was silent a moment. "You have no love for rogues and cheats, Una?" His tone was strange and made her pause. Suddenly she remembered his sister's words about Armand's conduct at the tournaments. *Oh.*

"I do not like to think of anyone taking advantage of you, that is all," she repeated after a pause.

He spluttered at this, muttering something she did not catch beneath his breath. Anxious to appease him for insulting his friend, she pressed forward. "Forgive me," she said contritely and dropped a kiss somewhere in the vicinity of his mouth. It was hard to tell in the dark.

"You'll need to console me more than that," he complained, falling back against the pillows. "I'm wounded to the core."

Una blinked down at him in alarm. "Wounded? I never intended—"

"Too late," he interrupted her. "I may never recover from this blow to my self-esteem. My wife thinks me an easy prey to those who would take advantage of my guileless nature."

Una bit her lip, for that was exactly what she had done. He suddenly laughed and caught her about the waist, dragging her half on top of him.

"You think me a tender gull for the plucking, my princess," he said silkily. "But you'll soon discover your groom is more fox than goose." His hands were roaming over the thin fabric of her shift, cupping her buttocks and softly squeezing her there. "Or maybe I should say cock pheasant," he said, his voice thickening as he took her hand from his shoulder and slid it down his body until it rested on the hard thrust of his arousal.

Una blinked in the darkness, striving to keep up with his mercurial mood. Clearly his self-esteem had not suffered too dreadful a blow, or he would not now be so inflamed, she thought as her fingers tentatively made out the shape of his thick shaft. His own hand over hers encouraged her to be bolder, and feeling grateful of the darkness, Una took him firmly in hand, making him gasp.

"That's it," he whispered. "Now stroke me, Princess." His fingers showed her what he wanted. *So firmly?* she marveled, but he should know what he liked, and she listened closely to his raspy breath as she familiarized herself with the handling he preferred. Suddenly his breathing hitched, and his hips thrust up. "Stop," he groaned. His hand returned to cover hers, stilling her fingers but keeping her hand lightly squeezing him. "Slow down or I'll spill in your hand."

"I don't mind," she admitted in the dark.

"You may not, but I would," he said. "There's a much sweeter spot I crave."

Una blushed deeply. He couldn't be talking about what she thought he was, surely? Emboldened by the enveloping darkness, she asked quietly, "Do you mean inside me?"

He groaned. "I do. But for now, you can pet me some more. But gently, very gently."

Una caressed him lightly with the pad of her thumb. "Like this?"

"That's good."

"Armand," she whispered. "Do you have a place…?" She almost lost her nerve, but plunged on, lowering her voice. "A place like I do? You know." She groped for the words, but she simply did not have the vocabulary. She did not think she'd ever heard the soldiers speak of pleasuring a woman. "My…bud?" she ventured.

He drew a ragged breath. "I don't have a pretty bud like you," he answered. "But I am especially sensitive at the head." He slid her hand up to the tip, where she lightly squeezed. "And at the base, between my ballocks," he said huskily.

Una's eyes widened. "Oh." She moved her hand down and let her fingers trace him lightly there. It felt curiously soft. "Tell me what to do."

"Cup them," he said tightly, and grunted when she did so. "Now roll them carefully in your hand." She gently massaged his ballocks until his breath grew raspy again and she thought she had better change strategy. "Is this nice?" She traced a figure-eight pattern around them, and he made a sound deep in his throat. She paused the progress of her fingertip and rubbed at the spot that had made him shudder.

"Fuck, Una!" he exclaimed, sounding shaken, and the next thing she knew, she was on her back with Armand astride her, bunching up her shift.

"I hope to gods you're wet, my princess," he panted, sliding a warm hand up her thigh. "'Cause I can't wait." He made a rumbling sound of appreciation in his chest as his fingers delved between her legs. "Thank fuck. Open your legs wider."

Una blinked at the coarse language, for he restrained it around her usually, but his blood seemed well and truly up. To her surprise, he did not settle his hips between her thighs at once, but instead shifted down the bed. Feeling his breath between her legs, she let out a surprised gasp. "Armand, what—"

"Shh," he told her. "I know what I'm doing. Trust me."

Una froze. He was kissing her down there! She tried to sit up, but he wrapped his strong arms about her thighs, keeping her firmly in place.

"Your hair's so pretty, Una," he said huskily, and her cheeks burned when she realized what hair he was commenting on. "Such a lovely shade of deep, dark red."

She could think of absolutely no response to this. Luckily, he did not seem to require one, as his soft kisses became a good deal bolder, his fingers opening her cleft to his tongue.

"Armand!" Una panted, her head dropping back onto the pillows. She squeezed her eyes shut and shuddered. "Oh!" *Oh my gods!* What was he doing? Her mind rebelled at the feel of lapping tongue. He couldn't possibly be licking her down there! But he was, and what's more he sounded like he was enjoying it. He groaned against her, and Una's body took over, her mind too shocked to comprehend the wicked sensations he was evoking. She went taut as a bow before the moment of release, and then she shot right up into the heavens with a muffled shriek.

The next thing she knew, Armand was guiding his throbbing staff between her legs and thrusting deep inside her. She gasped, but he had prepared her so well that there was barely any discomfort at all. "Ah gods," he groaned. "So good." Once he was planted deep, he held himself very still. "Wrap your legs around me," he urged, dragging her thigh over his hip.

222

Una opened her mouth to respond, but suddenly his fingers were between her legs again, his thumb seeking out that pleasure place, and soon he had her panting and twisting against him. The sensations streaking out from the pressure of his thumb, combined with the heady feeling of his hard shaft embedded so deeply within her, soon had her sobbing and trembling once more on the very edge she had only just descended from.

When he labored above her this time, she did not find his movements crude, but moved along with him. He was striving to please her, she realized, and simultaneously to stave off his own rapture. That was why his expression trembled between blissful and tortured. The ragged edge to his breathing, the kindling look in his eye, all served to twist the coiling pleasure in her belly higher still.

When he lowered his head to suck one pointy nipple into his mouth, Una broke again, and he drove into her hard, crying out. Their explosion seemed this time simultaneous, and it was a long while before Una felt herself drift back down from the ceiling into her tingling body.

Armand was lying half on, half off her, his face turned into her neck, one hand resting on her bottom. She should pull down her shift, she thought exhaustedly, and make herself decent, but she didn't want to move a muscle.

"My clever princess," Armand murmured, his voice deep and velvety with a rough edge to it. He kissed her collarbone.

She really ought to reprimand him for calling her princess, but her eyes were closing, and instead she lay in his arms, limp and sated.

10

Armand spent the next morning shut up in consultation with Fulcher again while they thrashed out the last details of their arrangement. Once the bargain had been struck to the satisfaction of both, they sat back and regarded each other thoughtfully.

Fulcher clicked his tongue. "You've the devil's own luck, and no mistake," he said with a small shake of his head. "Fort you was proper done up, my lad. Caught in the parson's trap like that and shackled to that—"

"Careful," Armand interrupted him, his eyebrows snapping together. "That's my wife you're speaking of."

Fulcher regarded him with surprise. "Well, that's what I'm saying. She ain't turned out a bad-looking gal at all. Some might even call her 'andsome in 'er own way," he said generously. "When she ain't glaring at a body across the supper table."

Armand suppressed a wayward grin. "She thinks me a tender lamb that needs protecting from a nasty wolf."

"Wot, you?" Fulcher demanded. "A tender lamb! Bullshit."

"Let's not forget, the last time I told her I was meeting with you, I came back sporting a black eye."

Fulcher avoided his accusing gaze. "Fort we was dissolving our partnership, didn't I?" he said, sounding injured. "Had to protect my interests."

"By setting a gang of thugs on me?"

"Only roughed you up a bit," Fulcher said with a shrug. "You broke poor Walt's nose and give 'Enry such a blow to his ear that he ain't 'eard nuffink but ringing ever since!"

"And, if that's not all," Armand added direly, "you stole my hat!"

Fulcher sat up. "Your 'at?"

"That monstrosity sat upon your greasy locks at one point was my hat," Armand pointed out with dignity. "Una made it for me."

Fulcher removed his hat and gazed down at it. "I love this 'at," he said sorrowfully. "Best 'at I ever 'ad. Now you tell me it was made by a princess, it sorta makes sense."

"Well, you needn't look like that," said Armand. "I don't want it back!"

Fulcher's expression brightened. "You don't?"

"Certainly not!"

After Armand had picked out some of the most distinctive pieces from his treasure collection and Fulcher inspected them before stuffing them in a sack, they made their way down from the attics together.

"'Ow comes you never told me you'd got a great big place like this, tucked away waiting for you?" Fulcher commented in an injured tone. "All these years I knowed you and you been keeping secrets from me."

"You never asked," Armand retorted. "Besides, I only inherited it four years ago. I think we'd had a falling out at the time over some money."

225

Fulcher's frown cleared. "Oh," he said without rancor. "That was that time you flung off 'ome to cool your 'eels. Makes sense."

Armand paused, turning toward him. "How did you find me, then?"

"Followed you, didn't I."

"So it was you following us? I thought there was someone…" he said, trailing off. Of course, he'd put that down to Otho in the end.

"I weren't the only one," Fulcher snorted. "There was at least two ovvers."

"Two?" Armand was startled.

Fulcher nodded. "One of 'em was a right shadowy bastard. Slipped in and out of view. I barely caught glimpses of 'im. Just when I fort he'd backed off, I'd catch sight of 'im again. Black 'ood he wore. Changed his 'orses regular. For a while I 'ad the notion 'e weren't even the same body every time I caught sight of 'im, but…" Fulcher scratched his chin. "I'd started to get the wind up by then, so I dunno. Seemed like a professional to me."

"Professional what?"

Fulcher looked cagey. "Scout mebbe. Or assassin."

Armand expression hardened. "I can't think why either should be on my tail."

"What about your good lady wife?" Fulcher suggested lightly.

Armand was alarmed. "Why the hells should they be?"

Fulcher threw up his hands. "Don't shoot the messenger, my friend," he said hastily.

Armand ignored him, swinging around at the foot of the stairs. "You said two others?"

"S'right," Fulcher said, lolling against the banister. "They didn't seem to be travelin' togevver or nuffink. Oh, and the second party 'ad a Novern accent."

"Northern?" Armand's spine stiffened.

Fulcher nodded. "I 'eard 'im talkin' to a stable lad one time. Soft-spoken 'e was, but you could 'ear it all the same. Unmistakable."

*

Armand was sufficiently disturbed by this piece of information to seek out Otho that afternoon. He found him directing Peter as to some fencing repairs that needed doing in the orchard.

"Have you been working at that fencing all morning?" Armand asked the lad pointedly. Peter nodded, round-eyed and apprehensive. "You haven't seen anyone skulking around the place?"

"No, sir," he replied with a puzzled frown.

"If you do, I want to hear about it. Immediately."

Peter nodded and made off with his tools as Otho gave Armand a sardonic look. "You surely don't believe that fine friend of yours's story? I caught him red-handed. *He* was the mysterious figure skulking in the bushes and none other."

Armand ignored this. "If a party of northerners was following us from Caer-Lyoness to Derring, who do you suppose they would be?"

Otho gave a start. "What? Northerners you say?"

Armand nodded. "A day behind us at most."

"They're nothing to do with me," Otho said aggrievedly. "If that's what you're thinking!"

"It wasn't," Armand responded dampeningly. "Now answer the question, for I don't want to put it to your sister."

Otho folded his arms and regarded him steadily a moment before he answered with a shrug. "Rebels, I suppose," he said gruffly. "It wouldn't be the first time they've sought her out. Why do you think I wanted to put her in a convent where she'll be anonymous? She'll know no peace now she's no longer under lock and key."

"I didn't know you *did* want to put her in a convent," Armand replied shortly. "It's the first I've heard of it. Are you actually suggesting Wymer should have kept her under house arrest for the rest of her life?" His tone was cutting.

"He was mad to marry her off," Otho said bleakly. "Surely you can see that. This whole scheme was doomed from the outset."

"Gods, you're a miserable bastard, Otho," Armand responded with disgust. "I've no patience with your constantly bleak outlook on life. Thank the gods Una is nothing like you!"

"You have no notion what you've gotten into," Otho persisted grimly. "Why do you think I'm sticking around? It's not like you've any intention of guarding over her for the rest of your life, is it?" Otho's lip curled. "I know your type."

Armand's fists curled, and he took a few calming breaths before replying. "Oh, do you?" he drawled. "It seems you know me better than you do your own flesh and blood. Una was *desperate* to get away from court. She was no more suited there than she would be in a convent."

"And where do you imagine she would be suited, then?" Otho flared up jeeringly. "Married to some obscure knight who can barely hold his own in a fight? I've seen farmhands wield a sword with more skill than you, *Sir* Armand! Maybe here in the south they'll bestow a knighthood on any fool, but where I'm from, it's a different story, let me tell you!"

Armand had heard of red mists descending and people losing control before, but never associated such things with himself. He always prided himself on his steady, even temper. More often than not, he was the first to see humor in a situation, and hard to stoke to wrath.

Which is why he really could not explain why the next thing he knew, he was driving his fist into Otho's face while the other lay sprawled out beneath him. It took an almost superhuman effort to stay his arm from landing another blow and he crouched over him, breathing raggedly, as he forced himself to roll away. He lay in the dirt, dragging air into his burning lungs and flexing his numb fingers. How many times had he hit him?

It was one thing for his wife to think him a gullible fool, but quite another for his brother-in-law to insult him like that. Of course, others had tried before in the field. You made mistakes when in a fury and Armand had always used this to his advantage. His had been the ready tongue and the mocking laugh that would provoke his proud enemies into hasty errors. Others never ensnared him with such tactics.

His fellow knights mocked him every time he went crashing out in an early round, and he shrugged it off every time. Such words had never dented his armor before. Why then had he completely lost control this time?

He glanced at Otho's bloodied face. He was still breathing at least. He propped himself up on one elbow and eyed the horse trough. He'd have to dunk him in it, he thought resignedly, dragging himself to his feet and grabbing Otho beneath his armpits.

He had just reached the trough and was propping Otho against the edge when he heard approaching footfalls and glanced around. It was Peter come running from the orchard, looking alarmed and out of breath.

"I seen you dragging him from over yonder. Whatever's happened to Master Otho?" he puffed, coming to a standstill.

"He's been attacked," Armand answered coolly. "Here, help me dunk his head in."

Peter hurried over, his mouth hanging open. "Was it one of them strangers on the prowl, like you was talking about?" he gasped.

"Yes," answered Armand. "That's exactly who it was. I shall need to hire more men to keep an eye about the place."

"And to think I never seen no one," Peter marveled aloud as he grasped Otho's shoulder and they lowered his head into the water.

After a moment, Otho's limbs started to struggle, and they pulled him back out and set him down upon the ground where he lay gasping for breath. "You bastards!" he growled.

"Nay, it weren't us, Master Otho. It was them intruders what Sir Armand warned us about," protested Peter.

Armand turned to him. "I want you to leave off mending the fence this afternoon and spread the word in the village, Peter. We're looking for strong and capable men to come and work and patrol the grounds here. They'll need to know how to handle themselves. It's no good bringing me old men or the infirm." He hesitated. "Former soldiers might work well."

Peter scratched his head. "We might need to widen the net to Upper Derring and Derring Lacey too, mayhap?" he suggested.

Armand nodded. "Good idea. Tell them I'll pay well and refer them to me or Otho here."

"Right away, Sir Armand," said Peter.

Armand watched him hurry in the direction of the house, before glancing again at Otho, who was watching him through wary eyes.

"Well, it didn't take you long to turn this to your advantage," Otho said sourly. "Your wits aren't lacking in any case." He spat a mouthful of blood onto the ground. "And your fists neither. Una said you were handier in a brawl than a sword fight."

Armand was silent a moment. "She's never seen me sword fight," he replied.

Otho's beat-up face showed surprise. "We both did. On May Day."

Armand shook his head. "Neither of you have ever seen me sword fight," he repeated and then walked resolutely back to the house.

*

Armand found Una in the solar spreading out pieces of fabric cut in different shapes. The smile she greeted him with dropped immediately from her face when she caught sight of his expression. "What is it?" she asked quickly. Abelard, who had been sat at her feet, slunk away to hide under a table.

Armand looked down at her broodingly. He didn't want to tell her what Fulcher had said. If a visit from his family could send

231

her into a cold sweat, what would news of one, if not more approaching northerners do to her?

Then again, he reflected, Una's reactions weren't exactly those of a normal woman. An unexpected knock on the door seemingly terrified her more than a band of murderous assassins swarming into their bedroom. She hadn't even mentioned that night at The Merry Wayfarer since it happened.

She straightened up. "Something is clearly amiss, husband," she said. "Please tell me."

Armand took a deep breath. "Fulcher says we were followed from Caer-Lyoness by at least two men," he admitted. "One of them was definitely northern," he added quickly before she could reply. "I'm hiring more workers for outside the house to keep an eye out for strangers. Fulcher says he saw someone else in our orchard yesterday. It may have been one of them. It may not."

Una kept her eyes trained steadily on his face. "Is that everything?"

"I just punched Otho in the face. Several times." He was more surprised by his confession than she was.

"I see," she said, coming to her feet and closing the space between them. She placed her arms loosely around his waist. "Are you alright?" she asked quietly.

"I'm fine. Your brother's face doesn't look too pretty."

Una hesitated. "Why did you hit him?" Armand didn't really know how to respond to that. "You don't want to tell me?" she asked gently.

"I'm not really sure myself," he answered gruffly, feeling a fool. He wasn't sure why she was comforting him at this moment. Shouldn't she be flinging recriminations in his face?

"You've been very patient," she said gravely. "Maybe it's the culmination of a lot of things."

And just like that, Armand felt like the worst kind of heel. He had been dishonest from the start, and Una had somehow mistaken his flippancy for something altogether more virtuous. That advice Bess had given her at The Stone Crow had not been far wrong. He was neither dependable nor a good bet for her in the matrimonial stakes.

He slipped his arms around her waist, pulling her close. "You give me too much credit," he admitted, resting his chin on her shoulder. "Sometimes I—" He broke off, unsure how to proceed. She waited patiently for words he was not going to be able to speak. "Una, how did you get taken by Wymer's forces?"

Una drew back to look at him with surprise. "Where did that come from?"

"It's been playing on my mind."

"Well, it was quite anticlimactic at the end, in all truth," she said with a grimace. "My father was dead, as were his most trusted generals. The last of us had been driven to a remote fort in the Braeburn Heights. There was barely anyone in a position to advise me, which turned out to be a blessing. Under siege conditions, we would have lasted a matter of mere days. When we received a request to parlay, I accepted at once. I was offered very generous terms for my surrender—safe passage and a dignified laying down of arms. I was only too happy to agree."

Armand scanned her face. That she was telling the truth, he did not doubt. He also knew she must be leaving out a good deal. "I can't imagine your soldiers would have been happy with that decision."

"No," she agreed. "But we were surrounded and vastly outnumbered. They were disillusioned, tired, and hungry and had homes and families to return to. They must have known deep down it was a lost cause. There is always the odd one or two who would fight to the death, but as I said, there was no one left in a position of command to oppose me by that point."

"You could not have known you could trust Wymer's generals to carry out their promise," Armand pointed out in a low voice, his fingers tightening at her waist.

"A prince's promise," Una replied lightly, "is something my father always laid great emphasis on, as a sacred trust that could never be broken."

"Did you believe that?" Una remained silent, but he felt the slight shake of her head against his shoulder. Wymer must have been sorely tempted to eliminate this rival claim to his throne, he thought starkly, and Una was the very last of the Blechmarshes. It was a miracle she made it out of the war with her life.

She drew in a deep breath. "Why the sudden curiosity?" she asked, sounding puzzled. "Did Otho say something? But he can't have done, he was on the other side of the country at the time, burying our father."

"It wasn't Otho," Armand said shortly. "It was that knock on the door. The other night."

She tipped her head to one side. "I said the terms of surrender were generous, but it wasn't so polite that they knocked on the door," she said with a humorous quirk of her lips.

Armand gazed down at her. Was she laughing at him? "I want to know why you reacted that way," he said abruptly. "When we were nearly murdered in our beds you were calm as could be. Why would a knock on our door frighten you to such an extent?" When Una lowered her eyes evasively, he caught her chin and tipped it up. "Tell me."

"I—it's hard to explain."

"Try."

Una colored. "I'm used to keeping my head in a crisis," she admitted slowly. "To things growing steadily worse, day by day, until all you can cling to is survival itself, without expectation of anything more." She paused. "It's the prospect of happiness I'm ill accustomed to," she said quietly. "Or rather, being so close to achieving it that I could *almost* touch it."

The sudden ache in her voice paralyzed him. All he could do was stare. "I've only known true panic twice that I can remember since childhood," she continued after a moment. "Once when I thought you would leave on the morning after our wedding—" She swallowed convulsively, blinking back sudden tears. "And that night when we were about to eat our first formal meal in the great hall, with our household." She smiled at him through her tears. "You see, both times, I was so…wildly happy, so crazily optimistic about a future I had never dared before to contemplate. Then on both occasions, suddenly out of nowhere, it looked as though that cup of happiness was about to be dashed from my lips before I'd had the chance even to taste it."

Armand murmured something, he wasn't sure what, and then he was kissing her face, which was damp with tears. She had been wildly and crazily happy just to be married to the loser of the May Day tournament? He kissed the tip of her nose, her two glowing cheeks, and that lovely, quivering full mouth. His heart twisted on the realization she had been frozen in terror because she had been so looking forward to eating pie with their servants at their own table. *A pie*. It should be laughable that a princess of the realm thought that the highest happiness she could aspire to. Why then, was laughing the last thing he felt like doing?

An aching pain throbbed in his chest that could only be assuaged by the feel of her in his arms. His kiss, which had started to placate and comfort her in her distress, dramatically changed. Suddenly, his heart was pounding, and he could not get close enough, even though he cupped her face and twined his arm about her waist until she was molded to him.

"Una," he whispered. "I'm going to give you everything. Anything you ever wanted." What was he saying? A small part of him, deep inside, wanted to shrink back in disbelief. He *never* made promises, let alone to women. But the rest of him was pressing forward, eager to forge himself to her with hasty, imprudent words. Words that negated entirely that promise he had wrung from her to be amenable in all things.

Una gasped at his words, possibly even at his alarming behavior. "You do," she strove to assure him. Her hands fluttered at his shoulders. "You are. Armand?" He drew back. "Should we not take this to the bedchamber?" Her cheeks were bright red and the high color suited her so well that he suffered another shock. He was fiercely attracted to his wife. Why hadn't he realized that before?

"Unless you don't want to," she said quickly, and it was only then that her words registered.

"Oh, I want to," he said thickly, scooping her up in his arms. Then he carried her to their room, stripped her naked, and made love to her with a tender thoroughness he had not shown her or anyone before. Una wept in the aftermath, which alarmed him, but when he held her close, she told him they were happy tears and he had to make do with that.

11

Una woke to find light still streaming through the wooden shutters and guessed it was early evening. She was lying naked with Armand's arm about her waist and he was fast asleep.

She turned carefully about so she could gaze upon his face. What on earth had gotten into him to make him so…gentle with her? She could not really think of the right word. He certainly had not collapsed grunting on top of her this time. He had acted like she was precious and in need of careful handling. It had been lovely, she thought, but she did not want him to get the wrong idea about her. She was not some fragile flower that needed cautious tending. She was a woman and she was his wife. Of course, weeping all over him like that afterward had probably not helped. She wasn't sure why she had done that, except that her emotions had been all over the place.

The fault had probably lain with those words he'd uttered. She felt breathless even at the thought of them now. *I'm going to give you everything. Anything you ever wanted.* Such an extraordinary thing for him to come out with! Her heart had seemed to stop for a moment before it had started wildly beating once again. She wondered with a pang if he would regret the words on waking.

The word of men could be undependable where women were concerned, or so her old nurse had warned her, when they'd been drinking or when they were trying to get under your skirts. But neither of those motivations applied in this instance. For though Armand had certainly been aflame for her, he had not been trying to seduce or persuade her into anything when he'd made his remarkable statement. As his wife, she had always said that his wishes would be considered law to her and she would oppose him in nothing. She had made that clear the morning after their wedding.

She hesitated before leaping to conclusions, but it seemed like he was now offering to rewrite their marriage bargain. Una bit her lip. It would be foolish to set too much store by such words spoken in the grip of some strong emotion. When he had come to her that afternoon, his feelings had probably been overwrought, and he had likely not been thinking rationally.

Just the fact he had even thought, let alone voiced such words was unspeakably precious to her. Unable to stop herself, she reached out a tentative hand and stroked one lock of dark hair from his face. His eyes flickered open and he smiled drowsily at her. Una caught her breath.

"My sweet princess," he murmured, tightening an arm about her waist. Una felt her chest flutter and swallowed. She really could not let him get away with calling her that. Some would consider it high treason! Her expression must have shown her thoughts.

"You'll get used to me calling you that eventually," he said, a glint in his eye. "In the bedchamber."

"I would much rather you did not!" she admitted, flushing hotly. "It's dangerous."

He cocked his head to one side. "What if I told you that men call women that sometimes, even when they aren't royalty?"

This took her by surprise. "Why would they do that?" she asked, puzzled.

"Much like calling someone a randy stable boy or a lusty tavern wench, I suppose." He shrugged.

Una felt she was in danger of entirely losing the thread of conversation. "You mean, even when they are not employed in a stable or a tavern?" she asked with a frown.

Armand smirked. "Now you're getting it."

"But why?"

"Just for bed sport," he suggested.

"Bed sport?" Una echoed, feeling mystified.

"For instance, if you called me Sir Lusty Loins, or called it 'riding my trusty stallion.'"

Una blinked. *Sir Lusty Loins?* She regarded him doubtfully. "I would *never* demean you in such a manner," she stammered hotly.

"Oh, but I would not find it demeaning me in the slightest," he assured her. "In fact, I'd like it."

Una considered this a moment, quite flabbergasted. He had a smile playing about his lips, and she wasn't at all sure he wasn't teasing her. It seemed like flirtatious Armand had returned with a vengeance. "At court—" she started painstakingly, but then stopped.

"At court?" he repeated quizzically.

She had been going to remind him how much she had disliked being called the northern mare but realized that would put a complete damper on his lightened mood. She liked playful Armand and was glad to see he was back. She just wasn't sure how to indulge or encourage him. She knew she had done a pretty woeful job of even attempting it so far. That had to change, she thought resolutely. Or he'd start treating her like a piece of glass every time he handled her. "You must be acquainted with the heraldic beast of my family," she improvised instead.

Armand's eyebrows rose. "The green wyvern."

"Yes," she agreed. "If we are to have different characters for our…bed sport," she said with a trace of self-consciousness, "then I would rather we called it…um…" She cleared her throat. "Sir Lusty Loins versus the Blechmarsh Dragon." Her face was surely crimson by now. Armand had an arrested look on his face, and she had a terrible suspicion he was trying not to burst out laughing.

"We could, certainly," he agreed, his voice a little uneven. "Let us discuss this further." He folded his arms behind his head. "How would that play out, do you suppose?"

Una bit her lip. She had not realized she was supposed to supply whole scenarios. "Well, er—" Her mind went blank. Had she made this situation ten times more awkward than it had been already? She almost wished she had let him call her princess and be done with it.

"Sir Lusty Loins could be sent along to vanquish the Blechmarsh Dragon with his mighty staff?" he suggested huskily when she remained tongue-tied.

"Yes…" she agreed weakly. Then suddenly she got the joke. *Oh! By staff, he meant…*

She flushed. He was definitely teasing her now. Una felt an overwhelming desire to vindicate herself and show she, too, could play this game! "Of course, he would find it no easy task," she said with a valiant attempt at airiness. "For I would be a very wicked dragon indeed and would entirely overpower him."

"Indeed?" He sounded more intrigued than alarmed by that, rolling toward her and running a hand up and down her thigh. "How?"

"Everyone knows a dragon breathes fire. I would—breathe on him."

"Breathe?" He cocked an eyebrow.

Una leaned forward with great daring, pressing her breasts to his chest. She knew he liked them, for he had told her so when he was drunk. "From my lungs," she whispered in his ear. "Like this." She blew gently against the shell of his ear, and Armand's own breathing hitched before he went very still. Something wasn't still though, Una thought, for something was definitely stirring to life against her thigh.

"I see," he said after a moment's pause. Was it her imagination, or did he sound a little breathless? Una felt secretly thrilled that she might be having some effect on him. "I imagine that might be effective," he conceded. "If you breathed like that against…my staff," he suggested, giving her a scorching look.

Una blinked. "If I breathed fire against your staff, it would surely disintegrate," she pointed out.

"Nay, you are quite wrong on that score," he said thickly. "I think it might *explode*."

"I would not let you burn to a crisp," Una assured him. "I am a dragon, and I like to devour my prey whole."

Now it was his turn to blink. "Gods, Una," he groaned. "You're bloody good at this, love." He rolled her underneath him. "By all means let's try it your way."

Oh, he wanted to play it now, she thought, gratified. She must be getting the hang of it!

He grabbed her wrists in a loose hold above her head. "Behold me now, wicked dragon," he rumbled down at her. "For I have been sent to battle with you. Prepare to be vanquished, for I have brought my trusty sword—"

"Sword? I thought it was a staff," Una corrected him, tipping back her head to look up at him. Feeling suddenly inspired, she arched her back and pressed herself against his hard cock. He made a surprised noise in his throat.

"In truth," Una mused breathlessly, "it feels more like a staff than a sword…" She rubbed herself against him like an abandoned thing, biting her lip. She felt him grow harder against her. "And yet, I am not sure…"

"You wicked, brazen creature," he groaned, and the way he said it sounded more like praise than censure. His big hands landed on her buttocks, kneading them, encouraging her to move against him in a sinuous slide. "You should know that all knights are pure in heart and cannot be defeated thus."

"Is that a fact, Sir Knight?" she panted. For the life of her, she could not remember his character's precise name at this moment.

"It is," he grunted. "Perhaps you do not know Sir Lusty Loins has more weapons in his arsenal than just his mighty staff."

Sir Lusty Loins, that was it. "And what weapons might those be?" she asked.

"My tongue," he answered. "My silver tongue that can soothe the most savage beast."

"Your tongue?" She shivered. "That does not sound very…scary."

"Oh, I'll soon lick you into submission," he promised.

243

Una caught her breath. "I do not think that will work on one such as I," she practically whimpered.

"Oh?" He quirked a brow at her before yanking her thighs apart. "But I am keen to try, for I have heard dragon flesh is so very succulent and juicy."

Una trembled as he scooted down her body. Oh gods, conversing with him like this was making her feel so very strange! She felt like she was poised on the cliff edge and about to tumble off it already. It was too much, too intense. He paused a moment between her thighs, and she felt his hot breath on her most intimate parts. "W-wait!" she squeaked.

He looked up at her; his hair tumbled forward and he winked at her. Una was lost before he had even started. It didn't take long before he had her squirming completely at his mercy.

"Oh! *Oh! Sir Armand!*" she screamed, completely forgetting the made-up name again.

He gave her a last lingering lick and then moved back up her body, breathing hard.

"That was a very naughty dragon to scream another knight's name as I give you a tongue lashing," he growled in her ear. "It seems I need to remind you who you're dealing with." Luckily Una was dead to all shame by this point, a heaving, roiling mess as he inserted his hips between her thighs and slid his hard cock between her wet cleft in a hot, teasing slide that made her sated body perk up again.

"Drenched," he breathed. "Well, well, maybe you will swallow me whole yet, my dragoness." He surged forward, and Una moaned deep in her throat as his thick inches penetrated her slowly, making her ache for him. She wound her arms about his shoulders.

"More," she groaned. "*Please*."

He gave a breathless laugh. "Shh, my insatiable dragon, let me make this good for you."

Una sank her nails into his back. "Dragons don't like it slow," she panted. "They like it fast."

"Who's conquering who here?" he demanded raspily as he eased into her. Una wrapped her legs around his back, canting her hips, encouraging his penetration in any way she could. She moaned again loudly, letting him know how needy she felt.

"Fuck, Una," he grunted as he slid the last few inches until he was buried deep. His breathing was ragged, and she watched as he closed his eyes. She wasn't sure if he was fighting for control or just savoring the moment. Her own eyes fluttered shut as she felt him so deep inside her, where she wanted him most. "Open your eyes," he grated out, and Una obeyed. He was gazing down at her so intently, she felt scorched.

"So beautiful," he ground out in what Una dimly realized must be part of their bed play, but she could not help how it made her chest throb almost as much as where they were joined. Her eyes swam; it was nice he'd decided her wyvern was beautiful, she thought. He was kind. And breathtaking. And utterly— Her thoughts broke off as his body flexed hard against her. *Oh!*

Her hips rose to meet his thrusts as he quickly fell into a punishing rhythm that had her struggling to match his pace. She kept falling out of time, only for him to seize her hips and jolt her back against him hard until she matched him thrust for thrust. The sensations rising in her soon had her spiraling out of control. He wasn't teasing or coaxing cooperation from her body this time. He was demanding it. There was no more dragon and knight talk either as he grunted loudly in time with each of his pounding thrusts. Una lost herself completely to sensation, the sounds, the pleasure.

She wouldn't even know how to describe the strange keening noise she was making. She ought to release her grip of his rippling shoulders and cover her mouth, she thought, her senses reeling. But if she did that—if she did that, he might stop. And if he stopped then she would surely die of disappointment. It wasn't as though he was trying to muffle her cries, she consoled herself. Between the two of them, they were creating quite a racket.

Then she gave up on conscious thought as her moans turned hoarse and her movements became frantic, and the tension building and building inside her suddenly burst in a blaze like a ball of flame that tore through her like wildfire utterly consuming her. She lay stunned and shaking as Armand shattered in almost the same instant. He gave a guttural cry before slumping over her with a low, spent groan and thus they remained for several long moments, intertwined and panting.

"Holy fuck," he breathed at last, kissing her brow. "That was…incredible." He gave a small chuckle. "Your dragon was certainly…formidable." Una tightened her arms around him, which had fallen slack. She didn't feel up to words right now. "We'll call that an even draw," he mused. "Though in truth I think you defeated me utterly."

Then he seemed to notice her silence and drew back, eyeing her almost warily. "Una?" She buried her face in his neck, unable to face his teasing. "Feeling shy?" he asked, sounding amused. She shook her head but would not look at him all the same. He blew out a breath. "Very well, I'll let you off the hook this once. But only because you were an absolute revelation." He drew a lazy pattern against the skin of her back with his fingertip. "I never thought dragon-slaying would be so—" He broke off at the sound of some noise outside. "What the fuck?" It was a gentle knock on the door. "Go away!" Armand bawled.

Una winced. "Armand," she murmured reproachfully. "They must be waiting on us to serve supper."

"Supper?" He glanced at the window. "Oh yes," he said, frowning, clearly displeased at the thought of venturing below stairs.

"I could ask them to serve ours to us here," she suggested. "At the small table in the corner?"

His expression cleared. "That's a damned good notion," he said with approval.

"And also to bring us a bath," she suggested, coloring slightly.

He looked thoughtful. "How large is the tub?"

*

They ate their supper intimately secluded in the privacy of their room. Armand's bare feet brushed her own under the small table, and after the first few passes, she realized it was by design rather than mere accident. By the time they were tucking into the roasted meats, her own feet were resting atop of his in an act of familiarity that quite took her breath away.

Feeling his eyes upon her almost stole her appetite, and he had to keep urging her to eat. "You'll need your strength," he teased, wagging his eyebrows at her, and Una felt her face grow hot. She had a terrible suspicion he was going to tease her about their dragon play, and she felt entirely lily-livered about the subject. It was one thing to be bold in the throes of passion, but quite another to have anything you might have said repeated back to you in the cold light of day.

His glinting eyes seemed to say he could guess her thoughts, for though she could see a jest tremble on his lips a time or two, he did not voice whatever it was, though his eyes brimmed over with wicked laughter. He ate voraciously, his eyes never wavering far from her face, and though she was dressed in a loose brocade robe over her shift and should have been quite comfortable, she felt as breathless as if she had been tightly laced.

When the bath arrived, Armand complained it was a good deal too small, though it looked to be of usual proportions to Una. To her surprise, he dismissed Rose and bade her take the hiding Abelard with her, for the dog must be wanting his supper. Una was relieved to see Abelard lick Rose's nose in a display of spontaneous affection that made the girl laugh delightfully, and she carried him off in her arms, singing under her breath.

Then Armand locked the door and set about undressing and bathing her as though it were some task for him to savor. He dragged the sponge over her neck and shoulders, then peppered kisses in its wake. He lathered the soap flakes in his hands and rubbed them over her body with his fingers and palms. It was more like an act of worship than a cleaning exercise and Una was both heated and bewildered by the time she emerged from the water and was wrapped in a drying cloth.

As he quickly stripped and climbed into the tub after her, she crouched before the fire and dried her hair. "Should I help bathe you?" she thought to ask belatedly as she heard him splashing the water about.

"Next time," he answered briefly. "We'll commission a larger tub."

Una glanced curiously over her shoulder. "I suppose you do make that one look a little small," she admitted. "But only because you are rather large for a man."

He grinned back at her. "I want one we can share."

"Share?" she repeated blankly. "At the same time?"

He nodded.

"Oh." Una turned back to face the fire. At least the flames gave her an excuse for her overheated cheeks. It suddenly struck her that he might have been covering her in kisses to show her how much she had pleased him. After all, that was what he had demanded from her the last time he had brought her pleasure. She bit the tip of her finger and ventured another quick glance at him as he rubbed a cloth over the expanse of his chest.

Remembering how she had shrieked his name a short while ago, she could only suppose he must be expecting his own reward on the morrow! When he joined her in front of the fire a few minutes later, kneeling on the rug beside her, instead of rising to go and don her shift, Una turned to him and started drying his hair with the cloth.

Armand angled his head toward her and sat passively while she moved down to rub his shoulder and neck. By degrees, he maneuvered her into his lap, until her back rested against his front and they sat wrapped in the same sheet, their naked skin pressed together in companionable silence before the fire.

A knock at the door was Peter and Janet come to carry the tub away. Armand kept his arms firmly around her, so Una remained where she was, facing the fire.

Rose brought in another flagon of wine and a bucket of logs for their fire, which she placed carefully down by the hearth, whilst scrupulously avoiding looking at their seated figures. She picked up the other wet drying cloths from the floor and hesitated at the door for just a moment. "Will I keep Abelard with me for the night, milady?" she asked.

249

"Is he content to remain with you?" Una asked.

"Oh yes, I let him have all the supper scraps."

"Then by all means," Una responded warmly. After the door closed, she murmured, "I expect she'll let him sleep on the bed. No doubt he'll like that."

Armand did not respond, merely dropped a kiss to her shoulder. She shivered and he asked quietly, "Are you cold?" Una shook her head. She felt warm and safe in his arms like this. She wished she had the nerve to say so, but it was hard for her to judge if such words would even be welcome. Armand's actions and his past words did not seem entirely in accord, just recently.

"You remember those words you said to me on that first morning," his voice rumbled behind her.

"Which ones?" she asked cautiously.

"About being amenable to me in all things."

How strange that he was thinking along the same lines as she had done earlier! "Yes," she admitted, still looking at the licking flames.

"I don't want that anymore." Una's breathing came a little quicker. "In truth," he carried on after a moment, "I feel like we already replaced that agreement, with our pact to be perfect traveling companions."

"I felt that too," Una agreed, remembering how overjoyed she had been at his suggestion.

He paused. "Good," he said gruffly, his hands seeking hers and intertwining with them before resting them on her knees. For a moment she thought he would say something else, but no other words were forthcoming, and they sat quiet until Armand

250

suggested they get under the bedcovers. When they did, he immediately pulled her close and did not let go until morning.

When she was very sure he was fast asleep, she found herself whispering in the dark. "You need never worry about being a heavy sleeper again. You have me now, and I will never let any harm come to you." His arm tightened around her for a moment and then relaxed again. She was quite sure that he had not made out her words at all, but it was a nice reaction all the same.

*

The next morning brought an invitation from Anninghurst for them to dine with Armand's family. Una received it with mixed feelings. On the one hand, it was an opportunity for her to redeem herself after the disaster of their visit. On the other, she rather dreaded the possibility that things might grow even more strained, for instance, if they grew aware of her real identity.

"'E's a fine peacock and no mistake," sniffed Fulcher, who was planning on leaving them shortly. He was looking out of one of the arched windows, and Una crossed the room to see who he was regarding with such interest. It was Armand's younger brother who had delivered the message from Sir Hugo inviting them to dine that night.

"That's Armand's brother Roger," she said, attempting to cultivate a more friendly manner with Armand's dubious friend. After all, if he would be collecting and distributing their ill-gotten gains over the next twelve months, she had better get used to having him about the place. "I suppose he is a well-favored youth," she said, surveying him critically. To her mind, his looks were nothing compared to his older brother's.

"'Old 'ard," Fulcher said. "I was wonderin' why he was loiterin' like that."

Una noticed Rose was skipping up the path with a basket of herbs she had been gathering for the kitchen. Roger started toward her hastily and Una saw Rose's step falter.

"Young dog!" Fulcher chuckled. "He ain't much different to his bro—" He choked off his words hurriedly. "Beggin' your pardon, milady, what I meant to say was—"

He didn't get much further, for the next thing Una knew, Roger had seized Rose clumsily in his arms and her basket had spilled its contents all over the path. Rose cried out in alarm, struggling wildly to get free. Una made for the door, Abelard close on her heels.

"Now, milady, you don't want to start interfering in what's perfectly natural high spirits in young folk—" Fulcher started uncomfortably, but Una already had the door open and was hurrying outside.

"Roger!" Una called censoriously as Abelard took off barking toward them. Una stopped abruptly, however, on realizing someone else had appeared on the scene before her. It was Otho. Quick as a flash, he had wrenched Rose free from the young man's grasp and had slung Roger across his hip sprawling into the dirt, coughing and choking.

Rose had her hands clasped together and was gazing at Otho with stars in her eyes. He turned to her direly. "Get back to the kitchen, Rose!" She fled at once, Abelard taking after her. Una, seeing a martial light in her brother's eyes, hurried over before Roger could clamber to his feet.

"Well now, that's quite enough," she said briskly. "I'm sure Roger will now offer me his apology for treating my maidservant so ill." Roger, who had opened his mouth hotly, closed it again, looking mutinous. "Otho, please extend a hand to help this young man to his feet."

252

Otho glared at her before remembering due deference. He grudgingly reached down, but Roger pettishly slapped it away.

"I want no help from this man!" he bleated. "I'll have my brother turn him away from his door for this insult!"

"You want your brother to turn mine away?" Una asked coolly. "That might be awkward."

Roger's mouth fell open. He looked from Una to Otho and back again. "I thought he was my brother's steward," he said grudgingly.

"And so he is," Una agreed.

"I knew of no other relationship." Roger gulped.

"No indeed, how should you?" she said pleasantly. "I will hear your apology now."

Roger rose stiffly and dusted off his knees. "I apologize, sister," he said, rigid with affronted pride.

Una nodded. "Very proper. Now see that it does not happen again."

"My—my attentions were not intended to be dishonorable—" he stammered, then broke off, his color very heightened. "Perhaps I might be permitted to apologize to the maiden."

Una glanced at Otho, who was looking at this point very forbidding indeed. The black eye and swelling about his face made him look somehow even more alarming. "Perhaps in a day or so," she said, addressing Roger kindly. "Rose is a very sensitive girl and I fear you may have overset her feelings far too much for one day."

He looked mortified, bowed again, and then hurried toward his waiting horse.

"Impudent young puppy!" Otho burst out furiously. "What other intentions would he have toward a servant girl?"

Una pursed her lips. "I think he's a little green where girls are concerned," she started tactfully. "His father intended him for the church, and I don't think he has much experience—"

"I don't give a damn if his father intended him for a eunuch!" Otho burst out angrily before checking himself. He bit back his words with difficulty. "Gods, Una, I'm sorry, that was unpardonably rude—"

"Not at all, Otho," she soothed him. "Indeed, I much prefer it when you speak naturally with me like this, without exaggerated civility."

He gave a bark of laughter. "I don't know why I got so worked up like that."

"Well, Rose is a very innocent young woman, surely it is only natural that you should feel protective about a member of our household."

Otho swung round, giving her a very sardonic look. "Una, that girl is destined to be some rich man's fancy, if ever any girl was." At her sharply indrawn breath, he continued damningly. "She's frivolous and good for nothing but ornamentation. Quite frankly, I've done nothing but delay the inevitable."

"Otho! I'm surprised at you!" Una plunked her hands on her hips. "Rose is a virtuous and kind young woman with many good points and does not deserve to have you speak of her in such a way."

He rolled his eyes. "Sister, you have led a—"

"Don't be ridiculous!" she cut him off. "If you mean to tell me I'm some sheltered virgin, then I would remind you I am a married woman."

He spluttered. "I never intended to say any such thing!"

"Then kindly do not speak poorly of that girl in my hearing or I will be quite cross with you!" Before he could respond, Una turned on her heel and marched in the direction of the house. She made straight for the kitchens in the expectation she would find Rose in floods of tears and in need of comforting. To her surprise, she found her sat at the table humming a tune and grinding herbs in a pestle and mortar.

"Rose," she said, crossing the threshold and ignoring the Mrs. Brickenden's disapproving look. "You are not feeling upset?"

She looked up with shining eyes. "Oh no, milady," she said with a smile trembling on her lips. "Was not Master Otho wonderful?"

Una felt a twinge of misgiving. Something about Rose's reaction seemed decidedly amiss. Abelard, who was sitting next to Rose, whined, and she reached down to pat him absently. "Master Roger said he would like to apologize to you in person, Rose. I hope that would not distress you?"

"Distress me?" Rose looked surprised by the notion. "Oh no, why should it?" she said vaguely, then started humming again, a small smile hovering about her lips.

Oh dear, thought Una. Roger might be young and handsome, but it seemed Rose's tastes ran to burly northern men with cantankerous dispositions.

*

When she tried to discuss the matter with Armand as they rode over to Anninghurst that evening, he seemed disposed to treat it lightly. "Yes, Fulcher mentioned something about it before he set off on his travels. I'm sure Rose will soon recover," he said dismissively. "Roger's a young fool. He should have told my father years ago he did not want to be a cleric. Then he'd have a bit more finesse with wenches than to try and wrestle them into his arms like that."

"Not everyone might find it easy as you to stand up to a strong personality like Sir Hugo's," Una pointed out.

"I told my father the church wasn't for me before I was twelve," he retorted, drawing in his rein. "Second sons are usually dedicated to the church. Stop here," he said, reaching for her horse's bridle.

She drew in closer. "What is it? What are we looking at?"

He pointed to an impressive gray stone property surrounded by its own moat in the distance. It had castellated walls and big square mullioned windows. "Anninghurst," he said shortly. "Where I was raised."

"It's a very impressive size," Una commented, though to her eye Lynwode was far prettier. The night was fine and mild, and they could see for miles as they rested the horses, taking in the view. "It's lovely countryside around here. I take it the surrounding lands are attached to the estate?"

Armand nodded. "That there is its own private chapel," he said, pointing to the left. "I'm sure you will get the official tour of the place when we arrive."

He spoke nothing but the truth, and Una was duly led on an hour-long exploration of Anninghurst's every nook and cranny by both Muriel and Henry, who were keen to point out its every superiority to their new sister-in-law. Una professed deep admiration for its every detail, indeed, they would not move on into the next room until she had done so. Armand declined the offer to reacquaint himself and remained in the great hall with his father and a sheepish-looking Roger.

By the time Una was brought back to them, Anne and her husband, Matthew Buxton, had also arrived for supper. Anne took great pains to greet her warmly, showing their prior acquaintanceship. Una could not help but respond with a smile when her sister-in-law took both her hands and kissed her cheek.

"Matthew is most keen to meet you, Una," she said, introducing her to the fair, solid man stood at her side. "For I told him how good you were with our children."

Una shook hands with Anne's husband, and they were led to the table where a rather spartan supper of cold mutton awaited them.

"You will have need of a second supper when you return home," Anne murmured behind her hand as they took their places at the long table. "Matthew always prepares himself by lining his own stomach before we even leave."

Una schooled her features not to betray a reaction to this, for Muriel was already addressing her.

"You will see, my dear Una," she said with a wintry smile, "that we do not permit our servants to dine with us here at Anninghurst. In my opinion it encourages waste and overfamiliarity between the ranks."

Una saw that Roger gave a violent start at his sister-in-law's words, and he sent her an accusing look. Surely, he did not think she had been telling tales at supper, she thought, and sent

257

him a reassuring smile. Unfortunately, as Roger was now staring at his plate, he could not receive her unspoken message.

"We prefer to run our house along more traditional lines," Armand said loudly, reaching for Una's hand and kissing it. "The old ways are good enough for us." He met her eyes and smiled.

Una saw Sir Hugo's eyes widen at this sentiment and Muriel turned quite puce. "I assure you that both Henry and I consider ourselves custodians of tradition here at Anninghurst," she replied quickly.

"Quite so, my dear," Henry echoed. "Armand mistook your sentiment entirely."

Sir Hugo interrupted at this point. "Armand speaks nothing but the truth," he said heavily. "In my day, the household always ate their supper together in the great hall, one and all."

An uncomfortable silence fell over the table, only broken when Anne commented how disappointed she was that Armand was not dressed in his court raiment this evening, for she had so much been looking forward to seeing it. Even Una could tell he was being ribbed by his sister, and once again realized that the outfit she had made him must not be suited for anything outside of a royal residence.

"No," Armand answered mildly, lowering his wine goblet. "For Una has not yet made me a second suit. The first was her wedding gift to me." He covered her hand with his and lightly squeezed her fingers. "I hope she will make me another very soon." He lifted his cup again, and looked at her thoughtfully over the brim. "Perhaps blue and white next time to match the family crest."

She had scarcely had chance to recover from the idea that he might welcome another outfit than Muriel was speaking to her again, this time with much more enthusiasm. She very much approved of the fact that Una had some practical skill and believed it must be very economical to make your own clothes. Tailors, she opined, charged such a shocking amount, it was little more than robbery!

The rest of the evening passed without much incident.

Henry and Muriel de Bussell were doubtless an eccentric couple, but to Una they seemed to exist in a state of deep accord. Their chief interests in life appeared to be the same; namely Anninghurst, and schemes of how to save money. Muriel's gown again was rather shabby and old-fashioned, but she carried herself with assurance and seemed to accord her husband the utmost respect and deference.

Roger cheered up after the eating was done, no doubt assured that his conduct that morning was not about to be brought up. He even managed to contribute some talk about horses, for his own was old and ready to be put out to pasture. Armand remarked that one of his tenant farmers had several mounts for sale, which might interest his brother.

Their father, Sir Hugo, cut in at this point, extremely surprised that Armand was familiarizing himself with the running of his estate. "You have visited your farms, Armand? I had feared you would be in a frenzy to return to your tournaments. That is your usual habit after all. Generally, you are itching to get away from us after you have been here a few days."

"No doubt," Armand returned easily, "I will in good time. There are still some matters to be sorted about the smooth running of the place."

259

Una looked at him fleetingly and then, realizing her father-in-law's eyes were upon her, hurriedly turned back to Anne to resume their conversation.

When they came to take their leave, Sir Hugo drew her to one side. "I'm pleased," he said abruptly. "Armand seems to be finally waking up to his responsibilities. I take it we have you to thank for that."

Una gazed back at him. "I am not—"

He waved her words away. "Do not bother protesting. We are only too familiar with Armand's many faults, I assure you. His mother ruined the boy and now we are all reaping what she sowed."

Una bristled. "I do not think he has any faults!" she found herself saying defensively. "Not any serious ones, in any case."

Her father-in-law seemed at a momentary loss for words. "You are very newly wed," he remarked dryly after an awkward silence.

"Yes, we are," Armand agreed cheerfully, coming to her rescue. She hoped he had heard only the latter part of their exchange. "Are you ready, my love? Night is falling."

Una collected her cloak from the hovering servant, and they made their way out of the gloomily lit hall.

"Thank the gods that's over with…excruciating conversation and unpalatable food," Armand said breezily as soon as they were out of the door and heading for the stables. "We need not consider ourselves duty-bound to visit again for at least a month."

Una breathed out. "It was not so very bad as all that." He made no response and she bit her lip. "Armand?" she said on impulse.

"Yes?"

"Is there any special reason we are not disclosing my true identity to your family?"

He looked confused. "What do you mean?"

"About my being a...northerner," she finished lamely.

He was quiet a moment. "You are Lady Una de Bussell now," he said with a twist of his lips. "And there is no secrecy about the fact."

"So, your father would not be very angry if he knew my background?"

"No. Why do you ask?"

"The King mentioned that the de Bussells have always been loyal to the Argent throne."

Armand snorted, tugging her toward the stables. "Is that what he told you? My great-grandfather was a champion, it's true, but my father has not been to court in over forty years. Henry only ever went once, to be presented. If you hadn't noticed, my family is a pack of country yokels these days. House de Bussell has sunk into rural obscurity." He squeezed her hand. "You need have no fear whatsoever on that score."

Looking at his warm smile, Una found that by some miracle, she was reassured and answered it with one of her own.

He laughed. "Now tell me, what did the old man say to get you so heated? I told you he was a damned cold fish."

Una looked away in confusion. "I forget now," she prevaricated.

He carried her fingers to his lips. "You must not cut up rough on my account. I know he doesn't think much of me."

"Then he is a fool," Una burst out hotly.

"Una!" He swung her round to face him, and she saw he was laughing.

"If he does not know what a good, true friend and faithful companion you can be, then—" she started, but he did not let her finish, snatching her up to kiss her lips soundly.

When he released her, there was a faint frown on his brow. "Friend and companion?" he echoed with some displeasure. "I'm your husband, Una. Make no mistake about that."

"I—I could not mistake the fact," she assured him breathlessly, and he pinched her chin.

"Good, now let's get home."

*

Una woke late the next morning and found Armand had already risen. When she descended to the great hall, Janet told her he was with some new hands outside. "Peter told me they're a right bunch," the garrulous maid confided. "He says—"

But Una was not to learn Peter's opinion on the new recruits, for the housekeeper came in at that point and pinned Janet with an accusing look.

"If you'll excuse me, milady," Janet said hastily, dropping a curtsey and scurrying off. Una eyed the housekeeper with some exasperation. She could not warm to the woman, who seemed to have as much personality as a chair.

"Have you seen my dog, Abelard, this morning, Mrs. Brickenden?"

262

"Yes, milady," the older woman answered repressively. "It was following that Rose about earlier. Now if you will excuse me, milady. I have much to do this morn." She made a hasty retreat.

It was not Armand but Otho who Una came across next. He hurried into the great hall with a hunted look on his face. "Otho?" she addressed him, and when he wheeled about with a start, she gazed at him in some surprise. "What is it, brother?"

"Oh, nothing," he said hurriedly. "I thought you were someone else."

"Who?" she asked curiously.

He cleared his throat. "Rose." Una glanced at his flushed face and bit her lip. "She keeps jumping out at me from around corners," he complained. "Asking if she can fetch me anything."

"No doubt she wishes to repay you for the kindness you did her yesterday in repelling an unwanted suitor."

Otho looked harassed. "That was not what I was doing! She should be focused on her work, not on dalliances!" A light step was heard in the distance and Otho took to his heels.

Una watched him disappear around the corner as Rose came blithely into the room.

"Good morning, milady," Rose sang out with a beatific smile. Abelard trotted from her side to greet his mistress.

"Good morning, good morning." Una stroked his sleek little head. These days he was starting to look a lot more presentable, as his coat was starting to grow back in and his ribs were receding as he put on weight.

"'Tis a lovely day," Rose told her earnestly. "The orchard's in full blossom. You must take a scented walk down there while it is so pretty, milady. There is nothing like it."

"You look in full bloom today, Rose," Una told her truthfully.

Rose beamed back at her. "I don't know why, but I feel as full of joy as a spring lamb," she admitted. Una thought she might know why and marveled at it. In truth, she had never seen a lovelier girl than Rose, and though she highly esteemed Otho, not even the fondest sister could think him handsome with his blunt features and savagely shorn head. Then again, she reflected, her own meager physical attractions were no match for Armand's. Rose drifted off again in the direction of the kitchen.

Una felt restless and though she knew she ought to schedule a long-overdue meeting with Mrs. Brickenden to talk over household matters, she found herself shying away from the task. Maybe it was the fault of the balmy weather, she thought distractedly. Then she remembered Armand's words about wanting another outfit and headed back upstairs, determined that she would spend the morning sewing instead.

She had been interested last night to see that the crest of the de Bussells was a white winged horse on a field of dark blue. She dimly remembered Armand's shield had borne such a device at the May Day tournament, but she had not seen it since that day. Certainly, it was not displayed anywhere at Lynwode. Of course, he had inherited the place from his godfather, who was not a de Bussell, so that was hardly surprising.

Perhaps she ought to sew a banner to hang from the minstrel's gallery in the great hall, she pondered as she looked over her remaining stash of fabric. She had not been able to bring all of it from the palace, but she had a good quantity of blue she thought might be the right shade. She was just walking over to the bedchamber window to hold it up to the natural light when she heard Armand's step in the corridor outside.

"You've missed some excitement," he said, striding into the room and heading for the chest against the far wall.

"What excitement is that?"

"Roger came by to give a much-rehearsed apology to Miss Rose."

"Oh?" Una lowered the cloth. "How, pray, was it received?"

Armand shrugged. "She didn't even allow Roger to finish, I felt quite sorry for the lad. Told him his cause was hopeless for she loves another."

Una gasped. "She did? Was...um...Otho present?"

Armand shot her an inquisitive look. "No, though that talkative maid was there, hanging on every word, so no doubt it will soon be all over the house. Why?"

Una bit her lip. "I think Otho might be the object of her affections," she admitted.

"Otho?" Armand was incredulous. Then he laughed. "Who knows, maybe she'll balance him out. He's far too serious."

"I was thinking much the same earlier," she confessed.

"I wouldn't hold my breath if I were you," he warned her. "They seem a mismatch to me."

Una watched him covertly as he opened his trunk and began rooting around in there for something. "I'm thinking of sending to Muriel to see if I could borrow some representation of the family crest," she said aloud. "Do you suppose she would have some token she could send me?"

Armand rolled his eyes. "Sure to," he answered. "They're stiff-necked with family pride and past glory." He regarded her with sudden suspicion. "I don't want it emblazoned across my new tunic, mind."

Una smiled. "I would be a bit more subtle than that," she assured him. "Perhaps a small badge might be acceptable?" When he made no reply, she asked, "Can I help you locate what you are looking for?"

"I have it," he said, brandishing several wooden poles. At her curious look, he explained briefly, "It's for training the new men."

Una nodded. "Did you really mean what you said about my making you another suit of clothes?" she asked, choosing not to dwell on the fact he thought their outside servants would need to bear arms.

"Of course," he replied lightly. "I think another hat too, while you're at it."

"A hat?" She looked at him quizzically, wondering if he was merely trying to keep her busy instead of worrying over impending northerners. "Only…I received the distinct impression that you did not favor the hat," she admitted.

He frowned. "When?"

"At that first inn." She paused. Pointing out he had seemed happy to lose it did not seem terribly diplomatic. "You did not seem devastated by its loss," she replied instead with tact.

Armand lowered the lid of the trunk. "I think it's a bit much that I'm expected to stand by hatless," he said sternly, "while Fulcher swaggers around, bragging it is the best made hat he ever owned."

Una blinked. "Fulcher said that?" she uttered, feeling suddenly a lot more charitable toward the weasel-faced Fulcher.

"He did. He is inordinately proud that he owns a garment made by a princess's fair hands. Meanwhile my own wife refuses to make me another," Armand said in an aggrieved tone, climbing to his feet.

"Of course I'll make you another!" Una protested.

Armand crossed the room to kiss her briefly on the lips. "I'll see you at supper," he said, and Una realized he must be taking the new men's training very seriously if he meant to be about it all day.

She spent that afternoon in the solar and sent for Rose to keep her company. Mrs. Brickenden pulled a face, but Una was firm. "Rose has duties as my companion to fulfill also," she told the tight-lipped woman. "I would have you put out word in the village that we require another servant to pick up the buttery and kitchen duties."

When she imparted this to Rose, however, the girl did not seem as pleased as Una would have expected. In contrast to that morning, she looked suddenly pale and wan. She helped carefully cut the pattern pieces with Una, but was quiet and subdued and declined the opportunity to demonstrate her skill with the harp.

Una left the window where she had been watching Armand and Otho briefing the new men and returned to the pieces of fabric she had already cut out and left ready for sewing. "I have not yet heard you play."

"I'm putting that behind me, milady," Rose said, looking up from where she was kneeling, smoothing the fabric out. She gave a sad smile. "And all such frivolous things."

"Is all well with you, Rose?" Una asked with sudden concern. "You do not feel ill?"

Rose shook her head. "I am quite well," she assured her, but Una saw how Abelard circled the girl and sat at her feet gazing up at her with concern. She was not the only one to notice Rose's spirits had plummeted since that morn.

"I do hope that Master Roger's apology did not distress you," Una ventured, resuming her seat opposite Rose. She was reassured to see a look of genuine surprise flit over her face.

"Oh no, he apologized most prettily," Rose answered with apparent truthfulness, and they spent the afternoon quietly sewing the pieces for a replacement black and gold hat for Armand and a new blue tunic.

At supper, Una noticed a good many new faces along the table, which seemed to be filling up more at every meal. These assorted men had a more hardened edge, though they were as country-born and local as Peter. It did not take Una more than a few assessing glances to realize they had a look about them she recognized well. It was one born of experience. *Soldiers*, she thought and glanced at Armand, who was seating himself next to her. Armand had employed soldiers to work on their estate.

It was not that they were grim or dour, for when Armand stood and gave a short speech welcoming the new men to his table, they sent up a rousing cheer. When Mr. Beverley presented a large game pie and a side of roast beef, a spontaneous round of applause went up that made the cook quite flustered as he took his bow.

No, they were not morose, Una thought, but that they *were* determined to seize on any celebration or good fortune that came their way, for they knew too well the harsh reality of bad times. Armand bade the cups to be filled with wine for a toast, and Lynwode was proposed and drunk to.

"Everyone seems to be settling in well," Armand said as he waved aside the task of carving to Otho and instead poured Una another goblet of wine. "What say you?"

Una accepted the cup and took a sip. "I agree," she said with satisfaction. "I liked your speech and the fact our table is growing by the day. 'Tis only Mrs. Brickenden I am not yet sure of." She eyed the expressionless housekeeper who was out of earshot.

"What do you find amiss?" he murmured back, arching a black brow at her.

"She is too distant. Too reluctant to share any village news with me, or discuss her family or—"

"She is from round these parts?" Armand asked, suddenly sharp.

"Oh yes," Una assured him. "For several generations I believe." He relaxed. "Though I had to thank Janet for that fact."

"Well, if Mrs. Brickenden talks too little, then Janet talks too much," Armand responded dryly. "You should not encourage her."

"I like Janet," Una said staunchly, glancing down to where the merry-eyed servant was teasing bashful Peter. "Why should I not enjoy some local flavor in my household?"

He paused to consider this, taking a swig of wine. "In truth, there is no reason in the world, if you enjoy it. Did you send your message to Anninghurst?" he asked. "About the coat of arms?"

"Not yet," Una admitted. "I thought I had better write an accompanying letter to Muriel explaining why I wanted it."

He winced. "Ah yes, she's so tight-fisted, it's not likely she'd hand over anything without one. We now have a gardener's boy named Wat," he said, gesturing in the direction of a youth with straw-colored hair. "He can run it over once your letter is done."

"I had the idea I might try and fashion Muriel a velvet hood as a gift," Una confided. "But I thought I had better make one for Anne at the same time, or your sister might take umbrage. Rose wields a neat needle and can help me in my task."

"You think of everything," Armand replied. "But make sure you do not neglect your priority when it comes to keeping family members happy."

"My priority?" She met his laughing eyes. "And by that, I take it you mean my lord and master?"

His expression, which had been amused, swiftly changed to something else entirely. Leaning in, he quickly captured her lips with his own and lingered there. Another cheer went up from the rowdy end of the table, and Una found herself blushing when he drew back.

"Who else?" Armand murmured and took her hand in his. Una's heart was beating hard for the rest of the meal.

When Una retired upstairs, there was already a bath waiting, for Armand's at least had been a day of physical exertion. Una washed first but did not tarry as she knew her husband was having some final words with Otho below. She was just donning her shift when he entered the room, making straight for his bath.

"Shall I come and help you wash?" she offered, willing enough.

270

"Nay, I can scrub off my grime, never fear." He made short brisk work of stripping and washing while Una draped her drying cloth over a chair by the fire. "Get into bed," he urged her. "You'll get cold."

Una climbed into bed with some reluctance. She would have liked to fuss over him as he had with her evening before, but he did not seem in the mood to linger over his bath tonight. A pity. She remembered she owed him kisses from the previous day and wondered how to deliver them. She did not think she would ever have that ease of manner that meant spontaneous displays of affection would come readily to her. She could only hope that in time she might grow better at it.

She watched him rub a cloth vigorously over his muscular shoulders and did not wonder that his sister had told her that he had always been successful with the fairer sex. How she wished she knew how to flirt and flatter as he did! She knew herself to be wretchedly stiff and unaccustomed to such things. Would he eventually grow tired of a wife who had not the smallest notion how to play coy or coquettish?

The bed dipped and Armand slid between the covers with a sigh. He scooted against her at once, and Una's heart caught at how naturally he reached for her.

"Armand," she said before she lost her nerve, "shall we play dragon and the knight?" She was gratified by his look of surprised pleasure.

"That's an offer I don't think I'll ever decline," he answered with a slow grin.

That was an admission that could not help but give her confidence. She straightened her spine, shifting against the pillows. "You won't slay my dragon this time," she told him. "I have your measure, *Sir Lusty Loins*." His lips trembled. "Don't

271

laugh," she warned him, narrowing her eyes. "For I mean to have the upper hand this time, I assure you."

His eyes kindled. "That sounds only fair," he agreed, rolling onto his back. "Have at me, then." He patted his thigh as Una eyed him speculatively. He was naked beneath the sheets. Did she really have the nerve to do this? She took a deep breath and moved over to him.

"I think I shall have to incapacitate you," she mused, and his eyebrows shot up. She nodded thoughtfully. "Yes, my dragon must be permitted to have free rein over you," she said, placing a hand on his chest.

"How would it be if I simply swore to keep my hands above my head?" he asked.

She considered this. "If you think you can withstand it," she agreed.

"Withstand it?" he echoed.

"My onslaught." She could see him struggle to hide his smile at her words.

"I believe I'll stand firm," he answered with a decided twinkle in his eye.

I shall make you eat those words, she thought with sudden determination. "Very well, Sir Knight, if you are thus resolved."

He stretched his arms above his head. "How's this?"

Una looked him over, letting her eyes travel slowly from his handsome face, over his broad shoulders and impressive chest, down to where the sheets covered him. Slowly, she slid her hand down his muscular belly until she drew the sheet down over his muscular thighs. Armand's breathing hitched and his manhood grew stiff and swollen before her very gaze.

"I believe I shall accept this charming tribute," she said thoughtfully and felt his eyes burning into her as she reached up and swiftly undid her braid, running her fingers through her veil of auburn hair. Only then did she turn back to Armand, who was watching her appreciatively.

"A very beautiful dragon," he murmured as his gaze roved over her. "But I won't spare you all the same."

Una laughed softly. "Neither shall I you," she vowed and leaned slowly forward, affording him a view of her breasts, which were threatening to spill over the neckline of her shift as she swiftly straddled his lap until she sat squarely on his thick thighs, looking down at him.

"Such a pretty knight," she murmured. "I believe the King must have sent me his handsomest specimen. But I believe you have forgotten something." She raised a finger to her lips. "Where is your trusty staff, Sir Lusty Loins?"

Armand's eyes gleamed. "Oh, it's here, if you only know where to look." His eyes dropped to the bold thrust of his erection as if she might need a clue. In truth she could hardly miss it.

"Hmm," Una said, letting her eyes follow his. Armand let out a grunt of surprise as she ran her hand over his cock, boldly making out his shape.

"Ah yes, I *see*," she murmured. "A formidable weapon indeed. I look forward to testing its mettle."

His breathing was coming rapidly now as his cock further thickened and lengthened in her grasp, practically knocking against her belly for attention. She remembered how he had tutored her in his sensitive spots before and ran her fingers over the bulbous head, before reaching down to lightly trace the sizeable hairy ballocks at their root.

He shuddered and she halted, looking up quickly to check she was not doing anything he did not like. His face was flushed, and he had a tortured look, but even with her inexperience, Una could tell he did not dislike the attention she was paying him at all.

Now it was *her* turn to smile. She closed her hand around his shaft and lightly squeezed his pulsating length. He huffed out a breath and thrust his hips upward with a muffled oath.

"Harder?" she asked with a moment's uncertainty.

"Fuck, yes," he groaned.

Una gripped him more firmly, and he gasped, squeezing his eyes shut, the muscles in his thighs and stomach jumping as he craned toward her. Remembering how he had handled himself before now, she gave his shaft a firm pump that had him jerking upright.

"Una!"

She placed a hand on his chest, pushing him back down. "Ah-ah, Sir Knight. You said you would be able to withstand this, if you recall."

He was breathing raggedly, his eyes fixed to her face as she fluttered her fingers over the head of his cock, which was now slick with his fluids. He made a strangled noise in his throat as he placed his hands back under his head, submitting to her ministrations, though he was no longer relaxed, but primed and ready.

"Wicked dragon," he said thickly.

Una smiled, for in truth, the way he said it sounded like a compliment. She slid her fingers, now slippery, back down his shaft and pumped his impressive length again and again until he made that noise in his throat that was something between a cry and a whimper. Armand's eyes blazed, and he threw his head back against the pillows. When she paused, it seemed he could not help but burst out, "Don't stop! Ah gods."

"You forget," she told him, "that I am not some willing maiden eager to please you, but a dragon who means to devour you." She shifted back, retreating down his thighs, past his knees, and he tensed as though to catch her back up again.

"Where are you going?"

She ignored his sharp words, instead peeling down the thin straps of her shift, pushing the neckline down so that her breasts sprang free. Her actions seemed to have struck him silent apart from the rasp of his breath, but she did not dare look at Armand's face as she rearranged herself over the top of him, lowering herself between his legs until her full breasts pressed into his hairy thighs.

"Una," he groaned, and she pinched his hip.

"You keep forgetting the game," she told him breathlessly. "Do you want me to stop?"

He swallowed and shook his head. "No."

She leaned forward and blew softly on his cock, and he gave another harsh groan. Una took a deep breath. She was actually going to do this. She knew men liked it. She had heard her the lewd, unguarded talk of the northern soldiers often enough. And Armand put his mouth to her with every sign of pleasure, so she could not be wrong in this.

She moved forward, and taking his shaft in one hand, she ran her tongue along the underside of his turgid length. Dimly, she heard Armand's choked cry and she repeated the action, letting her tongue linger over the raised vein she could feel there.

When she reached the tip, she found more fluid had gathered there and, without thinking, darted her tongue there to taste him.

He gave a muffled yell at that, and fearing he would try to stop her, Una opened her mouth wide and closed it over the head of his cock, engulfing him in her mouth. She felt Armand jolt beneath her, and then he was sat bolt upright, his hands on her, urging her up his body.

"I can't stand any more," he said shakily when Una tried to protest. "You win, just let me inside you."

"Well, but—" She found herself dragged into his lap in a rather undignified fashion, with her breasts out and her hair spilling around her shoulders.

"Gods," he rasped, his eyes roaming over her hungrily. "You're so—"

Catching the expression on his face, Una felt like the most desirable woman in existence. He captured her lips in a kiss of sheer desperation, crushing his mouth to hers. Did they kiss last time they played this game? Then his fingers were between her legs and he was groaning again to find her wet for him.

"Armand!" she gasped reproachfully, for her lead role had clearly gone by the wayside now as he lifted her thigh and urged her to straddle his throbbing staff. She knew a moment's alarm when he thrust up and lodged deeply inside her. He felt extremely large from this angle. She winced and he stilled at once.

"Una?"

She moved tentatively on him and felt him ease further inside. "All is well," she assured him. He remained still as she resettled over him, lowering herself until they were both breathless and face-to-face, their nether hair intertwined. Then he leaned forward and kissed her, his hands in her hair. She could feel the sheer strength and eagerness in his body, yet still he held himself taut, even when she could feel the urgency thrumming through him.

"Ride me now, Una," he said, bouncing her on his cock, showing her the motion he craved. "Bear down on me, my sweet. Use me for your pleasure."

There was no playful talk of dragons now, she thought as one hand came to rest over the swell of her breast and the other squeezed her bottom. He was ready to burst and wanted her to reach her peak first. Una started the grinding motion he'd initiated, and he lowered his head to suck one nipple into his hot, wet mouth.

Una moaned, clutching his head as his hand moved from her hip to slide between her legs, and he concentrated, circling his thumb on that one sensitive spot between her legs that soon had her panting and gasping with need. Her movements became jerkier and less controlled as the excitement steadily built inside of her. Everything felt connected, Armand's sucking mouth, the pad of his thumb, and the steady throb of his deep penetration, all of it spurred her higher and higher, until finally with a cry, she blazed right up and burst in a shower of sparks behind her eyelids.

Then and only then, did Armand roll her onto her back and drive into her four or five times before he joined her in sweet oblivion, collapsing on top of her with a loud groan. After a moment or two, Una found she could muster enough strength to lift a hand and stroke his brow.

"I definitely came out on top in that encounter," she said drowsily.

"You really did," he agreed in a gravelly voice, then raised his head from her breast with a slight frown. "Where did you learn to do that?" When she hesitated, he looked alarmed. "Don't tell me I made you do it on our wedding night."

"No, of course not," she spluttered. "You worry far too much about that encounter, you know."

"Of course I do," he said gruffly. "I can't remember it and you were a virgin." He narrowed his eyes at her. "Weren't you?"

Una gazed up at him, speechless for a moment. "Of course I was," she said, shocked and meeting his hard gaze unflinchingly.

He drew back from her. "Did you have any lovers before me, Una?" he asked, and Una saw a faint color rise to his cheeks. She shook her head. *Where was this coming from?* "Then how did you know men like that?" he asked.

She hesitated to tell him her knowledge was gleaned from the ribald talk of soldiers. "I...heard things," she admitted. "You forget I was surrounded by rough soldiers for a good deal of the time. They were not coy when they discussed women."

Armand's brows snapped together. "They surely did not discuss such things around their princess!"

"Well, no, but... They weren't allowed to converse with me, you see," Una said. "And the campaign was so dreary and long, of course they wanted to speak of their wives and mistresses. In the end they sort of became inured to my presence. I think they forgot I was a real person."

Seeing his thunderstruck expression, she flailed around trying to extricate herself from the hole she had inadvertently dug herself into. "I ought not to have listened, of course. It was wrong of me, but I could not help but be curious about such things.

Especially when they talked about how even ugly women could please a man."

Armand stiffened. "Why should that interest you?" he asked sharply.

Una's face fell in dismay. Clearly, she was just making things worse. "Armand—" She reached out toward him tentatively. "I—I did not put my mouth on you on our wedding night, if that's what you're worried about."

He huffed out a breath. "That's not—" He broke off frustratedly. "Gods!" He ran his hand over his face. "Forget it. Of course you were a virgin." She read the regret in his expression and nodded. "I was insulting," he added and moved away from her. For one horrible moment, Una thought he would get out of the bed, but he was only leaning toward the candle to blow it out.

When he resettled next to her, he slid his arm around her waist and drew her close against him. "I'm sorry, Una," he murmured, and she closed her eyes as her throat worked hard to contain the sob that rose up in it. She had meant only to please him. Gods, what had she been thinking of? She lay racked with self-doubt for a long time before she drifted off to sleep.

12

For once Armand woke first the next morning, while Una still slept the sleep of the virtuous. He felt consumed with burning guilt, shame, and confusion. He crept out of their room and dressed in an empty one next door before making his way downstairs.

He was being a jackass. Worse than that. He was being a jealous, suspicious prick, and he had no right to be. Reacting angrily when your lover is better in bed than you expect her to be is ridiculous, but he couldn't seem to help himself. He had never been the jealous type. The best of his past lovers had been either married or widowed. Not for him fair blushing maidens who'd expect him to fix his interests. Usually any passion he felt for a woman burned out after the novelty of a new partner wore off. He'd always been a fickle bastard.

She'd said she was a virgin before him, and he believed her. If he hadn't seen the bloodstain on the sheets the morning after their marriage, her clear, untroubled gaze would have assured him sufficiently on that score. But that didn't mean that someone couldn't have taught her a few tricks along the way, and that thought enraged him. It didn't matter how many times he told himself he had no right to feel this way. For all he knew, she'd been betrothed a dozen times to foreign princes who'd be far worthier bridegrooms than him.

He felt a twisting, burning feeling in his chest when he thought of Una in someone else's arms. He had no earthly notion why. He'd never begrudged his previous lovers their experience, and he was angry that this time he felt different. He knew nothing about the men in Una's life before him. She could have been in love, for all he knew, with some fine upstanding northern hero. He gnashed his teeth at the thought. Some principled, noble type who'd never put a foot wrong in his life and deserved to win the hand of a princess.

Not like him, who hadn't even had the sense to be grateful when she'd landed in his palm like a ripe plum. No, he'd looked a gift horse in the mouth and pulled a face. Hemmed and hawed about how inconvenient it was for him to take a wife right now. He had expected her to bargain and plead with him to even take her rightful place at his side. He turned cold inside when he remembered how he'd tried to wriggle away from his obligations and just leave her there in that nest of vipers. He felt so full of self-loathing that it stung. Gods, he was a fucking asshole.

It didn't help that he'd always felt guilty as hell for the wedding night he must have given her. Drunk and practically unconscious, he supposed, was marginally better than drunk and rampaging with lust. But was it though? At least if he'd been in the mood to swive, he'd have given her his tongue or his fingers first. She must have been dry as dust, and he must have hurt her a good deal. He swore again. And then, to crown his folly, he'd gone and practically accused her of feigning her virginity!

He was appalled that Una could think she needed to learn additional tricks as she was not pretty enough to hold his attention. Surely it was obvious that he was wildly attracted to her? Having said that, the poison of court had likely wrought some damage even before their disastrous wedding night. He only hoped she had not done anything she found distasteful in the belief he needed added stimulus to bed her. Had she even wanted to play that damned dragon game with him, or had she felt duty-bound?

Could it be that Una still thought she had to be amenable in all things where he was concerned? He felt gnawed by doubt and closed his eyes a moment, feeling overwhelmed. There was no way he could put all this to rights. The only thing he could promise now was to start treating her with the respect she deserved and should have commanded from him from the very beginning.

"Bad head?" asked Otho with sympathy, and Armand saw his brother-in-law was sat in the great hall buttering bread. Armand grunted and joined him. "You're up early," Otho commented, and Armand surveyed him with disfavor. Otho pushed the platter of fried fish toward him. "Help yourself."

"Is no one else yet up?" Armand asked, glancing about with surprise.

Otho shook his head. "Just you and I."

Armand eyed him speculatively as he loaded fish onto his plate. "You prepared this meal?" Otho assented. "Why are you up so early?"

Otho set down the loaf and poured two cups of weak ale. "Couldn't sleep," he admitted, just as Armand had given up all expectation of a reply.

"Why?" Armand asked, glad of a distraction from his own worries. As soon as he asked, he realized his mistake. Of course, Otho was worried about the approach of suspicious northerners. Hearing that would only serve in making Armand feel even guiltier for not focusing on their real concerns right now. He scowled.

"I...er...had to speak to Rose yesterday," Otho admitted, avoiding his gaze. Armand's eyes widened. He took a bite of bread and butter. The fact he made no verbal reply seemed to unnerve Otho into speaking further. "I may have been a bit too harsh," he continued in a voice that rasped.

"She's still chasing after you, then?" Armand asked shrewdly.

Otho colored furiously. "Of course not!" A telltale flush was spreading right up his neck. Una's brother wasn't very good at lying, Armand thought wryly. "She's not that sort of girl. She just—she doesn't know what she's about, that's all!"

"She does seem a bit backward," Armand agreed.

Otho's eyes shot daggers back at him. "What do you mean by that?"

"Well…" Armand shrugged. "Just that she lives in a bit of a dream."

Otho's shoulders relaxed. "Precisely," he rapped out, but he still looked deeply uncomfortable, and after pushing his food around his plate a moment, he thrust it away from him uneaten.

"Has Una ever been betrothed to anyone but me?" Armand asked heavily before he could change his mind or Otho flung off in another mood.

Otho looked startled. "What? Why?"

"Answer the question."

Otho scratched his close-shorn head, and Armand wondered not for the first time why he wore it like that. He wasn't a pilgrim, so was he performing some kind of penance? "There was some talk of pledging her hand to some prince of the Western Isles," he said slowly. "But that was years ago, when she was just a girl."

"No one since?" Armand asked quickly.

Otho shook his head. "Once we embarked on war, there was precious little time to devote to royal alliances," he said with a shrug. "Our father had other worries on his mind."

"What about unofficially?"

"How do you mean?"

"You know, champions, admirers, that sort of thing."

Otho snorted. "You're thinking of the southern court," he said flatly. "We had no fripperies like that on our battlefields. My father jealously guarded his heir in any case. None of his generals were permitted to grow too close to her. Her personal guard was rotated every seventh day."

Armand considered Otho's words suspiciously. Their side had been losing, he supposed, but he still thought Una's brother rather naive if he thought a man still wouldn't notice an attractive woman, even in the midst of battle. Armand knew he would notice. Well, if it was Una he would. Besides, there *was* a general she had been close to. The one who had told her about the hidden treasure troves. "What was the name of your father's general killed at Kettelbrooke?" he asked, recalling suddenly where Una said the man had fallen.

"General Brunold," said Otho in startled tones.

"What was he like?" Armand demanded. "Young? Handsome?"

Otho stared at him. "He had a hunched back and was sixty-five if he was a day."

"I must be thinking of someone else," Armand mumbled. Yes, jealousy definitely needed adding to his ever-growing list of faults as a husband. "Una's not fond of that housekeeper you hired," he said in a swift change of subject.

"I know," Otho answered glumly. "She's made no secret of the fact. Hasn't liked her from the start." He looked pained. "That might have been my fault too."

"How so?"

"I didn't consult her," Otho admitted. "She felt I went over her head and left her out of the decision-making."

Something was definitely amiss with Otho today, Armand reflected. He seemed filled with self-doubt and misgivings, not his usual brusque self at all. It was at that point that a sober-faced young woman appeared before them in a gray headscarf and gown. Had they hired a new maid?

"Good morning, masters," she said in a colorless voice. "There's a traveler at the door asking to speak with you, Sir Armand." Otho made a choked noise, and Armand glanced quickly in his direction to find him staring at the girl transfixed. He looked back to the maidservant and was astonished to see that it was Rose. She was almost unrecognizable with her hair scraped back and covered and clad in such drab clothes. "Shall I let him in?" she asked when neither of them responded.

"No," Armand said, rising quickly to his feet. "I'll first go and see who this stranger is." He half expected Otho to join him, but his brother-in-law sat staring after Rose, who had bobbed a curtsey and disappeared in the direction of the kitchens.

Armand paused in the passageway to strap on his sword belt and then made his way to the front entrance, where a bearded man of medium build dressed in a brown tunic was waiting for admittance. Instead of letting him in, Armand stepped out to join him outside. "You have business here?" he asked, warily sizing the stranger up. He wore no sword at his hip and looked far from threatening with his mild expression. "I would ask what that is?"

The man smiled pleasantly enough and showed Armand his hands first and the fact there was nothing concealed up his sleeves, then he reached slowly into a pouch attached to his belt and drew out a folded and sealed document. "I have here a letter of introduction from Lord Vawdrey," he said smoothly as he handed it over.

Armand's eyebrows rose as he inspected the seal showing the well-known insignia of the Vawdrey panther with the earl's distinctive coronet. He motioned for the stranger to follow him, and they walked around the side of the house. "I am not going to read this letter now," he said shortly. "What is your name and who the hells are you?"

"It's Walker, sir," the other answered readily enough. "Though who I am is not important. I am a mere agent of Lord Vawdrey's in this business, and by extension, the King's."

Armand stopped short and turned abruptly to face him. "What the devils does the King want with me?" he barked. "I fail to see why he should have any outstanding business with me."

Walker's eyebrows rose at this and he cleared his throat. "I am sure you have heard tell of Lord Vawdrey's reputation, sir," he said, dropping his voice, and Armand's eyebrows snapped together. Everyone knew the King's chief advisor was also his spymaster.

"He is a cautious man, Sir Armand. Naturally when you set forth from Caer-Lyoness with a certain personage of close relation to the King, he sent others to watch over you from a safe distance."

Armand stared at the man, who gazed impassively back. "He set spies on me?" he asked hotly.

Walker cleared his throat. "A rather harsh word," he said reproachfully. "For the task entrusted to us."

Armand suddenly remembered Fulcher's mention of a black-hooded figure who changed horses frequently and dipped in and out of view. *Professionals.* "Just how many of you are there?"

he asked hollowly. Fulcher had thought there was only one man on their tail, yet Walker spoke now as if there were several.

Walker shrugged. "The number is immaterial at this point. We were given specific orders to follow your progress and ensure you reached your home safely."

At this point Armand suffered another unpleasant realization. If they had been following them, then they must be aware of what had occurred at The Merry Wayfarer. He regarded the man narrowly. "If that is so, you must know we were nearly slaughtered in our beds at one point," he said damningly.

For the first time, Walker looked a little uncomfortable. He cleared his throat. "Alas, we suffered an unforeseen setback and lost some time en route. When we arrived the next morning, we had a hell of a jolt at the scene that met us." He lowered his eyes discreetly. "We were, however, happily able to tidy up the aftereffects. Perhaps you made inquiries? It was put about that the landlord and his staff fled into the night after the untimely death of a pilgrim on his premises."

Armand colored slightly. "I made no inquiries," he admitted. Perhaps if he had done, this would not come now as such a shock to him. "What did you do with them? Shallow graves?"

Walker looked shocked. "Certainly not, Sir Armand. They were decently buried as plague victims some fifty miles away from that spot and without hint of scandal."

Yes, they were professionals alright. Armand eyed him warily. "So, you followed us here," he said abruptly. "Why did you not return then to Caer-Lyoness once the task was done?"

Walker scratched his beard. "Following you here was only half of the job," he admitted and gave Armand a wry smile.

"Half the job?"

"Once you were settled, we were to ensure you continued that way. Untroubled, shall we say, by any who would 'unsettle' you."

"You mean northerners who might want to snatch my wife," said Armand forthrightly. He was tired of beating around the bush.

Walker sucked in a breath as one unaccustomed to such plain speech. "In short, sir, yes."

Armand was silent a moment. "Have you had many to deal with?" he asked harshly. Had he been living in some sort of fool's paradise? Otho was right. He had not had a clue what he was getting himself into.

"One or two," Walker said with a shrug. "Nothing me and the boys couldn't deal with." Armand found he could well believe him, despite the apparent affability. He looked sturdy enough and carried himself with a quiet assurance Armand was starting to think others would be foolish to overlook. "Any interested parties have dwindled away to a mere trickle now," Walker said easily. "We've been kicking our heels for the most part."

"Why have you made yourself known to me now?" Armand asked. That was the only part he couldn't fathom. Why had they come out of the shadows?

Walker scratched the side of his face. "For two reasons," he admitted. "The first, it seems to me you aren't as guileless as you make out, Sir Armand." Walker's gaze flickered over him speculatively. "Been taking on a few soldiers of your own recently, haven't you? As such, I reckon you might as well take some of our number in among your ranks. We're doing much the same job. What's the point of us sneaking around the vicinity when you've enough muscle gathered at your own table?"

Armand shot him a look. "Well, that's plain-speaking enough," he said dryly. "What's the second reason?"

Walker hesitated. "Has your lady wife ever mentioned her surviving siblings to you, sir?"

"She only has one left; he acts now as my steward."

"I do not speak of the bastard Otho Fitzroy," Walker replied swiftly.

Armand swung around to look at him in surprise. "Who, then?" When Walker did not reply at once, Armand stared at him keenly. "Una told me she had four illegitimate brothers. Two born to noblewomen and two to commoners."

"True enough," Walker agreed. "Forwin and Waleran were born to noble houses. Otho and Umrey to obscurity."

"Una said the first two were promised great riches and honor if their cause had prevailed," Armand continued slowly.

"Yes. Forwin was the elder and perished like so many others at Demoyne." Walker paused. "It was initially believed Waleran was also a casualty of that battle, but since then, other facts have emerged. In short, his life was spared, though he teetered on the brink of death for a while with a grievous head wound."

"He's still alive?" There was a lump in Armand's throat. "Are you saying he means to rally northerners to the Blechmarsh cause again?"

Walker shook his head. "He has neither the means nor the following." He hesitated. "Waleran's injury unbalanced him. No man of sense would get behind his banner now. Even his own kinsmen have renounced him."

"What are you telling me?" Armand asked harshly. "That my wife's brother is a madman?"

289

Walker looked grave. "It's hard to predict the course of action such a man will take. Lord Vawdrey would not have the Lady Una troubled by this matter," he said quietly. "Not for the world. He thinks it would be wise, however, to give *you* fair warning."

Armand had a bad feeling in the pit of his stomach. "And Vawdrey thinks this Waleran *will* try to approach her?"

"Lord Vawdrey is keen to eliminate any chance of that happening," Walker said staunchly. "However remote that possibility may be."

*

Una spent a miserable morning by herself in the solar with only Abelard for company. When Rose brought her up some midday refreshment, she was distracted from her own woes by the marked change in that young woman. Una had never seen her in anything so drab as the gray woolen gown she wore, with her pretty hair tucked away.

"Why, Rose, where is your pretty gown this morn?"

Rose bobbed a discreet curtsey, nothing like her usual one of sweeping grace. "I'm putting such foolishness behind me, milady," she answered, startling Una a good deal as she set down the dish of pastries and cheese. Rose bent down to return Abelard's greeting. "I mean to take Janet as my example in future. This gown is one she kindly helped me alter." She touched the headscarf to check none of her hair was escaping.

"But…why?" Una asked, mystified.

"It's high time," said Rose, promptly straightening up. "I'm not a girl anymore, but a woman of two and twenty. I've moved out of the larger bedchamber and in with Janet," she added. "She's happy to share with me and it's more fitting to my station."

Una regarded her silently a moment. "If this is because you think you somehow invited Roger's attentions yesterday, Rose, then I can assure you that you did no such thing."

Rose looked blank. "Oh, Master Roger," she said, as if she had forgotten his very existence. Then confessed quite simply, "I do not think of him at all, milady."

Una opened her mouth to ask if this change, then, was in response to something Otho had said. Something stopped her from voicing the suspicion. If it was, then clearly Otho's words held an impact for Rose that should not be taken lightly. "And you are not unhappy?" she asked instead.

Rose gave a reassuring shake of her head. "No, milady."

"And...you do not find Mrs. Brickenden unkind?"

Rose blinked. "Unkind? No, milady. She scolds, but only where it's deserved, and Janet agrees with me on that score."

Una considered this. Perhaps she had done Mrs. Brickenden a disservice. "Would you tell Mrs. Brickenden to come to me this afternoon, when it is convenient for her?" she asked at last.

"Of course, milady." Rose bobbed again, cast a fond look at Abelard, and was gone. Una could not help but feel deeply disturbed by the recent development.

Mrs. Brickenden appeared before Una had even finished her meal. She had just handed a meat pastry to Abelard when the housekeeper's thumping step was heard on the stairs. Abelard, showing a new boldness, circled on a rug before lying down to enjoy his treat.

"Milady," said the housekeeper, appearing on the threshold.

"Please come in," Una invited, gesturing to a chair. She could see Mrs. Brickenden's reluctance to take a seat but kept her hand extended. After a moment, the older woman seemed to accept the inevitability and lowered herself onto a chair. "I wanted to ask you how you think you are settling into the role here at Lynwode."

Mrs. Brickenden's cautious features became even closer if that was possible. "Tolerably well, thank you, milady," she said repressively.

"You have acted before as chatelaine to a large household, I think."

Mrs. Brickenden relaxed infinitesimally. "I have, for Lady Mildred over Upper Derring for thirty years."

"It must be difficult adapting to a different place," Una commented mildly. Mrs. Brickenden's lips tightened but she made no comment. "I presume that at your last place, you reported to the steward," Una plunged on. "Here at Lynwode, I expect you to report directly to me at least once a week. I trust that will not be a problem."

The color in the older woman's cheeks rose. After a moment, she gave a short nod. "This morning, Rose told me she has moved out of the old housekeeper's room. I understand you will not require it as you live in the village still with one of your daughters."

Mrs. Brickenden took a deep breath. "I do, milady."

Una waited, but nothing more was forthcoming. Really, it was like trying to draw blood from a stone. "Tell me, what do you think of this recent change in Rose?" she said aloud. "I would value your opinion."

Mrs. Brickenden snorted. "Girls get these wild starts," she said after a moment and shook her head. "I raised two of my own, so I should know."

"You do not think it anything we should concern ourselves about?"

Mrs. Brickenden's bushy eyebrows shot up. "Certainly not," she said forcibly. "The sensible thing," she said stoutly, "is to let it play out. She and Janet are thick as thieves at present. She'll soon settle down to some middle ground."

Una regarded her with something approaching approval. "That does sound sensible," she concurred. "Now, I should like to show you my lists for new furnishings about the place. Let us consult one another about what needs doing."

*

Una had felt a good deal cheered after her interview with Mrs. Brickenden, but as supper approached without the slightest glimpse of Armand about the place, she began to suffer misgivings. Their "bed sport" of the previous evening had gone badly awry. Clearly, she was not supposed to be the aggressor or show initiative, however much he had seemed to enjoy it at the time.

She would have to apologize and hope things straightened back out again on an even keel. Feeling foolish, Una relegated her efforts to be bold and flirtatious to the scrapheap. She was clearly not cut out for such things and had given Armand a disgust of her by even trying. Perhaps men did not want that type of thing from their wife after all?

She dressed for supper with some deliberation, choosing a deep red gown she had not worn before, which had beautiful sleeves decorated with gold thread. Her hair she caught up in a gold hairnet, and after attaching a short gold veil with a couple of pins, she thought she could delay the inevitable no longer and went below stairs. She had hoped Armand would come to their room to change before supper, but he had not appeared, so she would simply have to face him at table. She hoped to goodness he wasn't avoiding her.

At first, her fears were heightened considerably, for other than a perfunctory kiss to her fingers, Armand was distant. However, when he subsequently failed to notice the entrance of Mr. Beverley with the roasted meats, she realized he was simply distracted.

"This looks wonderful," she told the crestfallen cook and nudged Armand, who was gazing moodily at the far end of the table.

"Yes," he agreed belatedly. "Good work, Beverley." The cook beamed and took his place next to Mrs. Brickenden.

"Is anything wrong, husband?" Una asked when Armand continued abstracted. "Shall I pour your drink?"

Armand gave a start. "Naught," he said hastily and reached for the wine, climbing to his feet. "Fill the cups," he yelled down the table, and Janet sprang to her feet wielding a pitcher of ale. Armand started pouring wine into the cups of those around him. "Otho," he prompted when his steward seemed almost as slow to act as himself that evening.

Otho tore his gaze away from the same direction and set to carving the meat for the plates. Glancing down the table at what was absorbing them, Una was astonished to see even more men gathered at the foot of the table. They were packed in very close. Soon, Una realized, if their number kept increasing at this rate, they would need to start seating people at the other two tables that took up the length of the great hall.

A few of the new men seemed to be boisterously trying to catch Rose's attention with jests and sallies. Even that ugly headscarf could not distract from her pretty face. Una noticed Mrs.

Brickenden rap the table with her broad knuckles and the men's gazes dropped at once respectfully and order was restored.

Once the plates were filled with meat and passed down and the cups of wine distributed, Armand cleared his throat. Again, he gave a speech welcoming any newcomers to their table and toasted Una as mistress of the house. These sentiments were duly echoed, and everyone fell upon their food.

Supper was a noisy affair that evening, and conversation was only stilted at their end of the table. Elsewhere, the murmur of voices rose to the rafters and even the occasional ring of laughter was heard. Otho was tight-lipped and morose, though in truth, he was never exactly effervescent company. As for Armand, he fell into abstraction and even seemed to forget to eat, except in fits and starts.

Una found she missed the loquaciousness of Fulcher, who could always be depended on to keep a steady stream of conversation, but he was not due back with them for some weeks now. Una racked her brain for things to talk brightly about, but in truth she did not think her husband or brother attended her, until she mentioned a proposed trip to Great Derring that herself and Mrs. Brickenden had decided to take upon the morrow.

"No!" both Armand and Otho exclaimed at the same time.

Una lowered the wine cup she had been raising to her lips. "But tomorrow is the market that Mrs. Brickenden thinks we might be able to find the linens we require—" she started patiently. Again, she was interrupted.

"I forbid it," Armand said almost simultaneously to Otho barking out another negative. Armand eyed Otho darkly, and Otho lapsed into silence. "It's not convenient at this time," Armand continued after a slight pause.

Una was speechless for a moment. "Very well," she said at last, rather taken aback. He had never forbidden her to do anything before.

"The Brickenden woman can go if you like," he added as an afterthought.

Una wasn't sure she trusted the housekeeper's taste. "Perhaps next week," she murmured and got a heavy frown for a reply. Clearly, she thought, she was not in Armand's good books, but surely this could not stem from her woeful attempts to please him in the bedchamber. She eyed him uncertainly, but precious few other words fell from his lips for the duration of the meal.

Abelard trotted happily between Una and Rose in search of tidbits and found neither of them ate a great deal that night, so his belly was nicely rounded by the close of it. When Una announced she was withdrawing upstairs at the close of the meal, Armand nodded absently.

"I shall be up later," he said, and she thought his shoulders seemed to relax, as though he would be able to speak more freely without her around.

She felt a stab of pain at this telling reaction, but hoped she masked it with her tight smile. "Of course, good night all," she answered smoothly and departed with her dog trotting at her heels, mounting the staircase with a heavy heart.

Una had shut her bedchamber door behind her and was crossing the room, pulling pins from her veil, when she first realized something was amiss. Abelard started a low growl that startled her, and she turned around to find the little dog staring fixedly at the large carved cupboard in the corner.

As Una turned to contemplate it, someone stepped out of the shadows, confounding her. A likeness confronted her that she had believed had gone to the grave. She drew in a shocked breath, even as doubt came rushing in. "Waleran?" she muttered, falling back a step. "Is that truly you?" Somehow, he seemed altered. The boyish face had grown sharper and leaner and he now wore a pointed beard upon his chin. But there was something else she could not quite put her finger on that seemed changed about him.

"Hello, sister," her youngest brother muttered with a peculiarly unpleasant smile. "You seem surprised to see me?"

"I heard tell that you were dead. With Forwin at Demoyne," she added through lips that felt suddenly numb. Her brain raced. *What could Waleran be doing here now?* She glanced surreptitiously about the room, but could see no other men lurking, or indeed, any other places they could be concealed.

"I am alone," he said, deducing her thoughts. "I did try to rally some men along the way, but alas, none of them had the stamina required for our cause. I am all alone in all the world, apart from you, sister," he added. "Blood calls to blood."

It was an unpleasant notion. "Nay, that is not true, for we have another brother remaining to us," she said bracingly. "Otho is still alive," she told him. "He is below stairs; I could fetch him now—"

"Otho!" he spat. "What do I care for that lowborn churl?"

Una hesitated. There was an empty glitter in Waleran's eye that she did not think had been there before. He had been spoiled and indulged from an early age. His mother's family had been a prominent one in the north, but she had never found him as overbearing as Forwin. "How is your mother? And your grandfather?" Una asked, hoping to find safer ground.

"Do not speak to me of those traitors," he pronounced savagely. "They are dead to me now!"

Una regarded him with dismay. "Traitors?" She faltered. "You must be mistaken, brother. The House of Kimarne fought bravely to the end and lost many sons."

"End?" he seethed. "What end? If they were faithful, they would be fighting these southern dogs still!"

"The north was defeated," Una said softly. "And we laid down our arms."

"Lies!" he burst forth, and Abelard let out an indignant bark. Waleran lunged angrily at the little dog, and Una snatched him up, misliking the furious look in Waleran's eye. She ran for the door, but Waleran was on her in an instant, seizing her arms in a painful grip and wheeling her around.

"Do not try to escape me, sister!" he said, shaking her so hard her teeth rattled. "I come to free you from this intolerable oppression!" Flecks of spit were escaping from his lips and he looked quite crazed.

"No!" Una burst out as Abelard cowered in her arms. "I'm not going anywhere with you, Waleran! This is my home now!"

"Home!" he yelped angrily. "You dare to—" He broke off his words in a towering rage. For a moment she thought he would strike her. "Traitorous jade!" he flung at her. "You're a disgrace to our father, whose name you should venerate! Instead, I find you have taken another! You have besmirched his memory!"

Una gazed at him in alarm. This was not the Waleran she remembered, who had been the cosseted pet of his family. What had happened to him?

"Look at you!" he choked out, his eyes roaming over her. "I scarcely recognize you as a Blechmarsh anymore! So steeped are you in southern ways and wickedness, I would take you for one of *them*." The bitterness rose in his voice. "There is only one way for me to purge you of such sin," he muttered, nodding his head. "Just one way for you to be saved." To her horror he drew a wicked-looking blade from his sleeve.

"No, brother!" The words were wrenched from her, and his lips stretched horribly into a grimace she realized was a grin. His painful grip on her arm prevented her from retreating.

He pressed the blade to her side, and she felt it pierce the material of her gown and graze her skin underneath. "Open the door," he said softly.

Una drew a deep breath. She knew for two pins he would drive the blade into her. If she screamed, it was likely he would do it now. If he made her walk down the stairs, however, there were many men down there. Men with blades of their own. She reached for the door and opened it.

"Now turn," he said. "No, not in that direction. We will take the backstairs."

Una closed her eyes an instant. *Damn it.* He propelled her forward and she was forced down the corridor before him. She could feel the dagger at her waist with every step and Waleran's ragged breathing into her ear. "How did you make your way through the house?" she asked. "Without anyone seeing you?"

He sniggered. "Your fine husband has so many new men running round the place it wasn't hard to slip in among their number. I was always clever, even Father thought so. He just didn't think I applied myself as I ought." His tone turned brooding, and Una eyed him warily.

Every time she felt Abelard tense to spring, she tightened her arms around him. She would have to try to set him down somewhere safely, but if he jumped out of her arms now on the narrow staircase, she would not put it past Waleran to kick him down the remaining steps.

As they reached the bottom, Waleran inhaled sharply, and looking up, Una saw a shadow on the wall drawing closer to them along the corridor. Suddenly, Rose was at the foot of the stairs, gazing up at them. Her stillness seemed to unnerve Waleran. "Get rid of her," he gritted through his teeth at Una, and she felt the point of the blade pierce her skin.

"Rose, this is my brother," Una said, and felt the point dig further making her draw a pained breath. "You must let us pass out into the garden now," she choked out as her brother's hand closed tight about her upper arm.

Rose took a step back, but kept her gaze fixed on them. Seeing Rose was too much temptation for Abelard, and he sprang from Una's arms for freedom. As he landed on his feet, Waleran aimed a vicious kick at the small dog, and he went skittering into the wall with a yelp.

"Don't!" Una cried and Rose whirled about. For a moment, Una's heart froze thinking the slight girl would tackle Waleran. Instead, she seized fast on his other arm, breathing deeply through her nostrils as though trying to contain great anger.

"Get off me!" Waleran snarled, but Rose's face was fixed and white and she did not speak to him, just glared at him with grim determination. "What is this?"

Una shook her head, and when he pressed harder, she cried out, "I do not know." If Rose was not so unique, she might have run for help, Una thought despairingly.

"Keep your voice down, or it will be the worse for you!" he threatened her.

"Where are we going?" Una demanded. Surely, they would not get far. Not with Waleran, hindered now in his flight by two women.

"You'll find out," he gloated, half shoving her through a side door. He tried to shake Rose off his arm but failed. "Well, if she wants to share our fate, she can," Waleran sneered. When he shut the door in Abelard's face, preventing him from following, the little dog flung back his head and started to howl. At least he would take no further hurt, Una thought, and maybe eventually his cries would alert the household that they were missing.

To her surprise, Waleran did not take them around the front of the house but headed instead down the garden. Una craned her eyes to scan for waiting horses or more men, but she could see no one else in the shadowy grounds save for the three of them. He must have been speaking the truth, she thought, about being alone.

Suddenly, out of the darkness the ruins loomed far above them. With mounting dread, Una realized Waleran was making a beeline for them. She dragged her feet and shot a glance at Rose, whose eyes were still fixed sternly on Waleran's eager profile. Did Rose even realize the danger they were in? she wondered.

Una ran her tongue over her dry lips. "These ruins are treacherous," she said desperately. "I have been warned to stay far away from them."

"You need have no fear," Waleran assured her, coming abruptly to a stop at the bottom of the disintegrating stairwell. He flung them both before him, so both women stood at the foot of the steps. "They will serve our purpose. I have tested them."

Una stared, for surely she could see a glow of light around the first bend and in the remains of the chamber at the very top. Had he set torches in the old sconces? "You have tested the stairway?" she repeated weakly. "Waleran, the steps do not lead anywhere except into the sky."

He nodded gleefully. "They will lead to our eternal glory." He was mad, Una thought with terrifying certainty. Quite mad.

He stabbed the air with his dagger. "Get moving," he said with menace and walked toward them. Given precious little choice, Una reached her hand out to take Rose's and they started climbing the steps with Waleran following close behind them.

13

Armand was descending the stairs two at a time when Otho appeared at the bottom, ashen-faced. "Well?" his brother-in-law demanded.

"She's not in the solar or the attics," Armand replied tersely. They looked at each other grimly. Armand had told Otho of Lord Vawdrey's message that afternoon, and no doubt they were both thinking the same thing. The house was now in uproar with servants running hither and thither. Armand flung up a hand. "Silence!" he roared. "Where's that dog barking?"

"Sir, he's in the kitchens," Janet said, round-eyed. "Creating ever such a racket he is, none of us can quiet him without Rose and she's nowhere to be found either."

"Rose is missing?" Otho uttered sharply, but Armand was already making for the kitchen where Abelard was scrabbling at the back door.

"Do not let him out!" Mr. Beverley cried, not realizing who was snatching the door open. "If he runs away, there will be hell to pay!"

As soon as it had been flung wide, Abelard hurled himself outside and Armand followed, pursued by a mob. Abelard pressed his tiny nose to the ground and headed straight down the garden. Armand followed him, his eyes intent on the dog. Someone behind him let out a cry.

"Look! Someone is at the top of the tower!"

"They must be mad!"

Armand glanced up with dread and saw the tower was illuminated with golden light streaming out of the little chamber room poised at the top of the winding steps. His heart stuttered and then started beating again twice as fast. He could see Una's red dress and the glitter of the gold net in her auburn hair. She was stood at the very top, with a shadowy figure on either side of her.

Janet let out a lusty wail. "It's the mistress!"

The babble and clamor that greeted her words seemed to propel Armand out of his stunned horror. He ran until he'd closed the distance between himself and the ruin. Finding Abelard poised at the bottom step, he scooped up the little dog and turned, dumping him in the arms of the first servant he spied.

It was Janet's swain, Peter. "What will we do, sir?" He gulped.

"Keep hold of the dog," Armand told him in clipped tones and made for the steps. Walker and Otho were close behind him.

"Stay where you are!" a voice bellowed down from above. "Or the princess will suffer for it!"

"Princess?" Armand heard voices behind him murmur in confusion. Maybe he should have mentioned that prior to this. There were lots of things in retrospect he could not help but feel he had handled badly. First and foremost, his woeful attempts to secure his property. By taking on so many in such a short space of time, he had let this stranger slip into their midst and steal his greatest treasure. He had much rather he had emptied his attic strong room than taken Una. Icy fingers of dread traced down his spine as he gazed up at the figures so far above him. Was he not to get the chance to set any of this to rights?

"It *is* him!" Otho breathed in disbelief. "It's Waleran. He's taken them hostage up there."

Armand froze on the fourth or fifth step up. He could see Una holding out her hands palm up as she tried to remonstrate with

304

the bastard. What the fuck was she doing? He felt his throat constrict and gave an agonized groan. Even worse, she kept trying to step protectively in front of Rose. He ground his teeth, refusing to let these charades distract him from his pale wife. He focused on Una as if the force of gaze from his eyes alone could keep her standing upright instead of plummeting like a stone from the ramparts.

Armand felt the fear settle like a pit of dread in his stomach. He was going to fucking lose her. And she didn't even know, didn't have a fucking clue how he felt… A hand clutched at his shoulder. Otho was stood on the step beside him. "Una is a sensible lass," he heard Otho murmur desperately. "She'll keep her head." He was right. Una would keep her head in a crisis. But she would not put herself first. She never did.

Armand's gaze swept up the crumbling flight again as he furiously estimated how long it would take him to reach the top, but he knew he wouldn't stand a chance of interception. She was going to fall. He knew it in his heart of hearts. It was his punishment for not appreciating her until it was too damn late. He felt sick to his soul. Terrified. He realized he'd never even known true fear in his life until this moment.

He stared up at her, desperately trying to will her to have some fucking sense and not incite her crazed brother. He muttered an involuntary oath as the two women suddenly huddled together, seemingly trying to crane as far from Waleran as possible. The bastard flung back his head and laughed. There were only three walls fully intact of the small chamber, so you could see the three of them clearly outlined against the gray stone where a torch flickered from the sconce.

Waleran held out a hand, as though asking one of them to dance. Both Una and Rose shrank back. Then Una was speaking again, and Armand advanced a few more steps, his mouth drawn into a grim line as Waleran's attention was focused on his sister. Then it looked as though Rose had said something, for his attention turned to her.

Waleran looked to be ranting at both of them in turn. It looked like they were arguing or interrupting him for he flung out a hand in frustration. In truth, Armand couldn't tell which one of them was mouthing off, but he felt sick with fear it might be Una. *Keep your goddamn mouth shut, woman*, he raged inwardly as he heard Walker's footfall behind him. Glancing back in warning, Armand saw the man held a bow and arrow. "Can you reach him with your bow?" Armand asked hoarsely.

Walker paused, sizing the situation up. "Not without risk to the two women," he admitted.

Armand cursed under his breath, climbing further as the women now had their abductor's sole focus. He kept low and close to the wall.

Una was speaking again, and though Armand could not hear her words, he could tell her tone was both reasonable and measured. Waleran looked to be grinding his teeth with frustration, and he clapped both his hands to his head in a sudden fury. Armand froze, and Rose stepped swiftly forward, thrust out both her arms, and gave a mighty shove to their assailant.

Waleran's mouth opened wide in a silent shriek and his arms windmilled as he found himself suddenly stepping back and treading thin air. His footing lost, he made a wild grab for her but went sailing over the edge. For a horrifying moment, it looked like Rose's momentum would carry her over as well, but Una lunged forward and caught her about her waist, dragging her back onto the ledge. Both women collapsed onto their backsides and Armand found he could suddenly breathe.

"Rose!" cried Otho brokenly, some ten steps or so behind. It sounded as if her name had burst involuntarily from his lips.

"Sweet lord," murmured Walker, who was somehow close behind him now. *"Did you see that?"*

A dull, heavy thud behind them heralded the would-be assassin's ignominious landing on the ground. Ignoring the muffled shrieks below, Armand kept his eyes trained on the red figure, never looking away as he clenched his jaw.

"Stay where you are, Una," he called tightly as he closed the gap between them. He turned back seeing some of his men starting toward the staircase. "No more on the steps!" he ordered. "It is not fit for the weight of so many!" He saw them turn back and go instead to inspect the body that had fallen to one side of the tower.

Una and Rose were both sat now with their backs to the remaining wall. Una looked very pale. Armand found he could not tear his eyes from her face to check on Rose. Otho was here for her anyway. He took the steps two at a time, and the higher he climbed, the more his fear receded. It was swiftly replaced with a burning anger that gnawed at his guts and left a nasty taste in his mouth.

He couldn't take it out on that bastard Waleran, so that left only one recipient for his wrath. *His wife.* What the bloody hell did she think she was doing prancing around up there, risking life and limb and nearly giving him some kind of seizure?

"I'll remain here," Walker said loudly. "In case you should need another pair of hands if one of them should swoon."

And then, with another few steps, Armand was at the top. He stepped onto the stone platform and reached down to grab Una by her elbows, pulling her upright. "Come to me," he said roughly, and she came.

"Rose," she said, trying to turn back.

"Otho is behind me. He will help Rose down."

"Did you hear that, Rose? Do not stir a step," Una said, admonishing the maid.

Armand's arm about her waist propelled her forward. "Watch your step here," he ground out. "It's uneven."

"I know. I would have stumbled if not for Rose. She is as surefooted as a goat."

He ignored this, pushing her flat against the wall as Otho reached their step. He braced himself in case her brother dared to try to snatch her from him. Instead, Otho merely reached out a hand to squeeze Una's shoulder. She patted his hand.

"I'm fine, Otho," she reassured him. "You go and fetch Rose down." Her brother nodded and advanced to the top. Armand heard him rumble something but did not catch the words.

Rose's voice carried down to them clearly. "He was a bad man," she said mutinously. "He kicked Abelard."

Una made a choked sound. "He wanted us to die together," she said wonderingly. "As some sort of grand gesture."

Armand did not answer, could not. "No fainting," he called down to Walker, who was waiting at the midway point. "You go down and we'll follow."

Glancing back up, he saw that Otho was still crouched beside Rose, as though talking some sense into her. Perhaps he did not want to risk all of them on the steps at the same time. Armand kept his grip on Una's waist. They followed Walker's descent cautiously, five steps or so behind him at any given time.

When they finally reached the bottom, Armand waited with bated breath for the sick feeling of relief to subside, so he could once again breathe easy. Watching Una raise a shaky hand to her face and swipe her eyes made something inside him snap. Suddenly he felt a tide of feeling so strong that he grabbed her upper arms in a biting grip and yanked her forward against his chest, holding her tight and breathing deeply against her hair. He met Walker's gaze over the top of her head for an instant before the other man nodded. Armand responded in kind and then it seemed the spell of heavy silence around them was lifted.

An impromptu smattering of applause broke out among their household huddled around the foot of the tower. Armand glanced over and saw someone had spread their cloak over the dead body.

"Armand?" Una asked in muffled tones from against his chest. He squeezed her harder, not willing yet to loosen his hold of her.

Approaching footsteps made him look up to see Otho and Rose had reached the bottom. Otho's expression, too, was foreboding in the extreme. Strangely enough, that fact made Armand feel a little better. Once they stood on the ground, Otho crossed his arms and stepped back, allowing Rose to get swept into first Janet and then Mrs. Brickenden's capable arms. Rose had a look of bewilderment on her face when she was hailed as Una's savior.

"Where's Abelard?" Armand heard Rose ask plaintively. Peter stepped forward with the little dog, and Rose cheered up at once, reaching for him.

"I should like to check on Abelard too," Una said in a small voice. "He was injured trying to protect me from Waleran."

It took a ridiculous amount of effort for Armand to relinquish his grip and permit her to take those two steps from his side and run her hands over the little dog's squirming body. "I think his side is bruised," she said in a low voice to Rose, her hand hovering over his ribs. "Here."

"Just a little sore," Rose agreed. "I can put my granny's remedy on it and bring the swelling out."

Armand's gaze met Otho's. "Let's get them back to the house now," he suggested. Otho nodded, and Armand reached for Una, tugging her resolutely into in his wake. He was irritated to find a crowd following close on their heels, all babbling with barely suppressed speculation. He sped up and felt Una struggling beside to match his pace.

"Armand—"

"Not a word, Una," he cut in tightly. "I'm warning you." He tightened his grip involuntarily on her and heard her gasp before forcing himself to relax his hold. The contact helped. Just a bit. It made the taste of death recede. He knew instinctively he had to keep his hands on her until his murderous mood dissipated.

"I am quite well," replied Una softly, shooting him a troubled look.

"No, you're not," he growled angrily. "Someone just tried to kill you and I nearly let them!" He was almost shaking with fury.

"It's not your fault—" she started, but when she caught sight of the expression on his face, she lapsed into bewildered silence.

310

There was a wary look in her eye, which was probably why she was holding her tongue now. She wasn't stupid.

He stopped abruptly and swung her up in his arms. "Stop struggling," he warned her grimly, though she hadn't made any move to resist. Once they reached the house, he turned to confront the crowd. "Everyone," he announced loudly, and the conversation hushed at once as everyone looked at him expectantly. "Walker and Otho here will brief you as to why this man wanted to end your mistress's life. If any of you feel you no longer wish to remain in our service, then you can pack your things and leave before the morrow."

Everyone stared back at him open-mouthed. Otho shot him an exasperated look, while Walker merely looked amused. Armand set Una on her feet and hustled her halfway up the first flight of stairs before she'd even had a chance to draw breath.

14

Una's heart sank as they mounted the staircase. For some reason, Armand was angry with her. Blindingly angry. She could feel it pulsing off him in waves. His fingers clutched at her waist sporadically, not in a comforting gesture, but rather as if he was making sure of her substance. She shivered slightly in dismay. But why was he so mad? She bit her lip and noticed his knuckles were white from where they clutched the banister. Gently she reached out and touched his fingers in what she hoped was a conciliatory gesture.

"Don't!" he burst out, and she tried to turn back to look at his face, but he tightened his grip on her and prevented her. "Face forward," he ground out.

She froze. He was blaming her, she realized with dismay. He thought it was her fault! She felt a spurt of rebellion along with a pinch of pain. It was grossly unfair. She tried to stand straight and stiff on her step, trying to hold herself away from him, but he yanked her back roughly.

"Don't!" he repeated, his voice sounding raw. His arms tightened around her like steel bands. What in heaven's name was wrong with him? She forced herself to relax back against him and felt his hold loosen infinitesimally. It began to dawn on her that she was in serious trouble. By the time they reached the top of the stairs, she was fighting to remain calm.

It only made it worse when she got a glimpse of his face as he dragged her up the top step, his fingers biting into her wrist as he maneuvered along the dark-paneled corridor.

"It is a little hard on Otho to leave him to clear up that mess," Una said, lifting her chin. "It's probably the last thing he feels like going into right now."

Armand ignored her, wrenching open the door to their bedchamber and bundling her inside. Once he'd shut the door behind them, he let his gaze sweep over her, narrowing his eyes to mere slits. "What the *fuck* did you think you were doing up there?" he hissed at her furiously.

Una stared at him. She opened then closed her mouth in astonishment. "Are you trying to give me a fucking heart attack?" he snarled nastily. To her surprise, Una heard herself give a slight sob as she shook her head. A tear slid down one cheek. It didn't seem to appease him, not one bit.

"Take off your dress," he ground out, pushing her into the middle of the room. Una stared at him a moment before reaching for her laces. He wrenched the door back open and strode out of the room, bellowing down the stairs for hot water. She had barely started unlacing when he reappeared behind her and started yanking open her gown.

"You're tearing it," she burst out in alarm at a loud rip of material. He didn't answer but carried on pulling and tugging until it fell in a pile at her feet.

"It hardly signifies, since I never want to see you in this gown again," he said tightly. Then he spun her around and glowered down at her.

"What do you do when your life's at risk, Una, and I'm not there to protect you?" His voice was silky and calm now, and for some reason that set the already tinkling alarm bells into a clanging peal.

"Um, well…" She gazed up at him, clutching at her bare upper arms. She knew her thin shift concealed very little.

"I'm waiting."

"I act sensibly and rationally and—"

"*No!*" he burst out angrily. "No, you fucking don't!"

Una winced. "I don't?" She could hear the uncertainty in her own voice.

"What's the point in acting rationally when you're confronted by a *fucking madman*?"

She chewed on her bottom lip. "Very well," she conceded, licking her lips nervously. "What should I have done?"

"I'm glad you asked," he said with a forced calmness that was somehow even more disturbing than his violent cursing. "Because I'm about to tell you, and I expect you to take this fully on board, Una, as I *don't expect to have to tell you this again!*"

She stared up at him and swallowed. "Very well," she agreed.

He ground his teeth. "Let's talk about what you did today." His jaw worked a moment and Una felt herself quail on the inside. *Oh my gods.* He was really riled up. This wasn't just a burst of anger. He was trying to keep a lid on real rage here.

He took a deep breath "What the *fuck* did you think you were doing trying to get between that bastard and Rose?"

"I don't think I—"

"I saw you do it," he cut across her bitingly. "At least twice."

She took a shaky breath. "Rose didn't really seem to have the slightest notion what was happening, Armand. I don't think she realized the peril we were in."

"So?"

She gulped. "Pardon?"

"So, she's inexperienced with danger and you were brought up with it. Why did you have to step in her path?"

"Well, I didn't want her to jeopardize herself anymore. After all, it was me that Waleran—"

"That should not have been your concern."

She gaped at him. "I don't understand—"

"Your concern," he said, enunciating each word slowly, as if she was devoid of wit, "should have been to keep yourself safe until I or someone else could rescue you. *Do you understand?*"

Una jumped at the force of his words. "But it was my fault she was up there in the first place..." She faltered.

"No, it was not!" She watched in fascination as his nostrils flared and he fought for control. "What you should have been doing," he carried on in a low, seething voice, "was keeping your goddamn mouth shut and your eyes downcast and keeping yourself as low to the ground as possible. Do I make myself clear?" He was watching her intently, and at a loss of how to respond, she managed a faint nod. "If you had to say anything at all," he ground out, "it should have been to plead for your sweet little life. *Nothing else—do you understand?*"

Una's tongue was stuck to the roof of her mouth. She gazed dazedly up at him. "Y-yes," she managed to stammer. *Oh my gods*, she thought, her brain turning fuzzy. It was concern for her that was driving him out of his mind. She couldn't quite wrap her head around the notion.

"Set it down over there," he said, making her aware of others in the room. Una turned her head in alarm as Janet and Mrs. Brickenden came in carrying large pitchers of hot water. She tried to scoot behind Armand to hide her half-naked state, but his grip kept her firmly in place between his legs.

Una could feel her face burning with embarrassment. They must realize her husband had just stripped her from the state of her red dress lying on the floor. It was humiliating. "Now lay the fire," he ordered, still making no move to cover her up. She could hear the servants moving around the room behind her. She stared forward at Armand's chest in growing mortification.

"I don't have any clothes on," she whispered angrily.

"You're about to wash," he pointed out.

"I don't want anybody to see me naked!"

"They can't see anything," he told her dismissively.

Her mouth dropped open. "This shift conceals nothing!" she argued hoarsely.

He dropped his hands to cup her buttocks and pull her more firmly against him.

She let out a hiss of breath from behind her teeth. The servants' hall would have plenty to gossip about tonight, she thought, closing her eyes.

"Shut the door behind you," he said, and Una's eyes snapped open as the door finally closed.

"Why are you being so unreasonable?" she asked him in disbelief. "You're acting like a man half-crazed—" She broke off her words as his fingers slid into her hair at the nape, pulling her head back.

"Well, that's what I feel like," he said gruffly before his mouth descended on hers in a hard, punishing kiss.

Una reeled under the savage onslaught, clutching at his tunic front and holding on for dear life. When she didn't struggle, he eased up a little. Una tore her mouth from his to draw in a ragged breath. He backed her up against the nearest wall, plastering his length up against hers. The breath was half squashed out of her.

"Tell me again," he seethed. "What you do when you're in danger."

Her wide eyes flew to his. He was deadly serious. "I—I beg for my life and wait for you to rescue me," she stammered.

He considered this a moment with narrowed eyes before giving a small nod. "Close enough," he conceded tightly and then lowered his mouth again to hers in another hard, plundering kiss. Una gave up trying to hold her own and collapsed against him. It made no difference, he held her even harder to the wall. Suddenly there were tears streaming from her eyes and she sobbed into his mouth.

It took a few seconds for him to register that she was crying, and then he pulled abruptly back, holding her up by her upper arms. "Repeat after me," he said in a low, ominous tone. "I do not put others before myself."

"I don't," she objected.

"You do it all the fucking time!" he roared. "Right in front of my eyes!"

Una gasped and shut her eyes against his fury. She was past the point of rationalizing his behavior. Dimly in some part of her mind, she realized he had been scared she would fall to her death, and she felt the spark of something warm in her chest area. He hadn't even waited for anything else, she marveled. He had stormed right back to the house with her.

"I won't do it anymore," she said in a small voice. "I promise, Armand. I truly won't."

His grip tightened even more on her arms, making her wince.

"Do you even realize," he started unsteadily, "what it would have done to me if you—" He broke off his words impatiently, staring up at the ceiling.

"I'm sorry," she whispered. *My gods, he was really upset.* "Please—"

Suddenly he pushed her away from him with a hard shove. "I'll leave you to wash," he said in a different voice, completely devoid of emotion. Shutters down, his eyes hooded.

"No!" she burst out, desperate for him not to leave. "Don't leave me." Suddenly it was imperative that he stayed with her. "Please, Armand." When he remained planted where he stood, she flung her arms around his middle and hugged him, pressing her face into his chest. Her mind raced trying to think how to get him to stay. "I'm scared," she lied unashamedly. "I don't want to be alone."

He'd wanted to join with her when he'd first pushed her into the bedroom, she realized. He had wanted to feel physically close to her. That had been his first overriding instinct after his scare. Maybe she could use that? She pressed her lower body against his as blatantly as she dared. Was he hard? she wondered, her cheeks filling with color. "Please, Armand," she pleaded again,

318

rubbing her hips slightly against him. He let out his breath in a low hiss. His hand came up to force her jaw up so their eyes met. She willed herself not to look away from the burning expression in his own.

"I always knew," she whispered, "that Sir Lusty Loins would come to rescue his dragon."

"I can't play that game right now, Una," he said tightly. "I don't feel remotely playful."

"I don't care," she replied, winding her arms around him tighter. The next thing she knew, he had backed her against the tapestry again, but this time he scooped her up so only her back was pressed to the wall and her legs were about his waist. This time, she felt more stimulated than constricted by his weight.

"Una," he murmured between urgent, devouring kisses. It almost seemed like he was *burning* for her, she thought dazedly. And she was not the sort of woman to ever get men worked up like that. She knew her good points. She was practical and she was stout of heart. A legendary beauty she was not. Not that she was complaining. It was thrilling to have him so eager for her embraces. She returned them with enthusiasm.

He drew back again, regarding her with dark eyes, brimming with emotion. "I don't want to be your ideal traveling companion, Una!" he burst out frustratedly. "Nor your faithful friend either!"

She blinked at him, wondering where this was coming from. Then she realized he was quoting her own words back at her. She had meant them as a compliment! Had they rankled then? "I only—" But she did not get to finish, for his mouth was on hers again. Then he was yanking her away from the wall, back into his arms, where he held her tight.

319

"Gods, I do everything wrong where you're concerned, Una," he said against her brow. "I should be consoling you right now."

"No, you do not, Armand," she insisted. "You do just as you ought."

He was holding himself very still. "I should go down and make sure they have set men to patrol the grounds. And explain…what just happened. Why it just happened," he muttered tightly.

Una struggled with what to say. For one horrible moment she thought he was going to resolutely set her aside. Reaching for his arm, she took a deep breath. "Otho can see to that, I am sure. We have things to discuss right now." He did not argue, but he did not exactly look encouraging either.

"You say you do not wish to be my friend and companion," she continued desperately. "Well, I do not wish to be a princess," she said forcefully. "I simply want to be your wife, Armand."

A spark kindled in his eyes. "You will always be my wife *and* my princess, Una."

She inclined her head in acceptance of this. "Very well, then you must likewise accept that to me, you are both my husband and the very best friend I have ever—"

She got no further than this, for he scooped her up, crossed the room in three long strides, and flung her onto the bed. She watched flat on her back as he stripped off his tunic and unlaced his crotch. To her surprise he didn't strip off his braies, but instead came to the mattress with his legs still clad in the tight black leggings.

"Maybe talking is not the best way forward just now," he uttered. Reaching for her, he ripped her thin shift in two and threw it off the bed, leaving her totally naked before him. Then he roughly grabbed her knees and flung her legs open before settling between them.

Una felt a pulse of alarm along with something else, a sort of breathless, wild feeling when his hands slid possessively over her full breasts and down over the slight swell of her stomach to cup her between her legs. When his fingers slid into her, she bit her lip and arched into them, finding with faint surprise that she was already wet, despite his lack of tender ministrations. She panted in excitement as his own eyes narrowed and gleamed dangerously before her. This was not playful Armand right now, but it was still her husband.

"Tell me you want me, Una," he said tightly.

"I always want you." He seemed to shudder slightly at her words.

"Don't you dare to even think about leaving me now," he said thickly. "I won't stand for it."

Una watched the rise and fall of his heaving chest as she looped her arms about him. "I have never once contemplated leaving you and I never will," she responded truthfully. She did not think it prudent to ask if this meant there would be no more talk of *his* going off and leaving her at Lynwode. To her surprise, she found herself saying it anyway. "And what of you?"

"What of me?" he asked huskily. His thumb was circling that spot that made her pant and twist against him.

"What of *you* going off adventuring and leaving me alone?"

He gave a short laugh. "Not happening."

Una's heart raced. "No?"

"I will drag you with me," he promised darkly. "You will soon regret calling me your ideal traveling companion when you're forced to pee in a field and sleep in a wet pavilion."

"Do you think I will?" she asked breathlessly, arching against his questing fingers.

His hand stilled a moment. "No," he admitted, his voice thick with emotion. "I think, my darling Una, that you will be cheerful and sweet, whatever fresh hell I put you through." His mouth was on hers again, hot and urgent, as he aligned their bodies and, without more ado, thrust into her. His mouth on hers muffled her cry.

"Ah gods," he groaned, closing his eyes. "I could have lost you tonight. I so very nearly lost you." When he opened his eyes again, they were brimming over with both passion and emotion. "And you're everything." He sounded shaken. "When did you become everything to me?"

Una caught her breath. She was everything to him?

"It happened—I'm not sure when it happened." He sounded bewildered. "Before I knew it, you were already—" He breathed out again, his body starting to move against hers. "You were already there and there was nothing I could do about it."

"Armand," Una breathed raggedly. Did he even know what he was saying?

"I have never known anyone like you. Anyone who made me feel like you do." He paused, one hand at her jaw, tilting her head up so he could look into her eyes as he stroked deep inside her. "You're so beautiful to me, Una." He shook his head slightly. "I should have told you that before now, but I didn't know how to say it to someone when I truly meant it." He looked frustrated.

"And it's not just the way you look. It's who you are. You ought to be bitter and distrusting, but you're not." His words broke off as his voice thickened. "You always think the best of me and defend me, even when every impulse must tell you I'm undeserving. You make me want to deserve your good opinion, Una. To deserve you."

Una bit her lip, her breath coming fast. Was he telling her that he loved her? Or merely esteemed her above other women? Or was it much the same thing? It was hard to concentrate when their bodies were joined and he was moving in that way against her. She stroked her hands over his back, feeling his rippling muscles as her eyes fluttered closed.

As she lifted her legs to wrap them about his hips, she felt the dull ache at her waist where Waleran's knife had grazed her skin. Despite that slight discomfort, the pleasure was coiling low in her belly and climbing higher by the moment.

"Una," Armand groaned. "I want to hear your voice, my love."

"You do deserve it," she told him breathlessly. "No one could suit me so well as you. From the start, you gave me everything I needed. Every time."

He lifted his head. "I did?"

She nodded and she felt him pulse deep inside her.

"I can't hold off," he groaned, his hips thrusting against hers vigorously. "Come with me."

Una's eyes flew open as she blazed and caught fire, convulsing around him. Armand held her gaze, his own turning molten as their passion consumed one another. Afterward, the only sound in their room was their mingled panting breath. They lay in a close embrace for several long comfortable moments before Armand started kissing her again, very tenderly.

"You have the loveliest mouth, Una. I've thought so many times, and this is the first time it has occurred to me to tell you so." He stroked her mouth with his thumb. "It's this bottom lip that's the culprit. It's so full and plump and distracting." Una laughed, but ended on a wince. "What is it?" he asked quickly.

She was forced then to admit to the scratches at her waist from the knife point. Many exclamations followed, and Armand was roused to fetch a washing cloth and minister to it tenderly.

"It's nothing," Una protested, but Armand would not be consoled, and desperate to distract him, she was forced to cast about for a change of subject.

"You did say it to me once before," she confessed. "That you found me beautiful, I mean."

He lifted his face from his solemn contemplation of the series of tiny red crisscrosses against her skin. "I did?"

"On our wedding night."

She had caught his attention now. "Tell me."

"You lifted your head off the pillow and said, 'How did you make yourself beautiful?'" Una recalled as Armand flushed. "It was the nicest compliment anyone ever paid me," she responded stoutly. "For you looked so surprised and sincere when you said it. It quite touched me."

Armand was silent a moment. "Gods, why am I so hopeless around you, wife?" he groaned at last, flinging away the cloth and stretching out beside her to adjust the pillows behind them. "I swear, my address is meant to be quite polished, but around you it deserts me completely!"

Una hid her smile against his shoulder. Strange to say, she quite liked that thought. "Maybe because for once you are being

324

genuine," she teased. He did not look mollified, though one hand started to stroke up and down her thigh.

"Even drunk I must have noticed these long legs," he murmured. "And how good they feel tangled with mine."

"You like my legs?"

"Very much. I never appreciated tall women before you." He squeezed her rear. "I noticed your nice plump thighs when I woke bleary-eyed the next morn—and your sweetly rounded backside. I was annoyed I could not remember our tryst."

"Oh?" She was somewhat startled by this unexpected inventory of feminine charms. Why had she thought men appreciated things like dainty ankles and pretty hands? she wondered dazedly. Or perhaps Armand was just a different type of male.

"And I very nearly embarrassed myself at that first inn, when you bent over to wash in front of me."

"Really?"

He nodded. "The only time I wasn't attracted to you was on that balcony." He frowned. "But that was only the getup you were rigged out in. You didn't really look like a woman. More like a ship." Una gave a smothered laugh. "But if those strange garments meant you were preserved for me, then I guess they served their purpose," he concluded with a sigh.

Una opened her mouth to agree, but he interrupted her. "You would tell me if you really weren't recovered from what just happened, wouldn't you, Una?" Before she could speak, he continued swiftly. "If you wanted us to remove from here, or if you would feel safer at court—"

"What? No!" she interrupted him quickly. "I love Lynwode above all places in the world! It's my home."

"Even if you wanted us to repair to Anninghurst for a while," he started tentatively. "We could—"

"Anninghurst?" she objected. "Why would we? When Lynwode is superior in every way!"

"Anninghurst is surrounded by a moat," he pointed out. "You might feel more secure there."

"Armand." Una adjusted herself beside him to face him full on. "Waleran was not in his right mind," she said simply. "He couldn't even rouse any followers to join him. He wanted us to fall to our deaths together as martyrs to the Blechmarsh cause." Armand's arms tightened about her, but she continued calmly. "We were never close, and he was not the spoiled young noble I remember, but a complete stranger." She sighed. "Otho was always the best of my brothers, and thanks to you, I am blessed to have him in my life still."

"Thanks to me?"

"Few husbands would tolerate so antagonistic a brother-in-law at such close quarters."

A brief smile touched his lips. "He's a good steward, and truth to tell, I have grown used to having him about the place. I'm even growing quite fond of him."

"Truly?" It was more than she'd hoped for.

"Yes," he agreed. "Besides, even if I couldn't stand him, I'd bear his company for your sake."

"You see," she told him encouragingly. "How truly considerate you are."

He shrugged. "It's still self-interest, Una. I mean to keep you contented by my side. That is all."

Una bit her lip, realizing Armand was going to take some convincing that he was not selfish through and through. "I wonder how Otho's explanation went over," she said, shifting further up the pillows and adjusting the sheet to cover her breasts. "Do you think many will have left our service before morning?"

Armand followed her up the bed, resettling against her, as though he could not bear to lose contact. "I don't really care. We can always hire more servants from further afield. I can find more men if need be."

She thought about this for a moment. "It might be as well to get word to your family before it reaches them via an alternate route, Armand."

He gave no response, his hand shifted up and down her hip in a vaguely comforting gesture. She hoped it wasn't because he was still assuring himself she was there.

"This is like that attempt on our lives at the inn, isn't it?" he said suddenly.

"I don't remember you being quite so badly affected by that," Una admitted cautiously.

"I was talking about your reaction, not mine," he retorted.

Una raised up on one elbow to look into his face. "I suppose it is, rather. Unpleasant." She shivered. "But soon consigned to the past."

He shook his head. "Not for me," he said grimly. "I'll have that tower dragged down stone by stone. And I'll still have nightmares about it."

"Armand," she said, twining her arms about his neck. "If Rose hadn't...done what she did, I would have contrived to survive somehow, I assure you."

A shade of his former grimness returned. "I should have kept you safe. Had you watched more securely."

"You've assembled quite an army already," she pointed out. "I have no idea what duties you will give all these men to keep them occupied about the place!"

He was quiet for a moment before admitting, "The more recent of them were sent to us by Lord Vawdrey."

"What?" She drew back to stare at him in dismay.

"Apparently the King's chief advisor did not consider me a safe pair of hands either." His gaze fell from hers. "He sent me a warning this afternoon that your brother Waleran was still alive, so you see I *am* to blame."

"Nonsense!" She shook his shoulder. "You could not have foreseen that Waleran would sneak into the house like that. His actions were not planned out or rational."

"Apparently he suffered a head wound at Demoyne," Armand said, slowly recalling what Walker had told him. "It changed him by all accounts."

Una stared. "I have never heard of such things. Have you?"

"Once before," he admitted. "A bloodthirsty man of war greatly changed into one who shrank from spilling blood and ended his days in a holy hermitage."

Una fell silent. "It's a shame the change wrought on Waleran was of the opposite effect. We will have to have his body sent north to his family for burial."

He grunted, pulling her closer, his hand stroking up and down her back. "Apparently Vawdrey's men have been steadily repelling those who would approach you with treasonous offers," he said, avoiding her gaze. "I had no idea you would be plagued by them to such an extent."

Una mulled this over. "Nor I," she said. Though, she had been pleasantly surprised not to receive so much as a smuggled note since they had reached Little Derring. Had she been a little naive by this turn of events? Probably. She had been similarly guarded by Vawdrey's men back at the palace. Seeing Armand's expression, she asked cheerfully, "But if they have been so effective, then why can they not remain so? They have obviously been doing a good job, and Lord Vawdrey can surely spare them." Armand gave a faint smile at this, but nothing more. "Your pride is hurt?" she ventured softly.

He shrugged. "Maybe a little. A man should be able to protect his own wife."

"You did. You do."

"I will from this day forth," he vowed.

Una turned her head to look at him quickly. "I hope you don't mean to escort me everywhere with an armed guard," she joked. When he avoided her eye, she lightly thumped his chest. "Armand!"

"We do have several men in need of occupation, as you so justly pointed out," he said evasively. "Though," he said, facing her straight on, "considering how jealous I'm turning out to be, I may have to rotate the guard on you, as your father did."

Una stared at him. "Your disposition is not jealous," she started as his hand landed at her waist on the uninjured side.

"Oh yes, it is, Una," he said, stroking his thumb at the indentation. "Make no mistake about that, my love. What do you think that piece of foolishness was about last night?" His color darkened. "I could not tolerate the thought that someone other than I might have tutored you in bed sport. That's why I reacted the way I did. Like a damned fool."

Una stared at him. "Oh! But I—I mean, no one ever—" She took a deep breath. "You've really got nothing to be jealous about."

"I'm glad," he answered huskily. "But that does not excuse the things I said to you."

"Well," she said. "I know you are very sensitive with regrets about our wedding night and—"

"I only regret that I was blind drunk," he corrected her swiftly.

"Yes, but I wish you would believe me when I seek to assure you on that score." She took a deep breath. "And in any case, I accepted your apology about last night. We have no need to discuss it further."

"I will never say anything like that again," he said, taking her hand from his chest and kissing her palm. "And I vow if you ever fly into a jealous rage, I will be just as understanding."

Una saw the smile trembling on his lips with relief. She loved his smile and it felt like she had not seen it in an age. "I have never been prone to jealous rages before," she admitted. "But there is a first for everything. I was once informed you have a sadly roving eye, but I have yet to see evidence of the fact."

"By whom?" he asked with a swift frown. "That was before. You have no need to worry on that score."

She smiled. "Good, but I will never tell."

"Bess from The Stone Crow," he snorted. "Much she would know. In any case, my eye only dwells in one place these days."

"That's nice to hear."

His brows snapped together. "It was Anne, wasn't it? I knew she would be revenged after I forgot her blessed children's names."

"I hope you will not be so remiss with our own children," Una commented. For some reason, all playfulness seemed to desert him at her teasing words. Una suppressed a sigh as he drew back from her.

"I can understand why you might worry about that," he started, looking so grave Una could have cried. "But I swear that I mean to take my duties seriously from here on out. To do that, I think you need to face some hard truths about me." He swallowed and sat up in the bed, putting some distance between them as he turned to face her straight on.

"It's like this, Una," he started resolutely in the manner of one making some grand confession. "I'm not any of the things you think me. I've never tried to be decent or honorable or considerate of my family. I'm selfish. I'm a cheat. I'm a liar. My family is quite right about me. I'm the black sheep and I've always reveled in the fact."

She opened her mouth, but he held up his hand. "No, allow me to say it. You're too good for me, Una. Far, *far* too good. If this were a just world, I would never have won your hand that day by faking a loss to Farleigh." He spoke the name with disgust. "For god's sake, if I had even one spark of decency, I would return you now to Wymer's court and demand a better bridegroom for you. The bridegroom you deserve."

"Armand—"

"But that's not going to happen, Una. Do you know why?" His chest heaved. "It's because I don't give a *damn* about what's right or decent or what I deserve. Or even," he added with some difficulty, "what *you* deserve, my sweet. My father's quite right on that score. I'm a selfish bastard through and through. I want you, and I'm going to have you." He glared at her resolutely. "Forever," he added through gritted teeth. Una nodded. "If you've got something to say on the subject, you had best say it now. I don't measure up, but I vow that I will one day, and until that day you will just have to bear with me."

"That is all satisfactory to me," Una said calmly. "As I do not want anyone else but you."

He expelled an explosive breath, crossing his arms. "That's because you don't know any better," he said tersely.

"That is only a matter of opinion."

He flung her the look of an extremely goaded man. "One of these days, wife, the scales are going to fall from your eyes regarding me and you're going to be devastated."

Una took a deep breath. "Oh, I don't think so," she said bracingly.

"I know you don't," he said broodingly. "That's because you're naive as hell."

"I'm not really, you know," she said gently. "Not in things that count." He shook his head and muttered something under his breath. There was nothing else for it, she thought, looking at his grim expression. She was going to have to be brutally honest.

"I already know you're a cheat, Armand," she said frankly. He looked up, staring at her. "If someone hadn't told me, I think I would have deduced it myself eventually. I like to think I would have anyway." She paused. "At some point I suppose you realized you could make more money by playing the odds and faking losses at crucial moments," she mused. "And Fulcher, I take it, was your confederate in the ruse." He was sat very still, and she watched his throat work as he struggled for words. "No doubt it's very shocking, but I find I can't bring myself to care about it as I should," she admitted.

"Una," he said huskily. "You don't appreciate—"

"No, I do," she cut across him coolly. "I do realize that acting in such a way is most dishonorable for a knight. I also appreciate that it would not even cross the minds of a Lord Kentigern or a Roland Vawdrey to do such a thing as throw a match."

"They'd sooner die than dishonor the field like that," he said hoarsely.

"I doubt that very much, Armand," she said practically. "Let's not be too fulsome in speech." He looked up quickly at that, but she plunged on regardless. "I daresay you have been a vastly undutiful son in your time, an inconsiderate brother, and a thoughtless uncle, but I don't find that concerns me unduly either. Because at the end of the day, you *are* an exceptionally good husband to me, whatever you may think."

He opened his mouth to speak, but she hurried on. "As for being selfish, I daresay you are no more selfish than most men who like things their own way. You are certainly not the monster of selfishness my own father was, that much I do know." She took a deep breath. "You did not want to win my hand, but once you had done so, you were unfailingly kind—"

He rolled into her again, pulling her roughly into his arms. "Don't talk like that," he said heavily.

"Like what?"

"About being unwanted. I want you alright."

"*Now* you do," she agreed. "But at the time—"

He gave her a slight shake. "Stop it. I don't want to hear those words on your lips again." He paused heavily. "Or that I'm a cheat. That's all in the past."

She regarded him thoughtfully. "It had better be," she said serenely. "I don't know how you could have continued to disappoint the King like that, when you knew full well he was rooting for you to win."

"I don't give a damn about Wymer," he said frankly. "The only thing he's ever done worth noting was bestow you on me."

"Well, you can't return me to King Wymer now, for I won't go."

He stared at her. "I wouldn't let you go!" he thundered.

"And for all we know, there could already be a baby in my belly," she continued as though he had not spoken. "And I don't want to hear anything about how you will make a terrible father, and if you dare to go flinging off in a panic when it happens, I warn you, I will be furious with you!"

He glowered down at her with a fulminating stare. "Is that what you think of me?"

"It is what you think of yourself, Armand," she responded quietly.

He paused at that. "I am only thinking of what we will tell any children that arrive," he said gruffly.

"What *will* we tell our children?" she prompted hopefully.

"We will tell our children," said Armand gravely, "that their father was a useless scoundrel until their mother came along and took him in hand. We will tell them I couldn't find my form

334

until she was cheering me on, and we'll tell them that the gods answered his unspoken prayers that day when he won her hand."

Una swallowed. "So, you do not mean to abandon me here at Lynwode?" she asked carefully. "While you go off adventuring to find the hidden northern treasure?"

His eyes flared. "I had forgotten all about that cursed treasure. It is hardly uppermost in my mind. It has likely been dug up already, but if I ever do get the notion to venture north, then we will go adventuring *together*, wife. *You* are the only treasure I care about or need to be content in this life."

"And you will take me with you? To the tournaments you attend as well?"

"Have you not been listening?" His tone was a little testy.

Una inclined her head. "I have," she said quietly. "Most assiduously. Yet you have not spoken the words I most long to hear."

He looked at her blankly, then a dark flush scored across his cheekbones. "Why am I such an idiot when it comes to you?" he marveled, lifting his hands from where they gripped her upper arms to cup her face. "Una de Bussell, do you not know that your husband worships the ground you walk on? Not because of your birthright, but because of *you*, the only woman who ever captured my heart."

Her face broke out in a smile. "It seems I do not mind fulsome speeches when you talk of such things," she admitted. "And I love you," she said simply. "Though I think you already knew that."

He looked rueful. "I hoped you might. Both hoped and feared," he admitted. "In equal parts."

"You are not going to let me down, Armand," she told him firmly, placing her own hands on either side of his face.

"No, I know I'm not." He covered her hands with his own and turned one over to kiss the palm. "Though I don't know how you can know that, going on past form."

"Going on past form, you have *never* let me down," she said staunchly, before adding conscientiously, "even if that might have been your original intent."

"Una," he whispered. "I love you so, and I really don't deserve you at all."

Her chest felt like it would burst as her eyes filled with tears. "I love you too, but I feel like I *do* deserve you. You are my reward, and I mean to savor you for the rest of my life."

He caught his breath at that and just gazed at her, quite open and sincere for a long moment. Una tipped her head to one side. "Do—do you want to play dragon and knight now?" she asked, dropping her gaze shyly to his throat.

"No," he answered, tilting her head back up so their gazes met again. "I want to make love. You're the only woman I've ever done that with. Did you know that, Una?"

She was fascinated to see his expression had settled somewhere in between playful Armand and intense Armand. It was a devastating combination. She shook her head. "Have you played dragon and knight with anyone else?" she asked with sudden misgiving.

He laughed, looking like a great weight had been lifted from his shoulders. "No, for that game was of your invention, wife. Do you not remember?"

"So it was." She blushed. "I hope you will not be too serious to play it in future, husband."

Armand grinned. "I'm sure I could be persuaded with the right incentive." He closed his arms about her, bearing her back down to the mattress.

"What kind of incentive?" she asked against his shoulder.

"The right fire-breathing dragon. My very own one, that is."

*

They did not descend below stairs until early the next morning when they came downstairs hand in hand. Una was wearing a robe over her shift, her hair in one long braid over her shoulder. Armand's tunic was not fastened, and he could not stop yawning. They had been forced to wash in cold water from the previous evening as no one had wanted to disturb them by bringing them up any fresh.

It was Una's hope that barely anyone would be about after the previous night's excitement, but by the time they reached the great hall her ears had picked up the low buzz of conversation in there. She tried to hang back, but Armand was having none of it, his arm about her waist, propelling her forward. At their entrance there was a drag of benches as all present rose to their feet with warm greetings.

"Good morning," Una found herself coloring up and wishing everyone. "Good morning." It seemed no one present bore her any ill will for her northern or indeed her Blechmarsh birth. Janet beamed at her and Peter shyly nodded. She was disappointed to see Rose still clad in her drab gray gown, but the girl's smile was as sweet as ever. Abelard came dancing over to greet his mistress. Una patted his head and examined his side, but he seemed none the worst for his ordeal. Rose retreated to a low stool by the enormous fireplace, where she sat feeding logs into the growing blaze.

Armand sat in his seat, and when Una went to take the chair at his right, he pulled her down into his lap. "Let us remain informal this morning, wife," he told her with a wink, lowering his voice for her ears only. "I fully intend on taking you straight back upstairs again after this."

Una gazed at him. "Well, I guessed that was why you would not let me dress," she confessed and dropped a kiss to his lips. Janet plunked down cups of frothing ale before them and Mrs. Brickenden came hurrying in with another platter of fish and fresh-baked bread.

Una thanked them with a smile and noticed that the hall looked just as packed as the previous evening. If anyone *had* flung off in disgust at the revelation of her birth, she could not tell. Glancing down the table, Una saw the personable-looking man who had carried a bow the previous evening. He was surrounded by the rowdier element at the table.

"Who is that man?" Una asked Armand. "Is he one of Lord Vawdrey's?"

"Yes," Armand said with a dismissive glance at Walker, who toasted them.

"Do you think they will stay with us for long?" Una asked, passing Armand his cup.

"Hopefully for life," Armand answered swiftly. "You were right. Why should we hinder them from doing their job? It is no hardship for me to have more mouths at our table. We've plenty of gold, and I do not mean to be caught unawares again." She noticed he was looking about in some consternation. "But where is Otho?" he asked, and Una realized for the first time that her brother was missing.

No sooner had he spoken the words than they heard a hurried step enter the room. Otho marched into the great hall, his expression fixed and determined, his arms full of wildflowers.

"Otho?" Una uttered with surprise, but he made straight for Rose, who was seated next to the fire. On reaching her, he knelt down before her and reached out to unwind the gray headscarf from her head.

Una covered her mouth with her hands as she watched Otho start carefully placing the flowers into Rose's golden hair. "Oh," she murmured as tears began to roll down Rose's cheeks. "Oh, Armand," she whispered. "Look!"

Armand shifted in his seat beneath her. "It seems too private a moment for everyone to be watching," he muttered, but Una could see that neither Otho nor Rose had eyes for anyone else present. Her hand sought Armand's, and she squeezed his fingers tight. After a moment, he returned the pressure.

"If he wants her, then good luck to him. He'll need it!" he murmured.

"Armand! Rose saved my life," Una reminded him reproachfully.

Armand snorted. "She'll probably say the faeries told her to push him over!"

"Armand!"

"Besides, you saved hers right back," he pointed out. "She would have gone over the edge if you had not caught her." When she did not respond, he ran a finger down her spine. "Remind me to warn Otho never to inadvertently step on that

339

dog. She'll pitch him out the window faster than he can beg its pardon."

Una shook her head and stole another glance at the fireside. Rose was now in Otho's arms. She could have cried to see the look of tenderness on her brother's usually stern face. "Oh, Armand," she sighed. "We shall soon have another wedding feast here at Lynwode."

Janet and Mrs. Brickenden started clapping enthusiastically and soon everyone else had joined in, so the hall was buzzing with good cheer.

When a loud clamoring started at the door, Una did not even flinch. "Likely it's my in-laws," she murmured, tipping back her head to look at Armand when his arms tightened protectively around her. "I told you they would soon hear of last night's excitement."

In this, however, she was quite wrong, for it turned out to be a royal deputation. One herald blew a trumpet as the other unfurled a long list of items. Then a third clapped his hands and a staggering array of wedding gifts were carried into the great hall. The first herald cleared his throat and informed them their unexpected departure had prevented the King from bestowing them before they left court.

Una watched in amazement as a procession of costly raiment, linens, damasks, brocades, tapestries, and lavish furnishings were paraded into the hall. The servants were open-mouthed as the pile grew high and items were stacked up against the far wall.

"I think," Armand murmured in her ear, "that we must be grateful neither Muriel nor Henry are here to see this disgusting parade of extravagance."

Una choked back a laugh. "They would not approve," she agreed. "And it seems I no longer need to visit that marketplace. Only consider how well those vibrant tapestries will look in the solar!"

The second herald cleared his throat and approached them with a letter in hand. He bowed low and presented it. Armand made no move to take it, merely looked steadily at Una, so she plucked it from the herald's fingers and opened it.

"It's an invitation," she said steadily, "for us to attend the Autumn Tournament at Aphrany as the King's honored guests."

Epilogue

Three Months Later

The Autumn Tournament, Aphrany

Una sat in the royal balcony once more. This time she was seated at King Wymer's left while Queen Armenal sat on his right. It was both familiar, and yet also vastly different to how she remembered the experience.

At first, she had been heartily dismayed to learn that the King expected her to sit in the royal box. She was not a royal, as she pointed out firmly to Lord Vawdrey. She wanted to sit among the other sundry nobles in the less exalted stands. She neither deserved nor desired such a mark of distinction from the King.

Lord Vawdrey, however, had been equally firm, an amused smile playing about his lips. "Lady Una, I believe you must indulge the King in his wish. Since you have married de Bussell, he believes you have done him great credit and is very gratified to have you back under his aegis. He was most upset that you rushed off so precipitately after your wedding." Seeing she was unconvinced, he added softly, "I fear if he does not see enough of you on your month-long visit to court, then he might suggest you extend it."

His mildly spoken words hit their target, and Una sucked in a horrified breath. "Oh no, no," she blurted. "That would not be convenient at all!"

Lord Vawdrey tutted sympathetically, and Una pressed her lips together. "Very well, I will join His Majesty in the royal box," she had conceded with barely concealed ill grace and been rewarded with a singularly charming smile. "I only hope my husband will not be too displeased," she added darkly.

"Dear me, I am persuaded he will be thrilled at the opportunity to both impress you and cover himself in glory in one fell swoop," Lord Vawdrey had answered with an arched black brow. Una had felt suddenly an uncomfortable suspicion that Lord Vawdrey was fully aware that Armand had spent most of his competitive career dissembling. She felt herself color hotly and was glad to flee his presence at the first opportunity.

For the past two weeks, she had spent as much time in Wymer's company as she had Armand's. She had been expected to sit with the King at formal banquets almost every evening. She was urged to join him on his morning hunt and applaud his prowess in the saddle. She had been hawking with the King, and even summoned to breakfast with him, a high favor indeed and one extended to precious few.

The King only ever breakfasted attended by Bathilde, his treasured old nurse, and whoever was his current favorite. Bathilde had clucked over her and served her a revolting pap of milk and bread that Wymer had eaten as meekly as any child in the nursery. Then, he had taken her on a tour of the royal crown jewels. She had seen, with surprise, the two highly encrusted collars she had left behind encased beside the King's ceremonial crowns. He had nodded at them significantly and patted her hand.

"Well, well, you're a good girl," he had said, clearing his throat. "And a credit to me."

In short, the history books had been entirely revised and Una now figured in them, not as a foreign oddity and royal embarrassment, but as Wymer's most cherished cousin, a relation he prized so highly that he had bestowed her hand in marriage on one of his most-favored knights. Una, though bewildered by this turn of events, could only be grateful for it.

At the banquet the previous evening, there had been a ballad sung in her honor of her loyalty to the King, her royal cousin, and her beauty, which inspired devotion in a chivalric breast. Una had scarcely known where to look, but the assembly had enthusiastically applauded and demanded an encore.

Armand's own reaction had been somewhat mixed. "Aye, well, so long as he doesn't start getting any ideas," he had rumbled, pulling her into his arms as soon as they were alone. Una had hurriedly assured him that the King's attentions were far from amorous but seemed instead a bewildering mix of the brotherly and the paternal. He had been appeased, but Una could not help but be aware that Armand was as keen to return to Little Derring as she was. That fact alone made her able now to bear court and all its attendant nonsense.

She glanced to the side where Fulcher lolled with the royal pages, looking disreputable as ever. Really, she would have to make him another hat soon, for that one looked quite dreadful perched on his head. He was having a high time acting as Armand's attendant, for they had been unable to drag the newly wed Otho away from Lynwode or from Rose. Fulcher, noticing her regard, tipped her a wink, nodding meaningfully to the arena, and Una turned back to watch.

Armand's sword swung down upon Sir Garman Orde's with a mighty clash of steel. The King's hand simultaneously clapped down on Una's knee and gripped it so hard she nearly shot out of her seat.

"He's going to do it!" Wymer muttered excitedly. "*Always* knew he had it in him! I always said, did I not? That he could be a champion." Wymer's words were choked with emotion

344

and his eyes moist. Una marveled that he could feel so deeply about it.

Queen Armenal pursed her lips. "If he garners glory now," she said, "he does so, because he hath found something worth fighting for." She paused when both Wymer and Una looked back at her blankly. "His lady's honor," the Queen explained loftily.

"Oh aye," Wymer agreed, blowing his nose. "I take your meaning. It's for your sake, cousin, that he has found his form." He patted Una's hand and signaled for a page to bring forth wine. "My cousin, my cousin," he ushered irritably when they went to hand him the first goblet. He was determined that for her month-long stay she would be his most-honored guest.

Una took it with thanks and gazed down at Armand. Even if he had come in last place again, it would not have changed her feeling toward him in any way. His face beneath his visor was streaked with sweat and she could tell he would be exhausted after. She would have to insist she missed tonight's banquet to tend his wounds, she thought, perking up. Then she could bathe him and fuss over him to her heart's content.

"Look at him!" the King crowed, almost spilling his wine on his hose. "Driven. Purposeful. All the resolve he previously lacked!" He slapped his knee, then raised his cup to silently toast Una. "All down to you, Una," he concurred with a nod to his wife. "As my Queen pointed out."

"Of course, he could still lose," Queen Armenal said musingly, earning a ferocious glower from Wymer. "Sir Garman does not cherish the runners-up cup and his own wife watches on."

Una glanced across to the box opposite, where the once-famous beauty Lady Lenora Orde watched with her cousin Lady Eden Vawdrey. She envied them the large white banner they sat beneath with the black heart weeping three drops of scarlet blood. She needed to have a large banner made up for Armand, she vowed, with his white winged horse on its blue field. Then she, too, could watch her husband from beneath his colors.

They had a banner hanging at Lynwode now, but they needed one they could pack up to take to tournaments also. Una had accompanied her husband to only one rural tournament so far. She had watched him lift the victor's cup at Areley Kings in June and crown her tournament queen. Somehow, she had far preferred that tournament to this pomp-filled one at the palace.

The crowd had fallen painfully quiet now and waited with bated breath for the victor to emerge from the grueling battle. All that could be heard was the ring of steel striking upon steel. Both men were staggering now and on their last legs. The tournament had run three days and whoever won this final bout would emerge the overall champion of the Autumn Tournament.

Sir Garman lunged; Armand looked to retreat, but then brought his own sword up violently. There was a blur, then Orde's broadsword went hurtling to the ground. Armand side-stepped neatly, bringing his booted foot down heavily upon the blade, preventing its retrieval. The point of his own sword hovered in the air before Orde's throat.

After a tense moment, Orde held up both his hands in a grudging gesture of defeat. The King leaped out of his seat with a battle roar, the contents of his goblet hurled over the side and spattered over an unfortunate duchess whose shriek of dismay was drowned in the din of the crowd's celebration.

Una found she, too, was on her feet, the King holding her hand aloft as though she had scored some kind of victory. She laughed delightedly and found herself engulfed in a hearty royal embrace.

The three-day tournament had a fairy-tale ending. The ugly princess had transformed into a celebrated bride, and the knight who could not find his form had finally emerged a winner. Una gazed down as Armand dragged off his helmet. His eyes were seeking out her own. She raised her hand to her lips and sent him a kiss. Before her eyes, he reached out a gauntleted hand to catch her tribute and press it to his breastplate.

"Oh my!" breathed the Queen, whose interest had finally been snared. She fanned herself with her hand and cast a sideways look at Una. "*Finally*, I see what all the fuss is about," she murmured.

*

Of course, they had not been able to wriggle out of that evening's feasting. Armand was a mass of aches and sores by the time the first course was served. He could not use his right hand, which was so swollen he was forced to hold his wine cup in his left.

They were sat at the high table next to the King and Queen, Earl Vawdrey and his countess, and a bunch of other courtiers whose names Armand had not bothered to catch.

He kept his focus on Una as she sat beside him, intent on cutting up his food. Her hair for once was loose, for her decoration tonight was neither veil nor headdress. Instead on her head, she wore the autumn wreath of orange flowers that crowned his win. It suited her well, as did the happy flush upon her cheeks. Her auburn hair was so long she was sat upon it. She looked, he thought, like a bride. Perhaps, they could have a second wedding night later in the privacy of their bedchamber, to replace all memories of the first.

This time, he would be a winner in truth, and a worthy bridegroom, even if he was a mass of bruises. It had all been worth it. Even having to suffer Una's attention being monopolized by the King, which had slightly maddened him this week. In truth, Wymer vied as much for Armand's attention as he did for Una's. He'd never really understood why the King liked him so much, but he supposed he was more grateful for the fact these days. It had caused him to look favorably on their match after all.

After his win, he had been presented by the King with a golden cup, a large bag of coins, and a new banner, which when unfurled, showed his winged horse juxtaposed with Una's green wyvern. Una had gasped at the sight of the Blechmarsh dragon on her husband's standard.

"Your new crest, de Bussell," the King had said with a nod. "Marking the occasion of your marriage."

"It looks very well, sire," Armand had said, raising his goblet aloft. It amused him to wonder what Henry and Muriel would make of him having his own variation on the family coat of arms. They had been rather pompous about the fact their family now contained former royalty, even if it was northern. Even his father had been touting the news about all of Derring, bringing his cronies and acquaintances over to meet Una at inopportune moments and sending a ridiculous number of invites for them to take their meals at Anninghurst.

Armand had started debating if he needed to build a hunting box somewhere, simply so he could stash his wife away from intruding hordes of people. It had been nearly as bad at Areley Kings, with crowds dogging their every step and gathering around their pavilion to get a glimpse of the northern princess. Luckily, Vawdrey had agreed he should keep Walker on and five of his men to act as a personal guard for Una, otherwise she would have been swallowed up by provincial crowds. She took it all in her stride, however, with a kindly smile and word for all who approached her. Her reputation was slowly changing from warlike to benevolent in popular opinion.

"Aye, it does," the King agreed, interrupting his thoughts. "Your heraldic beasts look well combined. As do you." He beamed. "It was a damned fine notion of mine, that May Day tournament. Said it would turn out for the best, didn't I, Vawdrey? Eh?"

He turned to the enigmatic earl, who gave his wintry smile. "As you say, sire," his aide responded diplomatically.

A strange thought suddenly struck Armand. "Una," he said in a low voice. "Do you remember that role you asked me to play the day after we were married?" At her frown, he continued urgently. "The possessive groom, eager to wend his footsteps homeward?"

Her brow cleared. "Of course," she said staunchly. "You were wonderful."

"What if it was merely a glimpse of what was to come?" he asked, and her gaze turned inquiring. "What I mean is, what if I slipped so naturally into it, because it's who I really am?"

Una smiled. "You mean underneath the easygoing façade Sir Armand is a budding domestic tyrant?" she asked teasingly.

"Exactly." He brushed a kiss to Una's brow. "I think we should hang the new banner over our bed tonight," he said warmly. "I look forward to vanquishing my dragon later," he murmured in her ear. "For an even sweeter victory than this one."

Una tipped her head back to look at him. "I fear you will not find me so easy to defeat as Sir Garman," she answered with promise. "For I have your measure, Sir Lusty Loins, and will never be taken in by your tricks."

349

"Don't I know it," Armand agreed fervently. His wife certainly kept him on his toes when it came to the bedchamber. There had been a time when he had thought her incapable of flirtation, he remembered dimly. Now, she had only to call him *Sir Armand* with slow deliberation and she made him so instantly aroused that he felt light-headed. As for their dragon-slaying trysts, they had grown so hot, he would not be surprised if he were burnt to a cinder one of these days.

He rested his hand on her belly, where she barely showed as yet, under the flared skirts of her blue gown. They had not told anyone of their news, even at Lynwode, for it was early days and they delighted in the knowledge that only the two of them shared. Next spring there would be a baby. "Are you happy, my love?"

She nodded. "Next week we return home," she said longingly. "I cannot wait to see how Otho and Rose have set up their new quarters in the lodge house, though Rose is sure to have lured Abelard there with her. Then we have our news to tell your family. Your father will be pleased, I think. He loves to see you piled high with new responsibilities."

Armand grinned. "To be sure. But you must dance attendance on the King for another week first." His expression darkened slightly. "I don't like sharing you."

She sighed. "It's not so bad. In truth, I never thought I could be this happy in a royal court, but with you by my side, husband, it seems I could be content almost anywhere." She touched his cheek lightly in a caress. "Besides," she added bracingly, "now you're no longer competing, you can come and take bread and milk with the King every morning. He has target practice with the bow and arrow tomorrow and is determined to teach me."

"Impossible," Armand answered swiftly. "I cannot spare you on the morrow for you will be tending to my hurts."

350

"Hurts?" Her face fell. "Are they so very bad?" she asked, immediately solicitous.

He nodded. "Yes, I need you to reforge my sword with your fiery dragon breath," he said straight-faced.

"Armand!" She blushed prettily. "Your dragon will certainly tend to your needs later," she assured him, and he lifted her hand to bestow on it a lingering kiss. He did not care who saw how much he doted on her. In truth, he could not hide it even if he had wanted to. It was apparent to one and all.

He would not call her princess just now, even in a whisper for it would discompose her, but later he would. When it was just the two of them. "You always do, my sweet Una."

"And I always will, husband," she vowed.

THE END

If you want to read more about Karadok, then the next book in the series is Aimee's story:

Her Bridegroom, Bought and Paid For

Aimee Ankatel, oldest daughter to the richest merchant in all Karadok, has eyes only for the heavily scarred Lord Kentigern. He's a ferocious competitor, and her heart beats louder when she watches him compete in the field. Not one of the handsome knights draws her admiration like he does.

When her father lends funds to the Crown and promises her a glittering match with a nobleman, she daydreams of making the ill-fated knight fall in love with her. After all, if Aimee's father buys back Kentigern's lands and castle for a dowry, surely that would make her an acceptable bride to him?

Any idealistic dreams of youth Kentigern once had were lost long ago in battle when he was disfigured and blinded in one eye. His destiny was a cruel one; his homelands confiscated for his part in the northern uprising, he ekes out a lonely nomadic existence, traveling from one tournament to another.

Never would he have dreamed that all he had once lost could be restored to him by some upstart merchant wanting a stud and a title for his pretty daughter. Never in his wildest dreams would he have imagined a reversal of fortune that included a wife like Aimee.

If you enjoyed this book, please consider leaving me a rating on Goodreads, Amazon, Bookbub or wherever else you leave your reviews. I would be very grateful.

You can find my website at: www.alicecoldbreath.com where you can sign up for my monthly newsletter and find out what I am up to.

Also, please do check out some of my other stories!

Many thanks, Alice.